Dylan's Redemption

Dylan's Redemption

BOOK THREE: THE MCBRIDES

JENNIFER RYAN

AVONIMPULSE
An Imprint of HarperCollinsPublishers

Excerpt from *At Wolf Ranch* copyright © 2015 by Jennifer Ryan.

Excerpt from *Full Exposure* copyright © 2014 by Sara Jane Stone.

Excerpt from *Personal Target* copyright © 2014 by Kay Thomas.

Excerpt from *Sinful Rewards 1* copyright © 2014 by Cynthia Sax.

EPub Edition AUGUST 2014 ISBN: 9780062334787

Print Edition ISBN: 9780062334794

JV 10 9 8 7

For all the Jessies out there who have overcome hardship and found themselves on the edge of life and oblivion and found the strength and courage to prevail. I wish you all a happy-ever-after.
Life and love are precious. Hold on to both.

Prologue

Senior Prom ...

HE COULD HAVE *asked any girl*, Jessie thought and gazed up at the night sky. She couldn't believe Dylan McBride asked her to the dance. Based on all the whispers and backhanded comments, neither could anyone else.

The stars glimmered brightly overhead. Jessie stood out on the veranda. Rock and roll emanated from the elegant ballroom more suited to waltzes and string quartets than the sounds of rowdy teenagers and thrashing guitars.

If her father discovered her gone ... Well, it didn't bear thinking about. Hard to explain living with someone who'd rather drink himself to death than offer you a kind word. You learned to hate them as the love between you withered like autumn leaves and died.

Pushing aside her tormented thoughts, she focused on the stars above and the fact she was here, tonight, with

Dylan. She'd give anything to kiss him again, feel his lips on hers, warm and urgent, making her heart slam so hard against her ribcage it just might burst out of her chest. Breathless when the kiss ended, the corners of his mouth would tilt with that cocky half grin of his and melt her heart. Even now, she felt the unfamiliar flutter in her belly that made her both excited and anxious to kiss him again.

"I thought you wanted to dance." Dylan walked out the French doors and across the veranda to join her at the stone wall. "Might as well get your money's worth out of that killer dress." His eyes skimmed over her from head to foot, making her skin warm despite the slight breeze chilling the air.

"I needed a break from all the whispers and snide re-marks. They're taking bets on what I have on you. How in the world did the Queen of Geeks get the most popular everything to ask her out?" Her social-outcast status had reached monumental proportions freshman year and soared ever since.

"Don't listen to them. No one knows you the way I do. They don't see the real you," he said, looking away, em-barrassed by the words spilling from his lips. He gazed up at the night sky with her and brushed his hand down the back of her hair.

She cherished the light touch on her head. Normally, she didn't let anyone get this close. Her father would rather hit than be gentle.

She smiled and turned to face him. "You know, there's a little poetry mixed in with all that rough-and-tumble jock." She recognized the gleam in his eye and inhaled sharply, aware of how close they stood together.

"I don't have a single memory over the last ten years that doesn't include you. I think you've been following me around since the day we moved here." His husky voice drifted away on the wind.

She didn't know what to say. He'd been the butt of many jokes because of her blatant interest. Maybe it was the dance, or her first real date with Dylan—tonight she felt older, wiser.

"You're the only one who doesn't look down on me." Nervous, she smoothed an imaginary wrinkle on her dress.

Dylan was the only normalcy in her otherwise turbulent life, and he graduated in a few short days. She'd miss him come fall when he left for college. She didn't want to face her junior year without any friends, without Dylan.

"You didn't embarrass me. Well, sometimes," he admitted with that half smile again. "Mostly I like the attention. You're good for my ego."

"Like your ego needs my help."

Another part of his anatomy sure did. Dylan wanted to grab fistfuls of her chocolate brown hair and crush his mouth to hers. He loved touching her soft hair, did it whenever she came within reach. The sparkle in her more-green-than-hazel eyes and the sway of her black strapless gown as it ruffled slightly in the breeze made his body tighten and a small groan form deep in his throat.

Her hair never looked prettier, hanging free from its usual ponytail. For the first time, she wore makeup.

Tonight she looked like a girl, not another construction worker on her dad's jobsites. If nothing else, tonight he'd given her a chance to be Cinderella. She looked damn good as a girl.

He ached with wanting her and the hurt that in a few short days, he wouldn't see her again for a long time. She didn't know that. No one knew. He wondered if their friendship could survive the distance he was putting between himself and this town, his family's demands, and, reluctantly, her. Maybe she'd wait for him to come back. A constant in his life, one he hesitated to give up. He needed to go, but all of a sudden he wished he could take her with him.

Something inside told him to take her along. A whisper from his heart, though insistent, he ignored. What could he do? She was still in high school.

"Let's get out of here," he commanded, his voice rough.

"Fine by me. It's not like I'm friends with any of the girls. Can't exactly invite anyone to my house and hang out, right? My dad's not exactly the welcoming committee."

"In all the time I've known you, you've never complained about your old man. In fact, whenever someone brings him up, you change the subject."

"What's to talk about? He's a drunk, everyone knows it, so there isn't much to say. Between the kids at school and living with him, sometimes I wish I could just disappear. Lord knows, no one would miss me."

"I would." An ache welled from his chest to the back

of his throat. She wouldn't want him feeling sorry for her. But he did.

"Come on, Jess, let's go for a drive and look for shooting stars. There's something I need to tell you."

Jessie thrilled at the idea of being alone with him. He leaned in, took her hands, and pulled her to him. His arms went around her, lips settled over hers in a kiss so soft and sweet she ached with wanting to keep this safe feeling forever. She only ever felt this way with him.

The kiss ended with a soft brush of his lips over hers. He stared down at her and something inside her shifted and tipped. Her girlhood crush turned into a full-fledged love, bursting from her heart and filling her soul.

Dylan stepped back, grasped her hand, and took off for the exit. He didn't stop until they were in the front seat of his car. Caught up in the excitement, she giggled, and Dylan gave her another of those lopsided smiles that made her insides flutter.

They drove away from the dance and all his friends and settled into the cozy car, the music blaring, his hand holding hers, and the comfort of just being together. The town lights faded behind them. Turning off onto an old, dirt logging road, they rolled and bumped to a stop on a rise overlooking the surrounding hills and trees. He killed the engine.

Jessie stared into the night, at the land, and the glorious star-speckled sky, and sucked in a quick breath. "Dylan, this is gorgeous. How did you find this place?"

"Since I got my wheels, I've been scouting out the back

roads. I come here a lot. Day or night, you can't beat the view."

"No wonder no one uses this road. I don't know how we made it this far over all those ruts."

"My superior driving skills."

"There's something superior about you, but it's not your driving skills. More like your attitude."

"You think so, huh?" He poked her in the ribs to make her laugh. Instead, she inhaled sharply, winced, and pressed her arm to her side before she thought better to hide her response.

"What's wrong? Did I hurt you?"

His brow wrinkled as he studied her. She couldn't tell him the truth. "It's nothing. I got hit with a board the other day at work and it left a bruise. That's all."

His palms glided up her arms to her shoulders. He pulled her to him and whispered in her ear, "Let me kiss you and make it better."

She thought he'd take her mouth again; instead his lips brushed a kiss on her bare shoulder. His head dipped and his lips pressed to the swell of her breast above her gown. The zipper on her dress slid down her back, his fingertips following its progress over her skin. The silky material swooshed and pooled around her waist. He came back to her mouth and kissed her hungrily. Her hands seemed to have a mind of their own, and she let them have their way with him. While his hands roamed her body, she explored his, stripping away obstacles.

An unfamiliar shimmering kind of heat spread over her entire body like hot waves rolling over a road in the dead of summer. She didn't know how they ended up naked in the backseat together; she only remembered the minute he'd locked eyes with her, his gaze one of pure emotion and need. Nodding her head in agreement, she pulled him down to her again.

On a star-studded night, on a deserted stretch of road, and in the backseat of a car, she gave herself to him with her whole heart.

If she'd known the love she felt that night would be eclipsed by the agonizing pain she suffered after, she'd have done it anyway.

Chapter One

Eight years later . . .

"J.T., WHERE THE hell did you go?" Greg's deep voice
came from behind her. She hadn't heard him come into
her Hope Construction office. She sat at her desk, facing
the window, looking into nothing.

Swiveling around in her chair, Jessie glanced up at
him and mentally shook off her stupor. No matter how
hard she tried, whenever she was tired, her mind took her
back to him, to the hurt.

"Sorry, just thinking."

"From the look on your face, I'd say you were remembering again." Greg's voice held deep concern.

"Just reminding myself how everything can change in
a moment."

"I wish you'd stop punishing yourself for being
human."

"Human? I'm a cliché. I went to the prom with the high school's star quarterback, lost my virginity in the backseat of a car, ended up an unwed pregnant teen. Dumped by the quarterback, almost killed by my alcoholic father, and then to add insult to injury I lost . . ."

She couldn't finish. For some unknown reason, today her mind brought it all back. She'd let the ghosts out of the closet and didn't know how to usher them back in. They lashed at old wounds and made her bleed.

Jessie hadn't spoken of the past in a long time. Part of her daily existence, she tried her best to push through, cope. Today felt different. She wished she knew why, so she could put a stop to it.

"And you lost her. Not your fault. You did everything possible. No one could have asked more from you. It just happened. The doctors tried everything and did their best to save her."

"I still feel like I failed. Maybe if I'd taken better care of myself?"

"You did everything right."

She shook off her mood and the past and glanced up at Greg. Thick golden hair, blue eyes, square jaw, tall and lean, tanned from working outside, quite a handsome package. Rich, smart, funny, and a good friend. All the things a woman could want in a man. So why, when she looked at him, didn't she feel anything? No longing to touch him, or to be anything more than friends.

It was the same with every man she met. Maybe she died along with her daughter and lived as a ghost of herself in some warped reality.

Besides, she thought of Greg as a brother. An only child, he'd always wanted a sibling and adopted her as his sister. What could she say? For them, it worked.

"Why are you here?"

"Did you get any calls today?" His tone asked a lot more than a simple question.

"I get about a hundred a day. Any call in particular you're referring to? Did Pop outbid me on a job again, and he sent you here to rub my nose in it?"

"No." He chuckled, though with little enthusiasm.

Ever since Pop fronted her the money to start her own business, they'd cultivated a friendly rivalry between their construction companies. She'd worked for Pop and Greg starting at fifteen, pregnant and alone, looking for a job to support herself through her pregnancy. She'd started in the office, helping Pop plan and organize jobs since she couldn't do any manual labor in her condition.

Later, to their utter fascination, she'd taken on any and all jobs on the projects. They had no idea a young girl could do everything from frame a house to roof it. She'd earned their respect, their admiration, and their love. And one day she found she'd grown so close to them, they made her part of their family.

At eighteen, she'd even changed her last name to Langley to hide from her father, or anyone else who came looking for her. Not that anyone had, but she'd needed the security of knowing no one could find her.

"Dad says hello, but I'm not here about any bid. He called about some news he heard today. He wanted to come himself, but you know how poorly he's been feeling lately."

"Is it his health? Did the doctor say something about his condition?"

"No. Dad's fine. Nothing's changed. The news is about something else."

Pop suffered from a heart condition over the last ten years. Some days it got the best of him. Most days, he got the better of it. Greg took after his dad and his zest for life. You couldn't hold either of them down.

"How's that new job you've got going on the outskirts of Fallbrook?" he asked, stalling, though she didn't know why.

She eyed him warily. She hadn't wanted to take the job near Fallbrook. The last place she wanted to go back to was her old hometown. Granted, she hadn't moved far. She lived in-between the two towns, closer to Solomon, where most of her business projects were located. She avoided Fallbrook like cats did water and hadn't been back, except to sneak into town to her and her partner's antique and furniture shop.

"Running smoothly. Fifty track homes and a community park. My biggest project yet, thanks to Pop's recommendation. Why?"

"Just wondering if you've gone into town."

"You're wondering if anyone knows I'm working there?" Still stalling, she waited him out.

"Something like that. Have you heard from your brother?"

"Not since he walked out the door while my father pummeled me in the kitchen. Why? You're fishing, spit it out."

Grimacing, he said, "I hate thinking about what happened to you."

"You and me both." The images crowded her mind clear as day. Her father beating her, her brother walking out the door, leaving her to fend for herself. Not his fault. Not really, when staying would have only made things worse.

"Rumors are still circling that you're dead." The grin died on his lips before he added, "At times, I thought you were close enough to it."

Jessie didn't have an answer and waited to see if Greg's train of thought took another detour.

"Do you know who the new county sheriff is?"

"No. Should I? Did I break some kind of law becoming a business owner and building a new track of houses?" She didn't mean the snippy tone. Greg's hedging irritated her and made her nervous. "Out with it. What's this all about?"

"The new sheriff goes by 'McBride.'"

At the mention of his name, her breath stopped, and she stared at Greg as if he'd grown another head. "Mc—" She couldn't even spit out the whole thing.

"That's right. McBride. Looks as if your Dylan moved back to his hometown."

She slapped her hands down on her desk and squared off with Greg. "He's not *my* Dylan, first of all. Second, what's this got to do with anything? You know I've put it all behind me."

"Bullshit. Let's leave off the fact that when I walked in you were reliving prom night and its aftermath. You may have gotten your GED, graduated college, worked your ass off to start your own business, and transformed from a broken girl into a strong woman. What you haven't done is put the past behind you. You live with it every day. You don't smile, you don't date, you haven't had sex in eight years, as far as I can tell, you won't contact your family, and you spend all your free time alone in your workshop."

True. Every word. Greg knew her well. She hadn't realized just how good a friend he'd been to her all these years. He and Pop were the only people she allowed close.

With little choice in the matter, she'd told them what happened to her. When she'd gotten off the bus in Solomon, showed up at their office, fifteen and a lot worse for wear, they'd threatened to call the police and have her sent home. Once she spilled her guts, they'd given her a job and let her be the woman she'd become the night of the prom.

"Why are you harping on me today? Why are you bringing up my brother and Dylan?"

"Dad does a lot of business in Fallbrook. He got a call from a friend who mentioned something interesting. There's no easy way to tell you." He walked around her desk and crouched down in front of her. Taking her hands in his, he looked her right in the eye. "Your father died in his sleep last night. Heart attack."

She exploded out of her chair and almost toppled Greg. Coming to his feet, he held her in place. Her whole body filled to bursting with rage. Her head felt like a plug on a volcano, the pressure building until she might actually explode.

"Are you telling me that bastard died *peacefully* while he slept?"

"Damn, honey. I didn't want to tell you at all."

"Why is it some people can be as bad as they want, do what they want without regard to how it affects anyone else, and get away with it? I always thought, at least in the end, he'd get his due. Maybe he'd end up wrapped around a tree after driving drunk one too many times, or he'd die a miserable death from liver failure. Hell, even a heart attack on the job could have been excruciating, long suffering, and scary. Never, not one time, did I ever consider he'd simply drift off to sleep and slip into death without so much as a whimper. I should have picked up the knife he dropped that night and gutted him where he stood."

"Vivid image, J.T." Greg's shoulders shuddered. "What are you going to do?"

"What am *I* going to do?" She threw her hands up in the air and let them fall to her sides with a slap against her thighs. "Nothing."

"He's dead. You're not going to the funeral? Don't you want to know about his business, or your brother? Dance a jig on his grave?"

"The last is the only one that sounds appealing." She smiled, but let it fall away. "Why the hell should I clean up the mess?"

"What mess?"

"Oh, I don't know. How about the trouble my brother's gotten himself into? He's a drunk just like the old man. He got married two years ago, and they're expecting a baby. He doesn't work, and they have bills up the ass. My father sold the business four years ago to his partner. He worked off and on since then. Mostly off. As far as I know, he's been living off the money he got for the business and social security, not that it's much."

Amazed, Greg asked, "How do you know all this? You said you haven't been in contact with your brother. I know you haven't talked to your father, or he'd be dead already."

She'd kept some things to herself over the years. Things she didn't want anyone to know, because . . . Well, they might question her sanity, quite frankly. At this point, she'd given herself away in some respect. Several ways, actually. Look where she lived. She'd bought the property above the road where she and Dylan spent prom night naked in the backseat of his car.

How sane are you, Jessie? A psychiatrist would have a field day with you and the many ways you torture yourself.

Sighing, she looked at one of the two men she trusted with her life. Without Greg and his father, she wouldn't be where she was today. She owed him an explanation.

"You know how you tease me about locking myself in the workshop. Well, when I go in there I work. I work until I'm numb and nothing is in my mind, so I can sleep without dreaming."

"I've heard the tools."

"Yeah, but you don't know what I've been doing. I build furniture."

"I've seen all the furniture in your house. You've given Dad and me some really nice pieces for Christmas and our birthdays. I know you made it yourself."

"Once I finished the house, I kept making it. It's kind of an obsession."

"So you have a barn full of furniture. How does that explain how you know about your brother and father selling the business to his partner?"

"I have a store in Fallbrook where I sell the furniture." Sheepish, she fell into her seat.

Greg rested his hip on the corner of her desk, folded his arms over his broad chest, and waited for her explanation.

"Okay, fine. I heard through some business contacts a shop owner needed a business partner. She sells antiques and collectibles and wanted someone who made fine furniture. It started off small with custom curio cabinets, headboards, hutches, and things like that. Then, people started asking about matching pieces and bigger pieces. Now, I stock the store with all kinds of things. I make a lot of money, and my hobby has turned into a second business."

He continued to stare at her with his determined chin stuck out, waiting for her to continue.

"I'm a silent partner. She runs the store and I provide the merchandise. She takes a small percent, and in exchange, she's agreed to keep her mouth shut about where the furniture comes from."

"J.T., that's amazing. How long have you been doing this?"

"Six years."

"Since we were in college. I had no idea."

"I think Pop knows. I used to stay late sometimes at

the jobsites to use the tools. I'd buy the wood and set up in one of the unfinished houses. I'd spend a few hours making a chest or a table. It was just something to do. I'd imagine someone sitting at the table having dinner with their family, or putting a favorite quilt in the chest." She shrugged and tried to fight the crooked smile creeping across her face. "Stupid, huh?"

"No. Not stupid. I've never known anyone better with their hands and power tools. You have a gift."

"It's the only thing the old man ever gave me. He always demanded I be the best one on any jobsite. He'd ride me all day, every day, to make sure I did the job right. I hated that, but I always liked the satisfaction of seeing the finished product. There's nothing like stepping back and looking at what you've built out of pieces. I like it when those pieces make a whole."

She wished she could do the same with her heart. It seemed the pieces would forever lie scattered in the chasm of her soul.

"I know how you feel. I felt the same way the day we finished my house. I feel the same way whenever I work on something." Taking a deep breath, he asked, "Are you going back to Fallbrook now that your father is dead?"

"You won't leave this alone, will you?"

"No. Dad and I agree. Go home and put the past to rest. Find a way to be happy."

"I'm happy." She'd spoken too quickly. His disapproving glare told her he didn't believe a word. "I am, damnit."

"You're not. What you are is a successful businesswoman. You aren't that poor little girl who had the misfortune to grow up with Buddy Thompson for a father."

"Well, the joke's on me, because he wasn't my father."

That little gem came out of their last fight. Buddy, drunk and cussing her out, went over the top, revealing her mother confessed to an affair in her suicide note. She'd loved the man, and he'd left her to go back to his own wife and children. Devastated and pregnant, she passed Jessie off as Buddy's daughter, until she couldn't take Buddy's drinking, or the loss of her one true love.

Every passing day Jessie looked more and more like her mother. She'd been a living reminder of her mother's betrayal. Buddy spent eleven years making Jessie pay for her mother's mistake.

"He's the only father you had." Leave it to Greg to speak the cold, hard truth.

"Lucky me."

He and Pop wanted her to finish it. Tidy up her past and get on with the business of living. They wanted her to be happy. After all these years, she didn't know if she remembered how to do that seemingly simple thing.

"Fine. I give up. I'll go to Fallbrook and exorcize the demons. Satisfied?"

"It's a start." He pulled her up out of her chair and wrapped her in his arms.

Greg and Pop were the only ones she'd allow to touch her. "I'm not going to see any of the McBrides. Even you can't ask that much of me."

"Just go and put your father to rest and check on your brother. That's all I ask."

She hugged him tighter and thought he might be asking too much. Even of her. She'd been tough and strong the last eight years, but even she had limits. She reached and surpassed them when she lost Hope. She didn't know if she could ever survive that kind of hurt again.

"How about I take you to dinner?"

"Oh sure, come here and turn my life upside down, and then just take me to dinner like nothing's happened." She pretend pouted.

"Come on. We'll catch up. I'll make you laugh and maybe get a glimpse of that elusive smile of yours," he teased, still holding her lightly in a comfortable embrace.

She gave him a smile as fake as a pink flamingo lawn ornament. "Not tonight. I need to make some calls. I have to make funeral arrangements. Lord knows, Brian hasn't done it. He doesn't have the money."

"If I know you, you'll do a hell of a lot more than plan a funeral."

She hid a smile and the plans forming in her mind to get her brother moving down the straight and narrow. She'd already pulled herself out of the pit of despair. She could do the same for Brian. No way she would let her niece or nephew grow up with a drunk for a father.

Chapter Two

THURSDAY NIGHT AT his cousin's bar, McBride's, was busy and raucous. Rowdy men and women crowded the place, looking for a good time. The music blared, the drinks flowed. People danced, laughed, and occasionally got into a squabble or two. Mostly, they had a whole lot of fun.

Brody and Rain had certainly changed the locals' dive bar into a place everyone loved to gather. Some nights, Dylan walked in to check things out and make sure the crowd stayed friendly and no one started a fight. Tonight, he searched for a particular patron. Someone he hadn't seen in quite a long time. If he wasn't mistaken, someone who'd been avoiding him at all costs, since he came home nearly two years ago.

With his back to the bar, he scanned the room. Only the bartender worked behind him, and he tracked him with his peripheral vision. An old and safe habit of watching his back. It had saved him many times in the military, and he'd never gotten out of the practice, even while he served on the Atlanta Police Department, working the streets for two years. Unhappy living in the city, he'd wanted to move back to his hometown, where you knew your neighbors and they knew you.

Small-town living lent itself to a quieter life and certainly less violent crimes in general. Fallbrook had its share of drug dealers, robbers, and domestic abuse, though murders were few and far between.

He hated the domestic abuse cases. He couldn't stand to see women in the direst of circumstances and think they had no one to turn to in their time of need. Even when they did call the police, they often didn't press charges because they were too afraid and too used to making excuses for the person who abused them. A vicious cycle, one few women broke away from.

He'd seen the kind of damage a fist could do to someone's ribs or back or legs. Abusers, in many circumstances, avoided the head because it wasn't easy to hide that kind of damage. Stick to the body and limbs, where clothes hid the injury. Sick tactics an abuser used to hide his behavior, so he could keep doling out the punishment.

That first call left him ill and consumed with visions of Jessie as a young girl always covered in bruises and forever chasing after him to get away from her old man. He'd often thought she just wanted to hang out with him and her brother, Brian. Now, he knew the truth. She'd been looking for a protector. She'd chosen him, and he'd failed her.

He'd heard all the rumors about Jessie's disappearance, and all the speculation about her murder, and wished he'd known all those years ago about her father abusing her. Unfortunately, he didn't figure it out until he joined the military and met a guy with fading bruises that matched the ones he'd seen on Jessie's back and ribs. That disturbing enlightenment came too late for him to help Jessie. To this day he couldn't forgive himself for not seeing what was right in front of him, for not protecting her. For not knowing in time to save her from her father's murderous hands.

He'd dedicated his life to protecting others, but it wasn't enough to assuage his guilt.

I wish I could just disappear. That ominous statement she made on prom night still haunted him.

All anyone knew for sure is one day about a week after Dylan left town himself, people started noticing Jessie's absence. The sheriff brought Buddy and Brian in for questioning. Buddy claimed a drunken blackout with no recollection of the night in question. He couldn't account for the blood seen on his shirt or his black eye. The sheriff at the time released them. Lack of evidence. From that day on, they remained silent, despite many inquiries, and Dylan trying his best over the last months to nail Buddy to the wall for something, anything he could use to get Buddy to talk and tell him where he buried Jessie. The man refused to speak to him. Even threatened to file charges for harassment. Dylan refused to stop looking for the one answer he needed to know. Where was Jessie? She deserved a proper burial. He needed to tell her how sorry he was for everything and give her the goodbye he'd been too afraid to say to her when he left for the military.

Dylan spotted his quarry across the room nursing a beer and a shot at a small booth on the far wall. Brian sat alone with three empty shots lined up next to his beer. Dylan didn't think he'd stop with shot number four, not after finding out about his father's death.

Maybe the booze would loosen his tongue and he'd finally talk about what happened to Jessie.

"Mind if I join you?"

Brian looked up through bleary eyes and scanned Dylan from his black Stetson, down his sheriff's shirt and badge, to his black jeans and boots. Dylan noted his vision halted just that extra second on the gun at his hip. He hoped Brian hadn't sunk so far into despair that he thought better to suck on a gun barrel than a beer bottle.

"Have a seat. I'm celebrating. How's about I buy you a drink, *Sheriff*. We'll have ourselves a toast. Good riddance, and thank you, God. The devil came to take Buddy Thompson home to burn."

Although Brian slurred his words, and they were more than a little slow in coming, Dylan heard him loud and clear. He was glad of the old man's demise.

Dylan took a seat and pulled off his Stetson and set it on the table beside him. The waitress came by and offered him a hot cup of coffee. He accepted it gratefully and dismissed her wide smile and the flirty gesture as she swung her hair over her shoulder. He kept his gaze on Brian and waited while the waitress paused in hopes of gaining his attention. She left pouting, and he didn't give her a second thought.

Women threw themselves at him all the time because of his looks and dangerous job, and sometimes they figured out he was wealthy to boot. His wealth was no secret to any woman living in Fallbrook. From the minute he'd settled into his new house out near his cousins, Brody and Owen, he'd been every single woman's favorite target. And a few married ones too. His cousins' wives even tried to set him up a time or two, but he'd avoided their snares.

Dismissing his personal problems with the opposite sex, he addressed the problem sitting across from him. "You've been avoiding me since I moved back, Brian. Why?"

"I didn't have a need for the sheriff." Brian picked up his shot, draining it in one long swallow with a wince and a heavy exhalation

"You've been too busy drowning in a bottle to take a minute to say hello to an old friend." Dylan's sarcasm made Brian's head snap up and his eyes flare. Dylan thought he saw a spark of his old friend in there somewhere, and it was a welcome sight.

"Some friend you turned out to be. You took off without so much as a goodbye, and you expect me to come running when you suddenly decide to come home."

"You were the only one who knew I'd planned to leave after graduation."

"I didn't know you'd show up at the prom with my sister. I didn't know you'd leave three days later after avoiding her and me all that time. Hell, we hadn't even taken off our caps and gowns and you'd already left the gym, never to be seen again. Jessie disappeared five days later. In eight days, I lost my best friend and my sister. Now, you show up and want a hello. I'd rather she was sitting here. Maybe then, instead of 'hello,' I could say 'I'm sorry.'" He raised his beer in a silent toast to the heavens. "I'm so damn sorry, Jessie girl." He took a deep swallow.

Dylan wanted to steer the conversation in this direction, but seeing Brian look up to heaven made his insides go cold. She'd never been far from his mind in all these years. He had to know what really happened to Jessie.

Dylan avoided her for those three days after the prom because she'd scared the hell out of him. She'd given herself to him so completely and so freely, he'd lost his damn heart to her that night. If he saw her before he left, he wouldn't have left her. And he had to go. He had to get out from under his parents' expectations and demands, the plan they'd mapped out for his life without his consent or happiness in mind. Jessie had paid the price for his choices. Some people believed Jessie left town brokenhearted over him. Others told stories he didn't want to think about. Rumors abounded, but the circumstantial evidence all pointed to one thing. Buddy killed her. He wanted the facts from Brian, because without Buddy only Brian knew the truth. At least, Dylan hoped he knew what really happened.

"What did Buddy do to Jessie, Brian?" He didn't want to push too hard. Brian was drunk and sunk deep in a mire of misery.

"Well now. That's the million-dollar question, isn't it? Maybe the old man buried her in the woods, or dumped her in the quarry lake. Maybe he put her in the foundation of one of the houses, buried her under a mound of cement, and smoothed it out with no one the wiser. Maybe . . ."

"Stop it." Dylan banged his fist on the table, making the shot glasses jump. "I don't want to hear what you think happened." He'd heard enough wild, gruesome speculation from everyone in town. "Tell me what you know."

"Look at you, wearing the sheriff's uniform. What the hell does it matter now if anyone knows what happened that night?" Brian slumped in the booth seat, his face a mask of misery.

Fortifying himself with another swig of beer, his eyes locked on Dylan. "What I know? Hell, I don't know anything. Not for sure. If he did kill her that night, then I hope he's burning in hell and she was the welcoming committee." Brian shook his head and took another swallow of beer.

Everything stopped. Dylan couldn't breathe, his chest so tight his heart stopped beating. If Brian wasn't sure she died, then . . . No. He couldn't let himself think the impossible. Everything pointed to her death. He couldn't find a trace of her anywhere.

"She probably had a beeline straight to heaven. Did you know he'd pick a fight with her just to see if she'd fire and flash, or if she'd back down?"

"I never knew Jessie to back down from anything." Dylan remembered the girl he knew as a child and loved one night. The kind of person who planted her feet and met any challenge head on. Jessie fought hard for herself and what she wanted and put her whole heart into everything she did. Like loving him.

"That's just it. Something came into his eyes when he went after her. Like he hoped, just once, she'd back down. Let him win. Oh, he was drunk enough to delude himself into thinking he won in the end, but deep down, he knew."

"What happened that night?"

"Who the hell knows?" Brian took another swallow of beer and focused on a crack in the table. "We came home from a jobsite. He'd worked her hard that day. I think she framed an entire room. By herself, no less. He just kept picking at her. Wouldn't let up."

Brian took a swallow and lost himself staring at the table. "She was in the kitchen, scrounging for something to eat. The old man knocked the cupboard door shut, flipped her around, and slammed her up against the wall with his forearm braced across her throat. He got right in her face and her eyes were huge. And then she did something odd."

"What?"

"She smiled."

Dylan studied Brian, noting the sheen in his eyes that had nothing to do with the booze.

"She'd been miserable since the day you left. I don't know what happened between you two at the prom, but I know something changed about her. When she realized you were gone for good, she barely spoke. That night, when the old man went after her, she smiled, like she felt as if for once she deserved it, welcomed it. He backhanded that smile right off her face. Split her lip. I can still see the spurt of blood and the trail it left down her chin."

Dylan winced. He didn't want to think about what she'd endured that night, or all the other nights. What he hadn't known then about her situation, he sure as hell knew now. Brian confirmed all his worst fears. She'd borne the brunt of her father's anger, and Brian witnessed it all.

"What did you do?" Anger and sadness choked off his words.

Brian drained the rest of his beer. He stared down at the scratch on the table for a long minute. Tears filled his eyes. "Nothing I could do. If I said anything, tried to stop him, he only hit her harder. More. When we were young, I tried, but he'd shove me out the door and lock me out and he'd beat the hell out of her every time I screamed for him to stop." Brian went quiet, lost in the past. "Jessie would yell for me to go, stay out of it. Run, so he didn't turn on me too.

"That night, Jessie's bleeding from the mouth, the old man turns to me and says, 'Get out.' Jessie stares at me, her eyes pleading for me to leave. So I did."

"You left her there, you fucking bastard." Dylan didn't hide his outrage.

Brian shot forward and pounded his fists on the table. "What did you want me to do?"

"Save her."

"Every time I'd tried he hurt her worse. I felt the fury in him that night. I didn't want to leave her, but I didn't want to be the cause of her getting hurt worse if I stayed." Brian fell back in his seat, the drunken grogginess returning to his eyes. "Walking out that door is the hardest thing I've done, but living with the guilt of knowing what happened after I left eats away at me every second of every day."

You deserve it. And so did Dylan for that matter.

"I spent most of that night at the high school bleachers, planning a new future. I'd take classes in the fall at the junior college. I'd get away from the old man and make something of myself. Maybe start my own business. I had it all planned out. I'd never have to watch him hurt her again. I'd get away from him and the guilt I carried every time I looked at her, knowing what I didn't do. Then, I went home."

Picking up his glass for another swallow, Brian thumped the empty mug back on the table. His eyes roamed the room as if he'd just remembered the other people. He spotted the waitress and held up his empty mug. He waited for her nod. His eyes caught Dylan's, and he almost seemed surprised Dylan was still there.

Dylan reached across the table and grasped Brian's arm, his fingers digging into muscle. "What happened when you got home?"

"Nothing. The house was quiet and empty. I walked through the front room and headed into the kitchen to grab something to eat." His focus on the table, he shuddered. "I can still see it as clear as the day it happened."

"What? What did you see?"

"Smeared blood on the linoleum and a bloody knife."

Dylan couldn't believe the words stumbling out of Brian's mouth.

"She wasn't there, just a bunch of blood on the floor and that knife."

As impossible as it seemed, Brian's silence drowned out the music and people around them. Dylan released Brian's arm and fell back against the booth seat.

"The old man came home the next morning with a nice shiner and blood on his shirt and pants. I sat on the couch right where I'd been all night. He came in and went to the kitchen and stopped short in front of the blood, like he was surprised by the sight of it. He fisted his hand in his hair and shook his head like he was trying to remember something."

Eyes still on the table, Brian traced a finger over the scarred surface. "He found a bucket, filled it with soapy, hot water, and scrubbed the floor clean with a rag. Tossed the knife in the garbage, like it didn't mean anything. He changed his clothes, came back out with the bloody ones and burned them in the fireplace. He turned to me. I couldn't even speak, I was so scared. He said, 'Time to go to work,' like nothing happened. He never said a word about that night or Jessie. Not that day, or any day since. I never asked. I didn't want to hear the truth.

"He took to drinking even more. Only after that particular night, he drank in the kitchen. He'd sit at the table and look at that spot on the floor and he'd drink.

He'd stare at that spot like he was waiting for something. I think he couldn't remember if he killed her or not."

Possible, if Buddy blacked out, then passed out somewhere in his truck, and woke up the next morning with a raging hangover and no recollection of how he got there.

"But you think he did kill her."

"They were fighting when I left her there. When I got home, they were both gone. Only one came home," Brian slurred. "Add it all up, Sheriff, and I'm sure you'll come up with the same thing I did."

Dylan didn't want to come up with Jessie dead. He grieved for her all these years, but always held out hope she was still alive despite the rumors that painted just as gruesome of a picture as Brian's story. Maybe she'd been hurt and simply left. Wishful thinking. At this point, maybe that's all he had left to hold on to. He sure as hell didn't have Jessie.

"Why didn't you go to the cops and report what you saw right away?"

"He threatened me. If I said one word about the blood and clothes, he'd kill me. With Jessie gone, I believed him. First chance I got, I moved out of that house. Every time I saw him, he'd give me this look, like if I ever told, I'd pay.

"Besides, I didn't see anything. I don't know what happened. Even when they did find out and questioned us, they didn't do a damn thing. Can't prove something when the old man kept his mouth shut for the first time in his life. Weren't no body, or a witness."

Dylan had read the sparse details in the police report. Add Brian's fear to speak up and the past sheriff's piss-poor investigation and you came up with Buddy getting away with murder.

Brian tilted his head back and to the side, his focus turned inward. "He never, and I mean never, tried to start a fight with me. He always went after her. From the time she was five, he had it in for her. I can remember him screaming at her that she looked just like her. She'd end up just like her."

"Like who?" Dylan asked, trying to follow Brian.

"Our mother. She looked just like our mother."

"Didn't your mom die when Jessie was five?"

"Yep. I think the old man blamed Jessie for her death."

"How'd she die?"

"Took a bottle full of pills, slit her wrists. Dad found her in the bathtub. Come to think of it, the day she disappeared was the anniversary of our mother's death."

The catalyst that set Buddy off that night.

Hard to comprehend so much tragedy in one family. Jessie was gone, and it was eating him alive. The rumors were true. Buddy Thompson killed Jessie one night while in a drunken rage and hid her body. No one had ever found her. It made him sick to think of her out there, somewhere, and no one knew where. He didn't know where.

"Come on, man, I'll take you home," Dylan offered. "Your wife must be worried about you."

Brian laughed under his breath. "Sure she is. I turned out to be quite the catch. She's probably burning my clothes and poisoning my dinner as we speak."

Dylan got up, placing his Stetson back on his head. Most everyone in the bar watched him stand, probably wondering if he'd arrest someone or leave them to their night of partying.

He slapped Brian on the shoulder, put his hand under his arm, and hauled him up and out of the booth.

"Let's go, man. It's time for you to sleep it off. Things will look better in the morning."

Dylan hoped he spoke for himself as well. Right now he wanted to crawl into a bottle with Brian and drink himself into oblivion. After all these years of thinking and dreaming about her, Jessie was gone, absolutely beyond his reach.

Chapter Three

DYLAN TOOK BRIAN home, left him in the care of his wife. Nice woman, someone he vaguely remembered from high school. A pretty blonde cheerleader with a lot of spunk and sass. Her petite frame appeared even smaller next to Brian's six-foot height. Strong and capable, Marilee ushered Brian into the house. She'd be a good mother if she looked after the baby like she took care of Brian. Too bad Brian wasn't capable of looking after her, let alone himself. Living with a drunk couldn't be easy.

He drove away from their rented house and over to Buddy Thompson's place. The sun had set long ago, and he assumed the house would be empty. Except, maybe, for the ghosts.

The paramedics took Buddy to the morgue after a friend discovered him this morning. They'd planned to meet for a fishing trip. Buddy hadn't shown up, so his friend came calling. He found Buddy in bed, presumably sleeping off a night of drinking.

Buddy wouldn't be going fishing anymore.

Dylan pulled up in front of the house and sat in his truck, staring at the place. Dark and empty, the black windows stared back at him, cold and foreboding.

He'd been there a hundred times, a thousand times. His mother hadn't liked him hanging out with Brian and, especially, Jessie. For some reason, she, like Buddy, never thought Jessie good enough. Dylan had a feeling they knew she'd been better than them all. Jessie never looked down on others, was always the first to lend a hand, and was a true friend. He wished he could say he'd treated her in kind. He hadn't. He had no idea what she really felt about him when she'd died such a horrible death. It left a gnawing in his gut that constantly ached.

She'd died like she'd lived, with the whole town ignoring her.

No one would ever know what really happened to her that night. Not with Buddy and Jessie dead.

He pulled out his cell and called the one person sure to brighten his black mood.

"Hey, Lorena, is he still up?" Lorena took care of his adopted son, Will, after morning preschool and while Dylan worked.

"I just finished his books. Hold on."

"Hi Daddy. When you coming home?"

Dylan turned away from Jessie's house, focused on the street in front of him and his little boy and the joy he felt every time he saw him or heard his voice. "Not for a little while yet. I've got something I need to do."

"Come home."

"Soon. I promise."

"I didn't find the mommy today." Will wanted the same thing other kids had, a mother.

"Finding the right mom isn't easy, but I hope we find one for you." Choked up, he thought of Jessie, her life cut short before she'd ever really lived.

"Maybe tomorrow." Will yawned.

Dylan didn't want to get Will's hopes up, so he dropped the subject. "Sleep good. I'll be there soon. I'll see you first thing in the morning."

"Smiley-face waffles."

"Yes, I promise."

Will loved it when Dylan cut up strawberries and made a face on his waffles. Dylan loved the boy's enthusiasm for the simple things in life. He wished with every breath he took Jessie was here and he could introduce her to his adopted son. He'd tell her about his job, how it led him to a young girl in need and a boy he loved more each day. He'd dedicated his life to helping people like Jess. He tried every day to make up for abandoning her.

"I love you," he said to his son, and meant it to Jessie too.

"I love you, too, Daddy. See you in the morning."

"See you in the morning, buddy."

Dylan hung up and slid from the car, feeling better but dreading walking back into his past. He took the cracked and broken path bordered on both sides by overgrown and mostly dead grass and weeds to the front porch. Reaching above one of the side windows, he ran his fingers along the edge until he found the spare key. He snatched it, stepped back to the door to unlock it before replacing the key. He stepped inside the house and into his past and what had been Jessie's hell.

With a flip of a switch, a single lamp came on in the family room just beyond the tiled entry. Buddy's housekeeping skills left a lot to be desired. Beer bottles, two empty bottles of whiskey, a tumbler glass, and a dozen or more newspapers and food wrappers littered the coffee table and floor. A dead plant sat in the corner and the fireplace hadn't been cleaned in a decade of fires. Ashes spilled out onto the hearth.

Dylan didn't come to see this. No. He needed to see Jessie's room, see if there was anything left of her. Walking through the family room toward the kitchen, he stopped in the archway looking in before he proceeded down the hall to his left.

Liquor and beer bottles covered the kitchen table. A single chair faced the archway. Almost precisely where Dylan stood. He imagined the pool of blood Brian saw on the floor. He glanced back into the family room and the couch with the coffee table littered with bottles. Buddy could have sat there and seen into the kitchen to this very spot.

The butcher block on the counter had several empty slots. Searching the kitchen, he found one steak knife in the sink and several in the dishwasher along with a long cutting knife. He checked the drawers and cabinets, but couldn't find the other three missing knives. To his dismay, he couldn't find the butcher knife that fit the largest slot. He hoped that wasn't the bloody knife Buddy used on Jessie and threw away.

His mind played every scenario imaginable of how Jessie and Buddy went at it that night. No matter how he ran the scene, his mind conjured Jessie's image on the floor in a pool of blood with a knife stuck in her.

Shivering, he walked out of the kitchen and down the hall, skipping over Brian's old room and stopping in front of Jessie's closed door. Taking a deep breath, he opened the door and stood looking at her deserted room. Everything appeared untouched, like she'd never left, though a thick layer of dust covered every surface. A green quilt lay over the bed. Her backpack and schoolbooks sat scattered on her desk, along with makeup and hair bands. The dresser and night table had a few trinkets and mementos. Alongside some discarded change and a pack of gum sat a picture of her mother. Dylan took special notice of the woman he'd never met.

Jessie was the image of her mother, with long, dark wavy hair, hazel eyes, and that flawless satin skin. He wondered how a beautiful woman like Jessie's mother ended up with a man like Buddy. Maybe Buddy had been a different man when they were young. Time had slipped away, until Jessie's mother couldn't deal with the consequences of marrying an alcoholic.

Always a neat freak, none of Jessie's clothes littered the wood floor or hung from the drawers. Nothing out of place except the black gown she'd worn to the prom hanging on the closet door. Her high heels sat on the floor, one tipped on its side. He imagined her lying on the bed looking at the dress and remembering the night they'd shared together. He wondered if the few short days she'd had left after the prom were happy or sad. Did she miss him? Curse him? Hate him?

He hoped looking at that dress brought her happy memories of their night together. Standing there now, looking at the gown and imagining her wearing it, a multitude of emotions washed through him. Mostly anger because she wasn't here. He gripped the dress and buried his face in the material, inhaling deeply, hoping for even a hint of her scent. After all this time, even that was gone. He smoothed his hand over the material, adjusting it just so, his stomach in a knot, his heart heavy in his chest.

He'd always wanted a chance to make things right. He'd thought a thousand times what he'd say.

Ah, Jess. I was so damn young and stupid.

I wanted you to no end.

Why'd I have to fall in love with you right when I was leaving?

I'm so sorry, honey. I wish I'd been here for you. I wish I'd realized Buddy was hurting you. I wish a lot of things. I wish you were here.

I miss my best friend.

Dylan ran his hand over the dress. He remembered how he'd slid the zipper down her back, her soft skin at his fingertips. She felt so good in his arms. She'd given herself completely, trusted him completely.

The dress went out of focus, along with his memories. His eyes burned and his throat constricted painfully.

He missed her more each day.

He owed her for so much. The years of friendship they'd shared. The career he'd chosen. Most of all, he owed her for showing him just how much a person could be loved. He had no doubt she'd loved him with her whole heart.

Unable to look at the dress any longer, he opened the closet door, peering inside. Just like her room, nothing appeared out of place. What little clothes she owned were neatly stacked or hanging. Her work boots were gone. She'd probably been wearing them the night Buddy killed her. As far as he could tell, everything stood as if she'd just left.

For all intents and purposes, it appeared Buddy and Jessie argued and Buddy killed her, then hid her body. But where? Now, he'd never know. That thought disturbed him more than anything.

Dylan closed the door to her room and walked out of the house without a backward glance. Jessie wasn't there. He'd lost her. He couldn't feel her presence in that house, or in her room. The pressure in his chest grew so great, he collapsed into his truck seat. He sat and stared at the stars for a good long while before he could breathe enough to drive himself home.

Chapter Four

JESSIE SPENT THE evening making calls and settling her father's affairs. Brian hadn't done a single thing to set up a cremation or funeral for their father. No surprise there. She'd made all the necessary phone calls and doled out her credit card number. She spent the rest of the evening carving a chunk of wood into a horse, alternating between denying the fact she had to go back to Fallbrook and resigning herself to the fact she didn't have a choice.

After several phone calls to local lawyers, luckily avoiding having to call Dylan's cousin Owen McBride, she discovered her father actually had a will. Everything went to Brian. The house had a small mortgage, but nothing Brian couldn't afford if he worked steadily. She could spare a few workers from the housing development outside of town for a few days to put the house to rights and make it perfect for Brian, his wife, and their new baby.

Morning bloomed bright and cheerful, irritating her already crappy mood. She pulled up in front of Brian's rented house. Brian hadn't done anything to take care of it. An old dusty truck sat out front. She wondered if it ran well, or if he'd neglected it like everything else in his life. The little compact car probably belonged to his wife, Marilee. A nice girl, Jessie remembered her from high school. A good choice for Brian. Sweet and kind. A cheerleader. Jessie remembered her being tossed in the air, her golden curls flying while her petite, strong body struck a pose. If memory served, she'd had a crush on Brian since their freshman year.

"It's now or never, J.T. Get your ass out of the car and go talk to Brian."

Great, she'd resorted to talking to herself. She headed for the front door, knocked, and waited for whatever came next.

Marilee answered the door, swinging it wide. Her polite smile died and her blue widened with shock. She gasped. "You're alive." She held a dishtowel to her breast. "Oh my goodness. It can't be. We thought you were dead."

"Not so much. Alive and well. I hear the old man isn't though."

"How? Why? Oh my God. I can't believe you're here."

"May I come in?"

Marilee regained her composure and stepped back. Jessie entered and found Brian lying passed out on the couch in the family room, four beer bottles clustered on the coffee table. Completely dressed, including his work boots, he snored so loudly she didn't even worry about lowering her voice as she followed Marilee through the room into the kitchen.

"Would you like some coffee?" Marilee asked, her voice unsteady, unsure after Jessie's surprise resurrection.

"I'd love a cup. How are you? The baby?"

Marilee's hands shook as she took down a mug and poured the coffee. Seeing Jessie had shocked her. Brian would probably think her a ghost.

"We're both fine. I've got about two months to go." She patted her growing belly. Jessie felt a twinge of jealousy and held off the overwhelming memories.

"Have you been to the doctor? Everything is going well?" Jessie accepted the coffee.

"I've been a few times. They gave me some vitamins and said the baby is growing just fine. There doesn't seem to be anything to worry about."

Marilee frowned, squint lines appearing at her eyes. Jessie imagined all the things she'd worried about over the last seven months. Jessie understood being pregnant for the first time and not knowing if you were doing everything you could for the life depending on you. She imagined Marilee wondered how she'd afford to feed, clothe, and generally take care of a baby when her husband barely worked. They had bills piling up and no good source of income.

"Listen, Marilee, you don't know me. You probably don't want me poking around in your business, but I'm going to if you'll let me. I want to help straighten Brian out and get him back to the guy he used to be. If you want my help, I need you to step back and let me do my thing.

I'm overbearing and demanding. I'll really piss him off before he realizes I'm only trying to help. If you're up for it, I think I can make life for you and your baby better. Actually, a lot better if I can get him to cooperate."

Jessie glanced through the archway at her unconscious brother, snoring on the sofa, and thought this might take dynamite to fix.

Marilee admitted, "I was never your friend. We used to laugh at you in school. Brian was the exact opposite to your loner, outcast, but now I realize that's not who you were. We pushed you into that role because of the way we treated you. I know about what happened with your father. How he used to . . . to treat you."

Jessie cringed, but hid the instinctive reaction by taking a sip of coffee.

"Brian sometimes gets going when he's drinking, and there's no telling what he'll say. I guess I'm just trying to say I'm sorry I wasn't very nice to you in school. I've been married to your brother for more than two years and we were together before that for three more. I love him. But, Jessie, I'm desperate. I want this baby to have a good life with a father who loves him and isn't half in the bag by suppertime."

"Him. It's a boy?"

"I don't know for sure, but that's my intuition. I haven't had one of those ultrasound things. We don't have insurance because Brian won't work steady hours. He does fine for months and then goes on a bender and everything he's worked for is wasted. It's like he's afraid to succeed. He's smart and works hard. He's great with his hands. I don't know what to do, or how to get him to stop drinking. He's punishing himself because you died. Well, we thought you did."

"He might wish I were dead when I start on him. I've come here to bury the old man and set Brian straight. If you want my help, you've got it. If you want me to keep my nose out of your business, say so now."

"You really are a no-nonsense, get-to-the-point kind of person."

"I don't want to waste my time, or yours, trying to fix things if you don't want my help. I'll probably step on your pride, and I'll kick some ass with Brian. You probably won't like my style, but I have your best interest at heart. I have the baby's best interest at heart."

"I'm having a hard time getting past the fact you're sitting in my kitchen. And you're offering to help with Brian. Clearly, you mean business. It's just so hard to believe."

Marilee sighed so heavily Jessie felt the breeze from across the table. "Believe it. I know you've resigned yourself to the fate of being married to a drunk. I'm offering you a different future."

"I've asked my parents to help us more times than I can count. I can't ask them again. The rent is due, the electricity bill is past due, the telephone is about to be shut off, and that's not all." She stood and flung open the refrigerator to reveal the nearly empty compartment. Among the few condiments, an apple sat alone in the crisper. An almost-empty container of milk and a block of cheese occupied one of the shelves. The rest looked inedible and sad. Jessie would bet the cupboards weren't much better.

"Jessie, I'm begging you. If you can get Brian to be the man he was years ago before this baby arrives, I'll do anything you ask. You won't hurt my pride, because I don't have any left. I've used it all up trying to make ends meet and make a semblance of a life for this baby."

"Are you working?"

"Yes, at the insurance agency in town. It's a small business, so they don't offer insurance to their employees. Too expensive. Ironic, I know. I have no idea how we'll pay the hospital bills when this baby arrives. I started as the receptionist, but now I'm an assistant to one of the agents. I've been learning how to do claims. It's a good job and pays well." She bit her lower lip and glanced at her sleeping husband. "I want to go over there and throw his feet off the couch and choke him for making me worry about everything while he drinks himself to death."

Jessie could relate. "Will they give you time off when the baby arrives, then allow you to come back?"

"Yes, I've worked it all out."

"Okay. Then, here's the deal. I've got a job for Brian. He'll get insurance by the end of next week. I'll make sure of it. As soon as it kicks in, I want you to make regular appointments with your obstetrician. Have your ultrasound, and I want to hear all about it." Jessie took out some papers from her purse. "Directions to the jobsite. He needs to be there Monday morning at six. He'll meet with James. It's on the paper."

"I don't know if I can make sure he's there. Sometimes he drinks and I can't get him up."

"Don't worry. If he doesn't show, I'll come after him. He won't like that outcome." She winked at Marilee.

"The old man will be buried tomorrow morning at eleven at the old cemetery out on Poplar Way. If you guys want to come and dance on the old man's grave, I'll see you there. There won't be any pomp and circumstance, but it'll be done.

"He left the house and whatever else he had to Brian. I'll have a crew fix it up and get it ready for you to move into as soon as possible. Got a favorite house color?"

"White with blue trim." Marilee didn't hesitate. Like she'd said, she had no pride left. "I've dreamed of having a white house with blue trim since I was a little girl."

Too many of her girlhood dreams hadn't come true when she married Brian. He had a lot of making up to do with his wife.

"Could you have them take out that old stump and maybe put in a new tree?"

"Anything in particular?"

"Not really, just something that will provide shade to the yard when the baby plays. Something we could hang a swing from someday." Marilee smiled at the thought and it lit her whole face. "This is like taking charity, but I'm doing it for the baby. I'll take whatever help you're willing to give and be grateful to you the rest of my days. Someday, I'll find a way to thank you and pay you back."

Overwhelmed by the emotion behind Marilee's words,

Jessie got them back on subject. "Anything else you want for the house?"

"I don't know. The kitchen is outdated, and the bathrooms too. You used to work with your father; I'll trust your judgment to make the house livable, clean, and safe for the baby. That's the most important thing."

"Done. Now, I want you to go grocery shopping." Jessie pulled out her wallet and took out a bunch of cash and handed it over to Marilee. "Can you still pay the electric bill at the market?"

"Yes."

"There should be enough to pay that off and get the groceries. I'll write you a check for rent and the other bills. That should catch you up until you get into the other house in about two weeks. By then, Brian will have his first paycheck and things should get back to normal."

Marilee unfolded the bills in her hand. Her eyebrows shot up at the sight of all the money, over five hundred dollars. She crushed it in her palm and held on to it for dear life. "He'll be shocked to see you."

"That's why I suggest you go grocery shopping while I rudely wake him up. And I don't just mean from his nap on the couch. It's time he saw the light and went about the business of being a husband and father."

Marilee stared at Brian on the couch. So much sadness and hope filled her eyes. She truly wanted to believe this time Brian would turn himself around and do the right thing. Jessie knew all about that kind of desperation.

"Marilee, if this doesn't work out—if he won't stop

drinking, and you want to leave—I'll help you. No questions. No strings. No judgment. I'll help you leave him and make a life with the baby."

Marilee's gaze remained on Brian for a long moment. "I've tried to imagine my life without him. I can't. I love him. When he isn't drinking, he's such a nice and caring man." But for the sake of the baby, she nodded her agreement to Jessie's offer. "Brian better clean up his act, or he'll lose us. This is his chance, and our chance to get our lives back on track," she said with such hope in her voice, Jessie felt it in her own heart.

"I'll be gone about an hour. Um, maybe you'd like to come to dinner tonight?"

Jessie smiled softly. She didn't want to hurt Marilee's feelings. "Not tonight. I'm not staying in town. Maybe I'll see you tomorrow. I think it would be good for Brian to go to the cemetery. It's time to put the past behind us. I think we could all use a fresh start."

Marilee nodded and pulled her own purse off the counter.

"Are you partial to that couch?" Jessie asked.

"It smells like stale beer and sweat. It's old and worn like everything else in this house, including my husband. I'm partial to the man, not the couch." With that, she waddled out of the kitchen, blond curls bobbing at her shoulders.

Jessie laughed. Marilee still had a lot of spunk. She may be down, but she wasn't out. Not by a long shot. Jessie related, making her like Marilee even more.

Jessie finished her cup of coffee, set the cup in the sink,

and grabbed another cup out of the cupboard and filled it from the coffee carafe for her brother. Black. She took a pitcher out of the strainer next to the sink and filled it with cold water.

Standing over her sleeping brother, she held the pitcher in one hand and the cup of coffee in the other. She poured the cold water over her brother's face and chest. He sat bolt upright and yelled, "What the hell!"

Chapter Five

BRIAN HELD A hand to his wet head and one to his stomach. He probably had a splitting headache to go with his rotten gut. As far as Jessie was concerned, he deserved both.

"Good morning, brother. Nice of you to rise and shine."

Brian wiped a hand over his face and turned to sit on the sodden couch. His blurry eyes found Jessie standing over him. His mouth dropped open and his eyes rounded before he gained his voice.

"You're dead. I've hit that bottom people talk about. I'm dreaming, hallucinating after a night of drinking. It can't be you. You're gone, and it's all my fault." He covered his face with his hands. Choked-up tears filled his voice, his pain and sorrow sharp and piercing. She refused to let it get to her, despite her guilt for making him believe she died. Brian needed a good ass kicking, not a sympathetic ear.

"You're going to wish I died when I get through with you, you miserable drunk. What the hell happened to you?" She handed over the mug of coffee and shoved it up to his mouth to make him take a sip. Reality setting in, he needed the coffee and a shower before he'd concentrate and focus on her and what she had in store for him.

"Don't yell, my head is killing me." He pressed the heel of his hand to his eye, probably hoping his brain didn't explode.

Jessie sat on the coffee table in front of her brother between his knees and leaned forward with her elbows braced on her thighs.

"Listen to me, brother dear. It's past time you cleaned up your act. Starting today, you are going to quit drinking yourself into a stupor. You're going to take care of your wife and child. You're going to show up for work on Monday morning clear-eyed and ready to earn an honest day's pay."

"Work? I don't have any job lined up for Monday."

"Yes. You do. I gave Marilee the information. You report to James on Monday at the new housing development going up on the outskirts of town. You'll earn a decent paycheck and have medical benefits for your family.

"The old man left you the house. I'll go over tomorrow after the funeral to see what needs to be done to make it livable for you and Marilee. I, big brother, am going to make you be the man you used to be, because I can't stand to see you turn into the next Buddy Thompson. You got that?" She'd yelled at him to get his attention and to reinforce the fact he'd created his condition. His eyes rolled back in his head, and he groaned in pain, all the reward she needed.

"If you don't show up for work on Monday, I'm coming after you. And I'll keep coming until you get it through that thick head of yours, you are not him. You're better than that. So get your ass up, take a shower, mow the lawn, kiss your wife, tell her you love her and you aren't going to be this asshole you've turned into anymore. You hear me?"

"Your voice is ringing in my head." He stared into his coffee cup but glanced up to say, "You look good. Life's apparently turned out all right for you."

Jessie shrugged that off, focused more on the lost look in Brian's round, sad eyes.

"I thought you died that night. I left and he killed you. Where have you been?"

"Around. Mostly Solomon. I have a house about twenty miles outside of Fallbrook."

"You do?" The surprise lit his face.

"I started my life over. It's time you did the same."

Brian ignored that. Mired in the past, he asked, "What happened to you, Jessie?" His soft, anguish-filled voice pierced her heart and made it ache. She didn't want to go back. She wanted to fix things for him now and move on.

She stood and walked away and stared blankly out the window. She hated thinking about that night. She didn't want to talk about what happened, but Brian needed to hear it.

"What do you think happened that night?"

She'd heard some of the rumors, but she wanted to know what he thought. He'd been there at the beginning and on many other similar nights.

"Dad had been drinking pretty hard. After we quit for the day, he and some of the guys sat around knocking back a few while you put tools away and cleaned up the jobsite.

"We got home and you went in the kitchen." He paused, thinking back. "You were chopping an apple at the counter when he started in on you, slurring his words, yelling, cussing. I don't remember about what. Doesn't matter. Never did. He'd pick something out of thin air for no reason, except to get in your face."

He took a sip of the steaming coffee and shook his head, trying to clear the images from his mind. She knew from experience it wouldn't work. Some things were burned into your cells. "He threw you up against the wall and choked you.

"I'd seen him do that so many times before, I can't even count them all. I've seen him punch you and slap you.

"You never cried. Sometimes, I'd see the tears come into your eyes, and maybe one would fall, but you'd never cry. You took every blow, every nasty word, and you never backed down."

Brian's intense stare bore into her back. She hadn't moved from standing in front of the dirty window looking out at nothing but a past she didn't want to remember or hear about ever again.

"He wanted to break you. Beat you down and make you weak. He never could."

No, he never could. The harder he'd tried, the harder she'd fought to stay strong.

After losing Hope, she'd come close to giving up. Even then, she'd somehow found the strength to go on, but it had been a near miss, standing on the edge of life and oblivion.

"He was angry with Mother. Not me. He blamed me because she killed herself. Really, he blamed her for leaving him. I was here, she wasn't."

"He yelled you weren't his daughter. He screamed about how you look like her, and then he backhanded you."

She turned from the window and focused on her brother, a pile of misery sitting on the couch. "I reminded him of her and her betrayal every day she was gone. She had an affair, and then me. The note she left when she died said she couldn't accept the other man didn't want her, had left her, and she didn't want to live without him. The old man blamed me."

"So you aren't his daughter?"

She shrugged. "Who knows? Who cares? A friend of mine pointed out yesterday he was the only father I had." She held up her hands in a "whatever" kind of gesture. "What's important is you are my brother. We'll bury the old man tomorrow and be done with the whole mess."

"But all the blood. I left in the middle of the argument. I came back to an empty house, the kitchen floor covered in blood. I can still see it, smell it, like it was yesterday.

"You were nowhere to be found. When Dad came back the next morning alone, I thought he'd done something with you." Brian hung his head and stared down at his now-empty coffee mug. The alcohol had worn off, the fog thinned. The guilt hung on him, weighing down his shoulders, his very spirit. The turmoil in his eyes and laced in every word tore at her.

"Brian, listen to me. It wasn't your fault. He did it. Not you."

"I left you alone with him, and he hurt you!" Brian roared from the couch. "How many times did I walk out the door and leave you behind without so much as one word in your defense? Never once did I pull him off you, or stand between you."

"I don't want to do this with you. It's over. Done. Stop blaming yourself for something you couldn't have prevented or stopped. When have you ever known me to need someone's help?"

Well, maybe one time she'd needed Dylan, but he'd abandoned her.

Brian pulled her focus back. "Jessie. I need to know what happened that night. It's haunted me for too long. Did he stab you? Did you end up in the hospital? Where did you go?"

Brian stood up to face her. Time to put the past to rest and move on, but Brian couldn't do that until she told him what happened. She wouldn't get away without telling him.

"After you left . . ." She took a breath when her emotions backed up in her throat. She started again, "After you left, he kept at me. Usually, he'd wind down and start drinking until he passed out. That night he just kept at it. I don't know what set him off, but I made it worse when

I took a swing at him and gave him a nice shiner." She smiled a little, proud of herself for standing up to him. "I knew better than to provoke him. I'd never back down from an argument, but I also wasn't stupid enough to take him head on. That was the one and only time I took a swing at him." At least she had that. "He grabbed the knife I'd been using to cut the apple and came after me."

She stood there looking at Brian and seeing the past.

"Did he stab you, Jessie?" Brian's soft, sad voice had her choking back tears.

"I turned to run as he swung the knife down. He cut a gash down my back." The only way for him to know what happened was to show him. She turned around, crossed her arms over her middle, and pulled the hem of her tank top up to reveal the long scar down her back. Brian inhaled sharply. She put her shirt down and turned back to face him.

"As the knife went in, I fell to the floor. I rolled over and he stood over me with the knife in his hand. I could smell the whiskey on his breath. I thought he'd finish it then, but something came over him and the knife slipped from his fingers and landed at my feet. He grabbed a bottle from the table and rushed out the back door. He probably drove somewhere and drank himself unconscious.

"I dragged myself up off that floor and left. I refused to take it from him one more second of one more day. I'll spare you the gory details about how many stitches it took to close up the gash."

"Jessie, how the hell did you survive that?"

"I sucked it up and moved on. Which is exactly what you are going to do now." Overwhelmed with her past, she needed to get out of there. She knew this would be hard, but not like this. She hoped this was the last time she ever had to think about and relive that night. "Marilee has all the information for the funeral and your job. I hope you come tomorrow. We both need to bury the old man and our past. It's over. I hope you start new today. Either way, on Monday you better be at work, or I will come and get you, and you won't like it if I do.

"And another thing, I'd make things right with your wife. I've already told her I'd help her leave you. I'd be scared if I was you. She actually took a minute to think about my offer. I won't have another Thompson grow up with an alcoholic for a father. Clean up your act."

With that hanging between them, she walked out the front door and ran straight into the one person she never wanted to see again. Dylan.

Chapter Six

DYLAN PULLED UP to Brian's house and parked behind a sleek, black Porsche at the curb. Nice car, not exactly something you'd see in this part of town. He walked up the cracked path to the front door, but five steps away, the door opened and a beautiful woman walked out. They stared at each other. His heart stopped, his throat closed, cutting off his breath, and everything inside of him froze for a second before the relief washed over him and he realized he wasn't staring at a ghost.

"Jess." Her name came out on an exhale.

God, she was beautiful. And all grown up. Fifteen the last time he'd seen her, at twenty-four she was a knockout. He took her in from the fall of her rich-brown wavy hair pulled back into a ponytail, to the tight white tank top hugging the curve of her full breasts and slim waist, to the tight blue jeans that showed off the slender curve of her hips and strong thighs, down to her black cowboy boots.

No wedding ring. If he'd been relieved to see her alive, it was just as powerful to discover she wasn't married.

A gold chain hung around her neck and disappeared down the front of the tank top and into her cleavage. Light makeup enhanced her eyes and mouth. God, that mouth. He wanted to kiss her.

Dylan wanted her as much today as he had at eighteen. All the years he'd thought about her, wondered about her, dreamed of her, hadn't done justice to having her close. His chest hurt just looking at her.

"Jess? Is it really you?"

He reached for her, grabbing her arm to pull her close. She gave him the shock of his life and seized his hand, spun, and using his momentum and her leg, flung him to the dead grass. He landed on his back, and she stood over him.

"Hey!" Still shocked, he didn't know why she glared down at him with enough fury in her eyes to scorch him.

"Don't touch me. Don't ever touch me again."

Everything inside of him refused to accept that warning. All he wanted to do is hold her close.

"You can't toss people to the ground, you know. Nice move though." He tried to lighten things up, despite the murderous look in her eyes.

"You deserve to be dropped on your ass. No worse than what you did to me, and far less than you deserve. What are you going to do? Arrest me?" She waved her hand, dismissing the idea, but paced away and back again, her anger turning to uncertainty in her eyes.

"No, Jess. I just want to talk to you. Where have you been?"

"Why the hell do you care?"

Dylan rolled to his feet, raked his fingers through his hair, bent, and picked up his Stetson from the grass, setting it back on his head. "I thought you were dead." He stared at her wide, shocked eyes.

"Why the hell would you think I'm dead?"

Anger laced her voice. Her eyes fixed on his gun and moved back to him with a cold glare. He wondered if she could hate him that much because he'd left without saying goodbye. He owed her an explanation, but he hadn't expected her to be this angry. She really looked like she wanted to use his gun on him.

"Thinking about shooting me, honey?"

"The thought did cross my mind. It is tempting. *Honey*," she said with venom. "You of all people knew I wasn't dead." She pressed her hand to her belly and the color drained from her face. "Why would you think I'm dead?" she asked, less hostile and more hesitant.

Dylan didn't understand the stunned disbelief on her face, or why she'd ask that question when everyone thought she died. "You disappeared a few days after I left town. My parents said no one knew what happened to you. All kinds of rumors floated around. Your father and brother were questioned about your disappearance. Brian told me about the night you left. His story is pretty convincing your father killed you and took your body and dumped it somewhere."

"Are you serious?" She planted her hands on her hips. "All this time you thought I was dead?"

"Yes. I did. I'm so damn happy to see you, Jess."

"This can't be. I mean, I can understand why Brian might think something happened that night, but not you. You knew I was alive. You had to have known."

Dylan cocked his head, studying her. "I wasn't even here. I didn't contact my parents until two weeks after you disappeared."

"I tried your cell phone, but you'd canceled the service, so I emailed you." Jessie put her arms around her middle and held herself. Her eyes filled with so much hurt, he felt it in his gut.

"Jessie, someone stole my phone at the airport. I canceled the number and got a new one a few weeks later. I never got an email."

"Don't lie to me. You got it. You sent me an email saying you didn't want anything to do with me, you had a new life, and you never wanted to hear from me again. I emailed you back. I tried to tell you, but you shut down your email address too."

Dylan sucked in a shocked breath and took a step back. He couldn't believe she'd think he'd do such a thing after everything they shared. Yes, he'd left without a word, but he'd had his reasons and none of them had to do with her and the friendship and more they'd shared.

Busy with the constant drilling those first eight weeks in basic training, he'd barely had enough time to eat and sleep, they kept him so busy. His parents were beyond angry he'd joined the army and didn't go to their hand-picked college to earn the degree they wanted him to have. He hadn't questioned them about changing his email.

If his suspicions were right, his mother had done a hell of a lot more than change his email address. Anger flashed through his system.

"When your email didn't work, I called your parents' house and spoke to your mother. She told me you didn't want anything to do with me. She said it was my fault you left and joined the military to get away from me."

"Jess, I'm sorry. No. That's not true. I'd never say anything like that about you. After I left home, my parents changed the email service."

"Your mother's way of keeping me from contacting you."

His mother made it clear on numerous occasions she disapproved of, even hated, Jessie. Maybe that's why he'd been so determined to be her friend. Maybe that's why when he noticed her as more than a friend, and his mother figured it out, as mothers do, she'd been adamant he not see her ever again. He never told his parents he had a date to the prom, and even went so far as to ask Jessie to meet him there instead of picking her up. Sneaky and cowardly on his part. He'd wanted to be with her that night without instigating a fight with his parents in order to do it.

When he'd left town, a small voice inside him told him to take her with him. He'd hated leaving her behind, but what could he do? She was fifteen and still in high school. He couldn't ask her to run away with him and get away with it. If he'd known about the abuse, taken her away with him, she wouldn't have been hurt, almost killed.

"Shit. I think she sent you that email. I can't believe she'd do something so callous."

"I can."

"I'd never tell you I didn't want anything to do with you, Jess. That's the furthest thing from the truth. You have to know that after everything we shared. I have grieved every day for you, Jess." He wanted to wrap her in his arms. Whatever was between them now, this anger she had for him, he wanted to make it disappear.

Jessie ignored those poignant words. She'd hated Dylan all this time for turning his back on her when she needed him most. She had a hard time switching gears. She clung to her anger, but turned it in his mother's direction now. His mother sent the email. She choked back the bile rising in her throat. Even now, she felt the terrifying realization she was pregnant and unable to contact Dylan. His mother telling her he didn't want her in the email and on the phone, going through the pregnancy alone, delivering their beautiful daughter . . . and losing her. The bitch had done it all because she found Jessie lacking and unsuitable for her only son.

She turned to Dylan, her emotions a whirlwind in her gut. "If she'd just given me your phone number, let me tell you, everything could have been so different. I swear to God, I'll make her pay for this."

Overwhelmed with sadness for all he'd missed,

the anger washed over her again, and then came the misery she'd felt all those years ago when his mother told her Dylan didn't want anything to do with her. A whirlwind of feelings and emotions she couldn't hide from her face.

Dylan responded to her, his gentle tone coaxing her to talk to him, spill her guts, and unburden herself. "Jess, I don't understand what you're talking about. Is this about what Buddy did to you? I should have protected you. I'm sorry. You must have been so angry when I left."

"Hell yes, I was angry." She couldn't face the fact his mother lied. She wanted to deny someone, anyone, could be that cruel.

"There was more. So much more," she said, her voice quieting.

"Jess, I don't understand. Tell me why you called."

"I didn't come here to . . . rehash the past with you. I came to see Brian and set things right with him. I can't do this with you, standing in the front yard in front of all the neighbors."

"Let's go somewhere and talk."

She couldn't do this now, today, not when her emotions and the memories of what her father did to her, Dylan's mother's scathing words, and losing Hope swamped her every thought.

"As far as I'm concerned, all the anger and hurt over what happened has been directed at the wrong person. Am I angry you left? Hell yes." She jabbed a finger into his chest, punctuating every word. "I blame you for not having the decency to say goodbye and tell me you were leaving. But what your mother did is unconscionable. She knew I was alive and didn't tell you. She didn't tell you I called because I needed you. No matter what she says, there is no excuse for what she's done."

"Jess, why did you need me? What happened with Buddy? There was blood. You must have been hurt pretty bad. Were you in a hospital? On the streets? What?"

"None of that matters compared to what I tried to tell you. If she'd simply given me your number, I could have told you."

"Tell me now."

"I can't. Don't you get it? Hurting you the way your mother hurt me will only make it worse." He'd hate her. The thought closed off her throat and made the bile churn and burn in her gut. She pressed a hand to her stomach, unable to bring herself to speak the words.

Up until today, she'd have liked to hurt him, making his heart bleed the way he'd made hers tear to shreds, but not now. Not like this.

"Jess."

"I have to go. I have to take care of for my father's funeral. Excuse me."

Dylan stood in the middle of the broken path, staring at the back end of the Porsche as Jessie drove away, memorizing the license plate. He'd Googled her over the years, hoping for any sign she really had run away. He never found anything that linked to her. Now he'd go back to his office and dig for information on her, starting with the registration to her car.

Brian opened the door behind him. "Hey man, what are you doing here?"

"I was just catching up with your sister." Actually, he felt completely at a loss, with no idea what just happened. She talked in circles. One thing was clear, his mother had interfered in his life again.

Dylan turned to face Brian. He'd just come from the shower. He wore a clean pair of jeans, a dark blue T-shirt, and his hair was wet but combed. Brian raised a hand to his bloodshot eyes to block the bright sun and winced from the pain. Dylan bet he had a raging hangover headache and sympathized.

"Did you two catch up?"

"She showed me the long-ass scar down her back. The thing goes from her shoulder down to her hip. This nasty, ragged line. That bastard sliced her open."

"Where did she go after she left town?"

"Solomon."

So close. Yet no one ever found her. Probably because no one went looking for her.

"I thought she was dead. Now, I have a job and she's yelling at me to quit drinking and being like the old man. Apparently, my wife is considering leaving me. Damn." Brian threw up his hands in frustration. "Hell, I don't know what's going on. Did she tell you anything?"

"She tried to contact me when she left town."

"She did? What the hell happened with the two of you at the prom?"

"I thought I knew. Now, I don't think I know the half of it," Dylan admitted and hated being in the dark. He rubbed the tense muscles at the back of his neck. Jessie's words ate at him. "Listen, I have to go to the office. You all right?"

"Just peachy. I think I better clean up the house before my wife gets home. You may have to come back if she decides to kill me."

Chapter Seven

DYLAN SAT IN his truck outside the sheriff's office and stared at the building, thinking of all Jessie said and didn't say. He pulled out his cell and hit the speed dial for his parents' house.

"Hello." His mother's cheerful voice came on the line.

"It's me."

"Are you calling to ask me to watch Will again?" The hope in her voice made him smile, but it died on his lips the second he thought about why he really called her.

"No. He's with Lorena today. I went over to Brian's house to see if I could help him make funeral arrangements for Buddy."

"You die young when you drink like that man."

No sympathy. Not even an offer of condolences for his old friend, Brian. Typical, judgment with no sympathy.

"Jessie's back in town. I saw her at Brian's house."

Silence. It took his mother twenty seconds to spit out. "Is that right?"

"Why didn't you tell me she called?"

"What difference would it have made? You left your family and joined the military against our wishes. You wanted to get away from us. This town. Her."

"No. Not her. But that's what you told her, didn't you? You sent her that email, saying I didn't want her and never wanted to hear from her again."

"Who can remember what I said after all these years? You moved on. I told her to do the same."

"How could you do that when everyone in town thought her father killed her?"

"Well, he didn't."

"Did you even ask her what happened? Where she was? If she was okay?"

"She wasn't my responsibility or yours. If I'd told her where you were, she'd have clung onto you again and dragged you down with her. That girl is nothing but an anchor. You're better off without her. You've got Will to look after now. He needs you, so don't get distracted from the life you've built here with him. That girl is no good for you."

Dylan smacked his hand against the steering wheel, frustrated to have the same conversation he'd had with his mother about Jessie so many times when he was a kid. Arguing about Jessie never got him anywhere. His mother refused to see the Jessie he knew.

"Dylan." His mother said his name with that placating tone that meant she'd reached the end of her rope with him. "I'm sorry I didn't tell you she called, but there was nothing you could do for her. You had your life. She had hers. Things turn out the way they do for a reason."

"You let me believe she died."

"After I spoke to her, no one ever heard from her again. You were gone, busy in the military, and then with Will. I never thought to mention it again. You never asked about her."

No. Why would he when his mother made her feelings clear and led him to believe Jessie died. He'd suffered and mourned in silence.

"You should have told me. I can't believe you sent that email in my name. How could you do something like that?"

"I was hurt and angry after you left. I wasn't thinking. I'd check your email every day for a clue as to why you left the way you did. What were you thinking? Then she emailed you, and it became so obvious you two had a falling out and that's why you left the way you did."

"I can't believe you were checking my emails."

"You knew the rules when you lived under our roof."

Yes, he did. They knew his passwords, but he never thought he'd given them any reason to check up on him. Sometimes his mother could be overprotective. In this case, she'd crossed a line.

Furious she'd invade his privacy, send an email in his name, and then follow up with her lies by telling Jessie on the phone, he didn't want to speak to her ever again. He couldn't speak to his mother right now. He might say something he couldn't take back. "I have to go. I'll talk to you later."

"Dylan. I'm sorry. The last thing I ever want to do is hurt you."

"I know," he conceded, but she had hurt him. She'd hurt Jessie, and that was harder to ignore. "I'll talk to you later."

The damage had been done. Now, he had to find a way to make it up to Jessie. First, he had to find her.

DYLAN SLAMMED HIS office door, rounded his desk, and sat in his cracked leather chair.

The office buzzed with activity. After his call with his mother this morning, he'd been detoured from his objective to find Jessie for one emergency call and then another. When he finally returned to the office, he consulted with his deputies about ongoing cases, returned phone calls, and waded through general crap before he could look into Jessie's past.

Story of his life. Especially since he moved back to Fallbrook.

Well, nothing and no one would sidetrack him this time. Not a case. Not his cousins, Brody and Owen, and whatever drama they had going on in their lives, though things had calmed down now that both of them were married.

He'd come back to his office to find out where Jessie had been all this time. Her license plate was the one and only clue he had to work with, but he'd start there and follow her trail through the last several years and uncover all her secrets. He needed to dig up all the information and details on her before he saw her again. The next time they talked, he wanted to be prepared. This morning, she'd blindsided him. He didn't want that to happen again.

The aroma of fresh coffee surrounded him. Inhaling deeply, he rose and poured a cup from the pot his secretary made recently on the credenza. Returning to his desk, he frowned at the files piled in his in basket. To his dismay, they overwhelmed the number he'd managed to move into his out basket.

He took off his hat, tossing it into the visitor's chair. He ran both hands through his hair and swore under his breath. One hell of a morning. Jessie was back. Not only alive and well, but more beautiful than he imagined. And royally pissed. At him. At his mother because of that damn email. Even the thought of hurting Jessie with a letter like that made him sick. He'd never do anything to hurt her. That she believed it only showed how short he fell the one and only time he'd laid it all on the line to show her how special she was to him. Prom night. That night and Jessie haunted his memories.

He took a swallow of coffee and pressed the heel of his hand to his forehead between his eyes. A headache throbbed in time to his heart. The sun slowly descended into dusk, and still he hadn't done what he'd come in on a Saturday to do.

He thought of all Jessie had been through in her young life, ending with Buddy slicing open her back. An injury like that could be fatal. Just the thought of what Brian described made him cringe. He'd seen his share of gruesome wounds in the military, on the Atlanta police force, and as a sheriff, but nothing prepared him to even think of something like that happening to the woman he loved.

Oh, he had no doubt he loved her. It had taken him not two seconds to figure that out the minute he saw her this morning, and the relief had nearly sent him to his knees. Jessie had knocked him on his ass, figuratively and literally. He smiled thinking of it now. Tough. Strong. God, he'd missed her. He didn't know what he'd done to earn it, but he'd been given a second chance at a real life with Jessie, and he wasn't about to blow it again. To think he might actually have a chance to get her back after spending the last years thinking she was dead. More than he could hope for, that's exactly what he wanted and planned to make happen.

A knock at the door drew his attention. Lynn's robust figure filled the space between the doorframe. Her white hair and smooth skin didn't give away her age, except to say she was older than everyone in the sheriff's office. He figured her age around sixty. A nice enough woman, great assistant, but she tended to be nosy as hell and talked a lot. She knew everything about everyone in town.

Right now, he wanted thirty uninterrupted minutes to mine his computer's knowledge and find the information he needed to know about Jessie under whatever name she'd been using, because he'd never found anything in her name.

"What now?" He hadn't meant to snap it out like that, but damnit he needed some peace and quiet.

"In a foul mood, I see. You often get this way after a long day, or something's on your mind. Word is Jessie Thompson showed up out of the blue this morning. Most of the town is talking about it. Marilee told the cashier at the grocery store Jessie got Brian a job."

When he didn't remark, she continued. Who could stop her?

"I also heard you arrived at the house shortly after Marilee left. If memory serves, you and Jessie used to be close friends. You took her to the prom and disappeared just days later. Sure, everyone found out you'd joined the military, but Jessie had already disappeared herself by then.

"So, Sheriff. Did you see Jessie Thompson this morning? Is it true she's back?"

Jessie wouldn't like him, or everyone else in town for that matter, talking about her. They'd done enough of that over the years. Not one of those people, himself included, ever tried to help her. As far as he knew, no one knew what was happening at the Thompson house.

"She came by to visit Brian this morning and make arrangements for Buddy's funeral tomorrow."

The best course, keep it simple and not give out too much information. Lord knew, if Lynn had already gotten wind of Jessie's miraculous return, then the whole town already knew about it. Hell, Lynn probably knew more about it than he did, and he was there this morning.

"I heard from Frank, who lives two doors down from

Brian, he saw you two talking in the yard for quite some time, and she flew out of there driving one of those fancy cars. A Porsche," she said and nodded with her lips pressed tight together.

He neither confirmed nor denied anything about his conversation with Jessie. "She does drive a Porsche. It's nice. Black." He wondered how she could afford such an expensive car.

Drunk most of the time, Buddy had scraped by on construction jobs, always riding the line between prosperous and poor. He might have done better if he didn't drink away his profits.

Ten minutes, that's all he needed alone to find out about her past and present. Then he could decide what to do next. How to approach her and get her to talk about what happened, why he left, and apologize for being a dick and what his mother did, sending her that email. Jessie had something to tell him too. Something big. The stress settled firmly between his tense shoulder blades. His mind told him he'd failed her somehow and it had nothing to do with Buddy Thompson.

"Sooo, give," Lynn prompted. "What's she been doing all this time? Where has she been?"

"She didn't say." He wasn't going to say any more. Unfortunately, Lynn had other ideas.

"You know, some folks thought she left to find you. I think most people dismissed that notion when your mama told everyone you'd joined the military. Seems she told everyone just a couple weeks after Jessie up and left."

Interesting. Jessie called his mother after she'd left

town. Maybe his mother wanted everyone to know she wasn't with him. Had to keep up appearances and propriety. That's why she constantly told him to "stay away from that no-good girl. She's nothing but trouble."

"Other folks said she ran off with a boyfriend she'd met on one of those construction jobs she worked with her daddy. Course, no one said who that might be. She tagged along after you and her brother. Seems she stayed real close to you two as much as possible."

He knew, now, why. She wanted to be safe with them. In the end, she hadn't been. They'd both walked out on her. He couldn't believe he'd been *that* guy. Stupid, idiot, teenager. Well, he'd never be *that* guy again. This time, he wanted forever.

"Most folks believed her daddy finally killed her."

"Finally? What does that mean?" Lynn held his full attention now. "As far as I know, no one knew Jessie was being hurt. At least, that had been my perception."

Lynn let out a incredulous laugh. "You were just a kid, engrossed in your own life and teenage dramas. Sports, school, girls. Those things held your attention."

He had to agree. Self-absorbed described most teens, himself included.

"Weren't no big secret old Buddy Thompson was meaner than a rabid dog to that girl. After her mama killed herself and Buddy took to drinking as his full-time job, he was known to leave a mark or two on her. A couple of her teachers noticed a few times and sent her to the office. Nothing was ever done. Buddy would come in and say how she'd fallen or gotten hurt at one of his construction jobs. Jessie backed him up, afraid to say anything against Buddy. Without any evidence, or a witness to the abuse, nothing was ever done.

"Who could blame her? On the days she went to the office, she'd come back the next day with more than a few bruises. Teachers became too afraid to say anything for fear the poor girl would pay for it. From the third or fourth grade on, teachers ignored her and the kids stayed clear of her. They figured if the teachers didn't want anything to do with her, neither did they.

"I remember she was real smart. Brainy, most would call her. Quiet. Shy. I don't think that girl ever had many friends, except you and Brian."

On a roll, Lynn continued. "Now Brian, that boy got everything Jessie went without. You'd see him with new shoes and clothes. Jessie was always an afterthought with Buddy. Seems if he'd done better by her, others would have treated her better as well. Even your mama said more than a few unkind words about poor Jessie hanging around you. She didn't like it one bit. Thought Jessie was no good. I bet your mama never thought you'd join the military and become an officer of the law."

Surprised didn't begin to cover it. He'd had more than a few arguments with her and his father about his chosen profession. The only concession he'd made to his parents' dream for him was getting his degree in criminology. He'd worked damn hard to earn it, starting with correspondence and online classes during his military stint and finishing during his first year on the police force. He owed Jessie for that too. Her death made him think about what he really wanted for his life. He hadn't saved Jessie, but he'd dedicated his life to saving others.

"Your mother blamed your life choices on Jessie too. She discovered you snuck Jessie into the prom and afterwards you didn't even talk to her. Boy, that got her going, but good. A few days later, you graduated and disappeared." Lynn waited to see if he'd tell her anything about his relationship with Jessie and if he'd left because of her.

He'd already signed up with the army by the time he took Jessie to the prom. What was he supposed to do? They were kids, she was only fifteen. He couldn't run away with her. What would he have done with her? He had a contract with the military and lived in the barracks. He served a tour in Iraq and another in Afghanistan. At the time, he had nothing to offer her and no real way to take care of her. If he'd known about Buddy, he'd have found a way to make it work.

Hell, she'd scared him. He'd never experienced feelings that deep, ever, or since. For him, it had always been Jessie. During that time, it had always been him for her. Now, she didn't want him to touch her. She refused to stay and talk to him.

It made him ache to think about the anger and sadness he'd seen in her eyes this morning.

If anyone deserved to be angry about her past, it was Jessie. He wanted to help her heal some of that hurt. Maybe then they could make a life together.

"Sheriff, are you listening?"

He pushed those thoughts aside and tuned back into Lynn. "What? Sorry."

"Work slowed down. Get on home to Will before things pick up again."

"I have work to do on the computer. I'll head out shortly."

She turned to leave his office, but he called her back. "Lynn, is there anyone I should know about who's in the same situation Jessie was in when she was young? Anyone? A child or a woman who needs our help?"

Lynn kept her ear to the ground, knew who slept with whom, and who had skeletons hidden in the closet. Dylan hated to think he'd overlooked someone who needed help.

"You took care of Shannon for Owen, though that was a whole other twisted kind of thing."

Didn't he know it.

"You know about the Dobbs woman. Several calls came in about her husband knocking her around some nights. I heard there's a boy in the third grade. He's been having a real hard time of it. Seems he's gotten into trouble for bullying the smaller children in his class. His mama does her best, but she doesn't have any help. Her husband ran out on her a few months back. Ask me, the boy is neglected, and he's acting out at school because of it. Perhaps if someone stepped in now and gave him and his mama some help, you could prevent that boy from growing up and being more than just a bully. I'm sure a stern talking-to about being kind to others from the sheriff just might turn him around. His name is Jimmy Boyd. I'll get you their address."

"If you hear anything you think I should know, my door's always open."

He held back a laugh as she beamed and avowed, "Looks like you'll make a fine sheriff for the county, much better than Sheriff Leland ever was. A lazier man, I've never met."

Which explained why Buddy got away with everything that happened to Jessie. If the law didn't care, who did?

Alone, finally, he set to work on discovering some of the answers to his many questions about Jessie.

Chapter Eight

JESSIE PARKED BEHIND her brother's truck and cast a glance at the other twenty or so vehicles parked along the road next to the cemetery. Maybe more than one funeral was planned for today. Her gaze scanned across the expanse of lawn and headstones to where she'd picked out the plot. Everyone stood around her father's grave site waiting for the funeral to begin. She wondered how all these people found out about the proceedings. Who knew Buddy had so many friends?

Unprepared to see all these people, she hesitated but bolstered her resolve and moved forward. Just like she always did. About thirty men and women watched and waited. It didn't look as though any of them were particularly sad over Buddy's death. Too busy studying Brian, several of them spotted her and literally gaped.

Some of the faces she remembered: Charlie and Buddy, his longtime fishing cronies; and Toby, his old partner in the construction business. Buddy had been more a hindrance to business than help, but Toby put up with Buddy for years.

Dylan stood beside her brother and sister-in-law. Seeing him, her feelings jumbled into a fiery ball in her gut. He wasn't dressed in his uniform, or what he used as his uniform. He didn't go in for the whole getup. At Brian's, he'd worn black jeans instead of his uniform pants. He hadn't gone with the sheriff's hat either. Like today, he'd had on that dangerous-looking black Stetson.

Gone were the jeans in deference to the funeral. In their place, he wore black slacks and a white dress shirt opened at the collar. She loved the way he looked, especially his broad shoulders and strong arms. The dress shirt couldn't hide either feature. He stood with his legs apart, hands in his front pockets as he spoke with Brian, his clothes and stance, both casual and elegant.

Dylan had always demanded and expected respect. He'd always gotten it, because he earned it. She doubted he had to work to make a living. He came from money, had a large trust fund and inheritance from his mother's side of the family, and probably worked because he liked it. Just one of the things she admired about him, he didn't use his wealth to separate himself from people who had less.

Everyone loved him. Easy to love, he had a great sense of humor and treated everyone like a friend. She'd fallen for him. From puppy love, to girlhood crush, to all-out love, she'd given herself to him through every stage of her young life. From the time she fell on the playground, skinning her knees, when a pack of boys chased her under the guise of playing tag but were really tormenting her. Dylan pulled her up and brushed her off, glared at the boys, and told them to leave her alone. To the night of the prom when she'd given him her body, her heart, and her soul.

It hurt just looking at him.

His eyes tracked her progress from the moment she got out of the car. Ignoring him, she walked toward the grave site. To her surprise, Pop and Greg came to lend their support. Not that she needed it. Nice to have some friends among the many people who only came to see her miraculous return.

She never expected all these people to turn out, but if they stuck around long enough they'd get an eyeful of just what Jessie Thompson thought of her old man.

Dylan didn't miss Jessie's arrival. Who could miss a beautiful woman getting out of a Porsche? She wore black jeans and boots with a white blouse that softly flowed down her body and clung to the curve of her breasts and waist. She carried a black tote bag. He wondered what she'd brought along. She wore her hair down today and the mass of wavy brown hair danced behind her in the wind.

She didn't even look at him, but walked straight over to two men who recently arrived. He didn't know them, but they sure knew Jessie. They smiled as she approached, and she returned their smile. He wished she'd smile at him that way. Alarms went off in his mind.

Could that guy be her boyfriend, or worse, her husband?

She'd legally changed her name at eighteen. Why? To hide her identity from her father and anyone else curious enough to look for her. Or did she marry that man? If so, why didn't they show up here together? No. Not a husband, but someone close.

She walked into the older man's arms. Maybe she was seeing the younger one, but at least she hadn't gone straight to him. Irrational, but it made him feel better. Dylan couldn't hear the exchange and wished he could walk over, put his arm around her, pull her to his side, and tell them and everyone else Jessie belonged to him. He wished she did.

"POP, YOU CAME." Jessie hugged him tight. "What are you doing here? I told you to take it easy."

"Ah, darlin', I wanted to be here for you. Just in case you needed me."

"I'll always need you." She let go of Pop and went into Greg's arms.

He kissed her temple and held her tight. For a moment, she leaned into him and took in his strength. Her friend and confidant, he knew everything about her father and Dylan. He'd been the one to get her to open up about how she'd landed in Solomon in the first place. He'd listened and helped her put things into perspective. He'd been with her when she had Hope and when she lost her.

"I see Sheriff McBride is here. Shall I kill him now, or wait until after the funeral?" Greg's voice took on that dry tone he used when he made a joke but was really serious.

She smiled and kissed his cheek. "Why not wait until after the funeral. Once they lower the old man into his dark, cold grave, we can send Dylan in after him. I can bury two for the price of one," she quipped, not really feeling it. Dylan hadn't done anything wrong. Not really. Yes, he left her without a second thought, and that hurt, but what his mother did was far worse.

"That brilliant mind is always working, J.T." He cupped her face in his hands and gazed into her eyes. "Are you ready for this? Everyone's staring at you. They want to know what happened and why you left."

She put her hands on his arms and leaned her forehead against his chin. It never hurt to let someone love you, especially a good friend like Greg.

"I'm ready. It's time to put the past to rest, along with Buddy Thompson." Now that she'd come back to Fallbrook, she'd have to finish it one way or another.

She broke free from Greg and went to the preacher to ask him to begin the service. She'd made all the plans and didn't care what anyone thought. Like everything else in her life, she'd do this her way.

The preacher called everyone's attention to the graveside and they gathered around. No chairs; Jessie hadn't planned for anyone but her, Brian, and Marilee to attend.

Dylan watched her with the two men, and the intimacy between her and the younger one. The older man looked on like a father watching his children. Dylan had a suspicion the two men were indeed father and son. He wondered how Jessie fit into their family. He had to know if he'd lost her to that man.

He couldn't take his eyes off her. She stood beside the grave, her arms crossed under her breasts, face blank, eyes unfocused on the casket. No flowers. Nothing to pretty up this service. Her expression said it all. She was impatient to have the deed done.

The preacher said a silent prayer before looking up at those who had gathered to mourn the passing of Buddy Thompson. Clearing his throat, he spoke only a single sentence.

"Do unto others as you would have them do unto you."

The preacher's words penetrated the quiet group, and the silence in the cemetery took on a presence of its own. Everyone held a collective breath waiting to see what happened next.

Dylan smiled. Leave it to Jessie to get the last word and put her father in his place.

The preacher crossed himself, hung his head in another silent prayer, then turned to Brian and shook his hand. They spoke for a moment, the preacher probably offering his condolences. Next, he went to Jessie. No words exchanged, only an envelope and a handshake. Jessie had apparently been the one to pay for the preacher and the funeral.

She could afford it. She owned her own construction company. Last night, he sat in front of his office computer ferreting out every detail he could find about her. Or, rather, J. T. Langley. He didn't know where she got the last name, but he'd find out. What he discovered amazed him. She'd earned a college degree in business. In addition to having two business licenses and her contracting license, she owned the thriving company. Once he discovered she owned Hope Construction, everything else fell into place. Most of the information he found was under the company name, not her new name, including a fleet of vehicles. She'd never been arrested or even gotten a speeding ticket.

He gathered facts and figures, but it still wasn't enough. He wanted the details of her life, and only those could come from her. If she'd only talk to him. He wanted to know everything. Like why she'd called his mother to find him. Maybe today he'd get the answers.

If nothing else, he needed to say his piece. He'd thought he'd lost his chance when he believed she died. Now, he wanted to tell her how sorry he was for not knowing about Buddy. For leaving without saying goodbye.

For not being the kind of friend she'd been to him.

He often dreamed about her (prom night and the backseat of his Mustang), but last night he'd brought Jessie into the here and now. He dreamed of her as the woman she grew into and what it would be like to have her today.

To his surprise, the preacher announced Jessie would like everyone to leave. She stood with her arms crossed and her face blank, never acknowledging anyone. Not until the two men she knew approached her again, setting Dylan's back teeth to grinding.

Chapter Nine

"ARE YOU GOING to be all right, Jessie?"

"Yes, Pop. I'll be fine. I'm going to have a drink with the old man. I have a few things to say to him, and I'd like my privacy. I'll give you a call later."

Pop gave her a hug from behind. She hadn't turned away from the casket to talk to him. She didn't move when he embraced her, except to lean back against him.

Greg kissed her on the top of her head and wrapped his arm around her shoulders. She leaned into him and he held her for a moment. There for her when she needed him, he didn't have to say anything.

She worked a man's job and sometimes forgot she wasn't as strong as she always felt she had to be. Today, a piece of her wanted to weep for the injustices of life.

You can't pick your parents. Jessie ended up with a father who'd rather hurt her than love her, and a mother whose demons drove her take her own life.

Greg was lucky. His father loved him, encouraged him, and was a friend as well as a parent. He treated Jessie as his own daughter, which is why she'd changed her name to Langley. Yes, to hide, but also because she found a place she belonged and was wanted. For the last eight years, she'd had someone to treat her the way a daughter deserved to be treated. Pop loved her. She knew what that love should feel like now. It wasn't what she'd gotten from Buddy Thompson.

Greg would understand she hurt when she reached up and held his forearm and leaned her chin on his arm. He stood and waited for her to stand on her own again. The only show of weakness she'd allow herself. He'd give her the time she needed. When her hands left his arm and she stood without leaning back on him, he released her with another kiss on her head.

"I'd really love to punch him until he hurts as much as you did when he left you alone," Greg said close to her ear. She smiled ruefully. Today wasn't the day to confront the sheriff on her behalf. But she appreciated the sentiment all the same.

He and his father walked away, leaving her with her brother, sister-in-law, and the sheriff.

"Jessie, thank you for taking care of the arrangements. We really appreciate everything you've done," Marilee's soft voice came from behind her.

Jessie lost herself in the storm of memories brewing. Like pelting rain, each drop another bad memory coming to the surface in her mind.

"Sure, Marilee. No problem," she said absently.

Her brother stood across from her on the other side of the casket. His hands trembled, but his eyes were clear.

"Brian, I'm going by Dad's house later. I'll make a list of the supplies we'll need. I'll have a crew there on Monday to get things moving. If you want to meet me there and tell me what you want to keep and what you want to go, I'll have the crew haul it away."

Brian screwed up. As a little girl, Jessie looked up to him. She used to tag along after him and Dylan everywhere they went. He'd given her a hard time, called her names, and told her he hated having her around all the time. He did all those terrible things an older brother does to torment a little sister and all she'd wanted was someone to protect her.

A hollowness took over his inside, leaving him empty. Hearing her tell him she'd take care of everything only proved how much he'd failed her.

Time to swallow what little pride he had left and let her help him. Somehow, he'd find a way to pay her back.

His wife laid down the law yesterday. He either took his sister's offer of a job and her help to get them back on their feet, or he'd end up alone. Marilee vowed to take the baby and the money his sister offered and she'd leave him for good. He couldn't let that happen. He loved Marilee, and he looked forward to having the baby. He wanted to be a good husband and father. Better start putting his family first. That meant accepting his sister's help.

"Brian," Jessie coaxed.

"Gut the house. There's nothing worth saving. Whatever changes you think are necessary, make them. If you want me there on Monday, I'll be there."

Jessie didn't think his working on the house would be a good idea. Besides, she'd like to surprise him and Marilee. Her way of giving them a wedding and baby gift all in one, since she missed their wedding.

"Go to the jobsite and report to James like I told Marilee yesterday. I'll take care of the house. Did the lawyer contact you?"

Brian nodded. "Dad left everything to me, the house and all its contents. A savings account from the sale of Dad's business and whatever he had in his checking account. You should have gotten half of everything. You were his daughter."

She held back her automatic retort, *not really*. At least, not according to her mother. It didn't really matter. She didn't need the money or half the property. She had her own house and money. Brian had a wife and child to consider. He needed both more than she did.

"I'm fine with the way things turned out."

"You're fine with how things turned out? You're fine?" He put his hands on his hips and stared her down.

She felt his anger, which had nothing to do with their father or what he'd left to Brian. He suffered an attack of conscience. She didn't want to rehash the past and all the times he'd walked out the door while Buddy punished her for being her mother's daughter.

"Brian, listen very carefully, because you and I are only going to have this conversation once. Today *I* am burying the past. I hope you can too. What's done is done. I can't change it, and neither can you. As far as I'm concerned, you and I are starting over today. I expect you to show up to work tomorrow morning and be the man I always knew you'd be. Maybe you don't want to be in construction again, but I'm giving you a chance to get back on your feet, and I hope you'll take it. Whatever you want to do once you've gotten out of the hole you've put yourself in is up to you. You'll be able to provide for your family. I want us to get to know each other again. I'm going to be an aunt. I'd really like to watch my niece or nephew grow up. Nothing would please me more than to be a part of your life.

"We were kids. You were just a kid. You knew what would happen if you tried to step in and help me. I've grown up and I can look back without it hurting so much. I have a new life now, one I'm proud of."

"I hear everything you've said and everything you didn't. I am two years older than you and was just as big as Dad by my freshman year in high school. I had the height and the strength to stop the old man. I didn't. Never even tried. He scared me. I was afraid he'd hurt you more. At the time, it seemed so much simpler to turn my back and pretend nothing happened, so he didn't come after me.

"I can remember so many times he'd hit you and you'd stand your ground. Tears would come to your eyes and fall and I could tell you begrudged each and every one of them. Every time he hit you, and you didn't bend or cry out, he'd get angrier and hit you harder. Bruises. God, the bruises all over you."

Unable to move, her chest tight, she stood, listening. Her hands on her hips, she leaned on her right leg. His words and the hurt in them washed over her and she slowly raised her face to the sky and her eyes filled with tears.

"The more he'd argue with you and you countered everything he'd say, he'd just be meaner. So many times I wished you'd just back down one time. Let him win one time. You never did. It's taken me this long to realize even if you had, he still wouldn't have stopped. I don't know how you took so much and never broke.

"I don't deserve what you're doing for my family and me. I've never been more proud to call you my sister than I am right now. Somehow, I'll make it possible for you to be proud to have me as your brother."

She turned away from the sky and let the tears roll down her cheeks. She didn't want to see those images in her mind again. Brian needed to heal, like she'd tried to do over the years. He wanted her to know where he was in that process.

"You're not to blame where Buddy and I are concerned. As much as I regret the past, the only thing I'm thankful for is you didn't have to go through what I did." His eyes widened with shock, and he actually took a step back, absorbing an imaginary blow. "Better me than you. If you were in my shoes, you'd feel the same way. You wouldn't wish Buddy Thompson on someone else if you could help it. That's why I always nodded for you to leave.

"You want to make me proud. Quit killing yourself slowly with booze. Be a good husband and father. Be the man Buddy never was, but I know you are."

Stunned by her words, it took him several seconds to give her a nod of agreement. "I'll see you at work."

Chapter Ten

ONE OF THE grounds keepers uncovered the mound of earth by the graveside and stuck a shovel into the pile of dirt. After handing him some money, Jessie told the guy, "Take a hike." Bills in hand, he left without looking back.

Dylan leaned against a tree about ten feet behind her. Frozen, she stood with her back straight and her head bent, looking down at her father's grave where Buddy's casket had been lowered moments ago. Jessie felt Dylan behind her and wondered if he'd leave, so she could do what she'd come here to do in peace.

The longer she stared at that grave the more the memories came to the surface. Memories full of abuse and hate were all she had from the old man, and as hard as she tried, only a handful of good ones came to mind.

Her father took her and Brian fishing. She was maybe ten years old, they'd spent the day sitting by the quarry lake, poles at the ready, red-striped white bobbers drifted on the serene surface. Light and happy, her father hadn't been drinking that day. She remembered he'd laughed.

He'd helped her bait her hook and cast the line into the water. When it tangled on a rock, he didn't criticize or yell. After wading out into the water, he untangled her line and helped her cast off again.

Such a simple memory and an ordinary day for most people. Why did she still feel that anxious panic in her stomach? She remembered feeling this way all the time growing up, like a clock ticked down on a bomb while you watched and waited for it to explode. That's what it felt like to live with an alcoholic, only their clock was haywire. You thought you had an hour; in a blink it zeroed out and boom—all hell broke loose.

She'd felt it that day at the lake. As good as the day had been, she'd always been waiting for him to turn on her without warning.

She took a deep breath to relieve the fluttering in her stomach and tension in her shoulders and reminded herself those days were long behind her. Buddy Thompson couldn't hurt her ever again.

"You going to arrest me, Sheriff, if I desecrate this grave?"

"Here I thought you'd continue to ignore me. As for the grave, depends. You plan on doing something to the body?"

She grimaced and shook her head. "Gross. But it's a thought. He's lucky I don't bury him with my boot up his ass."

"Do what you have to do. I'll be waiting over here when you're done."

Relieved he wouldn't stop her, she wished he'd leave her alone to finish burying her past.

She tried to ignore the pull between them. Impossible. Even now, she could close her eyes and feel his hand glide down her hair like he used to do every time he was near. That was then. This is now. Too much stood between them for her to give in to her emotions and walk into his arms and let the past fall away and find that safe place she'd only ever found with him.

She'd seen the way he looked at her. The same way he used to, but with an intensity that smoldered and threatened to flash every time she looked back at him.

Ignoring everything, including him, she took out the bottle of whiskey from her bag and unscrewed the cap. Even the smell took her back to nights of terror and pain and so much hurt. She took a long, deep swallow. She wondered if her heart hadn't taken the worst of it, every blow and horrible word echoed deep into her soul.

One last swallow and Jessie poured the contents of the bottle over her father's casket. Her perverted way of sending the old man off in the manner befitting his life.

Dylan stood back watching her, his gaze boring into her back. She contemplated lighting a match to it. Dylan would have no choice but to stop her. Besides, in her mind he burned in hell. Anger burning in her gut along with the whiskey, she let it fly along with the bottle she threw at the casket with as much force as she could put behind it, smashing the bottle into bits. She'd have liked to do that very thing a thousand times over the years.

She pulled her blouse off over her head, revealing a

tank top underneath. Tossing the shirt on her bag, she walked over to the pile of dirt, took up the shovel, and began filling in the grave, dismissing the backhoe nearby.

At first, it was just hard work, but as each shovelful went into the hole, she remembered something horrible he'd said or done to her. She gave into the rage and the hurt and the sadness. Tears streamed down her face faster than she could shovel. Each memory a blow to her all over again. Each shovelful of dirt, her way of burying those memories forever.

This man could never hurt her again. That's why she'd never come back to town. Instead of facing him, she hid. She didn't like it that he made her feel weak and vulnerable. The only person in her life she couldn't seem to assert herself with enough to stop him from hurting her with his words or his fists. In the end, she'd chosen to cut him out of her life like some cancerous tumor. It had been the only way to save herself.

She shoveled in the rest of the dirt. Hard work, but nothing she wasn't used to. Her job conditioned her body for physical labor. She didn't ask anyone on her work crews to do anything she couldn't do herself. She often worked alongside them and did her office work after the crews went home for the day.

Once she filled the hole, she leaned against the shovel and studied the mound of dirt. He didn't deserve it. He didn't deserve to be buried beside good and decent people. A good person, she couldn't have done anything less. She gave him a proper burial. That was for her, not because he deserved or earned her kindness.

Tears continued to track down her cheeks and it pissed her off. Raising the shovel over her head, she swung it as hard as she could at the mound of dirt. When she got the resounding thud she wanted, she picked up the shovel, and did it again. And again. And again. She did it until her arms ached and every last tear on her face dried. Then she stabbed the shovel into the dirt at her father's head as if she chopped it off and left the shovel there buried almost up to the bottom of the handle.

"Feel better?" Dylan asked from behind her.

Just for good measure, she stepped up on the dirt and jumped up and stomped. She did that a few times, smiling to herself. The bastard deserved to be buried with her boot up his ass. Her little dance upon his grave was as good as she was going to get.

She flopped onto the grass beside the freshly filled grave with her knees up and pulled out a handkerchief from her bag and wiped her face and blew her nose. She reached into her bag and pulled out the two bottles of beer and popped the top on one and downed a huge gulp. Breathing hard, covered in dirt and dust, she didn't care. A weight had been lifted, leaving her lighter. Free.

Dylan sat next to her, and she offered him the other beer. She'd intended to pour her dad a beer chaser, but where he was, he didn't need it. Of course, if he was burning in hell, he probably wished for a cold one about now.

Dylan accepted the beer and popped the top. After taking a deep swallow, he bumped his shoulder into hers, then reached out and ran his hand down her hair. Unable to help herself, she leaned into his sweet touch. "All done?"

She smiled, sat straight again, missing his hand on her hair and neck when he took it away to give her some space. "I'm sure it looked pretty childish. And it was," she admitted, "but I feel better." She took another swallow and let the cold beer wash the dust from her throat. A slight breeze rustled the leaves in the trees nearby. Peaceful. It had been a long time since she'd felt it.

"It's not childish to get your anger out. I almost feel sorry for that poor shovel, though. It took one hell of a beating."

"Yeah, well just be thankful I didn't come back when he was alive. I'd have buried that shovel in him instead of the dirt."

"Is that why you've stayed away all this time?"

She thought about it and realized more than just Buddy kept her away. "There was nothing left for me here." That simple, and that complicated.

"Brian was here."

"At first, I was too angry with him. Then I had my own problems to worry about. There was a time I didn't care about anything, not even myself. It took a long time to come back to myself and begin to care again."

"What happened to you, Jess?"

So much happened in such a short period of her life, she wished she could make it all right just by telling him. It wouldn't be right. Not ever again.

"Life happened to me."

She caught his frown out the corner of her eye. She'd come back to put the past behind her. She'd made her peace with his leaving and what happened with Hope. She couldn't change it. Better to move on.

"I spoke to my mother. While she didn't outright admit to what I can only imagine she said to you in that email to make you so angry and upset with me, she did send it. I'm sorry, Jess. My parents were beyond pissed I gave up my scholarship to college and joined the military. She took it out on you."

"I get that. I'm sorry I yelled at you yesterday. Now that I know it was her, it changes things for me. I'm still angry, but now it's at the right person."

"I owe you another apology. Well, probably a couple dozen for everything stupid I ever did to you, but I'm sorry about prom. I should have told my parents I was taking you, stood up for what I wanted, for you, and done it right. I should have picked you up, taken you to dinner, and we should have gone to the dance as a couple. Making you meet me there only made it easier for everyone to tease you more, and for my parents to say that even I didn't want to admit we were seeing each other. That's not how I meant it, but that's the impression I gave to everyone. It contributed to my mother sending that email. I hope you can forgive me."

"Dylan, that's the past. It doesn't matter now."

"It matters to me." He took a deep sip of his beer, stared off across the cemetery, and sighed. He shifted next to her and faced her. "I'm sorry I didn't tell you that night that I was leaving for the military in just a couple of days. I wanted to. I knew you'd be the one person to understand why I needed to do it."

"Yes, poor Dylan had a full-ride scholarship to play football and attend one of the best colleges in the country. You'd earn your business and finance degree and in a few short years, you'd be your father, working in an office, bored out of your skull. That's what they wanted. You wanted the freedom to figure out what you wanted to do with your life. With your grades and money, you could do anything, but you chose the military where you'd be part of a team again. Not exactly playing sports, but still, something familiar."

"How is it you know me that well, yet you believed some email saying I didn't want you in my life?"

"I didn't at first. At least, I hoped to change your mind. I hoped what I felt, what I thought you felt wasn't just an illusion. I didn't want to be just a distraction for you one minute and forgotten the next."

"Jess, no. You were my best friend and then so much more. I fell so hard for you. All I wanted to do is take you with me, but—"

"I wish you had, but we were just kids, making stupid mistakes, and here we are living with the consequences. So, you're sorry. I'm sorry. You've moved on and so have I. What does it matter now that all these years have passed?"

"You matter to me, Jess. Tell me what you want me to know." Dylan took another swallow of beer and prayed she'd open up to him. About to say something to her, he lost the thought. The look of utter despair on her face left his mind blank and his heart shattered.

"Maybe it really is too late. I can't give you back what you've lost. I hated you all these years for leaving me. If I tell you now, it will only hurt you and make you hate me."

"Jess, I could never hate you. Just tell me. I'll listen. I'll understand whatever it is. I promise."

She stared off into the distance, silent, the weight of whatever burden she carried too much to unload on him. She didn't trust him with her secret. Why would she? He'd left her when she needed him most.

Maybe if he opened up about himself, she'd open up and share whatever it was that made her so sad.

"I chose to be a police officer because of you."

That got her attention. She turned her head and her eyes lit with disbelief. "You did?"

"I met this guy in basic training. We sat around one night, swapping stories about why we joined up. He pulled up his shirt and showed me his black-and-blue ribs. He joined the military because he had to get away from his old man. He said the next time he went home, he'd be just as strong, just as tough as his father, and he'd stop him from hurting his younger brother and sister."

"So you thought, 'Poor Jessie. Can't take care of herself.' You thought you'd come back and put a stop to big bad Buddy Thompson."

"No. Well, yes, but that was the moment I realized what a colossal idiot I was. I never knew he hurt you. I never saw what was right in front of me."

That also went for the fact she'd been right in front of him and he'd never realized he loved her. They'd been friends practically their whole lives, and he hadn't really seen her. She was always there when he needed to talk, when he wanted to have fun, just all the time. He took her friendship for granted.

"Yeah, well, you and everyone else. What does that have to do with you becoming a cop?"

"Everything. I realized you hung out with Brian and me because you hoped we'd protect you. Maybe we did in a way. If you were with us, you weren't alone with Buddy. It isn't enough to remember that's all the help we gave you."

He stared down at the grass. His need to say it all drove him on.

"The night of the prom, in the backseat of the car when you were naked, I saw the bruises on your ribs and back. I never thought twice about them. I dismissed them as nothing more than something that happened on the job. That's what everyone thought. That's what you wanted people to think."

"You were thinking of other things that night." She gave him a half smile to lighten things up and get him to stop talking about it. "What does it matter now?"

Serious, he refused to let her distract him. Finally allowing him to talk to her, he needed her to know she mattered. The past mattered.

He wished he could find the words to make Jessie understand she was everything. He had to make her see they could build a future together.

"When that guy showed me his bruises, well, they matched yours. I called your house to check on you. Buddy answered and told me you'd taken off. He wouldn't give me any information and said you'd been gone for more than a week already. I tried Brian the next day, but he refused to talk to me. I lived in Georgia, tied to the military, I had no way to come back and try to find you. I called home. Mom confirmed you disappeared and told me about the rumors spreading through town, that almost everyone believed Buddy killed you."

He downed the rest of the beer, trying to wash away the pain of living with the belief she was dead. "I thought I was too late. I wanted to believe you'd done what you said that night—you disappeared. You had every reason to after what that bastard did to you day in and day out. But the rumors and circumstantial evidence supported the reason for your father and brother's silence. I tried to hold out hope that you were alive, I Googled you, checked the police databases, and found nothing. I believed he killed you, Jessie."

"I'm sorry you thought I died. I tried to find you."

She didn't offer anything more, so he kept talking. "After the military, I worked as a police officer in Atlanta. The domestic abuse cases were the hardest. They reminded me of how I'd let you down."

He wanted to tell her about his son, Will, but decided now wasn't the time. A long, complicated story, they needed to put this subject to rest before they could move forward.

"I became a cop because I didn't want anyone else to suffer like you'd suffered without anyone helping them, without me helping them. I couldn't help you, but I thought I could help someone else."

"I never asked for your help, Dylan. It's been my experience people are more likely to turn a blind eye. They don't want to make someone else's problems theirs. I never expected you to do anything for me. Face it, when we were young, I had a wild crush on you."

"And now?" He hoped she knew just how important her answer was to him.

"Now? For you and me, there is no now. There's only a past I thought happened one way, but turned out to be a lie. I truly believed you didn't care. Turns out you didn't even know I tried to contact you. That hurts me more deeply than I can ever say."

Jessie took a swallow of beer and stared out across the cemetery, remembering the time she buried their daughter alone. Pop and Greg had been there, but not Dylan. She wanted to believe if his mother hadn't lied, he'd have stood beside her and grieved as deeply as she'd grieved.

"I've been angry with you for so long, I'm having a hard time getting used to not hating you."

"I'm glad you don't. I want you in my life again. I've missed you so damn much. There were days when all I thought about was you and nights you haunted me into my dreams."

Every word held a wealth of hurt. He'd thought she was dead. No doubt, he cared. Jessie would have to account for what happened to Hope. Not today. She couldn't do it. She couldn't bring herself to willingly hurt him. Maybe not knowing was better.

"It seems there hasn't been a day I haven't thought of you too." She rolled to her feet and stepped away, needing the distance. He stood and came after her. She held up her hands and stepped back when he reached out to touch her. She couldn't let him do that when he didn't know the whole truth. "I have to go." She grabbed her stuff and walked away.

"Jess, wait. Come back. Don't leave like this. You can tell me anything."

She turned back and faced him. The guilt and anguish threatened to swallow her whole and send her into a spiral down deep into the despair that had stolen months of her life after Hope died. "Maybe there's a reason you didn't get that last email. Some things are better left hidden in the shadows of the past. Please, Dylan, leave it alone. We're done. Go back to your life. I'm going back to mine."

Chapter Eleven

JAMES CAME INTO the trailer that served as the office for the construction site. Jessie sat behind her desk poring over papers and ignoring the ringing phone. Half past six in the morning, she'd been up for hours already. She couldn't sleep with her mind replaying the scene at the cemetery and Dylan calling after her, begging her to stay and talk to him.

"Get in early today, boss?"

Surprised to see James standing in front of her desk and not out getting the guys started on the jobsite, she refocused on the task in front of her. She scanned the contracts for her supply orders and verified due dates and delivery times. She changed the dates on some of the orders because a few of the foundations hadn't been poured, delayed by several days of rain.

"I got here before five. I have a lot of calls to make today and wanted to have everything set up for the cement guys. I knew they'd show up early."

"They always do," they said in unison and laughed together.

"What's up, James? Why aren't you out checking crews?"

"I came in to tell you Brian showed up on time and sober. I've got him over on ten framing. I put him with Bucky and Andrew. They should keep him busy and kick him into shape by the end of the day."

Bucky and Andrew were a lot like her. On the clock, they worked. No small talk or pleasantries. Put a hammer in their hands and they hammered until break time, lunchtime, or quitting time. Either way, they'd work a man to death who wasn't used to keeping pace. Brian would have a hard day, but it would do him good.

"Send him in here at lunch to sign all his paperwork with Paula. He'll need his pay and benefits set up."

"You sure about putting him on the crew? You don't usually hire guys who have a history of drinking. He's your brother and all, but he could be a problem."

"I'll see to it personally that he's not. If you catch him drinking on the job, or he shows up half in the bag, I want to know about it immediately. Then, I'll put him on my work detail."

"Oh, God. You make Bucky and Andrew look lazy."

"Don't you forget it."

"How can I? I've worked with you a few times when you've been pissed off about something. You're ruthless."

She didn't think she acted that bad, but she could have a single-minded determination at times that some of the guys found hard to handle.

"I guess I can be a little demanding."

"Yeah, and sugar is just a little sweet. Kind of like you, J.T. You're a little sweet and a little sassy."

"Are you flirting with me, James?" She smiled at the big man. In his fifties, her right-hand man on the jobsite, he oversaw every aspect of the larger jobs she took on. If she had a question about where a crew was, if they were running on time, and how the supplies were holding up, bet on James to know. She trusted his judgment and his opinion. If he'd had the business skill and the money, she had no doubt he'd own his own construction company. A hands-on kind of guy, James liked to do the job. Although he coordinated things for her, more often than not she found him swinging a hammer or sawing a board.

A hard worker, who took no guff from anyone on the site, he was also married to a petite woman who could put him in his place with a look. Whenever his three daughters smiled at their daddy, he melted. She loved those things about him.

James's flirting with her was his way of coaxing her to stop being so hard-core into her work and have fun. In his opinion, she didn't have any fun in her life. Maybe he was right. At twenty-four, she didn't go out with friends; she didn't really have any but Greg. She didn't have a fun hobby, unless you counted making furniture, and that was more work than fun. Only when she completed a piece and stood back and admired the finished product did she feel any kind of satisfaction.

"I wish I weren't the only one flirting with you. Have you ever been out on a date?"

He'd been working for her for the last four years and knew she didn't go out with any men. If one of the guys on the crew asked her out, she politely told him she didn't date people who worked with her. She'd change the subject, so as not to make them uncomfortable, and go on with business. For Jessie, it was all about business. Maybe too much.

"You asking me out on a date, James? You know that pretty wife of yours will tan your hide if you start stepping out on her. Not to mention, I'm not taking the chance she doesn't sneak up behind me and fill me full of buckshot."

"Trudy loves you, J.T. She'd love to set you up with some friend of hers."

"Just what I need, your wife playing matchmaker. No way. Not going to happen."

"The last few days have been rough for you. Everyone's heard by now why you left Fallbrook. Most of us have known you for years, and we never knew the terrible circumstances."

"Is that the polite way of saying you guys didn't know my old man liked to knock me around for kicks?"

Jessie had seen James many times with his girls. A kind and caring man, he'd never think of raising his hand to one of them. For any reason.

"I've been in the construction business a long time. I knew Buddy Thompson by reputation. The kind of man you never dared cross. To think he'd unleash his explosive temper on you, Jessie, makes me furious."

She wanted to get up and hug the big bear of a man.

But that wasn't her style, and she held herself back. Like she always did.

"I wondered how you're doing this morning." James waited for her answer, but she remained silent. "It occurred to me, no one looks after you."

She couldn't help it. It made her feel good to have this man come to check on her. Made her feel like one of his daughters. Unable to look right at her, shifting on his feet, completely out of his element, he cared enough to leave the crews to their work and come see her.

"I'm fine, James. I did what I had to do yesterday. I put the past behind me a long time ago. It's time to move on.

"Speaking of moving on," she said and focused her attention on Buddy's old house. "Who can you spare from the crew? I need three guys to come with me to clear out a house. I had the Dumpster delivered this morning. We'll gut the place, and I'll need the guys to help me fix it up over the next week or two."

"I'll have the guys meet you at your truck.

"Would you like to come to dinner tonight? Trudy's making her meatloaf and mashed potatoes. There's nothing like my Trudy's cooking."

Right about that. The woman made being a wife and mother look like an art form.

Jessie went home every night to an empty house. Cooking for one had lost its shine the first month she'd lived in her new house. She barely used her spectacular kitchen to cook an actual meal. She usually threw together a can of soup and a sandwich, or went really wild and ate a bowl of cereal. What a shame. She should cook more often. Maybe if she did, she could invite someone to eat with her. Dylan's face came to mind, both irritating and intriguing her. She wondered what he'd say if and when he found out where she lived.

Eating alone sucked, so she accepted the dinner invitation. "I'd love to come. What time?"

"Since you'll be in Fallbrook, let's make it seven."

It would take her close to an hour to get back over to Solomon, but Trudy's cooking was well worth the drive. "Sounds good. I'm going to talk to Brian before I leave. Round up my men."

"They aren't cattle, you know.

"Close enough." She winked and scooped up the blueprints and other papers she needed before heading out the door.

Chapter Twelve

SWEAT DRIPPED DOWN Brian's back. Not even seven in the morning and his muscles ached, his mind lagged. God, he needed a break. The guys working with him kept up a fast and steady pace. He tried his best not to fall too far behind. They didn't talk, except to call out a measurement or ask for a tool. He wanted to sit down and take a breath without his muscles going into spasm. He hadn't worked this hard in the last six months, and it had only been an hour since he arrived on the jobsite.

He hadn't seen his sister, had no idea if she'd check on him like she'd threatened. On time for the first time in a long while, he wasn't going to screw up this opportunity, so he ignored his screaming muscles and kept at it.

Marilee had made it clear: he needed to work hard, earn his pay, and make sure they had the medical coverage they depended on for her and the baby. If he didn't, she would leave and take the baby with her. Time was running out on the pregnancy. Pretty soon there'd be a baby to take care of and feed. He needed this job.

No way would he make his sister look bad to whoever she'd had to beg to give him the job. He didn't even know if she'd just gotten him the job with someone she knew, or if she worked for the company too. At the time, he hadn't been clear of mind to ask any questions.

"Let's lift this section into place. Brian, you secure the bottom and we'll hold it in place." Bucky gave the orders and expected him to obey. Brian understood that much about the quiet man and did as he asked.

"You're moving a little slow," Bucky chided with no real hint of a reprimand. "You're trying hard though. That's all I can ask from the new guy," he said by way of encouragement. "We'll have you up to speed soon enough."

That, or I'll be dead.

Brian eyed Bucky and wondered if they assigned him to break in the new guys. In past years, he'd have had no problem keeping up, or being better than the likes of Bucky. Drinking had sucked the life out of him. Out of shape, he hadn't been eating properly, and his hands trembled after sobering up over the last two days. Whatever alcohol lingered in his system, he'd sweat out over the next seven hours.

The two guys hefted the wall frame into place, and he screwed it to the floor.

"J.T.'s on the way over." Bucky let go of the new wall and headed over to start framing in another section.

"Is J.T. the boss?" Brian asked and drilled the last screw into the frame without taking the time to look up and see who Bucky was talking about.

"Owner and boss," Bucky said in answer and went back to doing his work. Brian waited for the piece Andrew cut to fit.

Jessie spotted Brian helping to put up a wall in one of the thirty-eight track homes. In the beginning stages, they still had to pour foundations for the twelve custom homes that would line the back of the park yet to be started.

She loved the noise on a construction site. Definite sounds of progress. Hammers, saws, drills, air compressors, engines, and men. A cacophony of sounds, all of which contributed to the building of family homes.

She made her way to talk to her brother. Several of the men stopped her to ask questions and update her on the progress of one project or another. She had good people working for her, and for the most part, she could let them do what they did best. Build.

"Hey, Bucky, Andrew. You guys breaking in the new guy?" She gave them both a smile and stepped up onto the newly built floor that now supported two new walls her brother helped put up.

"Yeah, boss," they said in unison and got back to work, knowing if she wanted to talk, or give them something to do, she'd get on with it. They weren't required to stand around and jabber with her.

"Jessie? You're the boss?" Amazed, Brian stared at her. "I knew you were successful, since you drove that

Porsche, but I never expected to find you in charge of a construction site."

Either he'd been too drunk when she'd told him about his job, or he hadn't figured on her being the one to give it to him.

"Brian, you did realize when I offered you the job you'd work for me."

"I didn't realize you still worked construction. I thought you'd get as far away from a construction site as you could."

"Yeah, well, when you're fifteen and the only skill you have is construction, you use it. The only thing Dad ever did for me turned out to be a blessing. I got a job right away, and while I went to school, I could work from sunup to the middle of the afternoon and attend classes into the evening. Once I had my degree, I borrowed some money from the man who'd given me a job and started my own company. He gave me a chance to prove myself. Pop believed in me. From that belief came Hope Construction."

"Are you saying you own this construction company? This project is yours?"

She smiled because Brian's fog had finally lifted. Judging by the look on his face, her accomplishments impressed him.

"Yes, Brian." She spread her arms to encompass the entire construction site of dirt and foundations and trucks and organized chaos. The site wasn't much to look at right now, but in a few weeks they'd complete several homes and have others well underway. Several of the custom home projects were her designs.

"All of this belongs to me. I have really great people working for me. I work closely with a development group. They find the land and do the work to get the building permits and zoning, and then I build. This is the largest project my company has taken on alone. Pop and I have worked on several projects together. He's been instrumental in helping me get started and build my company's reputation."

"Who's this 'Pop'?"

"Ever heard of John Langley?"

"Are you telling me you're backed by Langley Construction? They're the largest construction firm in the state."

"They did back me, but I paid off my last loan to Pop about a year ago. Since then, I've been running in the black."

"Is that who met you at the funeral? Those two men you visited with yesterday."

"Yes, John and his son, Greg. I went to work for Pop when I left Fallbrook. Pop helped me get a small studio apartment and made sure I got my GED. Then he helped me get into college. All the while, I worked in the office with him planning and organizing construction projects, and more often than not working a construction site. Pop taught me everything I needed to know about owning a construction company and what it takes to plan a job and see it through. I learned when to buy equipment and when to rent or borrow. He made sure I knew when to take on a portion of the job myself and when to sub-contract it out. I've done pretty well over the last couple of years. When I need help or advice, Pop and Greg are there to lend a hand."

"Is Greg your boyfriend?"

"He's my friend. He was there for me when I needed him. Pop is the father I wished I had. You'll like them. They're good people."

She didn't mean to hurt his feelings with the truth that strangers had been there for her when he wasn't, but you couldn't dispute the facts.

"Take a look at the changes I want to make to your house. Let me know if you like them, or if there's something you want to change." She laid the blueprints out on the subfloor and waited while Brian scanned them. She'd spent most of yesterday afternoon going through the old house and updating the blueprints.

"You want to extend the house on both sides?"

"Yes, it'll make the bedrooms in back bigger. On the other side, you'll have a larger family room. You're going to need it with the baby coming. If I take out this wall, here, the kitchen will open into the family room and it'll be like a great room. Marilee can cook dinner and still keep an eye on the baby while he plays. We'll add an island with a breakfast bar. The larger kitchen will accommodate some updated cabinets and appliances. No need for plumbing, so it should be an easy renovation." She looked at the blueprints and bit her lower lip as she studied the changes, pleased at how well they'd turned out. "I think it will work. The house will have a more open feel and it'll be big enough for your growing family. The additions will add another thousand square feet."

"I can't let you do this."

"Which part don't you like? I can change the dimensions on the expansion if you want it larger, but it will cut into the yard even more and building codes require at least twelve feet between the building and the property line. I thought we'd put up a fence, so the baby is corralled in the yard."

"I appreciate you're getting the house cleaned up and making the repairs that *need* to be done, but this is too much."

Stubborn. Brian didn't want her to make the changes. Too bad. She wanted to make the house a real home for him and Marilee. She didn't want him going back to the same house they'd grown up in. She didn't want the past to infect his future.

Let him think she'd only make the repairs. If a wall fell down and she had to fix it, so be it.

"If that's what you want." Relieved she agreed, or so he thought, he relaxed his shoulders and stance. "I'm heading over to the house to start the cleanup. I want to pack a few things from my room. I'll donate the usable furniture to charity.

"Go to the office at lunch and sign your paperwork with my assistant, Paula. She'll get your medical coverage set up and get your cards, so Marilee can see the doctor. I'll catch you later."

She gathered her papers and the blueprints and headed for her truck where two other trucks waited with the guys assigned to help her at the house.

"Jessie!"

"Yeah?"

"Thanks, sis." Brian picked up his tools and went to help Bucky and Andrew with the next wall.

Jessie smiled. He'd be okay. He just needed time to adjust to his new life. She would make sure he put his old life behind him, starting with the house.

Chapter Thirteen

JESSIE ROLLED HER shoulders and rubbed at the back of
her neck. After a week of running nonstop, she needed a
break and some sleep to recharge her tapped-out energy.
Between keeping things moving at the housing development and working on Brian's house until well after sun-
down, she'd barely eaten or slept in days.

Down to her last nerve, Jessie worked her way
through the round of questions with her foremen, all
three of them, and beelined it to her office to hide out.
The phone never stopped ringing, and her assistant
tried to put out one fire or another with suppliers and
subcontractors.

Jessie worked through her paperwork, entering figures into her computer spreadsheets. She needed to check
the progress of one of the custom homes the crew started
two days ago.

She glanced out the small trailer window just as

Sheriff McBride pulled up in his squad car. He got out, scanned the construction area, and headed for her door.

Great, just what she needed.

Not a word from him in four days. Why did he come today? She'd told him to leave it alone. Should have figured he wouldn't let the past lie. She wished he'd chosen a more private place to speak and braced herself to see him again. God, he looked good.

She decided to head him off at the pass the moment he stepped through her door. "Afternoon, Sheriff. What brings you to my neck of the woods?"

"Man, this place is amazing, Jess. You've done well."

"Thanks."

"Must have been a lot of hard work to build your company this big in such a short time."

"I had help."

"Yeah, and you're just that good. And smart."

She didn't know what to do with such compliments. She received them so rarely, so she ignored them. "Um, is there something you wanted?"

The smoldering look in his eyes as his gaze swept from her head down to her breasts and back told her he wanted her.

He cleared his throat. "I, uh, came to speak with you about one of the guys on your crew."

Surprised, she leaned back in her seat and asked, "Who?"

"Jay Bradley."

"What'd he do?"

"He got in a fight at McBride's last night and broke

up the place. Brody doesn't want to press charges, but he wants reimbursement for the damages."

"Brody? Your cousin? He's back in town?"

"Yeah. He and Rain bought the bar last year."

She'd wondered if Dylan owned the local hangout. He certainly had the money to buy anything he wanted. She'd met his cousins, Brody and Owen, a couple of times back in the day. She had a vague memory of Rain playing softball in high school. Dylan's life seemed so foreign to her now when once she'd known everything about him. Questions about his family, his life filled her mind, but she didn't ask a single one of them. She had no right. He left her behind. He'd do it again if she told him the truth about all he'd lost. Better to keep things like this, all business. Nothing personal.

She sighed and scrubbed both hands over her face and focused on the problem at hand. For the better part of two months Jay caused nothing but problems. Small things really, but they added up to cutting corners and laziness. She had yet to put her foot down and show him the line never to cross. Today she'd make him understand what it meant to work for Jessie Thompson.

She picked up one of the hand radios from the table behind her. "James, bring Jay Bradley to the office, ASAP."

"It'll be a minute. He's in the middle of something."

"Put someone else on it and get in here. The sheriff is here."

"On our way, boss."

She set the radio back in its charger, sucked in a deep

breath, and tried to ignore the ringing phone. Doing the same with Dylan was a whole other impossible feat.

The office door banged open and she expected James and Jay to walk in. Instead, Greg beamed a smile at her from the doorway. She caught Dylan's scowl out of the corner of her eye.

"Hey, beautiful. Got time to have lunch with me?" Greg asked, his eyes on Dylan, not her.

"No. I'm dealing with the sheriff here and an unruly employee, who thinks he can bust up the local bar among other unseemly acts."

"What else did he do?" Dylan asked.

"He thinks he can hit on his boss, slack off, and otherwise undermine my authority. It ends today."

"Are you putting him on your special work detail?" Greg winked at her.

"That's right. He'll either become a loyal employee, or he'll be dead by the end of the day." She gave Dylan a very insincere smile. "I mean that figuratively of course, Sheriff."

Dylan smiled and shook his head. "Not a mean bone in your body." He gave her another appreciative sweep of his gaze over her. The heat washed through her and made her yearn for things she had no right wanting. Not after what happened.

"So, you two talked. You told him—"

"No." She shut Greg up before he said too much.

"He knows," Dylan accused, glaring at Greg because he knew the big secret, but she had yet to spill her guts to him.

"Yes. Now isn't the time or place to get into this."

"J.T., you need to tell him," Greg coaxed.

"*I'll* take you to lunch." Dylan gave Greg a smug look.

James and Jay walked into her office, interrupting the tense situation. Jay glanced at the sheriff and immediately tried to defend himself.

"I swear J.T., that guy started the fight. I was having a beer after work, minding my own business."

She surveyed all the men standing in front of her desk. Dylan stood with authority. His dark hair brushed the back of his collar. His stormy gray eyes watched Jay with a predatory stare, making sure he didn't do anything stupid.

Greg, dressed casually in a pair of slacks and a dress shirt opened at the collar, his sleeves rolled up to his elbows, stood there enjoying the whole scene. As her best friend, Greg would like nothing better than to make Dylan pay for what he'd done.

James stood back, leaning against the wall, waiting for her to tell him what she wanted him to do with Jay after this meeting.

"James, did Jay arrive on time this morning?"

Jay cringed at the loud tone of her voice. His flannel shirt was half-tucked in, one sleeve slowly unrolling. Two days' worth of beard shadowed his jaw, and his tangled hair stuck up on one side. Hungover, he'd regret that very soon.

"He arrived ten minutes late. He's been out helping get one of the houses ready for the landscapers." James knew exactly where this ended. Her kicking Jay's ass.

"So he's enjoyed a nice quiet morning."

"Yes," James replied.

"Why didn't you tell me Jay's been taking it easy?"

"Well, now, you seemed tired. I didn't want to add any extra work to your day."

Pissed, she snapped, "He's supposed to Sheetrock one of the houses. Now, that crew is a man short. If he can't pull his weight, I want to know about it."

"J.T.," Jay tried to explain again.

She pointed a menacing finger at him. "Shut up."

Hungover, hauling Sheetrock and drilling in screws was sure to split Jay's head clear open. James let him slide. He was only trying to take care of her, but she had to maintain her position as boss and couldn't let anyone slide on the rules.

James frowned and his deep brown eyes held a look of apology. "I got tied up with some of the other pressing matters on the site, so you wouldn't have to come out yourself. I'm sorry. Won't happen again."

She nodded in acceptance of James's explanation and turned her attention to Dylan to take care of the situation with Jay.

The door to her office burst open again and Brian stormed in, red-faced, mouth set in a grim line, ready to explode. He didn't stop to consider the other men in her office. He only had eyes for her.

"Why the hell are you putting up new walls? I went by the house this morning. I told you not to do the addition."

"J.T., I really didn't start that fight. You have to believe me," Jay pleaded.

All hell broke loose. Jay whined, Brian yelled about

the walls on the house, Greg took the opportunity to tell Dylan, "Stay clear of her. If you didn't give a shit about what happened after you left her, why the hell do you care now?" James told Jay to "Shut your trap and wait for J.T. to make her decision." Dylan exploded at Greg, telling him, "Mind your own damn business, Jess and I will work things out our way. Stay out of it."

Unable to take it anymore, she put two fingers between her lips and let out a shrill whistle. The exceptionally loud sound made everyone shut up and stare at her. She stood, planted her palms on her desk, and leaned toward the men.

"Shut up. God, you're all giving me a headache."

Jay winced in agreement. He probably had the mother of all headaches after drinking last night.

"Here we go. Sheriff, what are the damages at the bar?"

"It comes to two hundred and thirty-five dollars. Jay told the manager he wouldn't pay. Brody knew he worked for Hope Construction, since he drove one of the company trucks. He asked me to handle it."

Jessie put her hand up to stop him and caught Jay in her gaze. "You took one of my company trucks last night to go drinking in town, you busted up the place, and you drove home drunk."

"I wasn't drunk." Jay stuffed his hands in his pockets. "Please don't fire me, J.T. I know I screwed up. It won't happen again. I swear."

"Damn right it won't," she fired back.

She sucked in a deep breath and swept the wisps of hair from her cheek, but only managed to pull more of her hair out of her ponytail. She addressed Dylan. "Tell Brody the crew and I will be in tomorrow night. I'll throw a little business his way to smooth things over. Any damages to the bar, let me know, and I'll take care of them."

"It's nothing like that, just a few chairs and tables that got busted up."

Jessie took out a large binder from the locked drawer in her desk, wrote out a check, and handed it to Dylan. "Fine, one problem down."

Jessie locked the checks in her desk.

"Next. Brian, I can't help it if the house had dry rot. It needed new walls. I'm putting them up."

"Dry rot, my ass. You completely disregarded what I said. I told you not to do the additions."

"Would you believe termites?" She gave him another fake smile.

"What?"

"If you won't believe the dry rot, how about termites?"

"You aren't listening to me."

"You listen to me. I spent six hours working on those blueprints for the addition. I called in several favors at the building permit office to get everything in order to do the job. I lined up all the supplies and deliveries. I put a lot of work into this project because I want to make sure when you and Marilee move into the house it's yours and not a bad memory. I gave you the job, so you can start fresh. Besides, it's too late to be mad about it now. I knocked down the walls yesterday and poured the foundation for the additions. There's no turning back. Get over it."

He snatched the baseball cap off his head and slapped it against his thigh, a sign of pure frustration. Nearly finished with the house, she'd completely transformed it. She'd torn out the old tree stump out front, planted a new tree—several, in fact—and put in a brick walkway up to the door. The wall between the kitchen and family room had been removed, the kitchen gutted, the bathrooms were almost completely renovated, and the addition was coming along. She'd done a lot of work. All he'd done was complain and piss her off.

Reluctantly, Brian gave in without her losing her temper. "I'll go by the place after work and help out wherever you need me. The place looks great. Sorry I yelled at you."

"I don't want you anywhere near that place until it's done. Go home to your wife and spend time with her before the baby arrives. You have a lot of making up to do. Take the time you need to put your marriage back on track. Get things packed. The house should be ready to move into by next Saturday."

"Next Saturday? So soon?"

"There's a baby on the way. Time is of the essence, wouldn't you say?"

"The time is way overdue."

Yes, past time he started living the life he should be living.

"Your lunch is almost over. I'd suggest you grab something to eat and get back to work. I hear your boss can be a real bitch." She smiled to help alleviate some of his upset.

"She's not so bad. I love her."

Touched, she caught her breath. They'd never been the happy family that expressed their feelings. After everything that happened, she didn't know what to say. She loved him, but the words didn't come easy for her, so she mustered up a smile and said, "Go, I have work to do," with as much cheer as she could put into the words.

Brian gave her a lopsided smile and a break, letting her out of the awkward moment, leaving her office to finish his lunch and get back to work.

Her office remained full of men, however, with Dylan, Greg, James, and Jay waiting on her.

She picked up her tool belt from the table behind her desk and strapped it around her waist. Jay's eyes never left her hips. She took off her flannel shirt to reveal the tank top she wore underneath. She wanted to be comfortable while she worked out in the sun. She tugged on her baseball cap, pulling her ponytail out the back. Jay looked like he'd start drooling soon. She'd make him see her as something other than a sexpot.

"J.T.? Are you about to institute the bloodshot crew?" Greg asked.

An apt name for the guys who showed up with bloodshot eyes and hangovers that left them unable to pull their weight and landed them on her crew. Jessie started working those guys on Pop's jobs. They never showed up hungover more than once.

Greg couldn't help himself, he razzed Jay. "Man, I feel sorry for you. Working with J.T. when you're a hundred percent is a test of a man's abilities. Doing it when you're hungover is a test of sheer will and determination to keep your job and your life, because when you're finished you want to puke up your guts and cut off your head to keep it from pounding anymore. You're in for a shitty day, my friend."

"I haven't had to do this in a long time." Jessie eyed Jay. "He's new. He thinks the rules don't apply to him. He actually smacked me on the ass the other day and called me sweetie."

Greg winced. "Big mistake, buddy. You're in for it now."

Jessie noted Jay had the presence of mind to look chagrined. He turned green as well. She'd work out all the bad boy and get to the heart of the man who wanted to do the right thing, or she'd fire him.

Studying the map on the wall, she picked a house. "James, take Jay over to number eleven. The roof has been framed. We'll lay out the boards and shingle it. Get everything set up. I'll be there shortly."

"Come on, boss. It was just a fight. You can take it out of my pay." Jay pouted.

"I'll take it out of your ass because that's the only way you'll learn I mean business. You'll either survive the next four hours, or you'll quit. You sure as hell won't show up late or hungover to one of my jobsites ever again. You will also turn over the keys to my truck. You just lost your privileges."

He cussed under his breath, fished the keys out of his pocket, and handed them to her before following James out the door.

She waited for them to leave, knowing Dylan still wanted to talk to her.

"Dylan, I don't have time to rehash the past. I told you, leave it alone."

"Not going to happen, Jess. If we're going to move forward, we need to finish the past."

"We aren't moving forward. It's done. Over. There's nothing left between us."

"We aren't done. We aren't over. We're just getting started again."

Greg read the fatigue and resignation in J.T.'s eyes. The office was busy, and J.T. needed a break. At the end of her rope, dealing with the sheriff and her employee tapped all her energy, making her shoulders slump. Greg had seen her like this a few times. She'd work herself to death because she had nothing else but work to distract her from what really bothered her. Dylan and their past.

She hated talking about the too-painful subject. She could tell Dylan the truth and get the whole thing done. She didn't want Dylan to blame her for what happened. She blamed herself enough. It wasn't her fault, but she couldn't help the way she felt.

Would he blame J.T. for not finding him and missing the opportunity to see his daughter? Maybe he cared enough about J.T. to understand she couldn't have prevented what happened. She'd been so young and done everything she could. Alone.

"Greg, I'll take a rain check on lunch, but thanks all the same," Jessie said by way of goodbye, and started past him and Dylan to get back to work.

Greg stopped her with his hand to her arm and turned her to face him. He wanted to see just how much Dylan cared.

He held her, softly running his hands over her shoulders to her neck, holding her in place. He peered down into her surprised eyes.

"You know, darlin', I have a weakness for a pretty lady in a tool belt." He leaned down and kissed her softly on the mouth. Shocked, she stood immobile. "You and I should get married. We'll roll your company up with Dad's, and take a nice long vacation. Dad would love it. He already thinks of you as a daughter. Think about it," he ordered, and then he bent his head and really kissed her.

She grabbed his forearms to steady herself. After the initial surprise wore off, she stiffened her spine. She might not have known what had gotten into him at first, but it didn't take her long to figure out he did it to push Dylan's buttons. It worked, making Greg happy.

Dylan exploded, unable to take one more second watching this guy put his hands on his woman. "Get your hands off her." His words held just enough unleashed rage to catch both their attentions.

Greg only smiled more broadly, looking over J.T.'s head.

"Why?" Greg asked cockily.

"Because she belongs with me."

"She may have gone for you back in the day, but she's all grown up now. I don't think she'd make the same mistake of falling into bed with you again, knowing you can't leave her fast enough."

"That's not how it happened." Dylan hated having to defend himself to this asshole.

"No? That's right. You went all out and took her in the backseat of a car."

"Are you guys finished talking about me like I'm not here?" Jessie tried to take a step toward the door, but Greg didn't let go. A silent order to stay put. Dylan wanted to yank his hands away from Jessie. He didn't want this man, or any man for that matter, touching her.

"If you cared so much about her, why did you leave and never look back?"

"It wasn't like that."

"Bullshit. You knew you were leaving the night of the prom and you still slept with her without any possibility of a future between the two of you. You didn't even talk to her afterward. Nice way of showing her how much you care. She thought that night meant something. All it meant to you is goodbye. So don't pretend you cared then or now."

Dylan felt every angry word pelt him in the heart. "You're right." He faced Jessie. "I was an asshole. I handled the whole thing badly. If I could do it over, I'd change so many things about that night, except what happened between us. I felt it. You felt it. We shared something amazing. Something like that doesn't just disappear. I've held on to it all these years. So have you. I see it in your eyes every time you look at me. Whatever it is you want to tell me, we'll get passed it. I thought I lost you once, Jess, I won't lose you again."

"Those are some nice words, but she fell for them

once. She won't fall for it again," Greg said, though he didn't put much certainty into the words.

"Enough. I'm not standing here while you two have a pissing match." She yanked her arm free. "I don't care who either of you think I belong with. I don't belong to anyone. No one wanted me." She slammed the door behind her and left Dylan, Greg, and her assistant staring, the phones ringing unanswered.

No one wanted me. Those words rang out in the silence.

"I don't think she realizes what she just said. She believes it though. I'll cut you a small break because I love that girl like she's my own sister. That's all there is between us."

Relief washed away some of Dylan's hostility.

"As long as I've known her, she's never gone on a date with anyone," Greg continued. "She learned the hard way from Buddy, Brian, and you she wasn't worth the trouble. She thinks men will just hurt her, or leave her. It took a long time for her to trust Dad and me. She was always wary and unsure of our intentions."

Greg ran a hand over his face and got lost staring at a past Dylan didn't understand anymore. Nothing he remembered added up to this much hurt rolling off Jessie every time he saw and spoke to her.

"Exhausted and hurting, Jessie came into our office to ask about a job. She'd been to some free clinic to have her back examined. By the time she came to us, she had an infection and needed to have all the stitches redone because the guy who'd stitched her up had done a piss-poor job of cleaning out the wound. Dad gave her a job on the spot, drove her to the hospital, and had her taken care of properly. He set her up in a studio apartment near work after it took almost an hour to convince her if she didn't tell us what happened, we'd call the cops and have them haul her back to Fallbrook. Scared to death, she believed our bluff."

Dylan understood Greg and his father wouldn't have sent her back to anyone capable of hurting her that way.

"She's one of the smartest women I know. When we hired her, we thought she'd be like a secretary, or do some easy labor, cleaning up the jobsites. We had no idea how much she knew about construction. She taught Dad and me more than a few things. She's got great ideas, and with help from my father, she's built a life for herself."

"Why are you telling me all this?"

"Because for six months Dad and I wondered if she'd live or die. She wanted to die and did damn near everything to wither away before our eyes."

"This isn't just about the fact I left, or anything Buddy did to her. Is it?" Dylan asked, looking grim.

"She believed, back then, you didn't want anything to do with her, or what happened to her. She tried. Once your mother gave her your message, she had no choice but to go on without you. Then, the unspeakable happened, and we almost lost her. She needs to share it with you because she can't carry the burden alone anymore, but I get why she's reluctant to tell you. She doesn't want to hurt you. She's afraid you'll hate her, and if you hate her, then everything from her past is tainted. She'll have nothing good left to hold on to."

Greg shook his head, a sad, desolate look coming over him. "Talk to J.T. and everything will make perfect sense. She's come back little by little, but I still see where a part of her is still missing. She's still alone." Greg sighed, stared up and away, thinking again before giving him another clue that told him nothing. "I can't tell you how important Hope is." He slapped Dylan on the shoulder. "That's all the help I can give you. If you love her, make it a point to find out now. Don't wait any longer. Don't let her get away with blowing you off. J.T. deserves to finally put the past to rest. She's done that with her father. Now, she needs to do it with you. Otherwise, she'll spend the rest of her life with it hanging around her heart, dragging her down, and stealing every ounce of happiness that comes her way."

Greg walked out with the sheriff right behind him. Before they each got into their cars, Greg asked, "Why didn't you tell her you were leaving?"

"She scared the hell out of me," Dylan admitted. "You don't find the woman of your dreams at eighteen. Except, I did and was too stupid to see it. I didn't deserve her then, and I sure as hell don't deserve her now. I will get her back though, and spend the rest of my life trying to make it up to her that I let her down and never protected her the way she needed me to."

Greg sighed. "Love makes us all stupid at one time or another."

They both looked out across the dirt road and found Jessie kneeling on top of the roof of a house nearby. Jay raised his face to the sun and sucked in a huge breath. Every hammer blow made him put a hand up to his eyes or head, his face red with the effort to keep up with Jessie.

"She's going to punish him for the rest of the day, isn't she?" Dylan asked.

"She makes it clear when anyone signs on. No drinking on the job and don't be late. Under no circumstances should you show up hungover and expect to get out of working as if you were a hundred percent. No one will cover for you. If you do, then you end up working with her. This is just a normal day for her. Poor Jay will wish he never hears a hammer again."

"She could use the pneumatic nail gun," Dylan suggested.

On the other houses being roofed and shingled, pneumatic nail guns went off like some kind of battle being waged.

"She could, but what fun would that be for poor Jay. He'll either make it to the end of the day with her, or she'll fire him."

"She'd fire him because of a hangover?"

"She'll fire him for incompetence and not following her rules. The guys that make it working with her are some of the best in the business. She pays them well and gives them every opportunity to improve their skills and their position. Some of them will have enough experience to become foremen, others will learn enough from her to start their own businesses. She gives them her time and her expertise. She doesn't take it personally when they leave to start out on their own. My father did the same for her. Most won't make it. It takes time and a lot of hard work to build a construction company. Jessie had the knowledge and the experience. My Dad fronted her the money, recommended her for jobs, and she did the rest. She worked her ass off to make this company what it is today.

"She's a good designer. You should see her house. You'd find her home—interesting." Greg tossed out yet another cryptic comment that Dylan hoped would make sense one day soon.

Chapter Fourteen

MOVE-IN DAY. EXCITED for Brian and Marilee, Jessie arrived at the house early, putting the final touches on the living room before her brother and Marilee arrived. She expected them any minute. Her crew had done a great job. The old hardwood floors had been sanded, stained, and varnished in a honey tone. New cabinets lined the kitchen to match, along with new white appliances. An electrician had come in and replaced all the light fixtures with new more fashionable ones, providing more light.

The expense didn't faze her. Not when she'd erased the look and feel of Buddy's house and transformed it into Brian's.

Jessie had a few pieces of furniture delivered to the house. A new sofa and chair sat in the family room along with a sage-green rug that complemented the soft oatmeal wall color.

She'd built them a table and chairs for the kitchen.

Nothing fancy. Just a few oak planks she sanded smooth and stained and varnished to a high polish. A bench seat sat on one side, two chairs on the other, and a chair at each end. The set would serve them well over the next several years, especially if they had more children.

She'd even made them a highchair that could be pulled up to the table. It sat in the corner of the kitchen waiting to be used.

Since Jessie spent most of her time making furniture and selling it in the store downtown, she had a couple of dressers delivered for the bedrooms and two night tables in the master bedroom.

The baby's room made her proud. She painted her old room a soft yellow. The handmade cradle sat near the window and the dresser stood next to the closet doors. A lower set of drawers with a rim around the top held a changing table pad she'd bought and built the piece to fit.

Simple Shaker style—no matter if the baby were a girl or boy, the furniture would suit them until they were much older.

She especially loved the rocking chair. She'd spent several days making it for Marilee and it sat in the corner by the cradle and window. Marilee could rock her baby by the moonlight or sunlight.

Tears slipped down her face unnoticed. It had been a long time since she cried for her baby. She had known setting up this nursery would be difficult, but her heart broke all over again as she stood in the doorway wishing for Hope and wanting to rock her in that chair.

A truck pulled up out front. She turned her back on the

chair and shook off her memories and stopped herself from wishing for something that would never be. She wiped the wetness from her cheeks and stepped out onto the porch expecting to find Brian and Marilee. Dylan slid out of his truck and approached, smiling his half-cocky grin she loved so much. She hoped he didn't notice her red, puffy eyes.

"Hey, Jess. If the inside looks as good as the outside, you did an outstanding job. Man, this is amazing."

Dylan hesitated taking the last few steps to her, unsure of the surprise that turned to something solemn in her eyes that tore at his heart. She stood on the porch, looking at him like she'd never seen him.

He didn't want to talk about the past and what she wanted him to know but was too afraid to tell him. Given time, she'd learn to trust him again. He just needed to show her he wasn't going anywhere. He'd take it slow, not push, but one day soon, he'd get her to tell him everything. Today, he'd spend the day with her moving Brian. They'd settle back into that easy camaraderie they had when they used to work together.

So pretty in her cutoff shorts and T-shirt, Jessie's hair fell over her shoulders and breasts. He wanted to run his hands through it until it spilled down her back. He'd give it a tug, until her face turned up to his, so he could kiss her. Long and deep, until she filled all the empty places in his aching chest.

"Jess, are you okay?" He closed the distance between them, leaving the unloading of his truck for later. She needed him. He felt the pull and gave into his own need for her.

Concern filled his eyes, making them narrow on her. Jessie wanted to tell him she wasn't okay. She was sad she didn't have a little girl with her to run and greet her daddy as he drove up. She wanted to tell him how her heart ached every day for a little girl who'd never gotten a real chance to live. She wanted to tell him just seeing him made that ache worse and better all at the same time.

Instead, she stood staring at him as he came up the steps to the wide porch she'd built herself.

He stood right in front of her, waiting with the infinite patience he'd shown her when they were kids and she chased after him. She gave in to her treacherous heart, went to him, wrapped her arms around his neck, and held him tight. He enclosed her in his arms, pulling her close. Everything inside of her melted along with her body into his. She exhaled with sheer relief. Back in his arms, the years, the heartache, the hurt washed away, leaving the way only he ever made her feel. Safe.

"I've waited a long time, too long, to have you this close again. I never want to let you go," he confessed.

"You did. You will again." The fear rose up, but she kept holding on, trying to forget he'd abandoned her, but it was no use. What happened couldn't be erased.

"No. I won't. Jess, come on. What's wrong? Tell me." He brushed a hand down her hair, and when he got to the back of her neck he pressed his fingers into the soft flesh and kneaded out some of the tension.

Brian's truck drew closer, slowly coming down the street. Turning her lips to his ear, she whispered. "I'm sorry. I'm really, really sorry."

She pulled away as the truck pulled up, leaving Dylan's arms and her insides empty again. The last time she felt whole he held her in his arms the night of the prom, and again just now. What she wouldn't give to have that every second of every day. But it could never be.

"Jessie, come back. Talk to me."

"Not now." She nodded to her brother and Marilee intruding on their moment.

Heading back down the porch steps, Dylan met everyone on the newly paved walkway. Like a light switched in Jessie, she was back to being all business, helping Marilee unload the front seat of Brian's truck.

Marilee stopped in front of the house and scanned the front yard and new brick path leading up to the porch with the white bench swing. The lawn sprang up green and lush around them, and where the old stump used to be stood a beautiful mature shade tree. At least twenty-five feet tall, it looked as if it had been in the yard for years.

"Oh, Jessie. How did you do this? It doesn't look like the same house."

"That's the point. I didn't want it to be or feel like the same house. This is *your* house."

"The tree is lovely. How did you get such a big tree?"

"A very large flatbed truck and a crane. In a few years, you can hang a swing from one of the branches."

"I don't know how to thank you."

"It's just a tree. Wait until you see the rest of the house."

Marilee put a hand on Jessie's arm, waiting for Jessie

to look at her. "It isn't just a tree. You made this place a home. I'll tell my child his aunt planted that tree the year he was born. I'll sit on the porch swing and watch him play in the yard in the shade of that tree. Everything is perfect." Tears rolled down Marilee's cheeks as she studied the new yard and house.

Dumbstruck, Jessie stared blankly at Marilee at a complete loss for what to say to Marilee's heartfelt words. Dylan grabbed a box out of his truck and set it on the driveway, still in awe of what Jessie and her crew accomplished in two weeks.

"Hey, honey, come help me with this mattress." He tried to rescue her from the emotional moment before she wore out her shoes, shifting from foot to foot, unsure whether to stay or run. She looked lost. He'd pull her toward him and give her time to get her bearings back.

Jessie gazed over at Dylan, standing beside the truck, that cocky half grin on his gorgeous face. She remembered the feel of his arms wrapped around her a few minutes ago. She needed to get away from the temptation of him and Marilee's overwhelming appreciation and overwrought emotions. She grabbed the armload of small boxes Marilee held and rushed into the house.

Alone in the kitchen, Jessie thought she'd be safe from everyone. Wrong. They stepped through the door, their arms full of Brian and Marilee's things, and stopped and stood silent. Their eyes roamed the room and settled on her. They stared with blank expressions, making her uneasy.

"What?"

Marilee found her voice first. "Nothing looks the same. Jessie, the house. It's too much. This room and the kitchen, they're twice the size they used to be. The furniture. It's beautiful."

"You have to stop. I told you both I'd take care of the house. I'm glad you like it. Go look at the rest. The bathrooms have been redone and the back rooms enlarged as well. You'll have plenty of space here. Go. Go see." *Please go. I can't take much more.*

Brian took Marilee's hand and led her down the hallway. A series of oohs and aahs went up as they made their way from room to room. Jessie continued to unpack the box of dishes and stack them in the cupboard. Unheard, Dylan come up behind her. His hands clamped on to her hips. He pulled her back to his chest and bent to her ear.

"You're a good woman, Jessie Thompson. You've done an amazing thing for your brother and Marilee."

"I did it for the baby. He deserves a father who isn't a drunk and a home to grow up in where he feels safe and protected."

A squeal echoed from the back of the house, and Marilee shouted for Jessie to come.

Reluctant, she didn't want to leave the warmth of Dylan's embrace. The sturdy wall of his chest pressed against her back, his hips snug against her bottom. His strong, warm fingers dug into her hips, holding her tightly to him. His breath washed over her cheek. His lips barely whispered against her skin. Reluctantly, she pulled away and headed to the back of the house with him on her heels.

"What's going on back here?" Jessie stood in the doorway of the baby's room. Marilee sat in the rocking chair balling her eyes out. Brian crouched on bended knee, trying to console her. They made the sweetest picture. Brian swept his hand over Marilee's hair and down her back, cooing, "Everything will be okay."

"It's beautiful. The furniture. This rocking chair. It's all p-p-perfect. I've seen furniture like this in the antique store downtown. It's expensive. Jessie, this is too much."

"Do you like it?"

"Yes. Oh, yes. I love it," Marilee said and sobbed harder.

"Then it isn't too much. It's just right. You look perfect in that rocking chair." Her voice broke, and she turned and fled past Dylan.

She managed to run into the backyard and take a few deep breaths to clear her head and stop the tears. To her relief, no one came after her. She didn't know what she'd do if Dylan had come after her and found her crying over a baby he didn't know they shared. She wanted to feel his arms around her again. It was so easy to let him touch her and make the years fall away until she was that young girl in love with a boy for the first time.

A long way from being that naïve, young girl, she needed to remember that and everything that happened because she loved a boy.

Chapter Fifteen

DYLAN WAITED OUTSIDE of Jessie's office trailer just like he had every other night of the past week. He alternated between seeing her and spending his evenings with Will. He hadn't told her about his son. He'd do it soon, but first he needed to repair the bond they'd once shared back into a friendship and hopefully more. God, how he wanted more right now, but he could barely get Jessie to talk to him.

The first night hadn't gone well at all. She walked out of her office, saw him standing there with a dozen red roses, and shook her head, and said, "Flowers do not make up for ditching me."

"Do they entice you to have dinner with me?"

"No."

She got in her truck and left. He let her. Short of following her home, handcuffing her, and making her go with him, what could he do?

He just might have to resort to handcuffing her if she continued to be this stubborn. Of course, he'd make it fun for both of them.

The second time he came by, he made sure to come after the crews left. He hoped he'd find her alone, working in the office. Luck was on his side. He brought her favorite, Gino's Pizza. Pepperoni, extra cheese, and a couple cans of Dr. Pepper. He walked into her trailer, sat in front of her desk, set the pizza and sodas right on her work, and plated up a couple of slices.

"What are you doing?"

"Having dinner with you. You won't go out with me, so I guess we're staying in. How was your day?"

Stunned, taken off guard, it took her several minutes to figure out what to do with him. Since he refused to budge and sat eating his pizza as if they did this every night, she took her plate, popped the top on her soda, and sat back and ate with him. They played Twenty Questions. He asked the questions. She evaded at first, but since he kept the topics about everyday things and nothing about her, him, or what happened, she went along. After about five questions, he figured out to stop asking her questions that only required a yes or no. Stubborn woman didn't want to like having him there, but by the end of the evening her soft smile came more easily and the wary look in her eyes disappeared. So long as he didn't push too hard, get too close, or ask anything too personal. They'd get there.

Tonight, he wanted to spend time with her. Maybe hold her hand. Find a way to break through the walls she'd erected and fortified with her refusal to talk about the past, or a possible future together.

He walked into her office without knocking. No sense giving her a chance to say no to him without him even asking her anything. "Hey, Jess, how was your day?"

She looked up from her computer and swept her gaze over him from his face to his boots as he closed the distance between them. "How did I know you'd show up tonight?"

"Admit it, you were hoping I'd show up. That's why you stayed and didn't go home."

"I'm working."

She tried to hide the fact she hoped he'd show up, but he caught the hint of a smile she turned into a frown and the appreciative glint in her eyes when she'd seen him walk through the door. He still affected her. The same way she affected him. Every time he saw her, he wanted, needed, to get closer. Like now, he'd like to walk around her desk, pull her up out of her chair and straight into his arms for a kiss.

"We have to go, or we'll be late."

"I'm not going anywhere with you."

"Please."

"No."

"Why not?"

"Dylan." She drew out his name with a world of exasperation behind it.

"Don't do that. Don't blow me off for no reason."

"There are a dozen reasons this is not a good idea. We had something. Once. It's over. It ended in disaster.

We can't just go back to being friends the way we used to be and forget everything that happened between then and now."

"Great. Then we are on the same page."

"I don't even know what planet you're on. You show up here with flowers and dinner this past week and you act like we're on a first date or something."

"That's exactly what it was. You know, two people who see each other for an hour or two and get to know each other."

"We know each other. We have a history."

"It's been years. For all intents and purposes, Jess, we're strangers. I don't know anything about you except our past. You don't know anything about me. All I'm trying to do is get to know you now."

"Why? To what end?"

"Because I like you and want to get to know you better. Because you're the only woman who ever made me feel the way I do when I think about or see you. Jess, I've missed you. I want my best friend back."

"She's gone, Dylan. Don't you get that? She isn't me anymore. So much has changed. Everything is different now. Why can't you just accept that and leave me alone?"

"Maybe I would if I didn't have a world of hurt to make up for causing you." That strange look came into her eyes again. Every time he even mentioned their past, her eyes darkened with fear and such anguish he felt it like a punch to the heart.

"Dylan, please."

"You are really making me work for this." He held up his hand to stop her from protesting further. "Answer one question."

"What?"

"If whatever it is you still need to tell me didn't hang over us, would you want to see me?" He held his breath for the answer. If she said no, he'd have one hell of an uphill battle to change her mind, but he would. Eventually. He'd keep trying until he did.

She let out a heavy sigh. "Yes. But it doesn't change—"

"Stop with yes. Okay, so let's make a deal. You have something you want to tell me, but you don't feel like you can because of what I did to you."

"Your mother is the one who sent me that email and said some things on the phone that made it clear you didn't want anything to do with me."

"As I told you, lies. I'm sorry she did that. I'll make it up to you. In order to do that, I need your cooperation. Let's put the past on hold. We won't talk about it until you're ready."

"I don't think that's a good idea. You're asking me to spend time with you, rebuild our friendship, and then you want me to tell you the worst thing that has ever happened to me, knowing it will hurt you and you'll hate me."

"That is not going to happen. Ever. But you don't believe that because I left you and you think I'll do it again. Give me a chance to prove to you that will never happen." He put it all on the line and added, "Otherwise, it's just you and me right here, right now. Tell me what happened. You'll see, it won't change anything."

She bent her head, stared at her hands in her lap, and sighed with such resignation his chest went tight.

Ready to tell him, she raised her head and looked him dead in the eye. "After you left, I . . ." Tears filled her eyes and choked off her words.

Dylan rounded the desk in a few long strides. He grabbed her arms and pulled her up and into his arms. She wrapped her arms around his neck and he pulled her close. He kept one arm banded around her waist and combed his fingers over her head and down her soft, long hair.

"Jessie Thompson doesn't cry." He tried to coax her out of this dark mood. She only cried harder, disturbing him even more. He had no idea what to do with a crying woman, but especially Jess. Tough as they come, whatever happened hurt her deeply. "Ah, Jess, come on now. It's okay. I'm here." He kissed the side of her head and ran his hand down her hair again and again. He turned with her in his arms and leaned back on her desk, bringing her close between his legs.

"I can't do this. It brings it all back and it hurts too much. You left and I was all alone. I got that email, saying you were done with me."

Dylan hugged her tight to his body and buried his face in her hair and neck. "It's okay, sweetheart. I'm so sorry. I'd never hurt you like that, Jess. You don't have to say anything, just hold on to me."

Nothing ever felt better than Jessie tightening her arms around him and holding on for dear life. He vowed he'd never let her go. He'd spend the rest of his life making her happy. She'd never feel this kind of heart-wrenching pain again.

She settled into him, the tears stopped, but she didn't let go. He waited her out, then took her face between his hands and made her look at him.

He fell into her somber gaze and lost his heart to her all over again. He'd never tire of looking at her. "You are so beautiful. You take my breath away, Jess. You've been through so much, and you've turned your life around and done some amazing things in such a short time. I wish I could convince you that the past doesn't matter anymore, that the connection we still share is enough to overcome anything and build a life together. I wish more than anything I could wipe away the hurt and sadness I see in you. I wish you could just say the words and get whatever it is off your chest."

Tears filled her eyes again. "Dylan—"

He kissed her quiet. "Shh. I can't bear to see you cry. No more talking. Not tonight." He stood, picked up her purse, and handed it to her. "Come on. We're still going out."

"Dylan, I don't feel like going out. We need to finish this."

"Not tonight. I want to be with you, Jess. So come on. I've got something planned. No talking required."

He took her hand and softly tugged to get her to come with him. She sighed and walked out of the office, locked the door, and got into his truck without a word. She didn't say anything on the way back into Fallbrook, or when they entered the movie theater. He bought the tickets, hot dogs, popcorn, and a couple of sodas and they took their seats. Trying to keep things light, he skipped the romantic comedy he thought she'd prefer, but might make her feel worse if it even touched on their circumstances, and they got lost in *Captain America*.

They finished eating during the opening coming attractions. He took her hand, laced his fingers with hers, and held on to her through the movie. At one point, she turned and looked at him and down at their joined hands like she didn't know how any of this happened. He smiled, raised their hands to his lips and kissed hers, soft and long, his eyes on hers. She turned back to the movie first and he kept her hand in his. She didn't let go when they exited the theater, or object when he took her hand again when he slid behind the wheel of the truck to drive her back to her car.

He kept his word. They didn't speak. Words weren't needed when he just wanted her to be with him. For now, it was enough. It took until they were settled in the truck on the way back to her office that he finally felt her completely relax next to him.

She tensed again when he helped her out of his truck and they stood next to her car. She opened her mouth to say something, but he cut her off. "I'm glad you came with me tonight. Can you get home on your own, or would you like me to follow you?"

"No. I'll be fine. Dylan . . ."

"I know, Jess. We'll get there," he said, meaning they'd get to that talk. "I'll call you tomorrow. Okay?" He pulled her door open and held it for her, giving her an escape, a way out of telling him what weighed so heavily on her heart and mind. She climbed in and started the engine, but turned to stare at him.

"Night, Jess."

"Thank you."

He got that she meant for making this easy and not pushing. "You're welcome. I'll see you soon. I'll call you." He closed the door and watched her drive away.

Eventually, they'd have to talk about it, but right now, she needed time to work it out. He could wait. He wasn't going anywhere.

Chapter Sixteen

IN TOWN ON business, Jessie walked down the sidewalk toward the antique store to check in with her partner. She usually went to see her at closing time, but since everyone knew she was back in town, today she went during normal business hours. A distraction from thinking about Dylan and what happened last night. She'd tried to tell him, but the words wouldn't come, and the pain of losing Hope rose up inside of her heart and made it bleed all over again.

Andrea had called to tell her she had some new orders.

Looking forward to making the new pieces, she desperately needed something to do to take her mind off Dylan. While she'd refused to admit to Dylan, or even give in easily to his plans, she liked that he came by this week. She thought the pizza dinner would be a quick way to show him the old spark was gone and she wasn't interested. Instead, his charm and easygoing openness disarmed her and drew her in. She should have known better, because any time she thought about him, or he was near, she wanted to let time fall away and go back to the days she loved him and everything between them was as easy as the half grin she adored seeing on his face every time he looked at her.

She needed to find a way to tell him about Hope. Soon. She'd barely gotten a few words out last night before her emotions swamped her and pulled her back to those moments in the hospital when she knew she was losing Hope and couldn't do anything about it.

The heat and pull still existed between them. She remembered the feel of his arms around her when they held each other close on Brian's porch, and the way he'd pulled her backside up against him in the kitchen, his heat and strength surrounding her. The tender and sweet way he held her hand during the movie and kissed the back of it to let her know he felt the buzz of electricity arcing between them, tingling her arm, and warming her system up to him.

Yes, she needed to tell him before things went too far. She'd lost him once. She couldn't fall for him again, build their relationship, only to lose him because she was keeping a secret he deserved to know.

She walked into the shop and spotted Andrea talking to Dylan. The rush of anticipation at seeing him again washed over her. She tamped it down, remembering her pledge to tell him everything the next time she saw him. She never expected it to be this afternoon.

Wondering why he was here, she put her finger to her lips for Andrea not to give her presence away. They stood at the back, so Jessie couldn't hear their discussion. She made her way through some of the antiques and collectibles. Andrea had some great pieces, and she'd displayed them in cabinets and other furniture Jessie had made. She liked seeing her furniture on exhibit like this with Andrea's pretty things. It always struck Jessie when she came into the store she had a talent for making furniture. Most of the pieces were simple. Clean lines, good construction, everything built to last. She used fine wood like oak, cedar, and walnut. Some of the children's furniture she did in pine.

Close enough to hear the conversation between Andrea and Dylan, he said, "I'd like a dresser, twin-bed headboard, and a toy chest. Something with a horse or western theme. Can the craftsman do something like that for me?"

Andrea discreetly glanced over Dylan's shoulder for a confirmation from her. Jessie thought about it and decided business was business. Dylan didn't have to know she made the furniture.

She nodded to Andrea she'd fill the order. She signed in the air for her to write down the details.

"We'll be happy to complete the order. It'll take some time for the pieces to be finished. The person who makes the furniture does all of the items by hand. If you want them carved with a special design, that's going to take longer."

"No problem. About how long will it take?"

Jessie held up three fingers behind Dylan. "Maybe three weeks," Andrea said.

"Sounds good. Call me when they come in and I'll come and pick them up. Should I pay for them now, or when they come in?"

"When they arrive will be fine. Anything else? You've practically bought an entire house full of furniture from us already. I can't imagine there's much more you need."

"I like the furniture. The craftsman is really into the details of each piece. You can't find this kind of quality in mass-produced furniture."

"I'm sure the person who makes the furniture would take that as high praise," Andrea said.

Jessie overheard and pretended interest in an antique vase and tried to hide a small smile.

Why does Dylan need a twin-size bed? Maybe he wanted the furniture for a spare room. It irritated her she didn't really know anything about him. She used to know everything.

Dylan turned around to see what drew Andrea's interest behind him. He didn't expect to see Jessie. He also didn't expect to see her in a dress and heels, like she worked in an office or was out to meet friends at a luncheon. The black dress, simple and elegant, like Jessie, reminded him of prom.

He'd describe her in that way. Strong too. The muscles in her arms were well defined. The dress ended a few inches above her knees, giving him a glimpse at the toned muscles in her thighs. Her job sure did keep her in shape. A very lovely shape.

"Jess, I didn't hear you come in. You look fantastic. How are you?"

"Fine, thanks. Getting some furniture?"

"Yeah. How about you?"

"No. I came in to get my orders from Andrea."

"Orders?"

Andrea handed her a bunch of slips. One of them she'd filled out with his request. The light dawned in his mind that she was the furniture craftsman.

"J.T. Designs. I thought that business name was for the custom homes you've built. You made all this furniture." He scanned the wide showroom.

"Guilty, Sheriff." She held up her hands like he'd arrest her.

"Funny." He smiled. His gut tied in knots just seeing her again. Last night was rough for both of them. Today, the wariness had vanished from her eyes. She seemed more at ease around him.

"Well, I'm glad I ran into you. I was going to call you in a little while and ask you to dinner. I need to tell you something." He couldn't expect her to open up to him about her life if he continued to keep secrets from her too. He needed to tell her about Will. How he adopted his son from a young girl in need.

"I don't know. I've thought a lot about last night. I know you said we'd leave the past for another time and get to know each other better."

"Yes. I thought we'd sit down to a meal together and I'll catch you up on what I've been doing."

"Before we move forward, we need to settle things."

He followed her out the door and onto the sidewalk in front of the shop. Andrea had been their captive audience. There wasn't anyone out on the street close enough to overhear them. If he could get her to open up, say yes to dinner, maybe he could convince her to take him back.

"Jess, if you're not ready to open up to me, that's okay."

"No, it's not. How can we, I, put the past behind me if I don't face it, tell you everything, and let the chips fall where they may. Holding this back is holding me back."

He reached for her, taking her by the shoulders, and drew her in close. Her breasts rose and fell against his chest with every breath they took in unison. His fingers gripped her tighter, and he pulled her closer. She smelled of flowers, fresh and sweet.

"If you're sure you're ready, I'll listen to whatever you have to say. I swear to you, Jess, nothing you tell me will change anything. Not the way I feel about you, or the fact I want us to be together again."

Jessie planted her hands on his hard chest and pushed away, unable to be that close to him and not give in to her need to move closer until they were one. Her body responded to the heat of his, tempting her to forget the words she still needed to speak and dive headfirst into the passion he always sparked in her. Everything inside her wanted to press closer, but she ruthlessly ignored the feelings. Instead, she focused on what she had to do. No more stalling.

"Why don't I follow you to your place? We'll talk."

"Uh, no, that won't work."

"Why not?"

"You see, I have something I need to tell you too. Before I take you to my place, I need to tell you about the person who lives with me."

"What? You're living with someone?"

A million thoughts raced through her head. Did he have a wife he forgot to mention? A girlfriend? Maybe she'd read far too much into him telling her he wanted her in his life again. Maybe he truly did only want his best friend back, not anything more.

Her unfocused gaze over his shoulder cleared and panic squeezed her belly tight. A little boy ran down the sidewalk on the other side of the street calling, "Daddy. Daddy." It took her a second to realize he wasn't going to stop when he got to the road. Fear gripped her throat and cut off her air and stopped her heart. She didn't think. She ran for the boy, hoping she got to him in time.

Dylan didn't get a chance to explain anything before Jessie bolted past him and sprinted into the street.

Horns honked and tires squealed. Dylan didn't know what happened, but he ran after her too late to catch her before she scooped up a child from the middle of the street. A car skidded to a screeching halt, hitting her, and throwing her up onto the hood and windshield with a loud thud. She held the child protectively in her arms. The car came to a jarring stop, and she flew off the hood and landed about ten feet away, hitting her shoulder and thigh, sliding several feet across the pavement. With her arms circled around the child's head and body, he could barely be seen. All Dylan needed to see were the child's shoes.

Panic squeezed his heart. His chest seized. He couldn't breathe. He recognized the shoes he put on his son this morning.

Stuck behind two cars that crashed, trying to avoid hitting him, the sense of unreality made everything around him quiet. Dylan came back to himself with an explosion of sound filling his ears. Several vehicles had rear-ended each other as traffic came to a jarring halt and Jessie had gone flying off one of the vehicles with his son in her arms. He tried to get around the cars, but they were a tangled mess. He jumped up and over a few before he made it to Jessie and Will.

From across the street, Dylan's mother called to Will and screamed for help. Dylan fell to his knees beside Jessie and Will in a few quick strides. Jessie lay on her back holding on to Will with all her might. Will cried out for him.

"Daddy!"

"I'm right here, son. Are you okay, little man?" He ran his hands over his boy, checking for scrapes, cuts, bumps, and—oh God—broken bones. He didn't find a scratch on him. By the way he moved, Dylan didn't think he broke anything. His son was safe, thanks to Jessie.

"Jess, don't move. You're bleeding." His training and experience kicked in at the sight of her blood oozing out of the gash on her head. He took out his cell phone and called his office.

"Lynn, it's me. I need four deputies on First Street and an ambulance. There's been an accident. A woman is down and my son may be hurt as well. Several vehicles are involved. Hurry," he ordered and hung up.

Jessie's eyes opened wide, her voice came out hoarse and disbelieving. "This is your son?"

"Yes. He's who I wanted you to meet. The person I live with. This is Will."

"She's my mommy. Okay, Daddy?"

Dylan smiled at his son and kissed him on the head to reassure his own distressed head and heart Will was okay. Jessie didn't look so good, and she grew even paler when he made the comment.

"He doesn't have a mother," Dylan explained. "Apparently, he nominates you."

Dylan's mother kneeled beside him and bent toward Will, placing her hand on his back. Tears streamed down her face. She pressed her other hand to her heart. "Will, I thought I'd lost you." Her hands shook as she sat back on her heels and held her hands tightly to her breast.

At three, Will was fast as lightning. Dylan's mother looked at her son. "Dylan, he must have spotted you across the street and took off without a word. I looked down to say something and he was gone."

"Mommy saved me."

His mother gazed down at Jessie, and her eyes went wide with such fear, Dylan didn't understand her reaction. "Jessie." She gasped.

Jessie focused on her, years of hate burned in her eyes. "You said he didn't want me. He never wanted to speak to me again. I was nothing but a distraction, discarded like the trash I am. You said he was tired of me using him. I believed your lies and I never got a chance to tell him . . . He's a father." The words came out haltingly.

The color drained from his mother's face. He'd never

seen her look this haunted in his whole life. "Jessie, you saved Will?"

"I need to tell you . . . about Hope." Jessie's eyes closed and her whole body went from rigid intensity to utter relaxation.

"She's confused," his mother said, her eyes pleading with him to understand something he couldn't comprehend.

Jessie's words rang in his head, but he couldn't seem to sort them out and make sense of them. Everything happened too quickly, chaos reigned around them, and he needed to get Jessie to the hospital. Panic overrode his common sense.

"Mom, I swear to God, if you know what she's talking about and you haven't told me, like you didn't tell me she was alive, this is your chance." He pinned her with a glare, disappointed when she stood on unsteady legs, opened her mouth to say something, but pressed her lips together, holding back whatever words she might have said in her defense to make him understand. She glared down at Jessie, then staggered away.

"Come here, little man. Jess is hurt. We need to get her to the hospital."

He tried to pick up his son, but he wouldn't let Jessie go. "Will, come on. She's hurt. Let me help her."

Will decided to let go and come to him. He wrapped his little arms around Dylan's neck and held tight and cried.

"Are you hurt, son? Are you okay?"

"I'm okay. It was really scary." His lip trembled. He

glanced at all the people watching them and realized he'd done something really bad.

"Yes it was." The accident had taken ten years off Dylan's life. He couldn't imagine his life without Will and Jessie. He'd just found her again.

The vision of her flying through the air with his son in her arms replayed in his mind. It would haunt him the rest of his days. He couldn't even think about losing her.

"Jess, wake up. Come on, baby. Wake up for me." He patted her face softly and held on to his son. His whole world was these two people.

The ambulance and deputies' sirens wailed in the distance. Several of his men were already at the scene. People milled around and a few of the drivers of vehicles had gotten out to inspect the damage to their cars. Mostly, everyone gawked at Jessie, lying sprawled in the street.

The woman who'd been driving the vehicle that hit Jessie cried and blabbered on and on about not seeing her and how she'd come out of nowhere. The woman didn't seem to understand she'd almost hit a child. No wonder. Will's head barely came up to the hood of the car.

Will sobbed quietly against his chest, and Jessie— Jessie wouldn't wake up. Blood smeared all over her arm and leg. Her dress was shredded on the bottom where she'd slid across the pavement and was pulled up to her hip.

He leaned over her and listened to her shallow breathing, then kissed her mouth.

"Come on, Jess. Wake up for me." Dylan pleaded now. He just wanted to see her eyes open. She had to be all right. The hood of the car that hit her was crushed in on top and had a broken windshield with a circular break, spreading out like a spider web. Blood splattered in the pattern. She'd slammed her head into the windshield.

"Will, I need to set you down next to me, so I can check on Jess."

When Dylan set him down, Will scooted close to Jessie and put his hand on her arm.

Dylan gently put his fingers under Jessie's head and tried not to move her neck. He didn't know how badly she'd been hurt. So far, she'd spoken to them, but she hadn't really moved, except to let go of Will.

He pulled his sticky, wet fingers covered in her blood away from her head.

He leaned over Jessie and tried to get a better look at her damaged shoulder. The street had chewed up her flesh and left it bloody and raw.

He moved down her side to check her thigh and noticed blood pooling at her waist and under her back. A lot of blood.

He peeled off his shirt and pressed it to Jessie's side and under her back. She didn't make any sound of distress when he pressed where she was bleeding. A bad sign.

He didn't want to move her in case she'd broken her back or neck. He pressed on the shirt and it quickly stained with blood. The ambulance should arrive any minute. He hoped the paramedics could stop the bleeding.

With one hand, he pulled up her dress to look at her thigh. A gasp went up from the crowd of onlookers. He looked up in time to see his deputy go white and turn away. Jessie's thigh was a mess. Road rash ran all the way up to her hip.

Leaning over her head, he whispered into her ear. "Jess, wake up. Please. Please, honey, come back to me. I can't lose you again. I love you."

"Dylan," she sighed. "Dylan."

"Yes, Jess. It's me. I love you."

"I'm sorry. Hope is gone."

"I'm here. You're going to be fine. The ambulance is here. We'll take you to the hospital. You're going to be okay. I'll make sure of it. I won't leave you. Stay with me. Stay with me, Jess." He cupped her face and held her gaze until her eyes fluttered shut again.

The deputies and bystanders stared and gawked as Dylan transformed from a tough no-nonsense sheriff into a desperate man in love, begging Jessie to wake up.

The paramedics shoved him out of the way so they could get to her. One of his deputies grabbed his arm and held him back. Will clung to his leg. He scooped him up into his arms and watched helplessly as chaos reigned around him. Today he wasn't a cop, but a father and a man in love with the woman lying hurt and helpless at his feet. He'd let his deputies handle the scene. He kept his eyes on Jessie. The paramedics staunched the bleeding wounds with bandages, strapped her to a gurney, and loaded her into the ambulance.

Rules, regulations be damned, he stepped up into the ambulance with the paramedics and Will, determined not to leave Jessie alone. Not again. Never again.

Chapter Seventeen

DYLAN SAT IN the waiting room slowly losing his mind. Someone in the ER had given him a shirt to wear when they arrived. He wondered if the doctor would ever come out and give him an update on Jessie's condition. Once they took her into a curtained cubicle, they hadn't let him see her again. No one came out to tell him anything, and it was eating him alive. Every scenario playing through his head turned into a vivid nightmare about how this could end. She had to be okay. He wished he'd wake up and find Jessie well and whole.

He'd been so worried about Jessie and had Will thoroughly checked out by a pediatrician that an hour passed before he realized he needed to make some phone calls. He took out his cell phone and called Brian first. Brian, understandably upset by the news, softly denied this could be happening before replying he and Marilee were on their way to the hospital.

His next call was even harder to make. He hated to admit Jessie may not want him with her when she woke up. He called Greg after getting his last name from Brian. Dylan had no idea he was a Langley from Langley Construction. Because Dylan loved Jessie and Jessie would want the closest people to her here, he'd suck up his own pride and jealousy and let them know what happened.

"Hey, Greg, it's Dylan."

"What's up?"

"I need you to come to the hospital in Fallbrook. It's not good."

"Jessie?" Greg croaked out.

"She was hit by a car. You need to come now. She needs you." Those words were more difficult than any he'd ever spoken.

"You do not leave her. You wait until I get there."

"I'm not going anywhere." Dylan hated that Greg thought he could leave Jessie. But he had left her once. He'd never repeat the biggest mistake of his life.

Greg hung up on him, leaving Dylan with nothing to do but wait.

Will slept next to him with his head resting on Dylan's thigh. It took all of Dylan's self-control to sit still when he wanted to jump up and pace the room like a caged animal.

Looking around the room, he felt as depressed as his surroundings. The walls were white and in sad shape, marked and scuffed. The pictures on the walls looked like they belonged in some cheap motel. The peach-and-sage-tone desert scenes did nothing to soothe his anxiety.

Several other people waited in the claustrophobic room. Paper coffee cups littered the small tables and old magazines lay strewn on empty chairs, the tables, and the floor.

The heavy feel of families desperate for news of their loved ones hung in the air, making waiting that much more difficult. Just when he thought he'd go crazy waiting alone, Brian, Marilee, Greg, and John showed up at once. They spotted him sitting with Will and made a beeline for him. Their faces wore masks of concern, but the anger on Greg's face set Dylan off. He didn't want them to blame him. She'd saved his son, and he'd gladly take her place in the emergency room.

Brian took a deep breath before asking, "What have you heard? Is she okay?" He rubbed his hand over his neck, his eyes pleading for a positive answer. "I can't lose her now. Not when I just started to get my life back on track all because of her. I haven't had enough time to thank her and pay her back for everything she's done."

"I haven't heard anything in almost two hours. She's with the doctors."

They stood over him. Under normal circumstances he would have stood and faced them eye to eye. His son lay asleep on him, and he couldn't stand without disturbing him. So he sat under Greg's accusing glare.

Disturbed by the conversation, Will sat up and rubbed his eyes, glancing around at the new people. "Daddy, who are they?"

"Jess's friends and family. They came to see her."

Greg just about lost it and gasped. "Son of a . . . This is your son?"

John and Greg exchanged looks of surprise and dismay. Dylan's anger intensified. They knew Jessie's secret. A secret she'd kept all these years and couldn't bring herself to discuss with him. If he had to beat it out of Greg, he'd make him tell him about Hope.

"This is Will. Will, these are Jessie's friends Greg and John. That is her brother, Brian, and his wife, Marilee."

"Hi. My mommy got hurt. We flew in the air."

Dylan sighed and picked up his son and held him close, standing to face the crowd of people waiting for his explanation.

"Will doesn't have a mother. When Jessie saved him today, he nominated her. Other kids have one, and he wants one of his own."

Greg actually took a step back from Dylan and Will and ran a hand over his head and put his fists on his hips. "Please tell me she didn't hear this."

"She did."

Greg swore under his breath and paced a couple steps away and back again. John looked just as upset and devastated.

Dylan thought about the accident and what Jessie said for the last two hours. Her words echoed in his head.

I believed your lies and I never got a chance to tell him. He's a father.

Hope is gone.

She hadn't meant that he was Will's father. He was Hope's father. A shudder ripped through him like a shockwave.

Greg's words at the construction site office came back to him too.

I can't tell you how important Hope is.

Jessie's breakdown, trying to confess her secret. Greg and John's concern about Will calling Jessie his mommy. It all made sense.

It hit him like a wrecking ball to the heart. It exploded into a million pieces that tore his soul to shreds. He'd left Jessie behind, alone and pregnant with his child.

"Tell me about Hope," he said to John and Greg at once.

Greg and John looked stunned and resigned at the same time. About to start talking, everyone stopped and stared when the doctor entered the room.

"I'm looking for J. T. Langley's family. I'm Dr. Williamson."

As a group, they stood together collectively holding their breath, waiting for the doctor's report on Jessie's condition. The worn, tired lines on the doctor's face told him the news wasn't anything he wanted to hear.

"We've moved her into a room," Dr. Williamson began, and Dylan exhaled his relief that she was okay. "I'll let you see her, but only a couple at a time." Things couldn't be that bad if they were allowed to see her.

Dylan took the lead. "How is she? What are her injuries?"

"Are you here officially, Sheriff?" Dr. Williamson eyed his badge and the gun at his hip.

"No," Dylan said tightly.

"You're going to break all the hospital rules to get to Jessie, aren't you?"

"I'm glad we understand each other, Doctor," Dylan responded, thankful he still held Will, so he wouldn't ring the doctor's neck to get him to start talking.

"She's unconscious. She has a major head injury. The fact she isn't in a coma is both a miracle and a rarity. We put ten stitches in her scalp. She'll have a massive headache when she wakes up and a bump the size of a small apple. We've cleaned the road rash on her shoulder, thigh, and hip. The scrapes were coated in dirt and grime from the street. She's on some heavy-duty antibiotics. Her skin will remain raw for a few days before it scabs over, leaving some lasting scars. Parts of her thigh and shoulder took the brunt of the skid on the pavement. Most of the gravel is out, but it's impossible to get it all. Her skin will heal over what's left and it'll feel bumpy rather than smooth as scar tissue builds up. Later, if she wants, plastic surgery can take care of most of it. I'm particularly concerned about the four-inch shard of glass we pulled out of her side. It probably came from a broken soda or beer bottle. We cleaned the wound and stitched it closed.

"We'll watch her for fever and infection over the next couple of days. The head wound is the most severe injury. We'll closely monitor her the next day or two and see how she does. She's very lucky.

"She's in room 211 on the second floor, a few doors down the hall. There's another waiting room upstairs. You can go in, but only two at a time. Only for a few minutes each. She needs to rest."

"Thank you, Doctor." Dylan shook his hand. As he left, everyone spoke at once.

Marilee became the voice of reason and called for quiet. "Let's go upstairs to the other waiting room. Brian and I will visit Jessie first, followed by Greg and John. Dylan, when you go in to see her, I'll watch Will. Now, let's go."

Dylan didn't utter a sound, and no one else argued or said a word. They rode the elevator upstairs, Dylan lost in his thoughts about Jessie . . . and Hope.

Chapter Eighteen

DYLAN WAITED FOR Brian and Marilee to go sit with Jessie before he demanded answers from Greg. He needed to know about Hope. If Jessie couldn't bring herself to tell him, Greg sure as hell would.

"Greg, tell me the truth about Hope."

Greg and John shared another look, and John nodded his head to Greg. "He deserves to know, son. You should tell him. Jessie's been hurting and angry for far too long. He should carry his half of the burden. She's carried it alone all these years. It's too much for her to carry alone."

Greg squeezed his father's shoulder, shook his head, and said, "I guess I'm the unwilling narrator to Jessie's story."

Frowning deeply, Greg continued. "Hope was your daughter."

"Was," Dylan said on an exhale, like that one word encompassed everything it meant. He took a shallow breath and leaned back in his chair, grief enveloping his whole being. He held Will a little tighter.

"No." Dylan's mother gasped. Everyone turned and stared at her, standing in the doorway of the waiting room. Her face pale, she used one hand to hold on to the doorway for balance. He couldn't believe she'd driven to the hospital. Everyone looked as surprised as him to see her there.

Panic etched into every line on her pale face. "She lied. That girl was no good from the start. She probably slept with every boy in town. She's the reason you turned your back on college, your family, the life you should have had. She sent you that email because she wanted to use you and get her hands on the McBride money. I wouldn't let her use a baby to reel you in again. Not then. Not now. The baby wasn't Dylan's. It couldn't be."

Dylan couldn't believe what his mother just admitted. Sick to his stomach, he spit out, "You knew she was pregnant."

"How did you find out? She never told Dylan," Greg added.

"The email Jessie sent didn't go through. The reason she called you"—Dylan turned his attention to his mother, raked his fingers through his hair in frustration, trying to put it all together and believe the unbelievable—"she called you to find me. You told her I didn't want anything to do with her when you knew she was pregnant with my baby."

"The baby wasn't yours. She lied to get your attention. When it didn't work, she left you alone."

"After the scathing things you said to her, the things you made her believe were Dylan's words, of course she didn't try to contact him again." Greg swore and hung his head. "Do you have any idea what you put her through?"

"It's her fault. She shouldn't have lied. She should have left Dylan alone and not filled his head with nonsense."

"Do you hear yourself?" Dylan asked, amazed this was his mother saying this bullshit. "You know, it was bad enough you sent her that email in my name, and were cruel to her on the phone, but this is unconscionable. You let me believe she was dead. You knew she was pregnant and you never told me. You let a fifteen-year-old girl, pregnant, stabbed, and alone, believe the father of her child didn't want her. How could you do this?" The low and soft sound of his voice did nothing to cover the deadly tone.

"I'd do anything to protect you from that girl. She's a liar and manipulator."

Greg and John stood behind Dylan. They both put a hand on each of his shoulders to hold him back. He strained against their grip and considered strangling his own mother for what she'd done.

"After what you've done, what does that make you, Mother?"

She gasped and clutched her hands to her breasts. "You've never spoken to me in such a manner. This is her doing. I did the right thing, protecting you from that girl."

Dylan turned to the men behind him. He owed both of them more than he could ever imagine. They'd been with

Jessie through her pregnancy. They'd been there when his daughter was born. Oh, God. They'd been there when Jessie wanted to die. It couldn't be. It just couldn't be.

"Tell me where my daughter is. Tell me Jessie gave her up for adoption, and she's out there somewhere. Tell me I still have a chance to see my daughter. Please."

Greg grabbed on to Dylan's arm to steady him, their eyes meeting. "There's no easy way to tell you. She died in her mother's arms five days after her birth. Complications from pneumonia. Jessie buried her at Saint Francis Cemetery in Solomon."

"Oh, God." Dylan staggered backward. He gripped Will tighter. Thanks to Greg's help, he managed to sit in a chair before he collapsed.

Tears rolled down his face and his son held him close. He stared into nothing and fell into the past, thinking of prom night and what happened to Jessie after he left.

"Her father tried to kill her, and she was pregnant with our baby."

Anguish and misery rolled off him as he worked things out in his mind, but it never dissipated, only grew more profound.

"Fifteen and scared to death, she had no idea what she was going to do, but she wanted that baby, with or without you," Greg said. "No matter what happened between you, she thought you deserved to know. Jessie begged your mother to give her your number, so that she could talk to you. You'd been friends for years, even if you didn't want to be with her, she hoped to at least change your mind about the baby."

No question Dylan wanted the baby and Jessie. Over the anger and despair he felt now, the longing for both of them grew. This couldn't be real. How could he want them this much and live with knowing he'd lost them? Jessie would never forgive him.

It wasn't fair that one person could interfere in two lives and change them forever. Dylan's mother had interfered, and he and Jessie paid the price.

How could he fix this? Greg said she'd closed herself off from people, men. He understood why, but he'd held out hope he'd find a way to convince her take the chance to love him again. With every damning word Greg spoke that hope faded.

"Jessie worked for Dad and me throughout her pregnancy. She went to the doctor and took care of herself. Dad and I helped her as much as she let us. We were with her the day she went into labor."

Dylan sat quietly listening, so Greg continued. "We took her to the hospital. You'd have been proud of her. She was a trooper through all sixteen hours of labor. Dad and I stayed, and Jessie brought that beautiful girl into the world."

The longer Dylan sat listening to Greg tell him what he should have witnessed firsthand, the angrier he got. Dylan added up everything, calculating just how much he'd missed out on and lost. Greg had been there and seen his daughter born, while he had been in the military and none the wiser, thinking Jessie dead and gone.

"Hope arrived, six pounds and ten ounces. She had dark hair like yours and blue-gray eyes. The nurse said most babies have that color eyes when they're born and they change. We'll never know what color they might have been. Hope wasn't breathing well, so they took her to the neonatal intensive care unit and a specialist checked her out. She got some fluid in her lungs during the delivery. They monitored her and gave her some medicine to clear her lungs.

"Jessie was frightened and hurting. She wanted her baby and they wouldn't let her see her for a few hours while Jessie rested and recuperated from the delivery. I stayed with her and over the next couple days I took her in a wheelchair to see Hope. She'd sit and hold Hope. She'd cry and tell her about her daddy."

Dylan groaned. After everything, to hear that Jessie told their daughter about him was too much to bear.

"Daddy, don't cry. It's okay." Will hugged him close.

"Daddy's very sad, little man. My heart is broken."

"Mommy will fix it. She can kiss it better. I'll ask her when she wakes up."

Dylan hugged Will tighter. He'd have to explain he couldn't just pick Jessie to be his mother. As much as Dylan wanted Jessie back, he didn't think she'd ever forgive him for not being there when their daughter died.

"Finish it," Dylan demanded, knowing there was still more to tell.

Greg took a deep breath, leaned his head back, closed his eyes, and held back tears. Dylan read Greg's pain and felt it as his own.

"You want to know how she died?"

Dylan nodded and Greg reluctantly finished the sad tale. "She was a beautiful baby. Her breathing and overall

health improved, and then on the third day she had a reaction to some medication the doctors gave her. It weak-
ened her even more. Jessie stayed with her every second
the doctors allowed. On the fifth day she stopped breathing. They tried to revive her. They couldn't bring her
back. Her lungs were too weak and damaged. Hope never
took another breath on her own. It took them the better
part of six hours to get Jessie to give her up. She wouldn't
let anyone touch Hope. She sat rocking her in her arms."

Greg wiped his eyes. "Sorry, the memory is too pain-
ful to bear." He cleared his throat, choking back the tears
as best he could. "I took Jessie home, helped her make
the funeral arrangements, and two days later we buried
Hope. It's like I told you. She lost Hope, her daughter, and
all the hope in her heart."

"What did she put on the grave marker?" Dylan asked
in barely a whisper.

"Do you want to know her name? Her whole name."

Dylan nodded.

"The gravestone reads, 'Hope Danielle McBride.' Below
the dates of her birth and death, it reads, 'Mommy's little
girl.'"

"She named the baby after me. She gave her my name."
Dylan's voice broke.

"Yes," Greg said. "There's nothing else to say. Jessie
loved you. She loved you enough to name your daughter
after you, even though at the time, she thought you didn't
want them."

"She was devastated. You said you thought she wanted
to die." Dylan could just imagine how Jessie felt. He wanted

to curl up and die right now too. The only thing that kept him from shattering and in one piece was his son now playing on the floor and Jessie lying hurt in a hospital bed.

"Yes. I don't know what finally brought her around, or if anything, except Jessie's inner strength finally pulled her through. Dad and I tried everything to bring her back from despair. Nothing we said or did worked. It was all Jessie. She never came back a hundred percent. She doesn't smile like she means it. She doesn't laugh with her whole heart. She doesn't live life to the fullest. She doesn't let any man get close."

"You said she hasn't dated anyone."

"No one. She's afraid to love again. Everyone she loved hurt her or left her. She won't allow that to happen again. I hate telling you this, but Dylan, you need to know just how much Jessie suffered."

Greg turned his hard gaze on Dylan's mother. "Are you pleased? Did she suffer enough, pay enough for having the audacity to love your son? I hope you rot in hell for all the pain you've caused."

Greg sighed, reining in his temper. "She shifted her focus, went to college and worked for Dad. She started her own business with Dad's help. All of that gave her a sense of purpose, but not the happiness she deserves."

"See, she just wanted to get money," Dylan's mother accused. "How'd she pay for college, or starting a business? That's the only reason she called, for the money."

John stood, arms crossed over his chest, and scowled. "I can't believe you're a mother. There's no love in your cold heart.

"She worked for me, and she got a couple small scholarships. When she would come up short, I gave her the money to finish her degree. When she wanted to start her company, I gave her the money. She didn't ask for it. I offered. She paid me back with interest. Every dollar. Every dime. Every penny. She worked harder than two of my men combined to earn her pay. She gave me more joy in my life, as if she'd been my own daughter. She worries about me, fusses over me, and generally treats me like family. That girl is better than any two people I know and a million times better than you'll ever be. You betrayed her. You betrayed your own son. Because of you, he never got the chance to see his daughter."

"Did you hold her, sir? Did you get to touch her?" Dylan asked, his voice raw.

"Yes, son. I did. Jessie honored me by placing that sweet baby girl in my arms. Besides holding my own son in my arms, there was nothing better. I'm sorry for your loss. More sorry than I can say."

Dylan didn't know what to say. He looked up at Greg with the same question in his eyes. He didn't know why it mattered so much to him to know these men held his daughter when he never got the chance.

"Yes, Dylan. I held her on one of the few times Jessie gave her up, even for a minute. Even at sixteen, you could see Jessie would have been a great mother. In those few days, she loved her little girl enough for a lifetime."

Chapter Nineteen

DYLAN FISTED HIS hands then opened them wide. Empty. He hadn't gotten to hold or love his daughter. He hadn't even known about her. His mother denied Jessie the simple courtesy of telling her how to contact him. Worse, she'd denied him the chance to know his daughter in the short time she'd been here. Five days. Five days that he'd never get back. Years that Jessie thought him so callous and heartless he didn't want her.

Years he spent thinking she was dead.

Will sat on the floor pulling pages out of a magazine. He made a mess, but Dylan didn't care. Let him wreck the place. He was a kid. They made messes.

Then it hit him. Will. He stood and turned to his mother.

"You knew about Jessie and the baby and you didn't say anything all these years. Not even when I adopted Will. You knew about his parents and how he came to me, and you never said anything. You accepted Will as part of the family, but you wouldn't accept your own granddaughter. Why? Why would you do that? Because you didn't think Jessie was good enough for me?"

"You deserve better. You're a McBride. As for the baby, well, we'll never know for sure she was yours."

Both men grabbed his shoulders again as he took a step toward his mother. He stopped, but the urge to slap her was so great he fisted his hands at his side to keep from following through with the impulse.

"I felt sorry for Jessie, but nothing could be done once the baby died," his mother said cruelly. "What good would it do to tell you after the fact? I didn't want to hurt you. It doesn't change anything," she said, further damning herself in Dylan's eyes.

Greg tapped Dylan's arm. "Wait a second, what do you mean you adopted Will? He isn't yours?" Greg asked.

"I chose Daddy and now I've chosen a mommy. When will she wake up? I'm hungry."

"Come here, sweetheart. Grandma will take you to get something to eat."

"No, you won't," Dylan snapped. "Do you really think I'll let you anywhere near my son, give you a chance to corrupt him with your cold miserable heart?"

His son was three years old. Hope never even saw her first birthday. "Little man, Daddy will get you something to eat in a minute. Jessie won't wake up for a long time. She's hurt real bad and the doctors are making her sleep."

His mother clasped her hands against her heart. "Dylan, you can't mean to keep me from my grandson.

You know how much I love him. You're upset. This will all be straightened out when Jessie admits she lied. The baby wasn't yours."

"Hope was mine. I made love to Jessie without even thinking about protecting her. I couldn't look past having her in my arms. If I didn't make love to her, I didn't want to take my next breath. I love her that much, Mother. I loved her then. I love her now. I will love her, and only her, the rest of my life. I'll never forgive you for what you've done, and everything you've taken from me." Which probably included Jessie, because she'd never forgive him after what his mother did.

He took a breath and tried to remember this was his mother. He tried to find the love he'd felt for her just hours ago, but he couldn't find it in his heart. Would he ever feel that way about her again?

"Jessie saved Will today. How do I thank her for saving my son when I wasn't there for her and our daughter? How do I say thank you for keeping my son safe when our daughter is dead?" He growled the last word, unable to contain his fury.

His mother tried desperately to explain herself again. "How could God be so cruel as to keep my grandson safe only to turn you against me? Don't you see, it can't be changed? It's in the past. That's why when you adopted Will I never said anything. The baby was already gone. You have to understand why I did it. The baby wasn't yours."

The more times she said that last part, the angrier he got. Hope was his, he had no doubt.

"Wait, you knew the baby died. Did Jessie call and tell you?"

"No. I checked with the hospital on her condition. I got a nurse to tell me about the baby."

"How did you find her? How did you know she went into labor?" Greg asked.

"I hired a private investigator to find her. He paid a man at the construction company to tell him when Jessie went into labor. If there was a chance the baby was yours, I wanted to know how she was doing."

"If there was a chance, you wanted to know? Did you ever plan to tell me?"

"It doesn't matter now. I didn't want to hurt you when nothing could be done."

"It doesn't matter." Dylan gasped. "Does it look like it doesn't matter to me?" He yelled at his own mother, but for the life of him she didn't look like the woman who raised him and cared for him all these years. Where was the mother that loved him?

"I expected your surprise when I adopted Will, but when I told you, there was something about the way you looked at me that I didn't quite understand. Now, it makes sense. The story so closely relates to the situation with Jessie and me. Doesn't it?"

He turned to Greg, desperate to have someone understand. "You see, I adopted Will in Georgia. I worked for the Atlanta Police Department. On one of my shifts, I found a teenage girl hiding behind some Dumpsters in an alley. She'd been mugged. Eighteen, more than eight months pregnant, she didn't have anything. She hid the pregnancy at home for as long as she could and ran away to have the baby. Her boyfriend didn't want to keep the baby. The girl wanted to give it up for adoption. She just wanted to go home and go to college in the fall like she planned and give the baby a chance to have a real family and a good life.

"I could have taken her to a shelter, or sent her back to her family, but she called to something inside of me. I had sworn to protect people like her."

"Because you thought Jessie was murdered," Greg guessed.

"Yes. I took her home and fed her. Her due date only weeks away, I told her I'd help her make the final decisions and get her back to her family. She lived with me until she delivered the baby. Then, she asked me to keep him. She said it was fate I'd found her and helped her. I took one look at that little man and knew he was mine. That girl loved him enough to give him a good life, but she wasn't ready to be a mother to him."

He studied the little boy at his feet, light brown hair, puppy-dog brown eyes when he wanted something, and a smile that melted his heart. He was perfect.

"Long story short, her parents arrived, agreed I could adopt the baby. A lawyer and a judge later, Will was mine."

"I chose you Daddy," Will said from the floor where he sat tearing the magazine pages and wadding them into balls, tossing them at Dylan and making explosion noises.

"That's right, little man. You chose me."

Greg rubbed his hand over the back of his neck. "That's amazing. Jessie will be surprised when you tell her," Greg said.

"What do I tell her? That I adopted a perfect stranger's baby, but I couldn't be there when she gave birth to my daughter."

"That's your anger talking. You didn't know. If you got her messages, you'd have been there." Greg made a point of staring down his mother as she stood by the doorway wringing her hands.

"Jessie thinks I'll be mad at her. Why would I be mad at her? She'll never forgive me for what happened. She'll never believe I love her," Dylan said, dropping his head and frowning miserably.

"She blames herself for Hope's death. She had a difficult delivery. She thinks that if she'd done something different, pushed harder, faster, or taken better care of herself before the baby came that it wouldn't have happened. It wasn't her fault. The baby got sick. That's all. Nothing she did or didn't do would have changed it."

"No, but it could have been better, if I'd been there to share her pain. If we'd shared our daughter and her death. I could have helped Jessie through her grief."

"Help her heal from this accident," Greg suggested. "Tell her you know about Hope and take it from there."

Greg tried to give Dylan something to look forward to. Something that would make everything a little more bearable, and Dylan grabbed on to it. "She has pictures."

Dylan looked up with interest. "Of Hope. She has pictures of Hope."

"Yes, Dylan. We took a lot of pictures at the hospital."

Greg squeezed his shoulder and Dylan sat, absorbing everything they'd told him. He leaned over his knees with his hands on his forehead and wept. It was just too much.

He didn't hear his mother sneak away or Brian and Marilee come in so that Greg and John could visit Jessie. He didn't realize Marilee bought Will a snack at the vending machine and sat with him in her lap while he ate. He sat with his head in his hands, silent tears falling, consumed by guilt and sadness for the woman he loved and the baby they'd lost.

He wondered if he'd lost Jessie.

He vowed he wouldn't let that happen. They'd lost enough. He wouldn't allow them to lose each other too. Now, all he had to do, convince Jessie he loved her. He always loved her.

Chapter Twenty

DYLAN SENT A very sleepy Will home with his nanny, Lorena. He needed to stay with Jessie. Dylan hated to be separated from Will. He wanted the boy close, so he could hold and love him and not feel so desolate at losing his daughter. The ache in his heart turned to a chasm of emptiness that threatened to swallow him whole.

He spent the night with Jessie in her room. Before they left, Greg and John gave him a bear hug and assured him they'd be back today with clothes for Jessie. The fact they knew where she lived and could get into her house irritated Dylan, but he had to face reality. They took care of Jessie. He hadn't been there for her, thanks to his own mother.

He was grateful to them for staying with her, helping her get through the desperate months she didn't want to live, and making sure she wasn't alone. They'd become the family she'd always deserved.

The nurses came and went through the night. They arrived often, checking her blood pressure, monitors, and changing out her IV bag. Jessie didn't stir at all.

They adjusted her position throughout the night, propping pillows behind her back and hips to keep her lying on the side that hadn't been ravaged by the slide across the road.

He caught on to the nurse's routine, and when it came time to move her, he helped the nurses in any small way. It gave him a sense of satisfaction to help Jessie and an excuse to touch and comfort her. He held her hand while she slept and stroked her face. He talked to her, knowing she couldn't answer him, but he hoped she heard him and took the opportunity to say all the things he'd wanted to say to her over the years. He poured his heart out about Hope and what happened, afraid she wouldn't give him the chance to say his piece when she woke up.

Sometime in the early morning, the nurse informed him they were cutting back on the sedative. They'd continue to taper it off over the next several hours and see if she woke up around mid-afternoon. The hours without sleep, the stress and worry over Jessie's condition, and grieving his lost daughter and a life with Jessie he wished for every second, he drifted off at dawn, shutting off his overtaxed brain.

Nearly noon, Greg walked in to check on Jessie, how she'd done last night, and check on Dylan too. He liked the guy. He'd gotten a bum rap over the years.

How could any mother be so cruel?

Jessie lay in bed, her back to the door, propped up on

pillows. Dylan slept, sitting in the chair next to her, his head resting on the bed, one arm wrapped over Jessie's calves and Jessie's hand in his.

Greg hated to wake Dylan, but he needed to know how Jessie did last night and what the doctors and nurses had in store for her today.

"Dylan. Dylan. Wake up." Dylan came awake with a start.

Greg gave him a pat on the shoulder to get his attention. "How is she?"

Dylan rubbed his hands over his face and scratched at his rough jaw. He stared at Jessie, his eyes red rimmed and bloodshot. Greg could almost hear him begging Jessie to wake up. The plea in his eyes disappeared when he turned and focused on Greg.

"She hasn't come around yet. The nurses kept her sedated all night. They tapered off early this morning. She should wake up soon. If she can't deal with the pain in her head, they'll knock her back out."

Greg stared at the bandages on Jessie's head and shoulder, imagining the ones wrapped around her sheet-covered leg. The hospital gown covered a lot.

Dylan caught him. "I hate thinking about what she looks like under that gown."

"You were the first to get to her after the accident."

"Yes. The blood. The damage to her beautiful skin." Dylan's hands shook when he scrubbed them over his eyes, trying to wipe away the gruesome images.

"She's tough. I'll bet she opens her eyes and demands to go home," Greg said to try to reassure him.

"At this point, I don't care if she wakes up just to yell at me. I need her to be okay." Dylan leaned over the bed and kissed her cheek.

"Where's your little guy? Do you have a girlfriend or someone to take care of him?"

"Subtle." Dylan half grinned.

Greg pulled the other chair up to the bed beside him. "Can't blame me, can you? I've been looking after her for a long time. Don't expect me to stop now."

"Fair enough. No girlfriend. Lorena, Will's nanny, takes care of him at the house after preschool and when I work. I've dated over the years, but no one special since Jessie. Every other woman never measured up to her. I could never feel for anyone else what I feel for her. I was a stupid asshole for ever leaving her."

"You were eighteen, and she only fifteen. It's not like you could run off, get married, and live happily-ever-after. She knew that."

"I would have found a way to make that happen for her and the baby."

"Not so easy to do when you were in the army. What made you join up?"

"When I took Jessie to the prom, I planned to tell her that night. She would have understood. My parents wanted me to go to college and turn into my father's clone. He works for a large corporation and spends all his time in an office making deals. I didn't want that kind of life. I joined the army because I needed to get out of my house and do some growing up on my own. I never expected to lose my head and my heart that night over

Jessie. Blame it on the dress or the stars. Maybe it was just seeing Jessie happy and carefree that night. I got caught up in the moment, and I didn't want to ruin it by telling her I was leaving. The next day, I was so far gone in love with her I couldn't bring myself to tell her. If I talked to her, or I saw her, I wouldn't be able to leave her, and I had to leave.

"It all seems so stupid now. None of that matters. When she needed me, I wasn't there."

"She still needs you. She loves you, though I'm not sure if she loves the boy from her past or the man you are now. You both need time to reconcile the past, everything your mother did to both of you, Hope, and find out who you are now. You want her back, right?"

"You don't beat around the bush, do you?"

"No point. She deserves better than she's gotten out of life. At one time, you were the only one who treated her with kindness. You loved her that night and she's held on to that all this time. If you can't or won't give that to her now, walk away before things get even more complicated and messy. She's had enough heartache and pain. She deserves to be happy."

"I intend to love this woman for the rest of my life. She can try to push me away like she's been doing, but sooner or later, I'll wear her down, and she'll realize I'm not going anywhere."

Chapter Twenty-One

"JESS. WAKE UP, baby." Dylan stood over her waiting for any sign she heard him. He needed her to wake up and look at him. He needed her to be okay.

Greg met him at Jessie's hospital room for lunch together for the last three days. He'd only gone home for a few hours each evening to have dinner with his son and put him to bed. He felt guilty twice over, for leaving Jessie for those few hours and being away from his son.

The doctor told them due to the concussion, she'd wake up when she was ready. The MRI scan showed the brain injury healing well. Every hour Jessie didn't wake up made Dylan worry that much more. They'd expected her to wake up days ago, but she went through groggy spells, never truly waking up, and slept for hours on end.

Greg stood from his seat and went to the other side of the bed. They watched and waited as she slowly started coming around over the better part of an hour. She'd moved and twitched. This was the first sign she might actually hear them talking to her. Once, she'd murmured something incoherently. Dylan hoped this time she'd wake up for real. The doctor said to give her time. He didn't want to give her another minute. He wanted to see her open her eyes, say something, anything, move so he knew she'd be okay.

Jessie heard voices over the throbbing pulse in her brain. She tried to lift her hand to her eyes to press them back into her skull. Someone held her hand down, and the pain, shooting through her arm and shoulder when she tried to move, made her moan. In her mind, she screamed.

"Jess? Honey, are you awake?" a voice crooned.

Honey? Funny, it sounded like Dylan. That couldn't be right. Maybe he changed his mind and came to see the baby.

Jessie's head pounded fiercely, making her think it might split clear open. She had a fleeting thought she must have gotten really drunk, and she'd have to kick her own ass. She wished she could remember what happened, but her mind was a blank screen, images flickering on and off like someone playing with a light switch.

"J.T. Come back to us. Wake up," Greg coaxed in a soft voice, his fingers rubbing her arm.

Greg's here. His voice came through the fog. It must be time to see Hope. Jessie wanted to see her baby. Hope needed her.

She tried to open her eyes, but the light and the pounding in her head hurt too much. Someone held her hand. Greg. She didn't know why her head hurt so much. Something she should know nagged at the edge of her mind and tried to crowd in. She kept holding it back because somehow she knew if she let it in, it would crush her.

She fluttered her eyes and squinted from the too-bright room. Someone turned the light off above her. The pain behind her eyes eased.

The impossible sound of Dylan's voice came again. "Jess."

"Dylan," she whispered, confused and so hopeful and happy he was here. "Did you come to see her? You changed your mind?"

She wanted to see his face. She'd missed him so much, and she'd been alone for so long without him. He'd finally decided to come. She'd hoped, prayed he'd change his mind. That he would want her and Hope. Groggy, she tried to focus. The doctor must have given her something to sleep because she'd been up all night with Hope in the NICU.

Everywhere hurt and something about that didn't seem right.

"Jess, honey, wake up for me." Anxiety and worry filled his voice. "Open your eyes and look at me."

She opened her eyes and gave him a half smile, worried how he'd react about the baby and if he'd stay or leave her again. She hoped he wanted to see his daughter and be a part of her life.

"Did you see her already? We can go see her together. She's so beautiful."

He glanced over her, and she followed his line of vision to Greg. She tried to smile, but it never quite tilted her lips. "We need to go see her. Will you take me?"

Greg winced. "J.T. You've been in an accident. You were hit by a car. Do you remember?" Greg asked, touching her cheek with his fingertips. At her blank stare, Greg finished. "I hate to break your heart again, but Hope isn't here."

She shifted her gaze from Greg to Dylan. Older now, he still had that strong hard jaw, the muscles in it working. Creases lined his brow and dark circles marred his eyes. He needed to shave and his hair was raked back in messy disarray. "This isn't right."

Greg's words sank in. She'd been in a car accident. No. She'd been hit by a car. The visions flashed in her mind. She'd scooped up a little boy. She remembered the thump of the car hitting her legs and back, the crack of her head hitting the windshield, and they'd flown through the air.

She glanced at Greg, her eyes filling with tears. His image blurred. "She's not here."

"No, honey. I'm sorry. She's gone. We lost her a long time ago."

"But, I saw her, held her in my arms. I could smell her," she sobbed.

"A dream, J.T." Greg wiped away a tear from her face. "A wonderful dream, honey. I'm sorry. I don't know what else to say. You've been through so much."

It washed over her. His words brought it all back. This wasn't the time she stayed in the hospital to give birth to Hope. Hope was gone and Dylan was back.

The car accident came back to her. She stared at him, but saw the little boy lying on her chest and calling for his daddy. Dylan's son. His mother standing over her. The guilty, horrified look on her face when she realized she'd just saved her grandchild. Dylan had a son. Her head spun. The room tilted. She turned back to Greg, her anchor. He helped her get through losing Hope. He'd help her now. He wouldn't leave her alone.

"Hope?"

Greg squeezed her hand. "He knows, J.T. I had to tell him after what happened. His mother came here and said some terrible things. I couldn't let it go. He needed to know the truth."

Pain and misery etched lines in Dylan's face and turned his lips into a deep frown. He knew about their daughter. He knew, and he hated her.

"I'm sorry. I tried. I tried so hard to do it right."

Her heart monitor kicked into top speed. Dylan listened to its steady beep for days and the sound of it stomping out this new rhythm worried him. She needed to calm down.

"Shh. You did everything you could, Jess. I'm so sorry you went through that alone. I should have been there for you and Hope."

"She said you didn't want me. She lied. Why would she lie?"

"Jess, calm down. You need to take a breath."

Tears streamed down her face and she gasped for air that never filled her lungs. He held her hand all this time, but now hers gripped his so tightly her nails bit into his skin.

Dylan didn't like this: the panic stealing her breath, making her skin pale, and her eyes wide with desperation. He leaned over the bed and pressed his palm to her cheek to make her look at him. "Jess, calm down, sweetheart. Please. Calm down."

"You didn't get to see her. She lied. You didn't get to see her because she lied. I only had her for five days. She lied." She gasped and the monitors started sounding piercing alarms. Two nurses and the doctor burst into her room. She desperately tried to suck in air, but never caught her breath.

Her eyes rolled back in her head.

The doctor ordered, "Get out. Let us take care of her."

Dylan didn't want to leave her. Not when she needed him.

Greg held him by the arm and tried to haul him outside so the nurses and doctors could tend to Jessie, but he struggled to stay.

"Come on. Let them help her." Greg pulled, but Dylan's hand still held Jessie's. He held on until the last possible moment before he had no choice but to let her go or pull her out of the bed.

They sat in silence in the waiting room. Both held cups of coffee neither drank.

"Gentlemen," the doctor said, bringing them out of their own thoughts and drawing their attention. "We've stabilized her. Can you tell me what happened before we came in?"

"She woke up confused and thought she had just given birth. She wanted to go and see her daughter. The baby died years ago," Greg said, concerned. "Then, she realized this wasn't the past."

Nothing else to say, and yet that didn't explain anything really. Leaning over, Greg braced his forearms on his knees and stared at his feet. "She came out of her confusion right away and realized this wasn't the past. But that didn't help her. It made things worse. Or better. Or the same." Greg shook his head, struggling to figure out what happened.

"Some terrible circumstances surround the death of my daughter." Dylan tried to clear up Greg's explanation. "Jessie woke up confused between the past and the present." He ran a hand through his hair. "It's complicated. She's had a rough couple of weeks and things are piling up on her. She couldn't catch her breath and the heart monitor sounded the alarm."

"That explains a lot," the doctor replied. "She had a panic attack. Her blood pressure skyrocketed and she passed out. Part of the problem is the concussion," the doctor told them. "There's a bigger problem now. She's got an infection. The antibiotics we've given her aren't working as quickly as I'd like. We've changed to something else and upped the dose. The next few days are crucial."

"Doctor, she thinks I blame her for our daughter's death. Are you telling me I might lose her before I get a chance to tell her that isn't true?"

"I'm telling you she's in a very fragile state and the next couple of days are critical. She needs to rest and remain calm. Her head injury is still a factor in her recovery. The fact that she's confused about what year it is tells us the concussion isn't better. I've sent her for another MRI scan, so we can take a look. The infection in her back from the glass is of grave concern."

"Tell us the truth, Doctor. Is she going to pull through this?" Greg asked.

Neither of them really wanted to hear the answer. She couldn't die like this. Not with all this mess just hanging out there unresolved. From the moment Dylan had seen her again at Brian's house, all he'd wanted was another chance, start where they left off and build a future together. How could he do that if he lost her before he even had the chance to say he was sorry?

"We're doing everything we can for her. She'll be back from the MRI scan in a half hour. Why don't you both go home and get some rest?" Shrugging, he added, "I know it's a futile attempt to make you leave. You aren't going anywhere until Jessie is back on her feet again. I wish I could tell you that will be soon."

"Thanks, Doc. We appreciate everything you're doing. Really," Dylan added. He took his seat in the waiting room next to Greg and sat back with a sigh.

The sun sank lower in the sky, darkening to night. Time passed unnoticed.

Greg's deep voice broke the silence. "She thought she'd just had Hope. She thought you'd come to see her." Greg took a second. "I can't get over that."

Dylan's thoughts ran much the same way. He hated that she'd finally woken up only to find herself in her worst nightmare, their daughter gone and him knowing the truth. The weight of it dragged his spirits down even more. She'd carried the burden of losing their daughter alone, thinking he didn't want her. His mother told her that . . . more than once. After he left her without a word, she believed it, because he hadn't done a good enough job of telling or showing her that could never be true.

Well, he'd spend the rest of his life proving to her that he loved her more than anything in this world.

He thought of Will and his throat tightened. He loved that little boy more than life itself. He couldn't imagine keeping something as monumental as a child from him. He swore when Will grew up, he'd never treat him so inhumanely. If he didn't like one of Will's girlfriends, he'd be objective and not interfere unless absolutely necessary. He'd never undermine one of his relationships the way his mother had done to him. He'd never harm another person the way his mother hurt Jessie. She'd practically destroyed her. He couldn't forgive his mother for what she'd done.

"I've never seen someone in so much pain. Then, she realized I knew, and she apologized to me. God. She apologized. I didn't get a chance to explain, or tell her I'd finally heard the truth from my mother. I didn't get a chance to tell her she had nothing to be sorry about, that I'm the one who's sorry. I wanted to tell her how much I love her, and how grateful I am to her for saving Will. I didn't get to explain how I got Will. And now I might not get the chance, and it's all because of my own mother. All she had to do was call and tell me Jessie was pregnant. I'd have been there for her, or had her come to me. I'd have taken care of her. I'd have seen my daughter."

Greg put a hand on his shoulder and offered what comfort he could. It wasn't nearly enough. Dylan had been dealt one blow after another. He was a man in love with a woman who had endured more hardship than one person should ever have in their life.

"She'll make it through this. She's tough. She pulled herself through losing Hope. She'll drag herself out of this," Greg tried to reassure him.

"She shouldn't have to. Again, my mother caused all of this. She was supposed to watch Will. She wasn't paying attention, and he ran into the street. Her fault. Again."

"Not that I want to defend anything your mother has done, but that could happen to anyone. Kids are fast."

"Exactly why you have to watch them every second." Dylan refused to give in or allow an ounce of sympathy to rise up for his mother. As far as he was concerned, this was her fault. If he lost Jessie forever, he didn't know what he'd do. A crushing force enveloped his heart at just the thought of losing her. If he thought he'd loved her eight years ago, and it had been so frightening he'd had to run away, it didn't compare to the love he felt for her now.

She was everything to him.

He'd learned his lesson. Leaving now wasn't an option. He intended to marry her. The day he'd stood on the new porch of her father's renovated house, he'd held her in his arms and known he only ever felt whole when he was with her. Without her in his life, he wasn't really living.

"She'll make it through this," Greg said again.

Dylan needed to hear it and prayed it came true.

Chapter Twenty-Two

So HOT. WAY too hot. She needed to take the covers off and turn on the air conditioner.

Why is the house so hot?

Maybe she left the heater turned up too high. She tried to throw off the sheets, but someone held her arm still. She tried to kick her legs to push the covers down and pain seared up her thigh, making her grab for her leg. Fire shot through her shoulder. She tried to roll over and found herself barricaded on both sides by pillows.

"Stop, Jess. Stop moving."

Someone put a cold cloth on her head and she raised her face to it. It felt so good to have something cool against her skin. She felt like she'd been in the desert for days, her throat dry and gritty, like she'd eaten sand.

"Water," she tried to say and knew nothing came out of her mouth. She tried to work up some spit and nothing happened. Someone's breath washed over her cheek. "Water," she said again on an exhalation

"Take a sip, Jess. Just a little. You don't want to make yourself sick."

The voice sounded so familiar, but she couldn't think past her desperate need for something to drink.

"That was an absurd statement, I know. Makes me want to laugh. Almost. You can't possibly get sicker than you already are."

The voice sounded lost and held a wealth of sadness. Drawn to the deep sound of it, she wanted to hear it again. A straw pressed to her lips and she drank deeply. Unsure of her surroundings, she tried to open her eyes. She managed a narrow slit, and discovered Dylan's hips and thighs nicely shaped in a pair of worn jeans. She wondered if there could ever be a time she didn't recognize him. Despite the pain and grogginess, a deep well of relief washed over her, knowing he watched over her.

He took the cold cloth from her head and turned and rinsed it in a bowl beside the bed. Then he ran the cool cloth over her neck and down her arm. With the room spinning, she felt like someone had put her on a spit and was roasting her alive.

Dylan rinsed then put the cold, wet cloth on her head and tried to cool her down. Her flesh burned under his hands. It went in waves. She could go for hours with a low temperature, and then it spiked. For two days, he'd stayed beside her trying to keep her cool while the doctors did everything they could to stop the infection ravaging her body. Drugs pumped into her hour after hour, and nothing. Every time he thought the fever had finally broken, it came back with a vengeance. Like now.

He needed to call the nurse to come and help him change the wet sheets before she started shivering. He'd cool her down with the water and wash away the sweat. She'd feel better if she were clean and cool. Her fever would go down. The shivers would come and they'd warm her again with another blanket. This same routine played out for two days.

The nursing staff gave up trying to shoo him away. It didn't work, and it was a futile attempt for them to try. Instead, Dylan did everything he could to help them with Jessie. He moved her position every few hours to make sure she'd be comfortable. He made sure to take care of her in every small way he could. He did it because she couldn't do it for herself. The longer it took for her to wake up, the more worried he became.

She moaned sometimes when she became uncomfortable. She even said his name a few times. It did his heart good to hear her call to him. In those moments, he'd hold her hand and kiss her brow. He'd talk to her about their past and the time they'd shared together. He tried to recall happy moments in their lives, like playing soccer as kids, catching a movie as teens, working together at a construction site. He remembered everything sitting there. The way she listened to him. She always laughed at all his dumb jokes. If he felt down or sick, she always cheered him up. He loved the way she turned into a puddle of goo when she saw a puppy or dog. She had a silly side and loved to make faces or talk in strange voices just to make him laugh.

Fearless, she'd climb the tallest tree with him. Kind, when they went fishing, she always released her catch.

The more memories that surfaced, the harder it was to think he might lose her. He wanted to build a future with her. He wanted to gather a thousand more memories.

The door opened behind him and he figured Greg or Brian came back to see Jessie. They'd been here every few hours to check on her, and him. He didn't mind their concern about him. In fact, he liked having them there to help him watch over her.

He turned to ask Brian or Greg to get the nurse, but found his cousins, Brody and Owen, standing there with their wives, Rain and Claire.

"I told you guys not to come."

"You were there for me and Rain when the mess went down with Roxy. You helped Owen when his wacked-out client went after Claire," Brody said. "Of course we came to check on you. We're family."

Those words hit Dylan hard. His mother had lied and deceived him. She'd hurt Jessie with her words and deeds. She'd made decisions for him that cost him ever knowing his precious daughter. Yet, here were his cousins, taking time out of their lives, away from their kids to come and check on him. He never went more than a few hours without one of them calling to check on him and assure him that Jessie would be okay. They didn't know her, but they loved him and wanted the best for him. It meant more than words could say to have them here, now, when Jessie's condition worsened with every passing second.

Rain stepped forward and wrapped her arms around his neck. Tired to the bone, he hugged her back and held on. "She's going to be okay, Dylan. Hang in there."

"I'm trying. She's getting worse."

"Well, if I'd known there was a party, I'd have gotten dressed," Jessie murmured from the bed.

Shocked she was awake again—and semi-lucid—he released Rain to go back to Jessie's side. "Jess, you remember my cousins, Brody and Owen. These are their wives, Rain and Claire."

"Go home, Dylan. Be with your family. Let me die in peace."

"Jess, no. You're not dying. You hear me. I won't let you, damnit."

Jessie looked him right in eye. "I tried to find you. I tried to tell you."

"I know, sweetheart." He kissed her lips softly. Her eyes fluttered, closing from exhaustion. "Rest." He ran his hand down the side of her head and held her cheek. "You're sick. You need to rest."

"My back hurts."

"You've got an infection where you were stabbed by the glass. You've got a fever. They're giving you some pretty heavy-duty medication. You're going to be okay."

"I want to lie on my stomach. My back hurts. My leg hurts."

"Do you want some more drugs?"

"Let's leave a few brain cells," she said sarcastically.

He smiled. "There's a little bit of my Jess. All right. Let me help you though. You can't move like you think.

You're weak. I don't want you messing up the bandages or your stitches."

"You're being ridiculous," she quipped, then tried to sit up and couldn't. Surprise and worry etched her whole face and her heart monitor kicked up a few extra beats.

"I told you. You've been lying in this bed for a week. The infection is bad, Jess." He hated to tell her like this. He wanted her to stay positive and use her strength to get better. He hoped if she understood how dire the situation, she'd fight. "I need you to get better."

Brody moved to the opposite side of the bed and stared down at Jessie. "Let's get you settled. You'll feel better."

"I don't think I'll ever feel better."

Brody moved the pillows to help her roll over. "I imagine right now you feel like shit. Trust me, I get it. I've been where you are right now." Brody had been wounded by a roadside bomb in Afghanistan. He suffered some burns and shrapnel wounds that put him in the hospital for weeks and rehab for months.

Dylan carefully took her leg at the knee and helped her roll her hips over. He settled her leg on the pillow. Unable to lie on her stomach all the way, her leg and arm had to be propped up to keep them from rubbing on anything. Brody helped raise her shoulders, and then settled her arm over another pillow. Satisfied, she gave a little moan of pleasure at the new position. Dylan and Brody both arranged the IV lines and the wires attached to her monitors.

Dylan brushed her dark hair away from her face. "I'm going to look at your back and see how the wound is healing. It's going to hurt a little." Breathing steadily, she'd gone back to sleep. Dark circles marred the skin beneath her eyes. Her skin had lost the warm glow of the fever, taking on a pale, translucent appearance. Sweat dried in her hairline. He'd have to clean her before it dried on her skin and itched.

"I'll go get a nurse to help change out the sheets and bring some new bandages," Claire offered and left the room.

Rain and Owen stood at the foot of the bed. Dylan appreciated their help and support, despite the fact there was really nothing anyone could do.

The sheet covered Jessie's legs and hips. He opened the back of her gown to look at the wound. Rain gasped. Brody and Owen both swore when they saw Jessie's back.

Dylan traced his finger over the long, jagged, knife wound. "I'd like to kill the bastard all over again for doing this to her."

"I'd hold him down for you," Brody said.

"I'd help you hide the body," Owen added, despite the fact he'd also chosen a job that required he uphold the law.

Dylan hung his head. "He tried to kill her. Look what he did to her. Pregnant with my baby and that man took a knife and slit her open from her shoulder to her hip. Greg told me she had it stitched up once, but it was a piss-poor job. She had to have the whole thing redone at the emergency room. Fifteen, pregnant, and almost murdered by her father. All alone. I wasn't there." Dylan gently traced his fingertips down the long scar again. Then he leaned over and kissed her shoulder.

"I know just how you feel, man," Brody said, coming around the bed. He clamped his hand on Dylan's shoulder and squeezed. "I wasn't there when Rain needed me. I wasn't there when Autumn needed me to protect her from that bitch, Roxy. We have more things in common now than we did growing up."

Dylan couldn't agree more. They'd had completely different family lives, but they'd both gotten the women they loved pregnant and abandoned them, none the wiser they had a child on the way. Or in Brody's case, two children.

"Like me, you've got a second chance to make this right."

"How do I make this right? My daughter is dead. Jessie has suffered that burden alone and the burden of thinking I didn't want her. She's lying here dying because she saved my son. I don't deserve that, but she's given it to me. I could have lost my son too. Maybe that's the punishment I deserved."

Jessie responded to his voice. Despite the pain, she lifted her hurt arm and grabbed him by the shirt and pulled him down to her. "No, Dylan. You don't deserve to be punished. She does. She lied."

He leaned down and kissed her cheek. "I shouldn't have left you in the first place. I was afraid of what I felt for you. I'm not afraid anymore. I love you, Jess."

Nothing could have made him feel better than the feel of her fingers sliding through his hair and grabbing on.

She pulled his face to hers and he touched his forehead to hers. "Please, Jess. Get better. I love you." Her hand went lax in his hair. She slept again. He sighed and wondered when she'd have enough energy to stay awake for more than a minute. These brief periods were being wasted. He still hadn't gotten to tell her anything important, like sorry and thank you for saving his son.

Bent over Jessie, stroking her hair, he pressed a light kiss to her temple.

Claire walked back into the room. "The nurse will be here shortly. We should go if we're going to make the movie on time."

"Date night?" Dylan asked.

"No, Pop's watching the kids right now. We're going to pick up Will and take him for pizza and a movie with all the kids. You stay here and be with Jessie," Rain said, giving him a hug goodbye.

"I've made you a roast beef and cheddar sandwich," Claire said, handing him the bag she brought in earlier and set on the table. "I put a couple of your favorite chocolate-chunk brownie bars inside too." Claire gave him a hug too. "Call me. I'm happy to bring you food anytime."

He tried to give her a smile, but he couldn't manage even half of one. It touched him deeply that they'd come today.

Owen gave him a bear hug and a slap on the back goodbye. "Hang in there, man. Anything you need, just call."

"I will. I'm glad you guys came."

Brody hung back as the others went out. "When I came back and discovered how deeply I'd hurt Rain and that I had two girls, I was overwhelmed with guilt and anger and so much more that I couldn't put into words. My own worst enemy, I vowed to make things right, like I know you're trying to do right now. Nothing you say or do will count as much as you proving to her how much you love her. Do that, and you can make this right. It's possible. Look and Rain and me."

"Your girls are alive and well. Mine died and I wasn't there for Jess."

"Not your fault. Not hers. You can't change that, Dylan. Neither can she. But if what you shared then is still alive today, *that* you can make thrive, make into a lifetime of love and happiness. After what you've lost, you both deserve that. Don't let the death of your child be the death of the love that brought her here, if only for a short time."

Brody hugged him and slapped him on the back. "I love you, man. Take care of yourself. Take care of her. That's all you can do. Everything else will come with time."

"Thanks, Brody. I really appreciate you coming today. I needed to hear those things."

"I'm sorry for your loss. I hope the two of you will be happy together again."

"Me too."

Brody squeezed his shoulder and left.

Dylan stood over Jessie, staring down at her pale face. "I love you, Jess." He didn't know she was still half-awake.

"I see why Rain forgave Brody. He's not what I expected."

"He's been through a lot. After he nearly died in the military, he came home and fought hard to win Rain back. I'm going to fight even harder for you, Jess, but I need you to get better. I can't live without you." Dylan took her hand, linking his fingers with hers. "Please, Jess, don't leave me."

"I'm not going anywhere."

Dylan believed her when she squeezed his hand, her grip strong, despite her dire illness.

Chapter Twenty-Three

TWO DAYS PASSED before Jessie's fever broke and the medication kicked in and killed the infection ravaging her body. Dylan never left her side, which made her both happy and annoyed.

Every time she told him to go away, he refused to acknowledge she'd said anything.

She stayed awake for longer periods of time. She didn't want to talk and often lost herself staring out the window.

Greg worried about her. He didn't like seeing her so quiet. "It brings back an eerie memory of you after Hope's death," he said the other day. He never wanted to see her depressed like that again. She had to admit, she didn't like scaring him, or feeling this way.

She shuffled back to the bed from the bathroom. The door opened and Greg walked in. Not exactly happy to see him, she'd finally had some time alone and didn't want to talk to him or anyone for that matter.

Dylan left hours ago to go to his office and do some work. He'd kissed her on the forehead and told her he'd be back and reminded her for the hundredth time they needed to have a long talk. She continued to stare out the window and ignore him. Her silence irritated him even more than her asking him to leave. She didn't care. She wasn't ready to talk to him, or hear what he had to say to her.

"I hear they're springing you from this place tomorrow," Greg said and pulled the chair in front of her. He sat and blocked her view of the window. "Stop ignoring me. Today, you'll participate in the conversation," he ordered.

"I'll give you a thousand dollars if you find my clothes and take me home right now."

Surprised, he fell back in the seat and stared at her. "This is new. Ready to leave so soon? I'd have thought nine days in the hospital would be quite relaxing."

"Relaxing? Someone is either jabbing a needle in my arm or torturing one of the many cuts and scrapes on my body. I'm tired of my ass hanging out the back of this gown, and Dylan won't leave me alone. He gave me a sponge bath last night that left nothing to the imagination. I'm too weak to fight him, and he's using it to his advantage."

"It's not the first bath he's given you. The man took care of you like a mother hen the whole time you had the fever. I've never seen anyone care so deeply for another. He loves you, honey."

"He feels sorry for me and guilty. He's grateful I saved his son. Those things I believe. Love? Not a chance. If he loved me so much, he'd have never left me. He'd have at least done the decent thing and told me he was leaving."

"Now you're just being stubborn and ornery," Greg said, giving her leg a pat.

"Back to my old self. Get me out of here. I have work to do."

"You can barely walk to the bathroom by yourself. Besides, I'm not taking you home until you stop all this self-pity crap. We're way past that. Just say what's on your mind."

"Work is on my mind."

"Say it."

"What?"

"You're pissed off because I told him about Hope. Yell at me. Scream. Cuss me out. Whatever it takes to get you out of this funk. Because so help me God, if you spend the next six months dying in front of me, I swear to God, I'll put you over my knee and paddle your ass."

"You'll have to get past me," Dylan said from the doorway.

"Bullshit." Greg stood and paced the room. "Damnit, Jessie. Snap out of this."

She threw the covers off and stood up in front of Greg and slapped both hands flat on his chest. "She's dead. I know that. I remember it every goddamn day. Don't tell me to snap out of it."

Greg's eyes sparked with mirth, but she could see the relief underneath. He took her face gently in his palms and held her softly. "There's my Jessie girl."

She didn't want to fight with him, or live with the anger anymore. She threw her arms around his neck and held on for dear life. "I'm not mad at you. I should have told him. I tried, but I couldn't get the words out."

"You did everything possible to find me and bring our girl into this world happy and healthy," Dylan said from behind her. "I don't blame you for anything, Jess."

"Everything I did wasn't good enough." Greg's arms wrapped around her tighter as she hid with her face in his chest from Dylan. Childish and unlike her, but everything that happened left her raw inside.

Dylan glanced at Greg. The same concern on his face Dylan felt inside. He had a hard time seeing her cling to Greg, but he kept his jealousy in check because at least she held on to someone. She hadn't drawn back into herself. If she couldn't bring herself to turn to him, at least she'd turned to her friend.

"Jess, I don't know what to say to you," Dylan said, at a loss.

She turned to him then, fire flashing in her eyes and her hands fisted at her side. "Go ahead and say it. It's my fault she died. It's my fault you never got to see her."

He sat on the edge of the bed, so she wasn't looking up at him. He wanted to pull her to him like Greg had done, but she wasn't ready to accept that kind of intimate contact with him. When she'd had the fever, and he'd taken care of her, she'd had no choice. Now she did, "Don't Touch" was written all over her.

"The stupidest thing I've ever done is walk away from you. Do you think I'd be stupid enough to think you had something to do with our daughter's death, or the fact I wasn't there?"

"You didn't get to see her." Tears glistened in her eyes.

"That will always be the biggest regret of my life. My mother knew and she didn't tell me. She's the reason I never got to see my daughter, not you. You'd never do something like to me. It's why you couldn't tell me. You don't have it in you to hurt someone like that."

He hung his head. He couldn't believe he'd never get to see his daughter or touch her. He'd gone home last night and fallen asleep with his son. Will missed him and they'd had a guy's night together, burgers and a movie on the couch. Will stretched out on his chest and fell asleep. Dylan had all the time in the world to look at his boy sleeping on him and wish he'd had the chance to hold his little girl the same way. He didn't have the heart to take Will to his own bed. He'd lain there for hours enjoying the feel of his boy in his arms and thinking about Jessie and Hope.

His eyes were soft and a little glassy. He swallowed hard, but then the muscle in his jaw jumped as he held back his emotions. Jessie remembered, for him, this was fresh grief. She'd had years to adjust to their daughter's death. He'd just found out. She'd felt Hope moving in her belly. She'd watched her come into the world. She'd held her for hours upon hours those five days. She'd been there when Hope took her last breath. She'd kissed her goodbye and told her she loved her. Dylan never saw her, touched her, smelled her sweet baby scent, or said his goodbye. He had nothing of Hope to remember.

She stepped in between his long legs and pulled his head to her chest and held him. She ran her fingers through his hair and kissed the top of his head. Greg closed the door, leaving them to their privacy.

"She was beautiful. She had pretty hands. Her little fingers were long, and even though she was just born, she had pretty nails. Her little feet were so chubby, her toes had dimples. Her hair was so soft, the slightest breeze made it kind of float. When she slept in her incubator, she'd hold her little hands together and put them to her mouth. When I held her, she'd turn her head to me and burrow as close as she could get. She liked to be against my skin the best."

Her voice cracked and Dylan stroked his hand up her back and held her close. She continued to comb her hands through his hair. He leaned into her touch. It had been too long since they'd shared this deep connection.

"I told her about you and how I used to chase after you when we were kids, and you were my best friend. I told her daddy was the best quarterback the school had ever seen. I told her how smart you are, and how you care about other people. I told her daddy liked fast cars, football, classic rock, French fries with ranch dressing, fishing, and taking long drives alone. I told her that one night we danced in a fancy ballroom and kissed under the stars. I told her on that beautiful night I gave you my heart and you gave me her." She took a deep breath and didn't even try to hide or stop the tears streaming down her face.

"When they put her in my arms and turned off the machines keeping her alive, I told her that her mommy loved her very much. I told her daddy loved her. I kissed one cheek for me, the other for you. I held her as she slipped away and a long time after that. I didn't want to let her go. I prayed to God to take me instead."

Dylan squeezed her so tight the cut on her back pinched with pain. She didn't care. It was nothing compared to the hurt in her heart cutting deep into her soul. Dylan leaned his head back, tears running down his cheeks. His anguish matched her own and she wished she could take it away. She cupped his face in her hands and looked him in the eye. "I told her you love her."

"After what I did, how could you possibly believe . . ."

"I knew you did because you loved me that night."

The earnest look in her eyes didn't lie. She meant it. She knew he loved Hope. "I love you still. I never stopped. I don't deserve you, and I want you all the same."

"Now isn't the time to talk about that. I just wanted you to know about your daughter. You were robbed of having any memories of your own of her. I only had five days, but I'll forever be grateful for those precious memories. It's all I can offer you now."

"We need to talk about what my mother did."

"There's nothing more to say. You left for your own reasons, none of which had anything to do with me. I know that now."

"I wanted to tell you I signed up with the army that night, but I got you alone, and I lost my head. I lost my heart." He gave her back her words so she'd know he'd fallen as deeply in love with her as she had with him. "I had to go, but I wanted to stay with you. I should have . . ."

She put her fingers to his lips and stopped him. "The 'should haves' are too many to count. Let it go. I'm tired of thinking about it."

He pulled her closer and kissed her fingers pressed to his lips. She dropped her hand, their faces inches apart. Drawn together, they met in the middle, and he kissed her softly, with a press of his lips to hers over and over again. Lightning shot through her system, spreading a warm and tingly feeling only he made her feel when they were close. His strong thighs pressed to the outside of hers and his hands rested on her hips. Their bodies were inches apart as she stood between his legs. Her own trembled a little. Maybe she was tired, or it was just having him this close again.

The years melted away, making her feel like they were teenagers again. His touch had always made her feel safe and loved.

He took the kiss deeper and sank into her. He wanted her. His need drew her in. Her breasts pressed to his chest and her fingers dug into his hair, holding him to her. His tongue slipped over hers, provoking her response. She could taste his need for her and it was an addiction she never wanted to overcome.

He trailed kisses down her neck and pressed a lingering kiss to the pulse racing in her throat. "I love you, Jess. Be mine again. I've missed you so much." He kissed her collarbone and pulled her closer. His hands skimmed up her bare back, his fingertips danced back down her spine, leaving a trail of tingling nerves. "I thought you were dead. I thought I'd lost you forever."

Thoughts of him muddled her mind, then, now, and everything in between. His warm mouth left soft wet kisses everywhere he roamed over her neck and shoulders and then back to her mouth.

His words rang in her mind. Before she'd thought he didn't want her, but he did. Then and now. He loved her.

It scared her to death.

There wasn't anyone else in her life. There hadn't been since him, and things had turned out so badly. He broke her heart when he left without a word after everything they shared. Although his mother was responsible for the rest, she couldn't help but feel that same hurt and sadness when she thought about the day she heard he'd left town.

She pressed her hands against his shoulders. Dylan kissed her one last time, a soft brush of his lips to hers, and then he released her. He wanted to crush her to him and make love to her, but Jessie wasn't ready. Not to mention they were in her hospital room where she was recovering from an almost fatal infection. The thought of his almost losing her again sent chills up his spine. He never wanted to feel that kind of fear again.

Dylan had to give her time. They still had a lot to talk about and work out, and that included Will.

"Come on, baby. Get back in bed."

She raised an eyebrow.

"You need your rest. As much as it would stroke my ego to say I make you tremble like this, I know you're still weak from the infection and fever."

"I don't think it's your ego you want me to stroke," she said with a sweet smile on her lips.

"You're right, it's not." He winked, loving seeing her playful side. It meant she was coming back to herself. To prove he wanted more than just her in his bed, he laid his cards on the table and hoped he didn't lose the pot for showing his hand too early. "I want you to be my wife, Jess."

Her mouth actually fell open in shock and her eyes went wide. He wanted to have a real talk with her about the rest of their lives, but the door swung open behind them and Greg's voice broke the tension.

"You need to deal with this, Dylan. She's had enough today, and I don't want her more upset."

Dylan turned. His mother, father, and Will walked toward them down the long hallway. His mother held Will's hand, and Dylan's anger flashed. He had to rein it in. His son didn't need to see him angry with his grandmother. Hell, he shouldn't be with them in the first place.

Chapter Twenty-Four

THEY WALKED AS a group down the corridor, but Jessie only had eyes for the little boy. Dylan's son. Her heart felt like someone had thrust a dagger into it, ripping apart old scars and making them bleed.

Dylan swore softly and put a hand to her cheek to get her attention. "Jess, I'm sorry, sweetheart, I haven't had a chance to tell you about Will."

She averted her eyes, unable to meet his gaze. "What's to tell? He's your son." She turned to the drawer next to the bed and took out her heart-shaped locket. She draped the long gold chain over her head and let the locket rest between her breasts over her wrecked heart.

"What's that, honey? It's beautiful. Looks old, the rose on the front is pretty. Is it an antique?" He kept eyeing his parents' progress down the corridor, ever getting closer.

Jessie wished they'd disappear.

"It's a picture of our daughter and a lock of her hair."

She turned away and lowered herself into the bed. Her muscles throbbed with fatigue. Her head was still spinning from that kiss Dylan planted on her. Most of all her heart ached for all they'd lost. It hurt seeing him break down and grieve for their daughter. This is why she didn't want to tell him. She hated putting that sad look in his eyes and breaking his heart.

He'd said he wanted to marry her, and she couldn't quite believe in the words or him. Unsure he'd even said the words, she found it difficult to switch gears and remember this was the man she loved with her whole heart. This was the man she'd given herself to, body, mind, heart, and soul.

Dylan reached out and touched his fingertips to the locket. His pinky brushed the swell of her breast, and her nipples hardened under the thin hospital-gown fabric. His eyes met hers and they stared at each other for a long moment. Electricity crackled between them. She wished they were somewhere else. Alone. A different time. A different place. A different past. She looked away first, breaking the spell and the building tension.

"Can I see?" he asked, his voice gruff.

She opened the locket and looked at their daughter's picture inside. She kissed the photo before turning it around to show him.

Dylan breathed in sharply at the first glimpse he'd ever had of Hope. His daughter. "She . . . She looks just like me," he stammered. He could see it immediately. A lock of her dark hair, the same shade as his, encased behind glass. A little pink ribbon held the soft, wispy strands together. Hope's little eyes were closed, her cheeks round and pink, her face soft and content. Like Jessie had told him, she slept with her little hands clasped together near her pretty bow mouth.

His eyes glassed over, filling with tears. Jessie wiped away the tear that slipped down his cheek with her fingertips. He leaned into her touch, needing her comfort, knowing she understood his pain.

"She's beautiful, Jess. You made a beautiful baby."

She held his face in her hands while he stared at the photo in her locket. "We. We made a beautiful baby."

"Son? What's wrong?"

Dylan turned partway and glared at his father, standing in the doorway with his mother. His mother stood rigid, back ramrod straight, hands clasped tightly in front of her. She could barely keep from turning away. Everything about her appeared defiant and guilty all at the same time.

"Nothing's wrong. I was just looking at a picture of my daughter. It's the first time I've ever seen her." Jessie gently slid the locket out of his grasp. She kissed the picture again before closing it with a distinct click. She tucked it down her hospital gown and stretched out in the bed on her side, ignoring everyone in the room. Including him.

He pulled the blanket around her. The dark circles under her eyes reminded him she wasn't a hundred percent yet. In the last few minutes, she'd withered before his eyes, tired beyond anything a person should endure. The last few weeks had been rough on her. She masked it well, but right now, everything had finally caught up with her.

He cupped her cheek in his palm. "Rest, honey. I'll get rid of them."

"Do that." She allowed him to take the lead when normally she'd have put her foot down and thrown his parents out herself. A take-charge person, it spoke volumes she was too tired to deal with his parents herself.

Dylan turned from Jessie and fixed his mother in his hard gaze. His father's eyes narrowed when Dylan didn't greet them with his usual smile. "Get out. I told you days ago you weren't to come here again. Jessie needs her rest, and I don't want to see you."

Will ran to him, raising his arms to be picked up.

"Son, we need to talk," his father said in that controlled tone he'd used to discipline Dylan when he was young. "Your mother told me what happened. In her attempt to protect you, I can see she's hurt you. We need to find a way to work this out."

Dylan pinned his father with his gaze. "It's too late to work it out. Did she tell you what she did? Did she tell you my daughter is dead, and she kept her existence from me?"

"She told me Jessie contacted her many years ago, but never said she was pregnant with your child," his father said, ever the diplomat.

Dylan couldn't believe his father's words. He took his mother's side. On one level he understood. His father loved her, and they'd spent over thirty years together. That kind of loyalty was admirable, even expected. However, Dylan didn't have to listen to him defend his mother's lies.

"Stop right there. If you came here to defend her for the lies she told you and make it seem like Jessie was anything less than up-front and truthful, then leave now and don't ever contact me again. If you take her side"—he pointed at his mother with an accusing finger—"or condone her behavior, we have nothing to discuss."

"Dylan, you're my son, and I don't want to lose you. Don't turn your back on us without even a discussion about what happened."

"Let me tell you what happened." He released Will into Greg's outstretched arms. They sat at the end of Jessie's bed. For his son's sake, Dylan tried to hold on to his temper. "Jessie sent me an email after I left, asking to talk. Mom sent her a scathing response that basically told Jessie I didn't want her, never cared about her, and never wanted to hear from her again. Jessie had no choice but to email *me*." He used air quotes, because she'd actually been responding to his mother, thinking it was him. "She wrote that she was pregnant and even if I didn't want her, I needed to know about my child. Mom sent her an email back, making it look like the email Jessie sent never got delivered and my email got shut down. Undeterred and determined to tell me about the baby, she called the house and got Mom. She was so rude and unbelievably callous to Jessie, telling her that it was Jessie's fault I left because I wanted to get away from her, that Jessie had no choice but to believe those words came from me. Me. The man who got her pregnant and left her without a word of goodbye, so why wouldn't she believe it." Dylan turned his gaze on his mother. "You knew exactly what to say to get her to back off and never try to contact me again. This, after everything she'd been through with her father. Everyone suspected she was dead. You knew something bad must have happened to her, but you did nothing. You didn't even ask if she was okay, did she need anything? Nothing. Not even a kind word. Hell, all you had to do is rattle off a few numbers for my cell." He turned back to his father. "When I asked her about Jessie's disappearance, she didn't tell me Jessie called looking for me. She led me to believe the ugly rumors that Jessie was dead."

He had to swallow hard. He'd grieved for Jessie, pined for her for years. Now, he grieved for his daughter.

The look on his father's face told Dylan he'd heard this part of the story a little differently. More half truths and lies from his mother.

"Your mother didn't believe the baby was yours. I have to say, I would have been skeptical myself."

"Then, I'd expect you to ask me if it was possible. I'll tell you, not only was it possible, it was the truth. Hope was mine. Jessie was fifteen and went through her pregnancy alone." He felt Greg's eyes on him and decided credit was due. "Well, not alone. She had two very good friends to help her out, but not the father of her child.

"I can't imagine what she went through. Sixteen years old, lying in a bed about to give birth, hurting and scared, and thinking the father of her baby doesn't want anything to do with her, that I've gone out of my way, shutting off my email and changing my cell number, so she can't contact me." He shook his head at his mother. "The more times I think about it, or discuss it . . . it makes my stomach turn and my heart bleed."

He ran both hands through his hair in sheer frustration. Why didn't his mother get it? Why couldn't she see what she'd done and be contrite about it?

"Jessie gave birth to our daughter, and I didn't get to see her come into this world. I didn't get to hold her. I didn't get to help Jessie pick out her name, or dream with her about what our child would be like when she grew up. I didn't get to hear her cry. I didn't get to hold her in my arms and feed her. I'll never know what she smelled like, or how soft her skin felt against mine. I'll never know how strong her little grasp was when she held my finger." He spoke to his father from his bleeding heart. "I never got to tell her I love her. I never got to say goodbye. Hell, I never got to say hello!" He raged at his father, because his mother didn't get it and he needed his father to understand. "Shall I go on? There are millions of things she took away from me. All because she doesn't like Jessie. It's unforgivable what she's taken from me."

"You have Will, son. I know it isn't the same, not even close, but at least you know what it is to have a child," his father offered.

"Don't you see, she was only here for a short time, and I didn't get to see her because Mom lied? She lied to Jessie. She lied to me. She lied to you. She knew that baby was mine. She just didn't want to accept the fact I love Jessie."

Will chose that moment to chime in. "I'm keeping her. She saved me. She's my new Mommy. I chose her like I chose Daddy."

Surprise and disbelief crossed both his mother's and father's faces. He turned to glance down at Jessie lying quiet in the bed. She stared up at him, eyes wide and devastated, and he knew. She'd never heard her own daughter call her Mommy. One more thing she'd never get. He wasn't sure how she felt about Will's declaration. He had a lot of explaining to do about Will, and how they'd become a family, one that needed a wife and mother.

"Will is adopted," he said to Jessie. "He chose me. I'll explain later."

She didn't say a word. She'd had no idea that he'd adopted the child. Will didn't look like Dylan. She'd figured he resembled his mother. It did something strange to her heart to know another woman didn't have Dylan's child.

Greg decided now was a good time to give her a push, and she'd have liked to smack him. "You couldn't pick a better mom than Jessie," he said to Will and gave him a squeeze. "You've got great taste in women, kid." Greg only smiled when she kicked him in the thigh.

"You don't owe her an explanation," Martha said to Dylan. "Jessie is better now and going home tomorrow. I'm sure she knows how much we appreciate her saving Will. We should let her get back to her life. After everything that's happened, I'm sure she'd be happier if we all just left her alone."

Jessie couldn't let that pass. "What you're really saying is you want Dylan to stay away from me. You don't want him around me because you think he can do better."

For some people in Fallbrook, she'd never measure up. She didn't care anymore. She'd spent too many years making herself into something *she* could be proud of. She'd overcome so much, and she wasn't going to let someone like stuck-up Martha McBride make her feel unworthy.

"You two have nothing in common," his mother said.

"We have more in common than what separated us. I grew up privileged. She didn't. What does that have to do with who she is as a person? She has the kindest, warmest heart of anyone I know. She's got more strength in her little finger than you do in your whole being. She stands up for what is right, and fights for what she wants. So don't tell me she's not good enough for me, because the truth is she's better than I could ever hope to be."

"Don't say that. You are a good and decent man, destined for great things," his mother said, her eyes filled with pride for a man she didn't know or understand. She didn't see the real him through her rose-colored glasses. "That baby wasn't yours. She wasn't yours," she tried to convince Dylan. "Jessie only wanted to use you to get away from her father. She used you to get to the McBride money."

"The McBride money has kept you well all these years, Mother. We have money making money. Tell me, how much is enough for three people? I mean, how much should Will get? He isn't blood after all. Maybe I should just make sure he gets the clothes and the food he needs. He can go to public school. Wouldn't want to waste any of that precious McBride money on a private school for him. I suppose college is out of the question.

"And what about Jessie? How much would it have cost you to give her my phone number? How much money would it have cost to pay her doctor bills? How much would it have cost to call in a specialist for Hope? How much would you have been willing to spend to save your grandchild?

"I'll tell you what your granddaughter was worth to you. Nothing. You threw away any chance I had of seeing her. All because you look down your nose at a girl born into a family you find beneath you. You were on the school board and head of the PTA. You knew that man was hurting her and you did nothing. Your indifference and position in the community led the way for everyone to turn a blind eye."

He brushed a hand over Jessie's hair. "The pretty girl I fell in love with turned into a beautiful woman, who runs her own business. Two, actually. She's successful. She put herself through school. She's been on her own since she was fifteen. Fifteen." He shook his head, unable to imagine what it must have been like to have everyone you wanted to love you leave you or treat you like you weren't worth a penny. He never meant to be one of those people. "What would someone have to do to be acceptable to you?"

"You left her. You didn't want her. It was just a phase."

"I don't call falling in love with someone a phase. You either love them, or you don't. I loved her then and I love her even more now. I left to get away from you and Dad. You were so busy pressuring me to go to college and be *him* that I couldn't breathe. I couldn't think about what I wanted. Jessie made everything clear and simple. I wanted her. I wanted to help people like her."

"That's just it. People like her. People who are poor and get drunk and break the law. Those are the people you help. You could be so much more."

"I'm enough. I'm a good father, who loves his son unconditionally. I help people who need help because someone hurts them. Do you know how it kills me to think that all those years we were friends she was being abused, and I never saw it? She wanted to be with me because she needed a safe place. I was her safe place. And when she needed me the most, I wasn't there. When our daughter died in her arms, I wasn't there." He hadn't meant to yell at her, but his frustration got the better of him.

"It can't be changed. It's time to move on and be a father to Will," his mother coaxed, like it was that easy to forget what she'd done and all he'd lost.

"I don't care what you think, or what you want. It's my life. Jessie is my life. She's my future. I don't want you here. I don't want to see you. I don't want you near my son. How did you get Will, by the way?"

"We told Lorena we were coming here to see you. We assured her you wouldn't mind our spending time with our grandson," his father said, unhappy with how this turned out. Dylan stood with his arms crossed over his chest, his mouth set in a firm line, letting his father know he truly meant to keep them away from him and Will.

"Dylan, I don't want to see the family fractured because of what happened years ago and can't be changed."

"Like the way she convinced you what Brody and Owen went through with your brother was none of your concern. You had your perfect family. No need to muck up your life by interfering in theirs. Not your responsibility to step in and help them when their own father couldn't help himself. If he squandered his money on booze and left Brody and Owen hungry, not your fault. If no one cared whether they did their homework, or went to bed at a decent time, so be it. If your brother went too far and smacked them around because they got out of line, they deserved it, right? Unruly. No discipline. No drive to be the best." Dylan shook his head. "No one to care and love them." He glared at his mother. "No one to step in and give them a better life. But hell, they're family and that's how we treat family we don't want. The way you treated my cousins. My daughter. We only care about the McBrides standing in this room. Everyone else, including Brody, Owen, Jessie, and Hope, can go to hell before you step in and offer the help they desperately need."

His father's eyes narrowed. Dylan had his attention. The thing with Jessie and Hope wasn't the first time his mother turned her nose up at someone she thought beneath them. She'd persuaded his father to dismiss his brother's drinking problems and the neglect and abuse inflicted on Brody and Owen.

Like with Hope, too late to do anything about it now.

"I won't change my mind. Not about this. I guess I wasn't clear with Lorena that grandparents or not, you are not to take Will."

"Dylan, you can't be serious. I worked so hard to make sure you never turned out like your cousins. We gave you every advantage and privilege."

"And offered Brody and Owen nothing but your back when you turned it on them. Owen, Brody, and Jessie all have one thing in common, amazing inner strength and determination to overcome the circumstances and consequences of where they came from. But you don't see or care about their achievement in becoming a successful lawyer, a businessman, a construction company owner. You only see where they came from, not where they are now, or who they are."

"You're better than them. Brody drank and caroused with women. He got two women pregnant and left without a word."

"He didn't know about his girls. Like I didn't know about mine. Except I would have known if you'd told me. I'm no different than him.

"You made decisions for me, and I'll never forgive or forget the consequences of those decisions. You can't make this right with an *I'm sorry*. You can't make this right by trying to make me believe you had my best interests at heart. If you did, you'd have told me about the baby before it was too late."

"How could I have known the baby would die?" his mother asked, as if it changed anything.

"If you'd told me Jessie was pregnant, I'd have been there to see Hope and I wouldn't hate you now. I wouldn't hate myself for putting Jessie through this."

"Son, there has to be a way to get past this. Your anger hurts your mother, and I understand you're upset, but we can work this out. Cutting us out of your life is extreme. This is spinning out of control."

Dylan sympathized with his father. "Dad, I'm sorry her decisions affect you too. She lied to all of us. I've lost my daughter and eight years with Jessie. I don't plan to live without her for another day."

"Will you come live with us like the other mommies live with the daddies?" Will asked.

His little face and eyes held so much hope Jessie would agree. She hesitated, her mouth open to say something before she closed it, then said, "I have my own house, sweetheart."

That wasn't going to stop Will from having her as a mother. "That's okay. We'll live in your house then. I'll bring my toys and Daddy can bring the TV."

Dylan's heart fluttered a bit when Jessie laughed. "You're always thinking, little man."

As much as Jessie wanted to hold him at arm's length, she couldn't resist Will as easily. She didn't want to open her heart to them, afraid Dylan would hurt her again, but he swore he heard it squeak open just a bit. That's all he needed, a foot in the door. Before long, he'd have her back.

"You and I will talk, Jess."

She closed up on him again. Already thinking and planning how to win her heart back, he'd take things one step at a time.

She used to be the one chasing him when they were young. Older and wiser, he'd chase her until she was his. No more running from her, only to her.

"Jessie needs her rest. You two can leave. I'll take Will home." He addressed his mother directly. "Do us both a favor, don't make things worse. Stay away."

His mother pursed her lips. "You've never spoken to me this way. I don't know how to overcome your temper right now, but I'll be here for you when you realize Jessie isn't the girl you think she is. You'll see, I'm right."

His father didn't let him respond to that outrageous statement. "Son, I don't want to leave things like this. I guess nothing will be settled this way. Perhaps you'll come by the house later so we can talk privately."

"I've made my feelings clear. I won't change my mind," Dylan said by way of answering without actually committing himself to another round of fruitless discussion.

"Jessie, may I see the photo of Hope? I'd like to see her," his father asked in earnest.

Surprised by the request, Jessie might have complied until Martha's eyes flashed with anger and narrowed on her. "No. You can't. I won't have you look at her the way you both look at me. I won't let you judge her."

"I wouldn't," he said, taken aback.

"Wouldn't you? You judged me because of who my father is and the things he did that had nothing to do with me, but somehow made me not good enough. It didn't matter I was a straight-A student, that I worked hard and was good at construction. All you saw was a girl who lived next to poor and had nothing to offer your son. Thank God we don't grow up to be our parents. Dylan is nothing like you," she said to his mother. "I am nothing like my father. But that doesn't matter to you because you don't see me, or know me.

"So no, I won't let you look at Hope and think less of her because of who her mother is."

"She's Dylan's daughter too," he conceded. "We'd never think she was anything less than perfect."

"Because she's Dylan's. Not because she was a beautiful, wonderful girl on her own. And how would you know? You never came to see her in the hospital. You could have. I wouldn't have kept you from her. Oh, but wait, you couldn't come see her because your wife refused to acknowledge her. Well, now it's my turn to refuse."

She expected Dylan to ask her to show them the picture. He didn't. He sat back against her bed with his arms crossed over his chest. Greg was beside him holding Will. They sat between her and his parents, making it clear the line had been drawn. His parents on one side, and they stood together against them for Hope.

Robert hung his head, and then focused on his wife with one of those looks that pass between couples who have known each other for a lifetime. The message was clear. He wasn't happy with what she'd done, or the results. Martha maintained her dignified posture. Grabbing her elbow, he turned her with him and escorted her from the room.

Jessie let out her breath. She didn't like being mean. She didn't like that someone had made her be mean. It upset her more knowing Dylan's parents' actions had forced her to do something she'd never do under normal circumstances.

"I'm sorry you had to deal with them again, Jess. I'll have a talk with my father and try to figure out a way to make him understand I mean what I say. I don't want them interfering in my life, or yours. Ours," he said to reiterate he meant to have her in his life for good.

"Go home and get some sleep."

Dylan shrank in front of her. His shoulders slumped and his face went lax. Dealing with his parents and her took a toll on him.

"I'm fine."

"You've been here every day and most of every night. You work and take care of me. Go home with your son and catch up on some sleep."

"I'll sleep when you're home."

"I'm much better, they're sending me home tomorrow."

Greg laughed as Dylan scowled at Jessie. "I think he means when you're home with him."

"I'm not going home with him—you." She looked from one to the other like they'd lost their minds. "I have my own home. I'm going to sleep in my own bed and not have people poking and prodding me all night."

The two men tried to hold back the smirks and the laughter, but it was hopeless.

"Shut up," she said to both of them. "I'm going home—alone."

"We'll talk about it tomorrow," Dylan said.

"I'll swing by and pick you up," Greg said helpfully. "Dylan doesn't know where you live, and I promised Pop I'd see you got home safe."

"I'm perfectly capable of finding my own way home and taking care of myself. I've been doing it a long time."

"Maybe it's time you let someone take care of you." She scowled at the very idea, making him chuckle and shake his head. Dylan ran his hand down her hair. He saw it in her eyes, that longing to be connected to someone again, to him, allowing herself to love and be loved. Afraid to accept it, or reach out for it, it had been taken away too many times. Not this time. He intended to give her everything.

He, Greg, and Will left to her many protests about them going home with her tomorrow. Greg slapped him on the back as they got into the elevator. "You've got your work cut out for you. She's afraid of being hurt again. Good luck knocking down all her walls."

"I plan on bulldozing them to the ground."

"I want to ride on the bulldozer," Will cheered.

"It's you and me all the way, buddy."

Dylan hoped he had it in him to heal Jessie's heart and win it back. He'd never stop trying, not until he had Jessie again. This time, he'd love her the way she deserved to be loved.

Chapter Twenty-Five

"DISAPPOINTED DYLAN DIDN'T come and pick you up from the hospital?" Greg tried to hide a smile, allowing only the corners of his mouth to tilt slightly, but Jessie caught the movement. "Since I picked you up, you've been quiet. Admit it, you wanted him to pick you up and take you home."

No way in hell she admitted that, but the disappointment settled in her heart and made it ache. "He's probably working. I imagine the sheriff's department needs to have their sheriff actually work. He spent a lot of time at the hospital with me."

She sighed out her worries. Before, she'd welcomed the quiet of the house and the solitude of her property. Looking out at the surrounding land as they drove, she guessed she'd get used to being alone again.

She refused to acknowledge the voice inside her heart saying, *You waited for Dylan to come back to you. He's here. You can make a life with him.*

She told that young girl inside of her, jumping up and down with excitement, to shut up and sit down.

"I don't know how he managed to keep everything organized. Besides checking in at work, he went home every night to take care of Will's dinner and bath and put him to bed, and then he came back to the hospital to be with you. If you ask me, I'd say he turned out to be a great dad."

"Does it make me a bad person that I'm happy someone else didn't have his baby? Is that stupid? I mean, he adopted a little boy who needed a home and a father."

"Honey, you aren't being stupid, and you aren't a bad person. You're happy he didn't fall in love with someone else. I'll bet you sat up there in your window looking out at the road and the land and wondered a million times if he was with someone else, loved someone else. You probably asked yourself a million times, why not you? Well, I'll tell you this. I've talked to him a lot over the last week and there's one thing that's clear. He loves you, has always loved you, and never loved another. Maybe there were other women in his life, he's a guy, but none of them stole his heart. You already have it."

Greg wanted to give her an opening to talk about everything that happened the last few weeks. She ignored him and stared out the window as they turned off the highway onto her private road. He stopped at the gate and punched in the code.

She'd had the old fire road leveled and graveled. He drove through the gate and took the curve up the hill to her house. Jessie looked out over the hills and trees as they came to the curve that left them on an open ledge. As far as the eye could see, she had a view of the surrounding unspoiled land. This was where she and Dylan parked on prom night and made Hope.

"Give him a chance to prove he loves you. Give yourself permission to be happy." Greg's voice broke into her thoughts of a past she saw in a different light, but still couldn't change.

"Are you telling me what to do?" she asked, being snotty.

"I'm telling you to give each other a chance to see if the love you both felt years ago is still alive today. Maybe it's grown into something lasting now. You shared a child. He might have missed seeing her and being with you, but he grieves for her as much as you do."

"He's only feeling guilty and nostalgic. He thought I was dead, for God's sake. He's just happy I'm alive. He might think he's in love with me, but now things will settle down. He'll realize you can't resurrect the past. Besides, we had one night. That's all it was. He left as fast as he could without looking back. The only thing linking the past and the present is Hope, and she's dead. Once he's had time to grieve, he'll move on with his life with his son."

"Who the hell do you think you're fooling, J.T.? Those are a lot of jumbled-up lies you're telling yourself. Do you really think he doesn't know his own mind? The man is in love with you and plans to make you his wife. He's declared himself, and he's coming after you. You better be ready, because he's not the kind of man who takes no for an answer."

"That's because no one ever says no to Dylan McBride. He's always gotten everything he wanted."

"Including you, so stop fighting it. He wants you and he aims to have you."

Greg got out of the car and came around to help her out, trapping her between his body and the car.

"You spent the last several years running from every man who tried to get close to you. You haven't been on a single date or slept with a man since Dylan. For heaven's sake, let the man catch you. Stop running away from the inevitable. You want him. I see it every time you look at him."

"Lust got me into this."

"Lust will get you laid again. It will also help you figure out what you both feel for each other now."

Conceding a little, she said, "I am having a hard time. Everything I thought was true isn't."

"There's only one thing you have to remember. He loves you both and is torn up about what happened. As devastated as you were by losing her, he's just as upset, and more so, because he's lost a daughter and the family he's always known. I can't imagine what it's like for him to know his mother betrayed him the way she did."

Jessie bit her lower lip. She'd warned Dylan, but she had no idea how it felt to have the one person who loved you above all else betray you. Sure, her father had been a rotten son of a bitch, but she'd never been one to count on him. He hadn't treated her with love her whole life and turned on her. For her, he was always bad news. Dylan's mother's betrayal had come out of the blue and that made it all the more devastating. She was used to being disappointed by her father. Dylan had grown up knowing only love and security from his parents. To have that love and trust betrayed probably made it just as hard to deal with as losing his daughter.

"I'll try to remember he didn't know. I'll remember his grief is fresh, and that I can help him through it the way I wished he'd been there to help me with mine."

"That's a start, honey." He escorted her into the house. "I set up a fire for you. Just strike a match and you're in business. I filled the wood box too. Do you think you can make it upstairs?"

Sore and still having trouble walking without limping, she'd get up those stairs if it killed her. "Even if I have to crawl up those stairs, I'm sleeping in my bed."

"Remember what the doctor said. Let the scabs heal. Only take a short shower."

"I'll manage. Don't worry."

She'd walked into the great room and stared out the bank of windows at her back lawn and the surrounding trees. The sound of an approaching car drew her attention back to the front windows. Dylan pulled up in her driveway.

"Did I mention Dylan said he and Will are coming over?" Greg feigned innocence.

She clenched her teeth to keep from yelling at him. "I don't believe you forgot at all," she said tightly.

Will raced in the front door. "This is the coolest house ever." He ran to Jessie and threw his arms around her legs. She flinched and clenched her teeth, but Will didn't notice. She recovered fast and gently pulled Will away from her injured leg.

"Will, you can't just run into someone else's house." Dylan walked in, carrying grocery bags. He stopped when he entered. The outside was spectacular, the inside even better. Twenty-foot ceilings towered over him with sky-lights letting in the natural light and making it appear as if you were still outside. The wood walls and floors gleamed a soft honey in the brilliant sunlight. The stone wall to the right boasted a huge fireplace with a stone bench run-ning the length of the entire wall. Large copper bins sat on each side of the fireplace filled with wood for the fire. A large vase on one end held ten-foot-tall branches that curled and twined together with white lights strung along them. They'd be a pretty sight at night. On the far end of the room, the bench housed several pots of varying sizes with a profusion of houseplants. The natural light made their leaves deep green and glossy.

Seating areas divided the great room into three sec-tions. Along the back wall where the sliding glass doors led out to a patio, the dining table sat with eight chairs surrounding an old plank farmhouse table. Closer to him were two seating areas, one for conversation, and the other for watching the big-screen TV.

The kitchen lay straight ahead. Glass-fronted wood cabinets in the same honey tone as the floors. The counter tops were sandy-colored stone. The sunlight streaming in made everything sparkle and glisten. The room was cheerful and homey, down to the soft brown leather sofas and yellow-and-white fabric chairs.

"Jessie, this place is amazing. You built it?" He noticed the huge framed picture on one of the walls. A set of blueprints for the house, showing the outside exposure.

Jessie stood staring at him like she'd never seen him before, so Greg answered. "She built it a couple years ago. Designed it too. Everything you see, she either built or picked out herself, down to the stones in the wall."

"What's in the barn outside?"

"That's her workshop. She builds furniture out there. You should see the rooms upstairs. The dressers and beds she made are amazing."

"I'll bet they are. I bought a bunch of your furniture. I sleep in a bed you made. I have an entire bedroom set, coffee tables, side tables, and a dining set. It all came from your store. You have the order for Will's new stuff. He's grown out of his baby furniture."

"I like horses. Daddy says we can't keep one in the house. Uncle Owen has two horses. He let me pet them."

Jessie's stunned silence faded. The little boy still held on to her leg, though loosely now. Coming out of her daze, his words penetrated her stalled mind. "No. You can't keep a horse in the house, but I have something you can keep." She asked Dylan, "Um, can I take him out to the barn?"

"Sure, honey. Be warned, he'll touch everything." She could only nod. "I'll put these groceries away and meet you out there. I'd love to see your workshop."

Jessie didn't know what to do now that they were here, in her house. She took Will by the hand and led him to the front door.

Dylan didn't let her get away from him so easily. He handed the grocery bags over to Greg and stopped Jessie before she passed him. He grabbed her wrist and turned her to him.

"Not even going to kiss me hello." He didn't wait for her to answer, simply leaned down and pressed his lips to hers. He pulled back just a fraction of an inch, enough to look into her eyes. Then he kissed her again and made sure she knew how hungry he was for her. He ended the kiss by touching his forehead to hers. He held the side of her head and looked into her wary eyes. "I've missed you."

"You saw me yesterday."

He gave her that cocky half grin she'd missed so much. "I missed you."

Those words were meant to convey a lot more than not seeing her for a day. He'd missed her a lot longer. She wanted to tell him she'd missed him too. She wanted to tell him she thought of him all the time and stayed up nights watching the road to her house, remembering their night together and hoping to one day see him drive up the road ending at her house.

It made her nervous to think he already knew. How could he not? Being here, at her home on the very land where their lives had come together and been torn apart, he knew how deeply she'd longed for him. Why else would she still be here waiting for him? And he knew it.

Will pulled her arm toward the door. So much easier to go with him than take a step toward Dylan.

"Come on. I want to see," Will said, tugging on her.

Dylan let her go. She passed him, but his hand softly slid down her arm to her hand before their fingers touched and dropped away.

Greg unpacked grocery bags in the kitchen, not even trying to hide his huge smile. "So, what's your plan of attack?" Greg asked.

"Every time she turns around, she'll find me. I figure the only way for her to believe I'm not leaving, and I want her with me always, is to make sure she knows I'm here, all the time."

"That sounds like a good plan. Are you going to talk to her about the fact she built her house here?"

"I'm blown away. She really has been torturing herself, since she left all those years ago."

"You should see what's in the garage," Greg said half under his breath, intriguing Dylan.

"What's in the garage?"

"Cars. What else would she keep in the garage?" He smiled wickedly. "You know, I never really believed there was one person out there for each of us. Not until I met her. For her, there's only you. You're the only man she sees and loves. The rest of us are just people to her, and a few, like Dad and me she calls friends. You are the only man that's been in her life since she was young. Remember that.

"Listen, man, I'm out of here. Take care of her. Her heart's as beat up as her body. Go out to the barn. See what an amazing woman she is."

"I already know how amazing she is. That's why I'm not letting her go."

"Good. I expect to be best man at the wedding. Dad

will walk her down the aisle. Nothing would please us more than to see her happy."

"That's all I want, to make her happy."

"I believe you will." He looked out the door toward the barn. Dylan followed his gaze. "Go slow with the whole mother thing. That area is still raw and sensitive. She only got to be a mother for five days. Will is going to remind her of how much she lost. Give her time to adjust."

"I've already spoken to Will about calling her 'Mommy.' He's determined to have her."

"Just like his dad." Greg slapped him on the shoulder and they walked out the front door. "I hope this works out, for the both of you."

Dylan intended to make sure it did.

Chapter Twenty-Six

DYLAN WALKED INTO the barn through one of the oversize doors and waited while his eyes adjusted to the darker interior. Will and Jessie stood off to the right beside a large cabinet. Will hid inside the bottom door and Jessie pretended she'd lost him.

"Will," she called. "Where are you? You disappeared."

The door flung open and Will peeked his head out. "No, I didn't. I'm hiding." He giggled.

"Oh my goodness." Jessie yelped, pressing her hand to her chest. "You scared me. I thought I'd lost you."

"Then you know how I felt when I thought I lost you," Dylan said from behind her.

She turned and took a step back. She hadn't heard him come in, and it made him smile to see her off balance.

"Daddy, look. I can hide in here." Will closed the door and shut himself inside the cabinet again.

"Handy. Now when he's bad, I can lock him up."

Will burst out of the cupboard. "No way."

Dylan scooped him up and hugged him tight. "I'd never lock you up, buddy. I'm only teasing."

"Only bad guys get locked up, huh, Daddy."

"That's right, and you're as good as they come." He nuzzled Will's neck with his nose and got a giggle from his little boy.

"Look, Jessie made a farm." Will pointed to the shelves along one wall. There were a dozen different carved farm animals along with small trinket boxes and larger chests she'd made.

"Jessie, oh my God. You did all of this."

She simply shrugged. "There are a lot of hours in a day. I don't like to sit idle."

Dylan surveyed the rest of the large open space filled with bedroom, kitchen, and living room furniture. Some of the pieces were finished. Others still needed to be stained. She had the barn divided into sections. Tools cluttered one area where she cut wood and put the pieces together. She draped another area in drop cloths where she stained or painted the pieces. The smell of freshly cut wood and varnish permeated the air. Finished furniture sat by the doorway until she took it to her store to be sold.

In one part of the shop, she had a seating area with a love seat and a chair. Several wood-carving tools and large chunks of wood lay on the coffee table. He could imagine her sitting in the quiet barn whittling away at the wood.

He walked over to some of the finished pieces. "Jessie, these are gorgeous. I love this dining table." He rubbed his hand over the carved wood. She had engraved a soft wave into the edge, rolling around the round table. The wave was mimicked in the base, only it swirled around and down until it met the feet. Unique. Like the woman who created it.

"I finished that piece several weeks ago. It's mahogany. Tough to carve because it's such a hard, dense wood, but it's beautiful. I haven't decided on the chairs yet."

"I think I need another house." He ran a hand over a large hutch. "These pieces are great, I'd love to decorate another house just to see them all displayed as they should be. My house looks great with all your furniture. I can't wait to see Will's new bedroom set."

"I haven't started it yet, obviously. I have some ideas in mind. I could sketch them out for you, so you can decide if it's what you want."

"I want a horse." Will said, moving back into the cupboard again.

"I think I'll make him a side table for his bed large enough for him to hide in." She leaned down and brushed a hand over Will's head through the door.

"I want this cupboard in my room." Will stomped his feet and listened to the echo inside the walls.

Jessie studied the cupboard critically and decided she could modify it a bit to make it suitable for a television up top and some storage on the sides. Maybe she'd leave the tabletop and shelves in a wood tone and paint out the sides in red. *It could work*, she thought.

Dylan watched her assessing the hutch. "I'll take it if you're willing to sell it."

"I have to make a couple changes." She pulled one of the notepads off her worktable and sketched the modifications. She made a list of things to do for the new furniture set to match. "What color is your room, Will?"

He opened the door and popped his head out. "Bright." He squinted, wrinkling up his nose.

She tried not to smile at his disgruntled, scrunched-up face.

Dylan had a silly smile. "It's a bright yellow. I guess he doesn't like it." He bent to Will. "Why didn't you say something?"

Will shrugged and closed himself up in the cupboard again.

"I'll paint it a soft wheat color. Then I'll paint out that cabinet in a deep red with wood shelves." She eyed the cabinet where Will hid. "I'll poke a hole in the back and run a strand of white lights inside, so he can see in there. The other furniture you wanted, I'll do in the same wood tone with the horse theme. Something that will grow with him and work when he's a teenager."

"Sounds good, honey. Will, let's go inside and get something to eat. We need to make Jessie dinner."

The door flew open and Will reluctantly slipped out. "She said I could have something."

Jessie set her drawing aside, remembering why she'd come in here in the first place. "Come here, Will." She waited for him to take her hand and walked him over to a large cabinet. She opened the door and laughed as Will said, "Wow." She took the horse from the top shelf and handed it to him. "For you. This one you can keep in the house."

Several animals and chests lined the shelves, but the cabinet held even more, all so very detailed and lifelike. The horse she handed Will looked like the real deal, only miniaturized. About a foot tall, it looked as if it were standing in a pasture smelling the breeze. The tail and mane softly ruffled in the wind. So perfect, you could almost feel it too. She'd sanded the wood so smooth it shined. Will pet his hand down the horse's back.

Dylan's mouth dropped open. "You amaze me. You did all of these."

"Like I said, I have a lot of time on my hands."

Will made horse noises with his new toy. Her chest grew tight thinking about all the things she'd made for her daughter, and Hope would never get to play with them. One in particular came to mind. She couldn't keep it hidden away in the barn forever. Someone should enjoy it. Dylan's son was a good choice. If Hope had survived, Will would be her brother.

Silently, she walked him over to an area separate from the other furniture ready to go to her shop. She stopped in front of one of the many covered pieces and bent down next to Will. Her throat clogged, but she managed to get the words out. "I made this a long time ago for a very special little girl named Hope. I think she would like you to have it."

She uncovered the rocking horse she'd made for their daughter.

Will squealed his delight, handed his horse to Dylan, and tried to get on the horse to make it go. A little bit big for him, he couldn't quite make it up. Jessie helped him on, and he rocked back and forth. He didn't see her crying, but Dylan did and stepped to her, his hands outstretched, to pull her close.

She walked past him, tears running down her cheeks and her hand up to ward him off.

Too much to bear, having them here, sharing Hope's things with them and remembering all she'd lost— she fled back to the house.

Chapter Twenty-Seven

JESSIE MANAGED TO leave the barn and get upstairs before Dylan and Will came back to the house. They moved around downstairs, but she needed time alone to collect herself. She hadn't been home in over a week and longed to get into her sunken tub and turn on the jets to work out the kinks in her back. Still sore from the accident, her scrapes not completely healed, taking a bath was out of the question. Instead, she turned on the shower and let the steam heat the room. Suddenly, she felt cold to the bone and weary.

She peeled off her T-shirt and bra before she caught sight of herself in the mirror. Her hair, tied up in a ponytail, came out in wisps at her neck and around her face. She tore the bandage off her arm carefully and took in the damage. Yellow, green, and purple bruises bloomed along her shoulder and down her arm in addition to the deep scrapes.

Kicking off her shoes, she carefully slid her sweat pants down her legs. Her hip hurt, making navigating the stairs a problem. She'd had to step up with her right leg and pull her left leg up behind her. Slow going, but effective.

Her leg had suffered the worst of the damage. She pulled the bandages off and turned to regard her backside's reflection. Red, raw, and scabbing over, the long deep scrapes ran down her thigh from the bottom of her butt on the outside to almost her knee. The same gory colorful watercolor display as her shoulder.

She frowned and turned away from her reflection. Nothing good to look at anyway. Too thin, too muscular from swinging a hammer and hauling wood, the same plain girl she'd always been. She was a construction worker, not a model. Disgusted with herself for even thinking she could, or should, try to compete with other women who worked in jobs that most people would consider the norm for a woman. That wasn't her. She was different. Not like the women Dylan probably dated over the years. She hated thinking about Dylan taking another woman to dinner, holding her hand, or kissing her. The thought brought on a dismayed groan.

Why would he want to be with someone like her?

The spray hit her back and she tilted her head, allowing the water to wash out the grime from her hair. The hospital shower wasn't more than a trickle, making it near impossible to get her thick hair clean. Her stitches had been removed, leaving a patch of stubble where they'd shaved her head. Hardly noticeable with her long hair.

She took her time in the shower, even though she shouldn't have because of her healing wounds. She loved the feel of the water, and after a time she actually relaxed.

Clean and dry, she creamed her skin with a softly scented citrus lotion. She liked the fresh scent and it lightened her mood even more. She made sure to put the ointment the doctor prescribed on her wounds and left the scrapes uncovered.

She slid a cotton T-shirt dress on over her head and savored the feel of the soft material against her skin. One of her favorite casual dresses, the navy blue faded from several washings, but it still made her hair flash red against the richer dark brown color.

She took her time drying her hair and pulling the sides up with a couple of clips. When she glanced in the mirror again, the same old Jessie stared back. Her face wasn't as pale and her eyes had a little sparkle in them again. She decided to forgo the makeup and simply dabbed on her favorite perfume.

She hobbled downstairs in her bare feet and found Dylan in her kitchen cooking. Will rode his new rocking horse in the great room near the fireplace. Dylan kept looking over his shoulder, watching him.

"You didn't have to stay." She leaned against the archway.

"Will and I wanted to make sure you had a good meal your first night home. I figured your fridge would need some cleaning out after you stayed almost two weeks in the hospital. I took the liberty of cleaning out everything spoiled or unrecognizable. I bought you some supplies.

You've got milk, eggs, cheese, butter, salad stuff, yogurt, pudding cups—those were Will's idea."

"I like his idea of grocery shopping." She smiled softly, watching Will rock, his enjoyment lightening her heavy heart.

"He'd have bought you cereal and pudding. He thinks that's all you need."

"Well, there's that and chocolate. Everything else is just for show," she teased.

Dylan laughed, a lighthearted sound that made her heart stutter. They'd both been far too serious lately. She'd spent too much time pushing him away, when she really wanted to pull him close, if only she had the courage to face her fear and believe he'd never hurt her again. She'd try, because pushing him away and never knowing if what they had could last scared her even more.

"I also got you some meat. It's in the freezer. I'm making spaghetti for us tonight with garlic bread. Oh yeah, there's a loaf of bread over there too. I wasn't sure exactly what you like, but I got you the basics."

"Dylan. Stop."

"What?" He glanced up from chopping the onions for the meat sauce. He stilled, and she came toward him. God, she was beautiful. Her hair hung soft and flowing down her back in waves of browns and reds. As the light caught the strands, it shimmered with the many colors. She wore a dress, and he couldn't help but look down at her legs. She had great legs. The dress barely hit her mid-thigh. He'd like to sit her on the counter and run his hands up the outside of her thighs until his fingers pushed the skirt up to her hips. He shook off the fantasy and concentrated on her face.

"You don't have to do all this. I can take care of myself."

He set the knife down and put both hands on the counter and leaned forward. "I know you're capable of taking care of yourself. I wanted to do something nice for you to thank you for saving my son. I wanted to sit across the table from you, share a meal, and catch up on our lives."

She opened her mouth, then shut it without uttering a word, accepting his kind gesture. She went to a cabinet and took down a bottle of red wine. She set it on the island where he prepared dinner and turned to get out the corkscrew. When she turned back, she ran right into him. He grabbed her waist to steady her. Bending down, he kissed her softly.

"Thank you for not putting up a fight," he said against her lips.

"I don't want to fight with you."

She stared at him with those big hazel eyes, more green than gold, and told him the truth. She didn't want to fight or argue with him about the past. She wanted to put it to rest. He kissed her forehead and released her and went back to chopping the onion, satisfied they'd moved another step forward. A first step toward each other—and, he hoped, their future together.

"Cartoons!" Will yelled from the other room.

Dylan put his head back and sighed. "I forgot to bring one of his DVDs to watch. He'll get bored, and then he'll get cranky."

"No problem." She headed to the other room, leaving the open bottle of wine on the counter to breathe. "What do you like to watch, Will?"

"I don't know."

"Well, let's see if that's on." She found the remote and turned on the satellite receiver and TV. Will's eyes lit up at the big TV. "Pretty cool, huh."

"Yup. Biggest TV I ever seen."

"Me too. Let's see what's on." She settled Will beside her on the couch and they surfed channels. He made her stop several times. Cooking shows, he loved them. She finally found a cartoon channel showing something he recognized. He snuggled in close to her side and sat quietly watching. She should help Dylan with dinner, but if he wanted to make it, let him. How often did she have someone around to cook for her? Hardly ever, and never often enough, in her estimation.

She loved having Will close, but warned herself not to get attached, not to start thinking he was hers. She tamped down thoughts of Hope and missing her. Wishing for her didn't do anything but make her sad, and she didn't want to be sad anymore.

She wanted to sit with this little boy and watch TV and let the warmth of the moment soothe her aching heart.

Dylan watched the two of them from the kitchen.

He surveyed the house again and smiled. He liked it here. It felt right. He and Will could be comfortable living with her. He'd thought he'd get her to marry him and she'd move out to his place near his cousins. On second thought, this place was perfect. Even more so because she'd designed and built it herself. He figured she'd never want to give it up. Add to the fact it she built it on the land they'd made their daughter.

He got chills driving up her driveway thinking about it. He wondered how she managed to make the drive every day and not remember their night together. Then again, she probably didn't try to forget. She'd picked this spot for the house for the very reason it was where they'd spent the night together. It gave him hope knowing she cared that deeply about their past. Now, he just needed her to love him in the present and for the next fifty-plus years.

Chapter Twenty-Eight

JESSIE DIDN'T REALIZE how much she'd missed having someone to share a meal with. Will was comical when it came to eating spaghetti. He got more on his face than in his mouth, but it didn't matter. He had fun doing it. Dylan kept the conversation moving, talking about his time in the military, serving in the wars overseas, facing life and death, finishing his degree during his police training, and living in Atlanta. She opened up about starting her own company, and how she'd worked while attending school. He understood how hard it must have been on her to accomplish it, and finish it.

They didn't discuss Hope or his mother. She wondered if he had more questions. She had a few of her own about Will. Did Dylan have someone special in his life? Did he really want to start over with her? Was it all just wishful thinking they could start over? Did he love her?

Afraid to ask, even more afraid he did, she didn't want to try again only to have it all fall apart. But what if it didn't this time?

They weren't impulsive teenagers anymore. This time, they had no secrets. They'd done their growing up and found their place in the world. This time, they could take the time, build their friendship and attraction into a sturdy foundation for a lasting future.

Looking at him across the table with the wine making her a little numb, she dreamed this was her life. Way too easy to think this was how she spent every evening. Dylan and Will had become a part of her home, seamlessly blending in without a ripple. Will played with the rocking horse and flopped on the couch like he owned the place. Dylan whipped up dinner without once asking her where she stored something. He'd simply made himself at home, rummaging through her refrigerator and cupboards. She regretted the late hour and found she already missed them, even though they hadn't yet left.

From the couch, Will said, "I'm not supposed to say so, but I want you to be the mommy. I get to choose. You said so," he reminded his father.

The blooming dream of a future with Dylan faded to gray. What if Will chose another mother? What if she couldn't be the mother he needed? Being with Dylan again meant being with Will. Surprisingly, that thought made her happy. She liked the little boy. Despite feeling as if she'd closed off her heart when Hope died, she found it open to Will, even if she still had her reservations about

Dylan. Loving a little boy was so much easier than loving a man.

"I know what I said. I also remember telling you we have to give Jessie time. She and I have some things to work out, and we're sad because we lost Hope."

"She died." Will pouted and frowned at Jessie. "My goldfish died. It was sad. I cried."

"That is sad, honey. Hope was just a baby when she died. I miss her very much."

"Daddy is sad too. He misses her. She can't come back from heaven."

"No, honey, she can't. Tell me how you picked your daddy." She thought changing the subject would be a good idea for herself and Dylan. Besides, she really wanted to know how these two became father and son.

"The belly mommy couldn't keep me. She found Daddy and he helped her. I didn't belong to the belly mommy. I belonged to him."

"The belly mommy." She smiled at Dylan, thinking it a charming way to tell a child he was adopted.

"I wasn't sure how to explain to him where babies come from. Since Heather carried him in her belly, we call her the belly mommy. Eighteen, all set to go off to college and have a brilliant future, she found out she was pregnant. She managed to keep it hidden from her parents and graduate high school with honors. When she couldn't hide the pregnancy any longer, she ran away from home, hoping to have the baby without anyone finding out. She had some trouble and wound up on the streets of Atlanta scared and alone.

"While on duty one night, I found her in an alley. I took one look at her and knew I had to help her. Something about her spoke to me and told me not to send her home, or to a shelter. After letting her parents know she was safe, she stayed with me a couple weeks, until Will came. Easier that way for her to go home without the neighbors and friends knowing she gave up the baby. When she went into labor, I was scared to death for her and the baby. We'd become good friends and her parents liked me. When this little man came into the world, she handed him to me and asked if I'd raise him. She'd already talked to her parents about it, and they agreed. I couldn't say no. I didn't want to say no. He was mine. I knew it the moment I saw him."

He studied her to gauge her reaction, relieved to see her interested and not upset by the events of his becoming a father.

"Heather went off to college. She's a junior. She's studying medicine and will someday be a great doctor. It's what she's meant to do. She wants to have a family someday. She just wasn't ready to have one at eighteen as a single mother. I keep in touch with her. We send letters a few times a year. I send her pictures of Will. I thought it important he know who his mother is and the courage it took for her to give Will to me. She wanted the best for him."

"She got it."

He sat back heavily at her words, letting out a deep sigh. Nothing could have surprised him more than to have her say he was the best father for Will.

"Don't be so surprised. You're a great father. It shows all over your face how much you love him. He's a lucky boy." She meant it.

"Does it bother you I adopted Will from a teenage mother? I mean, you were alone and I wasn't there for you. I stayed with Heather when she had Will. I took care of her the last month of her pregnancy." He couldn't tell her how guilty he felt about that, and at the same time what a blessing it was to be there to see Will come into the world.

"I wasn't alone, Dylan. I had Pop and Greg. But I really wanted you to be there." She shrugged and cast a glance past him out the window. "I'm tired of being angry about something that could have been, but wasn't. At least you know what it was like for me bringing our girl into the world. You were lucky enough to see Will come to you. I don't begrudge you that experience, or the fact it got you Will. In fact, it takes a little of the sting out of you missing Hope. You've had Will for three years. I only got five days. I know it's not the same. But it's something."

"It isn't the same. He's not Hope. I'll forever regret what happened."

"And what about your mother? Are you really going to cut her out of your life forever?"

"I don't know. All I know right now is the sight of her makes me so angry I want to punch something." Will abandoned the cartoons and climbed into his lap and let out a huge yawn. Dylan put his arms around him and held him to his chest, his chin resting on top of his head. Something else he'd never get to do with Hope. "What about you and my mother? You said you wanted to make her pay."

She smiled softly, her eyes eating up Will curled against him. "What is there to do about it? Hope is gone. I can't give you back those five days."

"Not just five days. Your entire pregnancy and eight years I could have been happy. I thought you were dead. She knew you weren't and could have let me know at any time. Do you know how many days and nights I thought about you? Too many to count. I regretted leaving you the moment I got on the bus and headed out of town. I regretted it even more when I thought you were dead. And, even more when I realized your father had been hurting you all those years. I have so many damn regrets about you. This isn't just about Hope for me."

"It can't be undone. I've spent years being angry with you, and the last month angry with her. I'm tired of all of it. As much as I hate to admit it, Greg is right. I cut myself off from others and I'm not happy. That's a hard thing to realize. It's hard to believe I've wasted so much of my life being angry."

"You've got more than your share to be angry about, Jess. Between your father, me, my mother, and losing Hope, it's a lot for one person to deal with, to live with."

"Yeah, well, it's over. Done. I need to move on and focus on my future. My business is doing well. Actually, both of them are. I like what I do. Professionally, I'm set. It's my personal life that's in shambles."

"It's not as bad as you think. You have me. I need you, Jess. I want you to be my wife. I wasn't kidding when I said I love you, or that I've thought of you all these years. Even when I thought you were dead, I loved you and wanted you back."

She could lie and tell him she'd only been angry with him all these years and she had no intention of making the same mistakes twice. Even though she thought he'd betrayed her and not wanted her or Hope, she'd always loved the boy who always let her win in a bike race, who chose her to play on his team when other kids overlooked her. The boy who made her smile again after her father hurt her, even though he didn't know that was why she was sad. The boy who held her under the stars and gave her Hope.

She didn't know the man like she knew the boy. But she wanted to.

Damn Greg for always being right.

"I've thought of you all these years too," she admitted.

"I'm sure you've thought of many ways to kill me," he said sardonically.

"Well." She smiled. "There was that."

Something inside her dared her to try again. Enough regrets stood between them already. She didn't want her inability to reach out to him to be another regret in her life.

She didn't want to end up alone for the rest of her life.

"I've spent a lot of nights walking through this empty house wishing you were here and these rooms were filled with our children. I built this house because of a dream. At the time, it seemed this house was the only piece of the dream that could ever be a reality."

"It's not, honey. We can be together. I like your house. I watched you and Will together on the couch tonight watching TV. I thought about how this is how things should be for us."

"Oh, yeah, with you doing all the cooking? I might consider it then."

He laughed at her enthusiasm. "I'd cook if it meant I had you in my arms every night."

She wanted to say yes. It was on the tip of her tongue to just give in and let the life she'd always dreamed come into focus as her reality. Something stopped her.

"A lot of years separate our past and today. I'm not sure what I feel. I don't know how much is wishful thinking and hope I can have the past back, or if it's real for me today." She leaned her head back against her chair and viewed the reflection of the house in the dark windows.

"Face it, honey, you still want me."

Blunt, but true.

"Fear is holding you back. I'll find a way to overcome it. The past is the foundation for what we'll build our future on now."

She had to admit, the man could be convincing when he wanted something. She didn't doubt he wanted her. The attraction between them crackled in the air and in her body even now. But this time it had to be about a hell of a lot more than hormones and lust. She wanted everything he offered, but didn't quite believe it. Cautious. Yes, but for good reason. This time, it had to be forever, or she'd never survive losing Dylan again.

The silence stretched. He was thinking, same as her. She enjoyed being with him like this in the quiet, absent any awkwardness. He gave her the space she needed because he needed time too.

"Why don't you stay tonight?" His eyes sparkled and a slow half grin graced his face. When his eyebrow went up, she knew his mind had taken a turn down the wrong road. "I mean, you could take Will upstairs to sleep. I realize it's not a far drive back to town, but he's wiped out. You can share the guest room. It's no trouble. It's just for tonight," she rambled.

"I think that's a great idea. I haven't seen the upstairs. I wondered what spectacular things you did up there."

"Nothing special, just five rooms and three bathrooms."

"Good God, Jessie. Why did you build such a big house?"

"Like I said, it was a dream. One I wanted very much," she said softly.

"Oh, honey. I'm sorry. Things could have been so different for us. They will be."

"Let's stop going in circles. Come upstairs. I'll show you the guest room."

"I'll settle for sleeping under the same roof. But, not for long. You will be my wife, Jess."

Looking at him now, his determined expression there for her to see, she believed him. He meant it. Nothing she said or did would put him off for long. He was just giving her time to get used to the idea. The moment she settled into it, he'd make her his wife. Relief and trepidation filled her at the same time.

They went up the stairs in silence. Dylan waited for her at the top when it took her longer to get there. He could be a patient man. She hoped those patience held out a while longer.

"I still can't get over this house."

"That's the master suite." She pointed to the door closest to the stairs. "The next two rooms share a bathroom between them, and then the other two rooms share a bathroom between them."

Dylan smiled. Leave it to Jessie to come up with the perfect floor plan. She led him to the first door on the right. The room was furnished and ready for company. The room across the hall had several pieces of furniture and a double bed, but there weren't any linens or decorations. The other two rooms were either the same or empty.

The guest room had two large dressers, a night table, a rocking chair, and a queen-size bed. He recognized the beautiful furniture as pieces she'd made herself. The bed had a light-green comforter with a cream-colored blanket at the end. It matched the cream paint on the walls. The painting above the bed showed a white clapboard house with a wide green lawn and trees in the background, making the room feel homey.

She pulled the covers back on the bed and he lay Will inside. He took off Will's little shoes and set them on the floor next to the bed. Leaning over, he kissed his son goodnight. It warmed his heart when Jessie did the same.

They stepped out of the room and stood at the top of the stairs. "Get some rest, honey. I'll go down and clean up. You look tired." He rubbed his palm up and down her arm and linked his fingers with hers. Her face turned up to his, her eyes soft and a touch sad.

"He's beautiful, Dylan. You're lucky."

"I hope so." He left her at the top of the stairs, hoping luck would bring him Jessie.

A half hour later, he walked into her room, carrying a cup of tea. The door had been left open and the massive king-size sleigh bed was empty. He made his way through the dim room, guided by the soft light glowing by the bed. The window was open and the breeze blew the sheer curtains into the room. Drawn in that direction, he found Jessie sitting on the roof outside.

"Jess, honey, what are you doing out here?"

"I sit out here most nights. It's the one mistake in the house I made. I should have put a balcony out here."

He climbed out the window and sat next to her. She was right. She'd miscalculated the balcony. What a spectacular view. The land rolled out before them and appeared to go on forever. Where the land ended, the brilliant stars sparkled against the dark night sky and spread upward. A beautiful, clear night, you could see for miles.

The curve in the road where they'd parked so long ago lay below them. Jessie had been torturing herself with the past for a long time. He put his arm around her shoulders and pulled her to him. He leaned back against the wall of the house. They sat together in silence long after she finished her tea. It was the first night in a long while the silence didn't make him long for things he couldn't have.

Tonight, the silence surrounded them like a cocoon and he sat content with the woman he loved snuggled against his side.

Late, they went back in the window and stood in the shadows in her room, drawn to each other. He pulled her close. Her body melted against his. He kissed her until both of them were hungry and wanting. As desperate as they were for each other, he could take her to bed and make love to her all night. He wanted to more than his next breath, but Jessie wasn't ready to trust him again. They needed time to bridge the gap between who they used to be and who they had become to each other.

Not wanting to rush her, feeling her hesitation when he took things just a bit too far, he pulled away and stuffed his hands in his pockets. He stared at her for what seemed like a lifetime, memorizing every line and curve of her beautiful face. He leaned down and pressed a soft kiss to her forehead and combed his fingers down her soft hair, ignoring the urge to grab fistfuls and draw her close again. "Goodnight, sweetheart." He fought his compulsion to be with her and left her room without another word.

Chapter Twenty-Nine

DYLAN HELD WILL'S hand and walked up the porch steps to Owen's front door. Will pulled him in the other direction, but Dylan held tight, tugging Will toward the door.

"Horsies," Will said for the hundredth time since they got out of the car.

"Later. Let's at least say hello to everyone first."

He knocked on the door and walked in without waiting for Owen or Claire to let them in. At Brody and Owen's house, his too, family was always welcome.

"Horsies," Will shouted, trying to escape his grip to run back out the front door and go to the barn.

"Hi Uncle Dylan. We'll take him," Dawn said, her sister, Autumn, nodding her agreement.

"Thank you, girls." He bent and made Will look at him, by holding his shoulders. "Do you remember the rules?"

"Pet nice. Stay outside the gate, not inside. Hand flat to give the apples."

"What else?"

"Do what Dawn and Autumn say."

"Excellent. Be good." He held his arms open and Will gave him a hug. He released his son and turned to the girls. "Where's my hug?" The girls launched themselves into his chest. He held them tight before letting them go. Each of them took one of Will's hands to take him outside. "Where is everyone?" he asked before they left.

"Out back," Autumn said.

Dylan walked down the hallway and through the kitchen. He stepped out the open back door onto the deck. Brody and Owen manned the grill. Rain and Claire sat at the holding their sons, David and Sean.

"Dylan," they all called, nearly in unison.

He laughed and accepted the beer Brody handed him. "Hey guys, how's it going?"

"Where's Will?" Rain asked.

"With the horses. And Dawn and Autumn," he added.

Owen chuckled. "You've got to get that boy a horse."

"Why? He's got yours to play with and I don't have to clean up after them."

"Where's your girl?" Brody asked.

"I didn't invite her," he admitted, wishing he had, but knowing he had to do something to draw her out.

"Why not?" Claire asked. "We expected you to bring her."

"I thought you two made up," Rain said.

"We did, but it's turned into this weird thing."

"So, what, it's not going to work out?" Brody asked. "You changed your mind."

"Hell no. The damn woman is stubborn. I thought we made real progress the day she went home from the hospital. Will and I stayed at her place—in the guest room," he added to wipe the raised eyebrows and knowing smiles off their faces. "We shared a meal and some real conversation. It was good. Better than good."

"So, what did you do?" Rain asked.

"I took her lunch several times over the last couple weeks. I sent her flowers. I left her some notes on her car when she came into town. I have gone out of my way to spend time with her every chance I've had between work and taking care of Will."

"Okay, so if we're having a family barbeque, why didn't you bring her? This is the perfect time for her to get to know us better and for you to spend time with her." Claire eyed him, looking at him like he was an idiot.

"I did all those things. She just goes along. Unless I go see her, I don't see her. Unless I call, I don't speak to her. Unless I start the conversation, we don't speak. The harder I try to get close to her, the more she stalls."

"You don't think she wants to be with you?" Owen asked.

"No. That's not it. When we're together, everything is great. But unless I'm right in front of her, it's like I don't exist. So, I backed off. I'm not going to call or go see her until she comes to me this time."

"Bad idea," Rain said.

"You're asking for trouble," Claire added.

"Back me up here, guys. I can't carry this whole relationship on my own."

Brody and Owen stood together and both of them shook their heads.

"Listen to the women," Brody said, nodding in his wife's direction.

Dylan turned to Rain. "Okay, what did I do wrong?"

"You answer that question first. What is it that you did that frightens her the most?"

"I left her."

"Yes. And?" Rain coaxed.

"She's afraid I'll do it again. But I've spent the last two weeks trying to show her that I'm here for her."

"Yes, I imagine you've been a very good friend," Claire said, though she didn't make it sound like a good thing in this case.

"I'm trying. That's where we started. If we get that back, then we can move forward."

"Friends is nice, definitely the foundation for what you have now, but friends aren't the same as boyfriends and husbands. They aren't there every day. They aren't the people you count on to be there at the end of a long day, or first thing in the morning."

"I'm trying to take things slow. For her."

"Is that really what she wants? Does she want a friend? Or does she want a boyfriend? Does she want you to be her husband?"

"I don't know. Not for sure. That's why I'm giving her time."

"Yes, and while you're giving her time, you're acting like her friend, which tells her that's all you want," Raid said.

"It's like that saying about dress for the job you want. In this case, you need to be the man you want to be to her. If you want to be her husband, you need to be that to her."

"So because I've been trying to be her friend, she doesn't believe I want to be more."

"After you left her once, why would she?" Rain asked.

"Crap." Dylan ran a hand through his hair. "What do I do now?"

"Well, it's too late to go and get her for the barbeque. She'll think it was an afterthought."

"She's my every thought," he admitted.

Rain and Claire both smiled and sighed.

"Thanks for that one," Brody said. "Go back to making me and Owen look like good husbands."

Dylan laughed and shook his head. "Hey, you're married to the women you love. I can't even get Jessie to call me."

"Stop taking things slow, or that spark between you will burn out. Fan the flames. Heat things up," Owen suggested.

Dylan glanced at Claire and Rain for their approval of that plan. "Okay, I'm definitely on board for that. This is taking too damn long as it is. I want her in my house, in my bed, in my life every day."

"Tell her that," Rain said.

"I have. Many times."

"Yes, and then you treated her like your best pal," Claire said. "If you mean it, show her in a way she can't misinterpret."

"Drag her to the ground and have my way with her," he teased.

"Less caveman, more 'I need you now,'" Rain suggested.

Dylan thought about the last two weeks and how'd he been so careful not to push for too much intimacy. They'd shared a few kisses, but they were far too chaste for his liking, and maybe Jessie's too. Maybe what he interpreted as caution in her eyes was really her confusion and trepidation to ask for more, or show him she wanted more, when he kept things so light and carefree.

Dylan dropped into the seat next to Rain. She put her hand on his knee and gave him a pat. "I think it's sweet you're taking things slow, but take it from someone who was left, all she wants to know is that you want her and only her. Don't tell her. Show her."

"Believe me, I want to. Bad." That admission made all of them laugh. "I'll take her to dinner tomorrow night. Something quiet, intimate. Set the scene, so to speak. Then, I'll take her home."

Chapter Thirty

JESSIE WORKED ON top of the roof of one of the custom homes at the back end of the park in the new housing development. It had become her special project and her own personal torture. With her shoulder and thigh completely healed, if still a little bruised, she'd gotten back to work with a vengeance. Mostly, she worked out her frustration over Dylan. Over the last two weeks, he'd begun a campaign of being there one minute and gone the next. She never knew when he'd show up or be missing. Disconcerting and a little—okay, a lot—annoying.

She hammered another nail into the tar paper and sat back on her heels. Scanning the housing development, progress continued even while she'd been gone. Several of the homes were finished, potential buyers arriving daily to walk through and hopefully buy. Work continued on the other homes. Everything ran smoothly.

Brian stepped things up while she was away, and he'd

become one of James's go-to guys. He worked hard and made his presence known to others. A good sign, he took his job seriously and worked hard to make things right in his life. On many occasions, he'd thanked her for the work she'd done on the house and told her Marilee was happier than he'd ever seen her. The baby would arrive in a few short weeks, and Jessie couldn't wait to meet her nephew.

That thought put an ache in her belly. As happy as she was for them, she wished the same for herself. As much as she loved Hope, she wanted to have more children. She thought of Will and smiled.

Dylan had been purposefully friendly and charming and maddeningly distant. He kissed her like a friend and not the woman he wanted. The last time he'd kissed her like he meant it had been the night he and Will stayed over at her house. He'd kissed her goodnight like it was the beginning of a good night and not the end. He never brought Will with him when he came to see her. "Popped up" described it more accurately. She missed the little boy.

Late into the night, she'd been building him his new bed, dresser, and night table. She'd sat for hours drawing out different horses for the carvings. She hadn't quite gotten it right yet. She planned to sort through what she had again tonight. She'd start on it this evening, since she had nothing better to do anyway.

Dylan had been conspicuously quiet for two days. No random calls to check up on her. No showing up with a bag lunch. No leaving her little notes on her car at the grocery store, or some other parking lot, telling her he missed her. No flowers left on her doorstep. She thought of the single red rose left on her roof where she liked to sit outside her window. That one had almost done her in completely.

She'd wanted to call him and tell him to come to her house. He made it easy, leaving all his numbers by her phone in the kitchen. For some reason, she couldn't bring herself to make a simple phone call. Probably because there was nothing simple about it.

Caught up in thought, she didn't realize Dylan had driven up in his sheriff's vehicle. The truck sat below her, but she didn't see him in it. A smile curled her lips when she felt him straddle her legs from behind and lean in close. His warm breath swept across her ear and cheek. She let the warmth sink deep into her heart.

"Hello, gorgeous. I called you from down below, but you were somewhere else. Thinking about me?" He brushed his lips across her earlobe. A shiver rippled through her. He traced the outer edge with his tongue and slid his hands over her hips and held her tight. His whole body curved around hers, his heat seeping into her bones.

"Actually, I was thinking about a very handsome man."

"Yeah, I like the sound of that, so long as that man is me."

His hands pulled her back to him and she leaned into his chest, his breath whispered over her skin seconds before he kissed her neck.

This is what she'd missed. The easy way they connected when they were together.

"It's not you." The breath came out of her when his lips sucked gently.

He set her away from him and studied her face. "You're not lying. You've been up here daydreaming about someone else."

His hurt reflected in his eyes, and she didn't have the heart to tease him. He'd been so sweetly maddening the last couple of weeks, and somewhere inside of her, she knew it was his way of giving her time and space.

"There's this really cute little man with light brown hair and a sparkle in his eyes. He likes horses and spaghetti."

Relieved, his rigid body went lax and rested against hers. His hands pulled her snug against him. "You were thinking about Will?" he asked, surprised.

"Yes. I was thinking about Will. I've been working on his furniture. It's all built. I just have to do the carving, sand it, stain it, and paint out the cupboard."

He wrapped his arms around her from behind. "You were thinking about Will," he repeated, though it was a statement and not a question.

"I was thinking about you too."

"Oh yeah. Do any of those thoughts include dinner with me tonight?"

"No. I'm busy." She didn't know why she said that. She longed to spend the evening out with him. Unsure of herself and his here-one-minute-gone-the-next routine. It left her confused. Did he want her to simply know he was there as a friend, or did he really want to have her as his wife? He'd said it enough times, yet he never asked her outright.

Maybe he changed his mind now that he was used to the fact she wasn't dead.

"Busy, huh? I can't persuade you to change your plans and go out with me on a date?"

"A date? After two weeks of you showing up out of the blue and disappearing into thin air? You haven't called, or been around in two days. You want me to just drop everything and be at your beck and call."

So his absence over the last two days had been felt. The hardest two days of his life. Every second of every day he thought about her and wanted to go to her. He wanted her to come to him more. He'd spent the last two weeks actively pursuing her, doing everything he could to show her how special she was to him without pressuring her. She'd passively gone along. He led. She followed. He needed her to participate, reach out to him the way he reached for her.

But like Rain and Claire told him yesterday, if he acted like her friend, that's how he made her see him. Tonight, he'd make her see him as the man who wanted her as his lover and wife.

"Now, honey, I'm asking you out on a date. I may not have seen you for a few days, but you didn't exactly call to see what I was doing. Please, Jess, go out with me. We'll have a nice dinner and talk."

"I have to shingle this roof. Why are you here so early anyway?"

Stubborn woman kept stalling. He wouldn't let her get away with it. It was like she was afraid to be alone with him. He'd put a stop to that line of thinking immediately.

"I got off work early to come and see you. I've been working like a maniac the last two days, and I want to spend a quiet evening with you." He noted the tar paper, hammers, and shingles spread over the roof. She had everything set up to get the job done. "If I help you shingle the roof, will you have dinner with me?"

"Dylan, you haven't done construction work in years. You've worked all day. The last thing you want to do is work with me. Besides, if I needed help, I've an entire crew to call on."

"Fine. Then let them do it and come with me," he snapped, losing his patience with her.

"This is my house. I've done almost all the work myself. I'm not handing it over to the crew now that I'm almost done."

He read it in her eyes. She wanted to do it herself and feel the satisfaction in knowing she could. Seeing the finished product made her love her work. He decided to try another tactic.

"You take that side and I'll take the other. If I finish before you, you go to dinner with me tonight."

She cocked her head and glanced over her shoulder at him. "And if I win?"

"You'll get half your roof done for nothing."

"Free labor, definitely a plus. I'd get the roof done faster and have more time to work on Will's furniture."

"Cocky, aren't you?"

She surveyed him from his black Stetson to his black-booted feet, looking more like an outlaw than a sheriff. The badge gleaming on his shirt said otherwise, but the dark hair brushing his collar and day-old beard said more about the renegade in him.

"You're talking to a girl who spends her days on top of roofs. I've been doing manual labor since I was old enough to hold a hammer in my hands and swing it hard enough to pound in a nail." She removed her gloves from her tool belt and slapped them onto his chest. "I wouldn't want you to get a blister on those soft hands of yours."

He took the gloves and smiled at her. "Honey, these hands are anything but soft. If you give me a chance, I'll prove it to you." He traced his fingertips over her cheek.

She felt the roughness of his skin and just how gently he could make those hands caress her. A tingling tickled her gut and warmed her blood.

"You'll have to beat me on this roof. Then, maybe, *maybe* I'll let you buy me dinner."

"If I beat you, you're going to dinner. Then, I might get my hands on that delectable body of yours."

She lost a little of her smile. The thought of making love to him again held a lot of appeal. She'd thought about it and him night after night. Always at the back of her mind was the result of their last time together and how badly it turned out in the end. She wanted him, dreamed of him, and was afraid of him all at the same time.

"You'll have to win first to get me to do anything."

"I love a challenge." He gave her a cocky grin and slid the gloves on his hands while she got things ready. To make the job go faster, she called down to one of her men to send up two pneumatic nail guns. Then, to his embarrassment, she insisted on tying a rope around him.

He had to admit, it felt good to have her worry about his safety. On the other hand, his ego took a hit.

He stood and moved to his starting position, his boots sliding on the roofing paper, throwing him off balance before he caught himself. She had a point.

Word spread like wildfire through the construction site: Jessie had taken on the sheriff. She was leading him, but only because he was slowed by not having all the tools he needed to open the packaging for the roofing shingles. Nail guns went off like automatic weapons, and he kept his head down and his pace steady. He worked his ass off trying to get the job done. At one point, Brian joined him on the roof to help him get things set up. Dylan caught up to Jessie; only then did she pick up the pace. At some point, Greg arrived and helped him too. The guys down below started placing bets, and Dylan wanted to laugh. The odds were still against him, even though he had Brian and Greg helping.

Greg laughed, loud and robust, as Dylan busted his ass trying to keep up. "I never imagined you two would be competing against each other like this. You know you aren't going to win this. She's been doing this a long time and could probably build a house in her sleep."

"Does she ever sleep?" Dylan asked, sweat trickling down his spine.

"I don't think so," Brian said. "Some mornings I show up here early and she's already working and looks like she's been here for hours. It's scary and intimidating all at the same time. She's some kind of witch when it comes to construction."

"Are you ladies going to sit over there gabbing at each other, or are you going to get to work?" Jessie snapped at them and finished another row.

Dylan breathed heavily, sweat glistening on his forehead, running down his neck. Greg and Brian both looked disgruntled at Jessie's jibe and called down for two more nail guns and started hauling ass on the roof. Even Jessie couldn't keep up with all three of them working against her.

"That's cheating!" she yelled from her side of the roof.

"You never said I had to do the job alone, only that you could finish before me."

"Do you really think I'm going to go out to dinner with a man who cheats?"

"I think I'm going to finish this roof before you, and you'll have no choice because I'll have won."

"That's not fair."

"Life's not fair. I thought you'd learned that by now."

"Don't I know it. Even the sheriff can't be trusted."

"You can trust that I love you, honey, and one way or another I'll make you believe in that and me. Even if it takes the three of us beating you at this stupid contest."

"You're the one who bet me you could do the job faster. The fact that I, a woman, can beat you must be a real ego buster."

Dylan laughed. It *was* a real ego buster, but he'd get his date, and in the end that's all that mattered. Greg and Brian busted their asses trying to get ahead of her, and after about half an hour they overtook her. After two hours, the roof finished, he turned to her side and smiled as she sat on the roof drinking a bottle of water one of the men had thrown up to her. She still had about four rows left to do on her side. The men below were exchanging cash between them and cussing about cheating and women who thought they could do everything themselves. Jessie hadn't asked for anyone to help her. It wasn't her style, and his accepting Brian and Greg's help wasn't Dylan's, but he had fun watching her try to beat them.

He sat beside Jessie and smiled at her, bumping his shoulder against hers. She didn't look happy. "Oh, come on. Admit it, we had fun."

She pressed her lips together and nodded, the truth eating at her. "You had fun. Just like old times. You and Brian fooling around and working together again. It always made things easier when the two of you had each other to throw insults back and forth and mess around. The job always went faster for you two. You even managed to get Greg on your side this time."

She stood and glared down at the men. Brian and Greg sat on the back of Brian's truck drinking water and talking. They looked like the best of friends. It hurt her feelings to see he'd taken sides against her. Greg wanted her to be happy, and he thought that happiness would come from being with Dylan. Still, it would be nice to have someone on her side no matter what the circumstances.

"I'll get cleaned up and we can go to dinner. I'll drive my truck, so you won't have to bring me back here to pick it up."

She headed for the ladder before Dylan called her back. "It isn't us against you."

"Sure looks that way to me. The three of you on one side and me, alone, on the other. You won."

"Did you really want to win, so you wouldn't have to go out with me?"

"No. I wanted to show you, at this"—she spread her arms—"I kick ass."

"I know you do. You don't have to impress me."

"No? I'm not exactly the woman of every man's dreams. I work a dirty job that leaves me looking and smelling like dirt, wood, and sweat. You're more likely to find me wearing dirty jeans and work boots than a dress and high heels. My hair is usually a mess, and I don't wear makeup. I cuss like a sailor when I'm pissed, and I can do this job as well as or better than any man on my crew."

"Where are you going with this?"

"I'm trying to tell you I'm not like the other women you've dated or had in your life. I don't know how to play these games and make you see I'd like to find a way for us to be friends and maybe turn that into something more."

She threw up her hands in frustration. "For the last two weeks you've been doing all these nice things for me, but you stay at arm's length. Every time I think I can expect you to be there, you aren't. Today, you show up here and want to take me to dinner, and then you challenge me to beat you, and you go out of your way to win by cheating because it seems really important we have dinner together. I can't seem to figure out if you want me to be close to you or not. Maybe that's what you want today, but tomorrow you won't be there. I'm just not sure what you want or expect from me."

Her frustration turned into anger at her ineptitude for a simple task like going out on a date and getting to know someone. Completely clueless, she didn't know how to make him see she wanted them to be close like they were years ago. She just didn't know how to go about getting back to that point.

"And why haven't I seen Will? Do you not want him to be around me? Did I do or say something wrong?"

He couldn't believe he'd finally gotten her to open up and talk about her feelings and they were up on a roof with about twenty guys standing below overhearing everything they said. One thing came through loud and clear: she was out of her element with him. He didn't like that at all. Instead of making her feel more comfortable having him in her life, he'd done the opposite.

He hated when Claire and Rain were right.

"Jess, I want you to have dinner with me tonight and every night. That's the truth. I'm not trying to confuse you, or make things difficult. What I thought you needed wasn't what you wanted." The blank look on her face prompted him to continue. "I made a mistake. Let me fix it." He went to where she stood on the roof in front of the ladder and held her shoulders. Her brows were drawn in a deep line, her eyes confused and angry. "Will you please have dinner with me tonight? We need to talk."

Her face didn't show she'd changed her mind, but her words gave him hope. She cut him a break and said, "Well, all you had to do was ask."

He busted up laughing. He took off his Stetson and wiped the sweat from his brow with the back of his hand. "Let me get cleaned up and meet you at your place. I'll bring dinner, and we'll have a quiet evening. We have a lot to talk about, and I have something I want to ask you."

"What do you want to ask me?"

"We'll talk about it over dinner."

"Okay. Are you bringing Will?"

"Not tonight. We need some time alone."

"He can come. I don't mind."

"I do." He hurried to go on before she got the wrong idea. "I haven't been keeping him from you, Jess. The last several times I've come to see you, I came straight from work. Will wants to see you again. He asks about you all the time. The other times, well, I was being selfish. I wanted you to myself. Like tonight."

She grabbed the rope around his waist and untied it. He sucked in a breath when her fingers brushed against his stomach. She let the rope drop, hesitated, then ran her hands up his belly to his chest. She leaned up and kissed him quickly before she turned and fled down the ladder. Her determined stride took her past her crew, their jeers and taunts silenced with one glare before she got into her truck and left without saying anything to Brian or Greg.

Dylan stood rooted to his spot on the roof, staring after her, completely stunned by her show of affection. For the first time, he hadn't been the one to kiss or touch her first. She'd come to him.

"You better get a move on, man. She's got a head start.

No telling how long it'll take you to chase her down," Greg called up to him.

"I know just where to find her."

As Dylan's feet hit the ground, Greg went on. "It looks like the two of you had some kind of breakthrough up there."

"I made a mistake. She didn't like having us on one side and her on the other. I forgot the one thing Jessie needs and has never had. Someone on her side."

"She's had me," Greg pointed out.

"And today you were on my side."

Greg swore as they stood watching Jessie's truck stop off at the office trailer.

"She thinks I'm playing games with her. I tried to give her some space and still let her know I was here. She's afraid to get close to me, and she's more afraid I don't want to be with her. It's a complicated mess I'll sort out tonight. I'm not leaving her alone again until she understands."

"She's never dated. She doesn't understand all the intricacies of attracting a man. You two were friends as children and that grew into love. I can see why she might be confused. You two need to get back that closeness you had when you were friends. She understands that."

"I'll fix it tonight."

Jessie came out of the office and jumped back into her truck.

"Go get her, tiger." Greg's encouragement made Dylan laugh.

He didn't need to be told twice. He had a couple errands to run before he went to Jessie's house and explained how things were going to be between them. Definitely. Absolutely. No more questions or confusion.

Telling her he loved her and wanted to be with her hadn't been enough. Tonight, he'd show her how much he loved her. Even if it took all night.

Chapter Thirty-One

JESSIE OPENED THE door and found herself staring at a huge bouquet of flowers with jean-clad legs. The scent of roses and Chinese food teased her sense of smell, and she took the bag of food from the hand she could see.

"I assume you're behind there, Dylan."

"It's me. I brought you flowers."

"It looks like you brought me the whole garden." She set the food on the hall table and took the vase of flowers from him. She stuffed her face into the blooms and inhaled deeply. Sheer pleasure shot through her. No one had ever brought her flowers. Dylan did so often over the last weeks and she never grew tired of it. In fact, she appreciated it more and more.

"I'm happy I stopped to get them."

While her hands were full, he cupped her face and kissed her over the bouquet. Electricity and fire shot through her as his lips touched hers. This kiss was different. Before, his kisses had been more like a "hello, I'm here." This one said, "I promise there's more to come." She wasn't sure how to respond, but she found herself leaning into him and his kiss and hoping there was more—a lot more.

"Hungry?" He pulled away just enough for her to see the humor in his eyes.

"Huh? What?" Off center, her mind felt drunk on roses and Dylan. He made her brain and body turn to mush.

"Chinese food, honey. Are you hungry?"

"Yeah. Um, yes. Let's eat." She stumbled over her words.

Happy to see her out of sorts, Dylan grinned and his eyes sparked with mischief.

She took a good look at him, noting he must have gone home to shower and change. His damp hair gleamed in the fading sunlight. His navy blue sweater molded to his wide shoulders and chest. Faded, well-worn blue jeans hugged his hips and stretched over his powerful thighs. He wore his favorite black cowboy boots.

"Like what you see?" He couldn't help it. Her casual perusal made his blood run hot. He'd like nothing better than to take her in his arms and make love to her. She needed time to settle into their relationship again. By the end of the night, he intended to show her how much he missed and loved her.

"You changed."

"I'm still the same Dylan you knew before, but yeah, I went home and got cleaned up." He pulled a folded paper out of his back pocket. "Will sends his love." He handed her the paper. Her eyes glassed over at the sight of the pictures Will colored for her. Horses. Lots and lots of horses. One of the pictures showed him, Will, and Jessie together holding hands.

"Thank you."

He took the flowers from her and headed toward the kitchen. "Don't thank me. He's been going on and on about you. I think he's in love." He came back to the entryway and grabbed the food. He took it over to the coffee table in front of the fireplace and set it down. He lit the fire already built before going back to the kitchen to get plates and forks. He smiled when he found Jessie in the kitchen putting Will's picture of them up on the refrigerator.

"Come eat, sweetheart. We need to talk."

She followed him into the great room and sat beside him on the sofa facing the fireplace. The fire burned bright and warm. The setting sun cast the room in shadows, enhancing the feeling of cozy romance. She leaned over to turn on the side table lamp, but he put his hand over hers, stopping her.

"Don't. Let's keep this just the two of us sitting and talking by the firelight."

"Okay. I like to sit and look at the flames for hours. Sometimes I sit here and carve."

"Will loves the horse you gave him."

"You left the rocking horse here." She pointed at it sitting in the room by the other seating area.

"For the next time Will comes over." Dylan filled their plates and handed one over to her.

"Why didn't you bring him tonight?"

"I want to be alone with you."

"Are you sure that's all it is?"

He reached for her, tracing his finger across her forehead and over her ear, tucking a lock of hair behind her ear. "That's all there is. I wanted us to have a quiet evening together, so we can talk and clear the air." He leaned in and gave her a soft kiss. She relaxed and gave him a small smile. He popped the top on her beer and handed it to her, and then did the same for himself. She took a bite of food and settled in to eat, making him happy.

"I thought I'd start off by telling you how sorry I am about the last couple of weeks. I never meant to confuse you."

"I can't seem to keep up with you. One minute you're there, or you leave me flowers and notes, and the next you disappear."

"You had my number. You could have called me."

"I didn't think you wanted me to."

"Did you like the flowers and notes?"

"I loved them. I know I work a man's job, and usually look like a guy—"

"You could never look like a guy. You're beautiful, honey. Everything about you screams sexy woman, even in jeans and flannel shirts."

He surveyed her with pure male appreciation. Her cheeks flushed at his blatant perusal.

She swallowed another bite, leaving her plate nearly empty. "Regardless, I'm still a woman. I like flowers and notes. I especially liked the rose you left on the roof."

"You sit up there and think about us. Wherever I am, I think about you."

Her eyes softened on him and she sighed. "I like it up there. You can't beat the view."

"We've shared a lot of history. It occurred to me today, standing on the roof, you've wanted to count on me for a long time. You haven't been able to do that, even when we were kids."

"That's not true. You were there for me when we were young. You'd have been there when I had Hope if you'd known."

"Let's not talk about my mother. I don't want to be angry tonight. What I'm saying is although we've always been close, there's been a kind of disconnect between us because we haven't been completely honest with each other. There have been things I didn't know about you and you didn't know about me." He took her empty plate and set it on the coffee table along with his own. He took her hands and held them while he looked into her eyes. "Here's the thing. I don't want there to be anything about you I don't know. I want you to know everything there is to know about me."

"That's going to take some time. I know a lot about you, Dylan, but it's been eight years since we've seen each other. You've grown up. I grew up. Things changed. Maybe we've changed too much and what we had isn't there anymore."

His fingers slid into her hair at the base of her neck. He drew her close, his gaze locked on hers. His mouth fit to hers and her eyes fell closed and she fell into him. He drew the kiss out, letting her feel the connection between them pulse and build.

"You feel what we have just as strongly as I do."

One side of his mouth cocked up in a grin when it took her that whole sentence to open her eyes again.

"We need a lifetime to know each other, and that's what I want with you."

He stood and pulled her with him. Moving around the coffee table, he pulled her down to sit between his legs. They faced the fire. He liked the way she settled against his chest without any reservations. He kissed the side of her head and gazed over her shoulder at the bright fire.

"Like I said, it's going to take a lifetime. We have something special. I love you, Jess. I always have, and that's never going to change."

"I love you too," she whispered.

He wrapped his arm around her shoulders and across her chest. She leaned her head down and rested her chin on his arm, watching the dancing flames snap and pop. The feel of his body down her back and his legs wrapped around hers made her feel safe and protected. Looking up through the skylights above them, night had fallen and the stars burned bright.

"I know you do. I've always known." He kissed her temple and squeezed her to him.

"You said you wanted to ask me something. What is it?" She settled into him and continued watching the fire. His breath whispered against the side of her face, and he sat behind her enjoying the fire and the closeness he'd tried to build over the last weeks, but all he needed was Jessie in this arms.

"Will you take me to see Hope? I want to put flowers on her grave and tell her I love her. I want her to have both her parents visit her."

She went to the grave often. She'd sit by the grave and talk to her. It always left her drained and depressed. The sadness of seeing her daughter's name etched in stone and thinking of all the things she'd never see her daughter do or experience overwhelmed her.

"I'll take you any time you want to go. I go several times a year, and always on her birthday."

"Let's go tomorrow. It's Saturday. We'll spend the day together. We'll pick up Will after we go to the cemetery."

"I'd like that."

"You like having him around."

"He's a great kid. You must have had a hard time taking care of him all by yourself when he was a baby."

"I had help." He smiled sheepishly. "I love the fact that you forget completely I'm wealthy. You know I could hire an entire army brigade to take care of Will, but you know me well enough to know I'm a hands-on dad."

Jessie didn't care about his money. She had her own, enough to keep her businesses running, a roof over her head, and food in her cupboards. She wasn't interested in Dylan because he could support her for the rest of her life. That had never been his appeal. No, it was the way he made her feel about herself, all the good he saw in her.

"I hired a nanny right away." He went on, "She took care of him while I worked and taught me what I needed to know about raising my son. The rest was a lot of luck and practice."

Jessie tried to get up, but he pulled her back down.

"Where are you going?"

"I have something to show you." She moved to get up, and instead he took her mouth and kissed her silly. The crackle of the fire faded and all she heard was his breath on her lips when his tongue slid past and glided over hers. He kissed her long and deep. His hand slid up her arm and over her collarbone before slipping down her chest to cup her breast. He weighed her in his palm. She sighed when his thumb swept over her taut nipple. Her arms found their way around his neck, and she held him tightly to her as his other arm banded around her back and pulled her even closer.

"What do you want to show me, honey?"

That soft, silky voice vibrated in her ear and his roaming hands sent warm tremors through her system. She couldn't think, didn't want to. She wanted to feel, and then she remembered what she wanted to show him. "Hope's chest," she stammered. "I have Hope's chest to show you."

He couldn't get enough of her. Warm and supple, her breast fit his hand to perfection, and the soft firmness of it made his fingers tingle to slide her shirt off and peel away her bra and find the smooth skin beneath. He squeezed her breast and took her taut nipple between his thumb and index finger and plucked at it until she sighed.

He took her bottom lip, sucked it into his mouth, and soothed her by licking the edge. He trailed small, soft kisses at the corner of her mouth and along her jaw.

Her head fell back and she rested her face against his cheek. He smiled into her neck.

"Go get it, honey. I want to see it." *Then I want to see you.* He didn't say the last part aloud, but it's what he intended. He didn't want to rush her. They had all night. They had forever.

She stood to walk away, but he kept touching her until she was out of his reach. His fingers trailed down her arm and over her hip and down her leg. She turned back to him and smiled, her eyes roaming over his entire body, making him want her so bad he had a hard time sitting still and not lunging for her. God, this woman made him crazy.

She walked to the seating area on the other side of the room. Next to a round side table on the floor sat a wood chest. She bent and picked it up by the metal handles on the side and brought it back. When she came toward him, he grabbed her hips and guided her down so she sat with her back to him again. The chest sat next to them.

He studied the simple design and knew Jessie made it. The name carved on the top humbled him: HOPE DANIELLE MCBRIDE. He couldn't get used to the idea that even though she thought he'd abandoned her, she'd still named their daughter after him.

"Why did you name her after me?"

"She's your daughter."

That was Jessie. She broke things down to the simplest truth. Hope had been his daughter no matter if he'd been there or not. It didn't change the facts or the love Jessie had for him. He should have realized that these last weeks and kept things simple with her. She loved him. He loved her. They should be together, so why hadn't he just been with her? Because he needed to know she wanted to be with him as much as he wanted to be with her. He went back to the simple truth. Jessie loved him and wanted to be with him. Done. End of story. Tonight, he'd stop all this complicated business, trying to give her time and drawing her to him. He'd go back to the easy way things used to be when they were kids. They'd be together. Tonight. Always.

"She was our daughter," he corrected. "I love her and miss her all in the same heartbeat." He traced his finger over the smooth wood.

"There's that little bit of poetry. Only now it's coupled with a tough cop."

"You said something similar the night of the prom."

"I'm a sucker for a poetic tough guy." She kissed his stubbly chin. "About Hope, I know what you mean. It's an ache that won't go away. Some days it's overwhelming and other days it simmers in the background."

The kind of pain only they could share because it was the loss of a child they'd created. The pain, like the child, was unique to them. He swept his hand down the length of her hair. She opened the trunk. He glanced over her shoulder and wanted to weep with sorrow. Inside lay Hope's things. Jessie pulled out a baby blanket, held it to her nose, and inhaled the lingering scent of their daughter. A single tear spilled from her eye and rolled down her cheek.

"This is the blanket I wrapped her in when she was born. They let her have it in the NICU where she stayed. I would drape it over the both of us when she nursed. I held her to my breast and looked down at her sweet face. She'd ball her fist and press it to my skin."

He slid his hand around her back and over her ribs to cup her breast. Heavy, her nipple tight. Even the memory evoked a physical response in her. He held her breast in his hand and kissed the side of her neck. She leaned her head back against him and gave him better access to her throat. He slid his hand from her breast and over her flat belly where she'd once carried their child.

He liked having her with him this way, sharing something deeply personal and intimate. She didn't resist, but relaxed into him, his hands on her body as natural as breathing.

She leaned over the chest and took out some of the clothes Hope had worn. He took one of the small pink sleepers.

"I forget how small babies can be. Will's grown so much. She wore this?"

"Yes. It's soft and warm. This was actually a little big on her."

"It's pretty with the little roses."

"She looked like a princess."

The chest held several other dresses and sleepers Hope never had time to wear. He tried to picture his daughter in them. It was hard since he'd only seen a single small photo of her. He hated that he couldn't bring her into his mind easily, there being only a single memory to recall. Jessie pulled out a thick photo album from the bottom of the chest. He inhaled sharply at seeing his daughter's name written on the outside cover with a close-up photo of her little face.

"Oh, Jess. You made this."

"We took a lot of pictures before and after she was born. Looking back, maybe we knew we didn't have a lot of time. We documented everything."

"We?"

"We," she confirmed. "Pop and Greg were with me all the time. I never went to a doctor's appointment alone."

He kissed her cheek. "I'm glad you weren't alone, honey."

About to open the photo album, she turned and fixed her gaze on him. "No fat jokes," she warned. The smile on her face bloomed bright and honest. The first real one he'd seen in a long time.

"Are you telling me there are pictures of you pregnant in here?"

"I'm saying there are pictures of me looking as big as a house."

It hit him again: just how much he'd missed. He'd never gotten to see her belly grow, or feel his daughter kick through her stomach. "Let's see," he said, choked up.

His throat constricted, heart aching, he inhaled deeply, catching Jessie's sweet floral scent. Just that small thing eased him.

Her hand swept over the cover. She opened the book and showed him the first page. It listed all of Hope's first information.

Hope Danielle McBride
Born: February 27, 2006

6 lbs. 10 oz.—19 in.

A photo showed her and Jessie taken moments after her birth. Jessie held Hope in her arms and smiled hugely at the camera, even though she looked worn out and exhausted.

She turned the page to several photos of her with her belly growing with each picture. They were in succession, starting at three months and every month after until she was, as she said, as big as a house.

"I can't believe how young you were."

"Fifteen, sixteen when I had her." She pointed to the picture of her at seven months pregnant. "This one is from just after we got back from eating at an Italian restaurant for my birthday. I devoured an entire platter of lasagna, I think. I had a real craving for Italian the whole time I was pregnant. I couldn't tell you how much of that baby bump is Hope and how much is dinner."

"Sixteen, alone, and a mother. I'm sorry, Jess. I should have been there."

"You would have been there," she said and turned the page.

He wouldn't let her get away with dismissing him and what happened so easily. He leaned his forehead to her hair and whispered in her ear. "I wish I'd been there with you. I'd have asked you to come to base where I was stationed and married you immediately. I missed you so much. I grieved hard for you every day. We could have had a life together. We could have shared our grief over losing Hope. I'm so sorry all these years were taken from us."

She leaned her head into his as his lips brushed her ear and hair. "I'm sorry too. I don't want to live in the past anymore. I don't want to live in what might have been, but focus on now. We've managed to find our way back to each other. We can share Hope this way," she said and indicated the book. "We can't get back what we've lost, but I hope we can keep a piece of her alive between us. Besides, neither of us would be who we are now. You wouldn't have Will."

Choked up, he kissed her temple and hugged her close.

The photos showed Jessie in labor at the hospital. Sweat glistening in her hair, making it stringy, her eyes squinted in pain, but she still had a soft smile on her face.

"This one is when labor was really bad. I couldn't even open my eyes because the pain overwhelmed me. See Greg's face. I'm squeezing his hand so tight I drew blood with my nails."

"Didn't you have any drugs?"

"Nope. By the time I said *uncle*, they said it was too late. She was coming and nothing was going to slow her down."

"Damn, honey. You're one tough lady."

"Look at the pictures, I was one scared girl. I was about to bring a baby into the world and I had no idea how to take care of her. I'd read a dozen books and made all her furniture. I had all the things I'd need to take care of her, but the actual how-to of it eluded me. Then, they put her in my arms and I looked at her and felt full, complete. I figured no matter what came my way, I could handle it because she was counting on me. When they told me she was sick, that mother lion thing kicked in and all I wanted to do was protect her. It was hard to sit back and watch the doctors take care of her. I felt helpless. I never want to see someone I love in that kind of situation again with me standing by helpless to do anything." Chills ran up her spine.

Dylan pulled her closer and tapped a finger on one of the pictures of his daughter having a bath. "I remember the first bath they gave Will. He screamed just like that."

"She wasn't excited about it either. Greg went with her to the nursery before they had to take her to the NICU. I made him promise to stay with her."

"So, Greg got to play dad."

"No. Greg wasn't trying to be Hope's dad. He was being my friend. I was scared and afraid to let them take her away from me."

"I'm jealous he and his father got to be there. They got to hold her." He stared at the pictures of Greg and his father holding Hope. They both beamed with pride, his girl in their arms. Two big, strong men holding his little girl like she was their greatest joy. It hurt. He let it sink in and hoped he never forgot how much his mother hurt him. He'd never let her do something like this to him again.

They flipped through the rest of the pictures, him making comments, her telling stories. The final photo broke his heart. Greg snapped the picture right after Hope died. Jessie sat in a rocking chair in the NICU with Hope lying on her chest. Jessie's eyes were red and swollen. Tears filled her eyes and rolled down her cheeks. Her nose ran and none of it mattered. Her daughter was dead. Jessie's hand rested on Hope's back. She stared down at Hope's pretty face, weeping for the loss of her daughter.

Jessie traced a finger over the image of her daughter lying in her arms. Hope was a beautiful baby. Dylan's chin rested heavily on her shoulder. He sighed and gazed down at their baby. His hand made a leisurely pass up and down her thigh. He hadn't stopped touching her as they sat together in front of the fire bringing their past into their present. A sense of peace settled over her like she'd never felt, especially when she thought of Hope. Sharing her with Dylan healed something long broken inside of her.

She carefully packed Hope's things back into the chest. Dylan's smoldering eyes never left her body. He wanted her, but allowed her the time he thought she needed to settle into the intimacy blooming between them. She didn't need time. She needed him.

She wrapped her arms around his neck and held him close. He squeezed her to him in a hug that made her feel like she'd either pop or meld right into him. Warm and strong and all hers. The man she loved, the father of her child. In that moment, she realized just how much she'd missed having him in her life and how lucky she was to have him back.

"I never want to let you go."

"Don't."

He pulled her down to the plush rug beside him. His mouth found hers, and he never stopped kissing her. He pulled her T-shirt up and over her head and trailed kisses down her neck and over her collarbone. He traced the ridge of her bra and over the swell of her breast with his tongue. He planted soft, wet kisses on her breast as he undid her bra and slid it down her arms and away. Her fingers dove through his hair and drew him down to her breast. When he took her straining nipple into his mouth, she arched in to him and held him to her as a soft moan escaped her throat.

Her hands ran down the back of his neck and over his shoulders. Her nails dug into his back muscles and down his spine. Her hands roamed back up, bringing his sweater with them, and she pulled it off over his head. He took the opportunity to give her other breast equal attention and traced a line from the underside up her breast to her nipple. He licked the tip and took it into his mouth, sucking hard and making her moan.

His hands moved over her body, leaving a trail of heat behind. His mouth, warm and wet on her skin, sent ripples of pleasure throughout her system. Tremors rolled across her bones as his hand smoothed over her stomach and his fingertips skimmed under the edge of her jeans. The button gave way and the zipper slid down with a quick motion of his nimble fingers. His hand dipped inside, his fingertips barely brushed against her sensitive skin. She pressed her hips up to bring his fingers where she most wanted them, but he retreated, and she felt the deep loss. His mouth trailed kisses down her stomach to her navel, moved lower, and so did her jeans until they landed across the floor somewhere. When his hot breath washed over the sensitive skin between her thighs, she realized her panties had gone the way of her jeans.

His hand moved down her thigh and over her calf. Every stroke and brush of his fingertips sent fire burning through her system. She wanted more. She needed to feel the weight of him on her and feel him move inside of her. His hand slid back up her leg and pushed her thigh out, allowing him better access. His fingers traversed her sensitive skin before one finger slid into her and she arched up to meet the intimate caress. The building heat low in her belly took on a new and explosive quality. He retreated and pushed back into her and that heat expanded even more.

Dylan leaned up on an elbow, his gaze roaming over her naked body. "God, you're beautiful." Her golden skin glowed from being in the sun. Her dark hair spread around her shoulders and trailed over the floor. Her arms reached out to him. She never stopped touching him. The feel of her work-worn hands was exhilarating. Gentle at first, then those lovely fingers of hers dug into his muscles to massage and coax him closer.

He leaned down and kissed her belly where she'd carried his child. Her soft, smooth skin tasted as sweet as honey.

His fingers caressed the slick folds between her spread thighs. So hot and wet for him, he throbbed with the need to bury himself deep inside her. His erection pressed to the fly of his jeans, and he wanted to strip and thrust into her to ease the ache in his body. In his heart.

"I've missed you so damn much."

He needed to take his time. He owed her that much. Their first time together had been anything but slow and sweet, stuffed into the backseat of his car. Here, he had room to roam her body and leisurely stroke and touch every inch of her. He meant to do just that.

"You're so sweet, Jess. I don't want to hurt you."

"You won't. It's been a long time, too long. Dylan, please. I need you."

He pressed two fingers into her and felt her give and shatter all at the same time. He moved up and took her mouth as she pulled him to her. She reached between them and undid his jeans, slipping her hand inside to cup him in her palm. She rubbed her hand up the length of his hard shaft, and he almost lost control. He pulled her hand away and tore off his jeans while her hands, those ever-moving and roaming hands, ran over his back and hips.

"Dylan, please. I want you now."

He snagged his discarded jeans and dug out a condom from his pocket. No way he forgot to protect her this time. He'd love another chance at being a father to their baby, but that required planning. They needed time together, and he had every intention of using that time wisely to rebuild what they'd lost.

Cradled between her thighs, he leaned down and took her mouth. His tongue slid over hers as he thrust into her hard and deep. She bent her knees up and slid her hands over his hips and pulled him deeper, making him feel— full, complete in a way he couldn't describe. He belonged right here, in her arms always. His mind emptied of all the anger and pain he'd felt for weeks. Replaced by so much love for her, it was a wonder he didn't burst from loving her.

Finally, the past and present converged. They were right where they belonged. Together.

She felt the subtle change in him. Opening her eyes, she gazed up at him as the fire cast a soft orange glow over his skin. Something magical filled his eyes. Love. Love for her like she'd never seen in anyone else's eyes. He wrapped one arm around her shoulders and the other hand gripped her thigh and pulled her closer.

His lips pressed soft kisses into her neck. She gave herself over to him, moving her hips to the rhythm he set, the heat building between them until she couldn't hold back. His breath came out heavily against her throat, and he called her name. She rocketed over the edge with him and stars exploded behind her eyelids as she gave into love completely.

She hadn't stopped trembling when the world tilted and she landed on top of Dylan, lying down his full length. Her head rested on his chest, his heart thundered beneath her ear.

"God, woman. I think you tried to kill me."

"I'm not entirely sure this isn't heaven."

He smiled and followed the line of her spine with his fingertips. She laughed and squirmed and it felt good to giggle. She sank her teeth into his chest and used her tongue and lips to sooth the small hurt.

"For a woman with limited experience at love play, you're doing a good job of driving me crazy." He cupped her bottom and pressed her hips down to his and let her feel him growing hard against her belly.

She circled her hips to tease him. He adjusted his back against the carpet again and she smiled and playfully nipped at his chin.

"Do you think we might actually make love in a bed one of these days?" Her husky voice didn't mask the teasing tone.

"Oh, I don't know. We seem to do just fine in cars and on the floor. Eventually, we'll make it to a bed."

"The car was difficult to maneuver. I couldn't touch you like I wanted," she confessed.

"You did just fine tonight, honey. You're doing fine right now."

Unable to help herself, she never stopped touching him. Strong muscles bunched beneath her hands as she rubbed up his arms and over his chest.

"We could try the whole car thing again," she teased.

"Your Porsche might be a little cramped."

"The Mustang is in the garage. I don't drive it often, but it's one of my favorite cars."

He leaned up and stared down at her, resting her chin on his chest. "Are you telling me you have my old Mustang in your garage?"

"It came up for sale last year. I drove through town and saw it with a FOR SALE sign. I contacted the old guy who owned it and bought it. I took it to a garage and had them fix it up. It's not the car you remember. It's better. I had it repainted. Cherry red with black racing stripes. Greg calls it a hot rod. He's lusted after it ever since I brought it home in mint condition."

"How did I get so lucky to find a woman who loves muscle cars?"

"I love *that* car. We can take it to see Hope tomorrow. I think it would be appropriate."

He couldn't help it. He kissed her softly on the lips and held her to him and softly kissed her again and again. "I love you." He couldn't get over how romantic she could be. He'd never have guessed she'd have so much sentiment when she endured so much heartache. She cherished the good things in her life because she'd had so much bad. She gave up the bad and hoarded the good.

He sat up with her, settling her in his lap. He picked her up and carried her to the stairs.

"Where are we going?"

"Upstairs to bed. I'm not finished with you yet."

"Don't you have to go home to Will?"

"He's with Lorena tonight. I'm staying with you. I have a lot of making up for lost time to do." He kissed her all the way up the stairs and loved and worshipped her long into the night.

Chapter Thirty-Two

THE MORNING AFTER their first night back together, they went to the cemetery as planned. Dylan drove the Mustang with her sitting quietly beside him. He held her hand, keeping the intimate connection between them. They placed flowers on their daughter's grave and stood at her marker for a long time, Dylan brushing his fingers softly through her hair. Both silently said a prayer for Hope, letting her know her parents were there. Dylan held Jessie's hand in quiet comfort. Before they left, he finally got to tell Hope how he felt, softly whispering, "I love you, sweetheart. I'm sorry I wasn't there for you. I promise I'll take care of your mother always." He kissed his two fingers and pressed them to her name etched in stone.

From that day on, she and Dylan committed themselves to each other. They spent every weekend at her home. For three months, every Friday night he and Will showed up for dinner, and they'd spend every moment together until Dylan and Will left again on Sunday evening. During the week, she and Dylan both worked and kept in touch. Dylan came by her work site and ate lunch with her. She still found sweet notes on her car in parking lots and flowers on her doorstep. In every little way, he let her know that although they weren't together every night, he thought of her every day.

She worried about him and the work he did. He'd had to break up a few fights and stop some hairy domestic violence incidents. He always reassured her he was trained for his job and always careful. He reminded her he had a lot to live for, namely her and Will. Still, the gun strapped to his side constantly reminded her something could happen to him. The calls in the middle of the night asking him to come and help with a situation always put her on edge. He always came back in one piece, if a little banged up on occasion. She couldn't help the worry. She loved him.

They'd talked about getting married. Both of them threw it into casual conversation, but they never made the commitment to move forward. She stalled, needing to be sure their new relationship carried them through the next fifty years. She told him time and again when she married him, it would be for life. He'd smile and tell her that's all he wanted, a lifetime with her.

In little ways, she gave into the idea and the fear. Will's furniture had been completed and ready for Dylan to take home. Instead, one weekend he and Will showed up and she'd led them upstairs to one of the bedrooms. She'd painted it during the week a soft wheat color and put Will's new furniture in the room. She got him a red-bandana comforter and a wrought-iron lamp with a cowboy riding a bucking bronco. She made a toy chest for him to match his bedroom set. Each week when he came, more and more of his toys ended up staying in the chest. She bought him a few new ones. He was in heaven each time he came to stay and found a new toy on his bed. Dylan just smiled and told her she spoiled him. She told him too bad, and they'd laugh.

More and more often, Will slipped and called her Mommy. She and Dylan had agreed not to encourage him until they officially decided to get married. Life for them became a routine, one she liked. Lately, she grew more and more restless when they were gone during the week. The nights dragged with wanting Dylan in her arms, in her bed, with her always.

She wanted to ask Dylan to come and live with her.

He wanted the whole deal, marriage and more babies. The babies worried her. She didn't want to lose another child, but she was even more afraid of not having Dylan and Will. She wanted more babies, and in the last week, she'd simply taken the condom out of Dylan's hand and put it back on the nightstand. He never said a word. That cocky half grin of his said it all. He wanted another baby with her and willingly complied with her silent request.

Only a few weeks from completing the housing development, she planned a celebratory barbeque in the nearly finished park.

Today, she'd taken the day off to take care of Dylan's birthday present. His birthday was a few days away and she wanted to make him something special. She drove to his office to pick up Will so he could help with her special project. It would be the first time she had Will to herself, and she looked forward to having him for the day. Dylan would join them for dinner and stay the weekend as usual.

She pulled into the sheriff's office parking lot, but didn't see Dylan's car. She'd either beaten him to the office, or he was out on a call.

Several of the other officers waved to her as she came into the office. Dylan's secretary, Lynn, typed furiously at her desk and she walked over.

"Hey, Lynn. Is Dylan out on a call?"

"Hi, honey. Yeah, he'll be back soon."

Jessie spotted Will with one of the officers. He waved at her and said, "Hi, Mommy." She smiled, her heart tripping a bit, and waved back.

"That little munchkin is so excited about spending the day with you," Lynn said cheerily.

"I'm looking forward to it myself."

"You did a real kind thing, speaking to Mrs. Dobbs, trying to help her after her husband knocked her around again."

"Dylan thought she might relate to me better than him."

"She said you helped her. She's staying with her sister over in the next town and might actually divorce her husband this time."

"Is he still in jail?"

"He gets out in a few days. I hope she goes through with the divorce for her own good. Dylan asked Owen to talk to her about signing the divorce papers."

"After what happened with Owen and Claire and the last divorce case he handled with domestic abuse, I'm surprised he'd agree. Still, Mrs. Dobbs is a nice woman. I hate to think of her staying with her husband, but it's hard to break out of the mindset you caused the abuse somehow."

Jessie looked at Will and thought about all she'd endured to get to this point. It hadn't been an easy road, but she'd worked hard to make a good life for herself. Mrs. Dobbs had a long, hard road ahead of her.

"She's strong. She can make it, and with help from her sister, she'll do just fine. The first step is the hardest. It's hard to break out of what you know and try something new," Jessie explained.

Which made her think of marrying Dylan. So easy to try something new when it's what you wanted more than anything.

"You did it. You've become a huge success. Those fancy houses you built are beautiful. I hear you designed a few of them yourself."

"Thanks. I did." Proud of herself, it was nice to have someone else recognize what she'd overcome and her accomplishments. "I made a life for myself because I had John Langley and his son, Greg, to help me. I was lucky."

"I think Sheriff Dylan is the lucky one. The man has been downright happy since the two of you started seeing each other again. I know you all are trying to keep things quiet, but it's nice to see the two of you together." Lynn beamed an approving smile.

Dylan and Will made her happy. What was she waiting for? She needed to talk to Dylan about getting married. She'd surprise him and bring it up first this time. Tonight. No more stalling and waiting for something they already shared. Love.

"Did Dylan want me to wait for him before I take Will?"

"I'm not sure. He said you'd be here soon and were spending the day with Will. He's been gone for a while now. Why don't you just take him? I'll tell the sheriff Will's with you. He can call you if he needs you."

"Okay. I'd really like to get back and get started. Will and I are making Dylan a birthday present."

"I'll bet he'll like anything you make. I have my eye on a round side table over in your store."

"Oh, yeah. Tell Andrea I said you can have it at a thirty percent discount."

"You mean it?"

"Absolutely. You take such good care of Dylan when he's here. You always make sure he gets out on time on Fridays. I appreciate it."

"It's no trouble. You young people need time together."

Jessie touched Lynn's hand lightly in affection and headed over to pick up Will. He sat, looking through a book of mug shots. "Come on, you little hoodlum, we have work to do." She scooped him up and blew kisses on his neck and made him laugh. She grabbed his backpack and car seat before walking out the door. They drove to her house and went straight into her barn. Will loved being out there with her.

Boys and power tools, she thought with a chuckle. Today, he'd get to help her use some of them to make a surprise for Dylan.

Chapter Thirty-Three

JESSIE THOUGHT IT sweet Will felt at home. He went from room to room and played with his things. She'd put several snacks on a low shelf in the pantry for him so he could help himself, which he did often.

Dylan missed dinner with them. Will asked her half a dozen times when his father would be home. She'd tried calling Dylan, but his cell went straight to voicemail. She left him several messages. Something wasn't right. Why didn't he call her back?

"Will, do you want ice cream while we wait for your dad to get here?"

"No. I want Daddy. Where is he?"

No ice cream. Not a good sign. He yawned hugely on the sofa where they watched TV. He had a blanket over him and his little face rested on her thigh. She absently stroked his hair, worried too about Dylan's silence and absence. He usually called to let her know if he had to work late. It wasn't like him not to call, especially since she had Will. Something tingled up her spine, warning her something was wrong. All of a sudden, that feeling she'd had for hours grew beyond her capacity to hold it down. She picked up the cordless phone from beside her and called his office.

"Oh thank God, Lynn. I've called twice and couldn't get through. I'm trying to find Dylan."

"Didn't they call you? I thought the hospital or one of the deputies would have called you by now. Oh, honey, I'm sorry."

"Hospital? Why would the hospital call me? Where's Dylan?"

"I'm so sorry, honey. He's been in an accident. He was chasing down a drunk driver who decided to take a high-speed joyride. Dylan lost control of his car and crashed into a guardrail, and then a light pole."

"Oh, no. No. Is he okay?"

"I'm not certain of his injuries. They took him to the hospital by ambulance just after three o'clock today."

"Three o'clock? That was almost four hours ago. I'm going down there."

Will climbed up on her lap and leaned against her with his head on her shoulder. Tears slipped down her face, and Will wiped her cheek with his palm.

"Don't cry, Mommy."

"It's okay, sweetheart. We're going to see Daddy."

"I've been trying to get out of here myself," Lynn went on. "This place has been a madhouse since the accident. Two deputies caught up with the suspect and brought him in. Another couple of deputies went to the hospital to be with Sheriff Dylan. I sent another to his parents' home to notify them."

"Why didn't you notify me?" she snapped.

"I'm sorry, I thought the hospital called you and things have been crazy here."

Lynn hadn't meant to leave Jessie out of the loop. Things happened and she'd done her best to keep the office in some semblance of order. It was an oversight Jessie hadn't been called, and one Jessie hoped never happened again. She'd make sure of it.

"There's only a few people who know Dylan and I are seeing each other," she said frantically. "I'm going down there. I'll see you whenever you can manage to get out of the office." She hung up and stood with Will still in her arms.

"Come on, buddy. We're going for a ride."

"Daddy got hurt?"

"Yes, honey. He did. He's in the hospital and we need to make sure he's okay."

"Will you kiss his owie better?"

"I'll kiss him a million times when I see him."

"Me too." Will held her tighter, and she hugged him close. Both of them needed the comfort.

She strapped Will into his car seat in the Porsche and peeled out of her driveway. He asked a hundred times as she drove if his father would be okay. She tried her best to reassure him. She just didn't know. She tried calling the hospital on her cell to get information. They wouldn't give her any because she wasn't family or his wife. She thought about calling back, lying and saying she was his wife, but she needed to concentrate on the road. She hoped the police didn't pull her over and give her a ticket for speeding. She couldn't afford the time it would take for them to issue the citation.

A couple of the sheriff department's cars sat parked in the emergency parking lot when she pulled in. She got Will out of his seat. Carrying him in front of her, she ran into the emergency room desperate to see Dylan.

"I'm looking for Sheriff Dylan McBride. They brought him in several hours ago. Can you tell me where he is and if he's okay?"

The nurse working the desk barely took the time to look at her before asking, "Are you family?"

"This is his son. I'm his girlfriend." She hated having to use that term. She'd much rather be his wife. No one could stand between her and Dylan then. The thought of losing him and never being his wife hit her hard.

"They took him upstairs to the third floor about twenty minutes ago. A couple of officers went up with him along with his parents."

"What is his condition?"

"I'm sorry, ma'am, I don't know. Check in with the nurse's station on three."

Jessie took off for the elevator. "Let's go find Daddy, Will."

Concerned and nervous, she didn't know what she'd find when she located Dylan. The elevator doors opened. Down the hall, the two officers entered the elevator at the other end of the hospital. She rushed to the nurse's station and waited while the nurse finished a phone call.

"I'm looking for Sheriff Dylan McBride. Is he here? Is he okay?"

Someone came up behind her, and she turned. "I'm Dr. Tanner. Are you the sheriff's wife?"

"No, she's not," Martha McBride snapped.

Dylan's mother exited one of the rooms a few doors down from the nurse's station.

"Is he okay? Is he hurt badly?"

Martha disregarded her concern and focused on Will. "What are you doing with Will?"

"Is Dylan okay? Please, just tell me if he's okay." Jessie walked to the room Martha exited. The doctor moved on to his next patient. Jessie's gut twisted. No one would tell her about Dylan.

Martha blocked the door. "Stop. Jessie, you can't go in there. Dylan needs to rest."

Jessie glared at the woman who cost her and Dylan so much. "Dylan and I have been seeing each other for more than three months. I love him and he loves me. I just want to see he's okay. Will wants to see his father."

"Come to Grandma, Will. I'll take you to see your dad."

Will clung even tighter to Jessie, burying his face in her neck. "Mommy, let's go see Daddy."

"We are, baby." Jessie took a step toward Martha, but she didn't move. Dylan's father, Robert, stepped into the hall and stood beside his wife, a wall, blocking her from entering the room. "Why are you doing this? I just want to make sure he's okay."

"He will be. Give us Will. *You* can go." Martha dismissed her.

"No. Dylan doesn't want you to have Will. I'm not leaving him with you when I don't know how Dylan is doing, or how long he'll be in the hospital. Just let me see him." Her heart pounded. She needed to get into that room and see for herself that he was okay. He needed her. She had to tell him how much she loved him.

Her heart thundered so hard in her chest that it echoed in her ears. The panic rose up and choked her.

Robert flagged down a nurse. "Please call security. This woman isn't family and refuses to release our grandson to us."

"Mr. McBride, don't do this. Dylan would want me here," she pleaded.

"The way I see it, it's because of you our son refuses to see us, or allow us to see our grandson. He treats his mother as if she doesn't exist."

"That's her fault, not mine. She kept your granddaughter from you, from Dylan."

"If she was our granddaughter," he accused.

His eyes betrayed the lie he just told. Easier to brush aside the truth than believe his wife did something so heinous. She could talk until blue in the face, but he refused to listen. They would never let her see Dylan. They'd moved him into a regular room, not the ICU. She had to believe that was a good sign. She'd come back later. No one would keep her and Will from him.

She turned on her heel and walked away, trying to think what to do next. Maybe she'd call Dylan's lawyer cousin, Owen. He'd know what to do. If nothing else, he'd get her into the room.

Both Martha and Robert yelled, "Come back here! You can't take Will." She ignored them and walked straight into the elevator with Will safe and secure in her arms.

"We'll come back and see Daddy in a little while," she assured him, hugging him close.

Will held on to her, his face buried in her neck. She tried to stop thinking all the horrible thoughts she conjured about Dylan lying in that hospital bed. Alone. She never even got a glimpse of him. She didn't know if he was just resting or seriously hurt. Sick to her stomach, she didn't want to leave, but she had to think of Will and take care of him. An all-out yelling match with Dylan's parents in front of Will would only make things worse.

She stepped off the elevator into the lobby. Several security and police officers waited by the double doors leading out of the emergency room. They turned to her, making her extremely nervous. They drew their guns, sending a lightning bolt of fear through her system. She held Will securely to her chest and tried to protect him with her arms.

"Hold it right there!" one of the officers yelled. "Put the boy down and walk toward me."

"What is this about? This is Sheriff McBride's son. He left him in my care today." Nothing but a misunderstanding— they'd check with Dylan, or his office. Everyone would tell him it was okay for Will to be with her.

"Put the boy down and step toward me," the officer repeated. They meant business. They wouldn't let her leave with Will. Resigned, brokenhearted, defeated, she knew what she had to do, but she hated feeling helpless to stop this. She hated even more putting Will through this. She loved him and would protect him with her life.

"Mommy, I want to stay with you." Will clung to her, trembling in her arms, scared of all the men with guns pointed at them.

"I have to put you down." She'd let him go to keep him safe, but it crushed her heart to do it.

His father was in the hospital, his grandparents made a scene upstairs, and now these officers trained their guns on them. She'd sort this out once the guns were put away.

The McBrides rushed down the hallway right toward the officers. Martha called out, "Stop her. Don't let her take my grandson."

"Will, honey, listen to me carefully. I want you to walk to that policeman right there." She chose the officer closest to her, who didn't have a weapon drawn. She bent to put Will down and kissed his temple. "I love you, honey. You'll be okay. They'll take you to see your Daddy."

Will went to the officer, but turned back to her, his eyes round, sad, and filled with unshed tears. She'd never forgive the McBrides for doing this to him and her. It broke her heart to see the little boy so sad and confused.

She dropped her purse to the floor and put her arms out from her sides. The officers rushed her, taking hold of her, pulling her arms behind her back and cuffing her. Resignation kicked in. She wouldn't get to see Dylan. Worse, Will watched them arrest her, tears streaming down his chubby cheeks. The cuffs bit into her wrists and she didn't feel anything but overwhelming anger and sadness. The officer handed Will over to his grandmother.

"Mommy! Mommy!" He held his arms out to her, screaming for her. Martha and Robert walked away with him and another officer. She vaguely heard the officer leading her out of the hospital say she was being charged with kidnapping before he read her her rights.

Her thoughts stayed with Will and Dylan.

I love you. Please be okay.

That phrase became her mantra as they drove her to jail and booked her for the kidnapping of Will McBride, the boy who should be her son. She decided then and there, as soon as she saw Dylan again, she'd demand they get married. She'd call Owen and find out how to adopt Will as her own. No one would keep her from Dylan or Will ever again.

Right now, his parents would direct his care. Dylan would want her there. He'd want her to take care of him.

This was the second time she'd been powerless to go up against Martha McBride. She wouldn't let this happen again.

Chapter Thirty-Four

"Sheriff Dylan. You have to wake up, Sheriff."

Dylan opened his eyes enough to see Lynn beside his bed. His parents had been there earlier. He heard them talking and ignored them. He wanted Jessie. He hadn't heard her or seen her the few times he'd woken up in the night. Why wasn't Jessie here with him? He needed to see her face. He hurt everywhere and knew if he could just see her, hold her hand, he'd feel better.

"Sheriff, you have to wake up. They arrested Jessie."

That terrible news came through the haze loud and clear. He opened his eyes wide. He squinted at the light and pain shot through his head due to the concussion. "What?" he croaked out, sounding funny, even to his own ears.

"Oh, thank God, Sheriff Dylan, you're awake."

"What about Jessie? Why isn't she here?"

"She came last night. No one called her when you got

hurt. She called the office looking for you, and I told her what happened. She came down here with Will."

"Slow down. Where is she? I haven't seen her."

"She's in jail. They arrested her."

Dylan had trouble following Lynn. His head hurt, but it got better the longer he stayed awake. "Why the hell did they arrest her?"

"For kidnapping Will."

He sat up and grabbed her wrist with his good hand. The other was strapped into a brace that went nearly to his elbow. "What do you mean, kidnapped Will? Where is Will?"

"He's with your parents. They had her arrested for kidnapping him. I tried to talk to the officers at the police station, but they won't budge. Your father has a lot of clout with the people of this town. They said your parents filed charges and insist she took Will against your and their wishes."

"That's crazy. You know I left Will with her."

"They won't listen to me, and with you lying in this hospital unconscious, they aren't likely to change their minds. Your parents have been here all night. I couldn't get to you. Will looks devastated."

"You saw him? He was here?"

"Your parents just took him away a few minutes ago. I understand Jessie had Will in her arms when they arrested her downstairs at gunpoint. It's all the hospital staff is talking about."

"They drew their guns on her and my son." He threw the covers off his legs and peeled the wires off his chest, setting off squealing alarms. He wore nothing but a hospital gown. "Find my clothes," he barked, taking a moment to settle his spinning head by pressing the heel of his hand to his left eye just under the stitched cut that ran across his forehead along his hairline.

This can't be happening.

He remembered Jessie telling him she never wanted to have someone she loved sick or hurt and her unable to do anything about it.

"Does she know what happened to me?"

"I told her you were in a car accident and you'd been hurt. I don't think she knows the details. I heard a nurse say your parents wouldn't let her in the room to see you." She handed him his clothes and turned her back so he could dress. "Are you sure you should leave? I mean, you could just make a call to the police department and get them to drop the charges against her. They'll let her out, and she can come here to you."

"She's been arrested and spent the night in jail. Do you think she's going to rush down here to see me when my parents are the ones who put her there? Hell, she's been there all night not knowing if I'm okay. She knows I didn't want my parents around Will, and she had to give him up to them last night. This is such a fucking mess." He tried to button his bloodstained shirt, but his swollen fingers didn't work. He gave up and decided to just leave it half-done.

A nurse came into the room to check on him and why the monitor wasn't registering his heartbeat any longer. "Sheriff, you have to get back into bed. You can't leave. You have a concussion."

"I'm leaving. I have to do something."

"No. You can't. I'm getting the doctor," she said and fled the room.

He stomped his feet into his boots and took his hat from Lynn. "Let's go."

Lynn took his arm and helped him to the elevator and her car. Unsteady on his feet, he leaned heavily on the older woman.

"This is too much," she said for the tenth time during the short drive to the police station. "I should take you back to the hospital. You look terrible."

"Drive," he ordered, refusing to let her turn around.

Dylan got out of the car and staggered before righting himself. Lynn held him around the waist. "Dylan, maybe this isn't such a good idea. You should be in bed."

"I agree. I'll get Jessie and she can take me to bed."

He managed to wink at her, even though he felt light-headed and groggy.

"You're fooling around now? Stop messing with me," Lynn scoffed.

"Better that than tearing a hole in someone." If his parents thought having Jessie arrested and taking Will would make him come around to their way of thinking, they had another think coming. Why would they do something this stupid and sure to piss him off?

"Well, you just keep your temper when we go in there, or they'll arrest you too."

"I'll be good. I just want her back."

"Well, let's go get her."

They walked up to the desk. "Where is Jessie Thompson being held?" he asked the Sergeant.

"You mean Langley?" At Dylan's nod, the officer said, "She's downstairs in a holding cell. You'll want to check with the lieutenant in charge of the case." The sergeant pointed to an office.

Dylan needed to get that Langley changed to McBride—fast.

He burst into the lieutenant's office, shoving the door open and letting it bounce off the wall.

"I'll have to call you back," the lieutenant told the person on the phone. He hung up and stared up at Dylan standing over his desk. "I planned to come and see you today. How're you feeling, Sheriff?"

"Like shit and getting worse the longer you hold my fiancée in a cell."

"Well, now. I had a hunch something didn't add up about her arrest. Your parents insisted the two of you weren't seeing each other and she took Will to get back at you for the baby she lost several years ago."

"That's a load of bullshit. She and I have been seeing each other for months. We lost our baby about eight years ago, but she doesn't have any hard feelings toward me. It's my mother we're both pissed at. My parents are just trying to keep us apart." God, he felt like a teenager again, having to explain every damn thing he did. "I've denied them access to Will over the last few months. They're angry at her because of it." He hated having to explain himself and his life to a fellow officer, but he didn't have a choice. He wanted Jessie out of jail. Now.

His mind didn't work as fast as he'd like, but something occurred to him. "Why didn't she call a lawyer and have him get her out of here?"

"She didn't ask for a lawyer, just wanted to know if you're all right. She said if you weren't here today to call Owen McBride. After that, she exercised her right to remain silent, and we took her to a holding cell downstairs. We checked with the hospital and gave her an update on you last night. After that, she said you'd clear everything up when you were able and she'd wait."

"She's just going to sit in a cell and wait for me?"

"That's what she said. I called the hospital this morning. They said you were still unconscious. I went down to see if she wanted to change her mind about the lawyer and told her you were still out cold. She hasn't slept. She's worried about you. She begged me to call and check on Will. I tried your parents earlier, but didn't get an answer."

"You need to let her out. Now. She didn't kidnap my son. I left him with her yesterday."

"He did," Lynn confirmed, trying to help. "She came to the station and picked Will up. The sheriff knew she had him. They've been seeing each other for months now."

Dylan wanted this to be over. He leaned heavily on the desk and got angrier by the minute. His head hurt, but his heart ached even more thinking of Jessie locked up and worried about him and Will.

The lieutenant picked up his phone and dialed. "This is Lieutenant Stowe. I'm sending Sheriff McBride downstairs to see Jessie Langley. We'll release her as soon as I get the paperwork together."

Dylan let out the breath he'd been holding and stood

up to his full height. He extended his hand to the lieutenant and they shook. "I can't thank you enough for not making this difficult."

"I couldn't imagine that woman stealing anyone's child. She was more concerned about him than herself. I'm sorry your boy had to see the officers arrest her. I understand your son screamed for her all the way down the hall when your parents took him away. He yelled for his mommy. The officers suspected something wasn't right when they heard him calling her that."

"He loves her very much. He wants her to be his mother, and I'm doing my best to make that happen."

"This wouldn't have happened if she were your wife. She'd have rights then."

"Don't I know it." Dylan thanked him again and headed downstairs while he left Lynn to get the paperwork sorted out.

Several of the officers he knew said hello and told him he looked like hell. He knew it and felt it. When he got downstairs to the holding cells, a woman officer greeted him and led him down a hallway, her keys clinking against her thigh as she walked.

"She's down here, Sheriff. She didn't eat this morning, and she's asked about you every chance she gets."

He came to the cell where Jessie sat on a cot with her knees pulled up and her chin resting on them. Her arms were wrapped around her legs, her eyes shadowed and half-closed, her shoulders slumped. Completely wiped out, she stared blankly at the wall.

"Jess, honey." The words barely made it past his lips.

He choked up seeing her this way. When she lifted her head and found him with wide eyes brimming immediately with tears, he couldn't get past the cell door fast enough to get to her. He dropped on his knees beside her and gathered her into his arms, ignoring the pain radiating through his body.

"I'm so sorry you had to be here. They're going to let you out in a few minutes. I cleared it all up with the lieutenant."

She pulled back from him and ran her fingertips over the cut on his head and the scrapes and bruises. She kissed each one softly and took his hurt arm and kissed each of his fingers. "Are you okay? Are you really all right?"

"I am now. Lynn came and broke me out of the hospital. I had no idea what happened to you."

"It doesn't matter. Where's Will?"

"He's with my parents still. I haven't seen them. I came straight here to get you."

"You should have gotten Will first. Oh, Dylan, you should have seen him. He was so scared. Your parents wouldn't let me take him in to see you. We didn't know how badly you'd been hurt, and then the police took me away from him."

"We'll go and get him right after I get you out of here."

His eyes fluttered and he had a hard time keeping them open. He kept squinting and held himself rigid to stop the pain.

"Did the doctor say you could leave the hospital?" she asked, brushing her fingers through his hair at his temple.

"He doesn't know I left. Lynn told me you'd been

arrested for kidnapping Will and I got here as fast as I could."

"Dylan. You need to be in the hospital. You have a concussion."

"I only need you." He gathered her as close as he could get her. "I'm sorry they wouldn't let you see me. I can only imagine how scared you were I'd been seriously injured."

"You were seriously injured."

"Yeah, and the only medicine I need is you, and they wouldn't let you see me."

"About that." She held his face in her hands, careful not to press on any of the bruises or scrapes. "Marry me, Dylan McBride. I want to be your wife. I don't want anything to ever happen to you again, but if it does, I want to be the one there to help you. Marry me because I love you and I never want to be separated from you ever again."

He kissed her and held her tight. She'd just answered every dream he ever had. "When?"

"As soon as possible. Today. Tomorrow. I don't care as long as it's soon. I want you and Will to move in with me. His room is all ready and you can bring all your stuff, and we'll be a family. I think we could all be comfortable in the house together. I always wanted it to be a home. It's not home unless you and Will are in it."

Dylan never answered. The officer arrived, saying, "Sheriff, I'll escort you and Miss Langley upstairs. The paperwork is ready, and she's free to go. The lieutenant wants to discuss the charges and your parents." Dylan sighed, but nodded his agreement.

They left the cell and followed the officer upstairs.

Dylan never took his arm from around her. He didn't want to let her go and hated to admit it, but today, he needed to lean on her too. Physically he wasn't all there, but more so, he mentally needed to lean on her. She'd trusted him to come and get her when he could, and she'd put Will first. She expected him to go to Will and take him away from his parents before he came for her. Nothing could have made him love her more than knowing she trusted him again.

She'd been so sweet and earnest about getting married as soon as possible. What she didn't know was that for weeks, he'd had everything ready for when the time was right.

He couldn't think of a better birthday present than Jessie becoming his wife.

Chapter Thirty-Five

DYLAN MARVELED AT the way Lynn took care of getting the local police to move quickly on the paperwork. She drove them back to the hospital where Jessie parked her car. Jessie insisted he see the doctor before going home. Lucky for him, the doctor released him with a prescription for some pain medication and orders that he rest for a couple of days.

The ordeal with his parents couldn't be overlooked. Dylan pounded on their front door, then turned back to see Jessie leaning against the hood of her car watching him. Worried and upset, he wanted to go to her, wrap her in his arms, and tell her everything was all right. But first, he'd have to make it all right, and that meant finishing this with his parents.

Will's little feet pounded on the floor in the entry hall as he ran to the door. Dylan's heart skipped a beat. The wait for the door to open took too long. He needed to grab hold of his son and hug him.

The door finally opened, and his father stood in the doorway, Will beside him.

"Daddy."

Dylan scooped him up and held him close despite the pain it caused his sprained wrist and aching body. He felt a weight lift from his shoulders just having Will close and out of his parents' grasp. "Hey buddy. I missed you."

"They took Mommy away." Will's bottom lip trembled.

"I know." Dylan's voice held a deadly edge, but he held back the anger roiling inside him for his son's sake. "I got her back. She's right over there. Go see her. She needs one of your special hugs real bad."

Dylan set his son down. He ran like the wind into Jessie's open arms. Tears trickled down Jessie's cheeks. She held Will close, her face turned into his neck. Every one of her tears tore at Dylan's heart and made him rage against his parents for putting her through all this in the first place. And so he turned to his father. His mother stood just behind him to his left.

"Dylan . . ." his father began.

"Don't. I don't want to hear anything you have to say." He swallowed hard. He couldn't believe it had come to this. "You had the woman I love, the woman I'm going to marry and spend the rest of my life with, the woman who gave birth to your granddaughter, arrested. In front of Will. At gunpoint."

"We were only looking out for your and Will's best interests."

"Bullshit." Dylan had never sworn in front of his parents, and their faces reflected their shock at his outburst.

"If you cared about my happiness at all, you'd know that I'm only happy, only whole, when I'm with her. She's everything to me. But you couldn't set aside your petty dislike for her for my sake, or Will's, because she's what we want."

"She's only going to hurt you," his mother said, the corners of her mouth dipping into a deep frown.

"No. She won't. She's just not capable of it. But you are. You've hurt me for the last time."

"Come inside," his father coaxed. "You should sit down, take it easy, and we'll talk about this."

"There's nothing left to say. Maybe someday I'll find a way to forgive you for what you've done, but I'll never forget. Stay away from me and my family." God, it felt good to know Jessie and Will and the babies to come would be his family, everything he'd ever dreamed of having. "If you don't, I'll file for a restraining order. Push me, and I'll arrest you for filing false charges against Jessie. As it is, I'm the only reason you aren't in jail right now."

His mother gasped.

"That's the last favor I'll ever do for you," he said, meaning every word.

"Will is our grandson. You can't take him away from us," his mother pleaded.

"You kept me from my daughter," he snapped. "After everything that's happened, that's the one thing I'll never forgive. I'm not a vindictive person, and it pisses me off that you've pushed me to this, but you will stay away from Will and whatever children Jessie and I have in the future."

"Dylan, son, you can't mean this," his father pleaded.

"I mean every word. You sided with her." He pointed an accusing finger at his mother. "You took her word for everything. She didn't want my daughter as her grandchild. Why would you want any I have in the future?"

"Dylan, please," his mother said, the weight of his words and the lonely future they'd face finally sinking in with her.

Nothing else to say. They'd turned their back on Hope, kept him from his daughter and Jessie, and now Dylan was going to hold on to his family, expand it with whatever children Jessie gave him, and build a life with them.

He turned his back on his past and walked down the driveway to his future and Jessie's open arms. She knew how hard it was for him to walk away from a life and family he'd thought he'd known. He buried his face in her neck, took in the love and warmth she offered, and left his parents' home for the last time.

The sun glared through the windshield. Dylan had to put a hand over his brow to keep the worst of the glare from his eyes as a headache pounded through his brain. Jessie sat quiet beside him and drove.

"Let's stop by my place and pack up some things for me and Will. We're moving in with you this afternoon." His tone didn't leave any room for argument. Jessie gave him a soft smile and made the next left toward his house. Her easy acceptance helped ease some of the strain after his confrontation with his parents.

Efficient as ever, Jessie helped them pack his truck in record time, making sure he didn't do even a quarter of the work. They stopped off for fast food and ate in the truck on the ride to Jessie's house. Finally home, they walked into their house together as a family.

"I need to make a few calls," Dylan said.

Jessie lugged in the hastily packed bags from the car, because he couldn't, and she wouldn't allow it with his injuries.

"Dylan, honey, please go upstairs and rest."

The warmth and caring in her eyes seeped through his skin and straight into his heart.

"Take Will up and get him settled in his room. He's exhausted, so he'll probably fall right to sleep. I'll be up after I take care of some business," Dylan promised.

His whole body ached with exhaustion. He trudged up the stairs to the master bedroom nearly an hour later. Jessie was there, putting his clothes into a dresser drawer.

"Finished with your calls?"

"All set." He hoped he'd covered all his bases. He had a surprise for Jessie and with his head aching and foggy, he hoped he hadn't forgotten anything important. He didn't want to ever disappoint her.

She closed the drawer and came to him then, taking his face in her hands. "You need to sleep."

"Come to bed with me." His words came out a hoarse plea.

Her hands slid down his chest, undoing buttons as she went. She spread his shirt wide and carefully helped him out of it. He let her undress him, her hands smoothing over his skin. He sat on the edge of the bed and she pushed his pants down his legs before she took off his boots, socks, and jeans. She tucked him into bed before standing beside him, his eyes roaming over every inch of her as she stripped. His whole body warmed and grew tight. So beautiful, he wanted to sink into her warmth, but knew he didn't have the strength. She slid under the covers beside him and took him into her arms. With his cheek pressed to her bare breast, so soft and welcoming, he exhaled and let go of the last of the tension knotting his muscles.

Groggy, he slid one hand up her thigh, over her hip and up her ribcage to cup her other breast in one long, hot caress. "I want to make love to you," he told her, knowing she'd understand he didn't have the strength right now.

"Shh. Sleep, I'm here."

Dylan fell asleep in her arms. Jessie stroked his hair and lay along his side in their bed. He woke the next morning with the sun shining on his face. He reached out for Jessie and came up with only a handful of cold sheets. Just after eight o'clock, according to the bedside clock, she was probably downstairs with Will.

Will laughed and Jessie joined in. Dylan sat up in bed carefully, relieved his head didn't pound and throb anymore, but settled into a dull ache. Naked, he grabbed his jeans from the chair Jessie had thrown them over last night. Pulling them on, barefoot and shirtless, he went looking for Will and Jessie. Surprisingly, he found them on the stairs. More specifically, sliding down the sides of the stairs. It hit him then why she'd built the stairs so wide and put a slanting platform on each side of the staircase. An odd setup, but the perfect indoor slide. She and

Will ran back up and took their positions. Will counted to three and down they went, laughing all the way. Will won, only because Jessie slowed herself down, and he raised his hands and yelled with victory.

"Shh. Your father is still sleeping."

"No, he's not," Dylan said.

Jessie glanced up the stairs at Dylan and a bolt of lust hit her low in her gut. So handsome, his bare chest and wide shoulders set off little fireworks in her belly. He sauntered down the steps, his gaze locked with hers, that cocky half grin on his face. He stopped inches away, and she put her hand over his heart and leaned up and kissed him good morning. She dipped her head and planted several soft kisses along the bruise from his shoulder and down across his ribs from the seatbelt that locked against his chest during the crash.

"Mmm. This is the first Sunday in a long time I woke up and didn't dread the day because I have to leave you tonight. This is the first day of the rest of our lives together."

"I love the sound of that, and you. I'm so glad you're okay. Happy birthday, Dylan."

"It's going to be," he said cryptically. They both looked down at Will with his arms wrapped around her and Dylan's legs, hugging them together and grinning up at them.

"Mommy made breakfast. We have a present. I helped. I got to use the tools."

"You did, huh. Okay. Breakfast it is. Then, we have a big day ahead of us."

"What do you mean?" Jessie asked, suspicious. "You need to rest and recover."

"I need you more." He took her hand and brought it to his lips. "You'll see. I have a surprise for you. I hope you like it."

"But, it's *your* birthday."

"Doesn't that mean I get to do whatever I want today?"

"I guess so." She wondered what he was up to, especially when that cocky grin spread across his handsome face. She was glad to see it. He'd slept so deeply last night, she worried he wasn't getting better. Today, his eyes were clear and bright, a healthy glow brightened his skin, despite the bruises and cuts.

"Good. I'm glad we agree. Now, what's for breakfast? I'm starving."

She smiled and led him into the kitchen. She made him sit at the breakfast bar while she got him his coffee and made him a big stack of pancakes. Will, who'd already eaten, had another pancake with his father and watched the wrapped present like it would grow legs and walk away.

She sat next to Dylan while they ate, unable to stop touching him. They'd had several conversations about his job and the dangers he faced. She assured him she understood his need to help others, but his accident brought it home he could be hurt at any time. Life with him would never be boring and would require a lot of faith and trust in him. She was willing to give him both and so much more.

After the breakfast dishes were cleared, she sat down with Dylan and Will again. "Open your gift," she told him with a sheepish grin.

He carefully ripped away the paper and saw the lid of a box. His face lit up when he pulled out the wooden box she'd made for him. He set it in front of him and leaned over to kiss her.

"It's beautiful, Jess."

"It's made from oak. Strong, sturdy, enduring, like you."

He smoothed his hands over the lid. It had a raised edge, but she'd sanded it smooth as glass.

"Open it. Open it. Look inside." Will bounced on his seat next to his dad and pulled on his arm.

"Okay. Okay. Calm down." He opened the lid, revealing multiple sections inside the box. Beyond amazed, he stared at Will's name carved into the lid and above it, a perfect outline of his little hand. It appeared so lifelike he traced his fingers over Will's carved print. Next to Will's hand and name, Jessie included Hope's name and a perfect carving of her footprint. He found himself tracing his fingertips over the impression of her tiny toes.

"Jessie, how did you do this?"

"I helped," Will announced proudly.

"Yes, honey. You helped me a lot. I made an outline of Will's hand and traced it onto the wood. Then, I carved it out to look like his real hand. Hope's footprint I took from her footprint card the hospital made when she was born. That's how tiny her little foot was with her little toes. I wish I had one of her hand. It would have been sweet to have both their hands. Will's foot was too big for the cover. She had pretty hands," Jessie said with a touch of sadness in her voice.

"It's beautiful. I love it, Jess. Thank you."

"There's more. There's more. See?" Will pointed inside the box.

"I see." He smiled to his son and ruffled his hair. Nothing like a child's excitement about opening gifts, even when they were for someone else.

One part of the sectioned-off box could hold several watches. Jessie had bought him a really nice stainless steel watch. "Wow, Jess. It's got all the bells and whistles, perfect to wear all the time." He pulled it off and noticed the morning was getting away from him. He had a lot planned and needed to get moving, so everything would run on time.

"It's inscribed on the back," Jessie said.

He turned the watch over and read the engraving. *We'll never lose another second.*

He didn't know what to say. They had lost more time together. Again, because of his mother, and this time his father participated. That would all end tonight. He'd ensure no one kept her from him ever again.

He pulled her off her seat and between his legs. He took her mouth and held her face with the watch pressed between her cheek and his hand. Her breasts pressed against his bare chest and he wanted to take her upstairs and make love to her. He settled for kissing her socks off. He pulled away and rested his hand on her chest, feeling her heart thunder under his palm. "Never again. We'll be together always." He kissed her forehead, released her, and turned to his son. "And you, my little man. I love my presents. You're the best."

"Mommy helped me carve my name. She held my hand and the chisel and we did it together."

"It's perfect."

"Mommy helped me spell my name."

"You did a great job. Now, I have another job for you, and we need Mommy to cooperate with us by not asking lots of questions."

"What are you up to? You've got mischief written all over your face," she said, grinning.

"I have something special planned. Will you go out to the barn and, I don't know, do something for a little while. I have to get a few things set up."

She took his injured arm in her hands and kissed his swollen fingers again. "I'll be in the barn. Do you want me to take Will?"

"No. He's my accomplice."

She laughed and his gut tightened at the lighthearted sound.

"I like seeing you like this," she said. The bright smile on her face did his heart good after what his parents did and the night she spent in jail worried about him.

She cupped his face in her warm hands, kissed him quickly, and left him and Will to conspire against her.

Chapter Thirty-Six

JESSIE SMILED TO herself, thinking of Dylan, his eyes dancing with mischief. He'd practically bounced on the balls of his feet when he sent her out to the barn. He didn't say how long she had to stay here. Not that it mattered. She had a lot of things to work on and had even finished a couple pieces already. She decided to use the time to start on a new idea she had for a side table for a bed or sofa.

She ran the wood through the table saw, sawdust spewing out the bottom onto her shoes. She flipped the switch to turn the blade off and stepped back and right into Dylan. He'd showered and changed. She glanced at her watch, surprised she'd worked for a couple hours.

"Hey," she said.

"Hey, yourself. You did all this in two hours?"

"Did you think I'd just kick back and wait?"

"I didn't think you'd build an entire table from scratch."

"Well, see, there are still a few things you need to learn about me. I'm not good at doing nothing. Unless I want to," she qualified.

He shook his head. "Come with me. I have something else I want you to do."

"Are you kicking me off my property altogether?"

"No. I want you to go and get ready for something special. I have everything for you to wear upstairs." He ushered her into the house and pushed her toward the stairs. "Do your hair and makeup. This is a very special occasion."

People worked in her kitchen, wearing black slacks and white coats, fixing trays of food. "Caterers? What's going on?"

"Just ignore them. You don't see them, or anything else. Go upstairs and do yourself up all pretty."

"Are you kidding me? What's going on? Dinner isn't for hours."

"This is different. You'll see."

She took another look at the people milling around in her kitchen. Important enough for him to risk her wrath by ordering her around, Dylan swatted her on the butt and pointed his finger up the stairs. She headed up to do what he asked. She hated to disappoint him on his birthday. If he wanted her to fix herself up for something special, she'd go along.

She went into her room and found a garment bag hanging on the door to the bathroom. A shoebox sat on the floor. She opened the shoebox and gaped at the jeweled-strap high heels. They sparkled beautifully. She unzipped the garment bag and found a beautiful strapless white gown inside and gasped. "He didn't."

Excitement made her smile so big her cheeks hurt.

She came out of the bathroom a half hour later with her makeup done. She put her hair up on the sides and let the rest fall down her back in thick waves. A couple of crystal-encrusted combs held her hair up. They sparkled like stars in her dark hair. The simple but elegant style complemented the dress.

Time for the moment of truth, she slipped the dress from the hanger and tried it on, pleased to see it fit perfectly. The white dress fit tight across her breasts and dropped to her feet. Soft, see-through material mirrored the dress beneath and had small pearls and crystals sewn in randomly. She felt like a princess. Once the shoes were on and she studied herself in the mirror, she held back tears. The dress, the shoes, everything was perfect. She felt beautiful. She couldn't wait to show Dylan.

She descended the stairs. Dylan and Will stood at the bottom. Both dressed in gray suits with red ties, absolutely handsome. She beamed a smile at them as they smiled up at her. She reached the bottom and they both kneeled in front of her holding up black velvet jewelry boxes. She caught her breath and held her hand over her gaping mouth. Beyond beautiful, Dylan had to swallow hard when he caught sight of her coming down the stairs. His cousins' wives, Rain and Claire, picked out the perfect dress and shoes. He'd called in reinforcements last evening and begged for their help. They'd come through big-time, not only for him, but for Jessie. A beautiful bride, and from the look in her eyes, she felt it.

"Jessie Thompson, will you marry me and be my wife?" He opened the box and revealed the diamond ring he'd bought her weeks ago.

Will bounced on his feet beside him excited to finally have a real mom. Dylan felt his enthusiasm, too.

"Mommy," Will began, "will you be my mommy?"

He opened his box just like Dylan showed him, revealing the necklace inside. Then, he looked to Dylan to make sure he'd said and done everything just right. Dylan brushed his hand over Will's head, and Will smiled hugely at him and Jessie.

Her eyes glassed over, Jessie pressed her fisted hands to her chest to still her pounding heart. Her tough guy with a touch of poetry, he'd pulled off the best surprise.

"You said as soon as possible. This was the best I could do in about twelve hours."

That cocky grin again. Staring down at him and Will, this was perfect. Everything she needed.

"Yes, I'll marry you." She ran her hand over his cheek and turned to Will. "Yes, I'll be your mommy. Nothing would make me happier than for all of us to be a family."

"Then come out back and let's get married." He stood and slid the ring onto her finger, kissing her knuckle to seal it in place. She held her hand in front of her and let the diamonds catch the light. He didn't know what sparkled more: her eyes with delight, or the diamonds. He took the necklace from Will and went behind her and draped it on her neck and closed the clasp. His fingers caressed the soft skin at her shoulders. He turned her to him and touched each stone with his fingertip. "They're Hope and Will's birth stones, an amethyst for Hope and a peridot for Will." The two round stones separated by a gold bead sparkled brightly.

"They're lovely, and the sentiment means so much. You thought of everything."

"I hope so. My brain wasn't firing on all cylinders yesterday afternoon while I made phone calls. We'll see how I did. Come with me."

He took her hand and squeezed it to assure himself she was real. He'd dreamed of this day for a long time and wanted to savor every moment. He wanted to remember the smile on her lips and the surprise and wonder in her eyes.

"How did you get the ring and the necklace and the dress and, well, everything?" She glanced at the diamond on her hand again as he held it loosely in his grasp.

"The ring and necklace I've had for weeks. I waited for the right time to propose for real and make things official." He brought her hand to his lips and kissed her knuckles again. "The rest was a lot of phone calls and help from family and friends." He led her to the back door and showed her the small group of people gathered in the backyard on the patio.

John and Greg Langley were there, along with Andrea from her shop. James, her foreman, and his wife and daughters had come. Brian and Marilee and their little baby boy, Jesse, named for his aunt. The day he was born, Dylan accompanied Jessie to the hospital to see them and she'd cried and held her nephew, a huge smile on her face for her brother and his family and future, so bright now that he'd turned a corner.

Dylan invited Brody and Rain and their girls, Dawn and Autumn. Rain held their son, David, in her arms. Owen was here to take care of the paperwork. His wife Claire stood beside Owen, holding their son, Sean. Owen held his family close to his side.

He asked a couple of buddies from work, along with their wives. Lynn held a bouquet of red roses for Jessie to carry down the aisle. The preacher stood by to perform the ceremony. A photographer snapped pictures of everyone.

He didn't invite his parents. They'd gone too far and forced him to push them out of his life. He hoped one day he'd find a way to forgive them for what they'd done. Today, he was marrying the only woman he'd ever loved. He'd have the happiness his parents had always wanted for him, even though their idea of his happiness differed from his own. Jessie and Will were everything he needed. As long as he had them, he would be happy the rest of his life.

"Claire and Rain got you the dress and shoes. Lynn picked up a bouquet of flowers for you. John and Greg have come to take you away if you don't want to marry me. If you do, then they're here to give us their blessing, and John will give you away." He grinned down at her as Will held her hand on her other side. "I called the caterers. Claire made a cake for us to cut later, and we'll have a quiet meal. Have I forgotten anything or anyone?"

"It's perfect. If it were just the three of us and nothing else, it would be enough." She looked down at Will, who looked up at her, and then to Dylan. "Shall we get married?"

"I thought you'd never ask," he teased.

"I did. Yesterday."

"Exactly. You said as soon as possible. I hope in about two minutes is fast enough."

She slid open the glass doors and stepped out to greet their guests. She'd met Dylan's cousins and their wives and the girls and babies several months ago. She recognized the men from the sheriff's department and met their wives.

She greeted Pop and Greg with hugs and kisses for both of them. "I'm so glad you're here. I don't think I'd have made it to this day without your help. I love you both."

She turned to Brian and Marilee and bent to kiss her sleeping nephew in Marilee's arms. Seeing him made the ache in her heart a little more pronounced, but it was better now that she'd shared the loss of Hope with Dylan. She no longer had to carry the burden alone. Looking down at her nephew, she placed a hand over her own belly and sighed with contentment. Today was perfect. Today, she was happier than she'd ever been in her life. She gazed up to the sky and sent a silent prayer to her daughter, letting her know today her parents would be married and joined by love forever. It's what Hope would have wanted for them.

After she and Dylan signed the marriage license, everyone got set up. She waited on the patio as Dylan took his place on the back lawn with Will at his side and Greg as his best man. She thought it appropriate the two men who loved her and had been a part of Hope's life stood together waiting for her to walk down the aisle. Pop stood on her left and Brian on her right. Arm in arm the two men walked her down the aisle to Dylan. Her past and present had finally converged with a clear path ahead of her, leading straight to Dylan and Will.

The ceremony took only a few moments with simple words of love, family, commitment, and connection from the preacher. Dylan slipped another diamond ring onto her finger to complement the engagement ring he gave her not even an hour ago. It came time to give him a ring and she panicked, but Dylan handed her a gold band that she slipped onto his finger with a brilliant smile. She had to put it on his right hand, because the fingers on his left hand were still too swollen. His wrist was still in the brace and would be a few more weeks. He didn't mind. He just smiled at her with that half grin of his and made her feel like everything was perfect.

He kissed her with so much love her heart filled and overflowed. The preacher declared them husband and wife. Everyone in the crowd cheered and Dylan kissed her again. Will hugged them with his little arms wrapped around both their legs.

The crowd of well-wishers enveloped them and she got separated from Dylan, talking to Rain and Claire. She loved seeing their babies, David and Sean. Dawn and Autumn kept Will busy, playing tag on the grass.

"Jessie, come over here," Dylan called to her from the patio.

She excused herself from Greg and Pop and went over to Dylan and Owen.

Owen handed her a stack of papers and a pen. "Mrs. McBride, if you'll sign here."

"Oh, I like that—Mrs. McBride."

"There are quite a few of you now," Owen teased, now that Brody, Owen, and Dylan were all happily married.

She scanned the legal papers and asked Dylan, "What are these?" not believing what she read.

"These are adoption papers. If you sign them, Will is yours. You'll be his legal mother."

"*If* I sign them? There's no *if* about it." She signed her name *Jessie McBride*. "Fitting the first time I use my new name it's to make Will my son."

He kissed her senseless after that beautiful statement.

"I'll file the papers with the court. We'll have a court date to finalize everything, but it's mostly a formality. From this moment on, you're Will's mother," Owen announced.

"You're the mother I always wanted for Will," Dylan said.

"Good thing Will picked me," she said, mimicking his words.

"I love you." He laughed and kissed her again. "Mrs. McBride." He leaned his forehead to hers. "We've waited a long time to make this happen."

"It was worth the wait," she said, brushing her lips against his.

The rest of the day went by in a blur. They had a lovely early dinner. Dylan turned on her stereo and they danced in the great room by the fire where they'd made love again for the first time. Everyone had a great time. They cut the cake and fed each other the first piece. Then, she'd led everyone in singing "Happy Birthday" to Dylan. Today was a double delight for them.

When the evening came to an end, Greg held his glass aloft along with everyone else. "Today, my best friend married the love of her life. Dylan got the wife he always wanted, and Will the mother he chose. Though circumstances tore them apart, love brought them together. Second chances are rare. Take care of each other. Love each other. I wish you love and happiness for the rest of your lives," he toasted them and everyone cheered, "Here, here!"

Greg kissed her goodbye that night on the forehead. "Be happy."

"I already am." She meant it for the first time in a long time.

WHAT A PERFECT day.

Everyone left an hour ago and the house was quiet. She left Dylan to read a story to Will and put him to bed after she kissed her son goodnight. In their room, she hung up her dress and put away her shoes. She slipped into a satin robe and went out on the roof to gaze at the stars.

She stared down at the road, the trees, the hills, and back up to the sparkling sky. Happy, she put her hand over her belly and thought of Hope and everything that led her to today. Grateful for it all, everything that came before had finally brought her Dylan and Will.

"Today was a big day," she said, and Dylan came through the window. "Your birthday, our wedding day, and I became Will's mother."

"You've been his mother from the start. You two took to each other immediately."

"That's because a car almost crushed him."

"Don't remind me." He sat beside her on the roof. He'd long ago discarded his suit jacket and tie. Will had practically undressed during dinner, trying to get out of his uncomfortable suit. Still, he thought they all looked nice when they'd taken pictures during the wedding. He didn't care about his banged-up face and arm from his accident. Nothing mattered except Jessie becoming his wife. He thought that all in all, a wedding put together in a matter of hours had turned out all right. Of course, he'd done a lot of preplanning.

She leaned into his shoulder. "Today was perfect."

"It's not over." He kissed her temple and squeezed her to his side. "Come to bed. Let's make a baby."

Leaning her head back against his arm, she smiled up at him. "Too late. We already did."

He gazed down into her beautiful face. The truth of it so clear to see in the joy filling her smile and eyes. Still, he couldn't quite believe it. "Tell me again."

"I'm pregnant. We're having a baby. I found out on Friday before I picked up Will. I wanted to tell you on your birthday, but it's been kind of hectic today." She leaned in and kissed him softly on the lips. He groaned when her arms crushed him to her and her breasts pressed against his chest.

"We're going to have a baby," she said again.

He smiled, unable to help himself. "I didn't think I could be any happier today. A baby. I'm going to be a father. Again," he said, smiling. "Are you okay?"

"I'm good. Nervous, but excited."

"Me too, but we'll get through this together. Come to bed. Let's celebrate." He kissed her again before he helped her through the window, back into the room and straight into his arms.

He held her tightly against him, walking her backward to the bed. Kissing her deeply, he sank into her sweet mouth. A shiver ran through her, and the joy in her eyes matched his own.

"We have a lot to celebrate." She smiled up at him, her back hitting the mattress as he lay down the length of her, his heart pressed to hers.

And celebrate they did through the night, and every day they were together, but especially on the day they welcomed their daughter, Faith, into the world.

If you loved the McBrides, head on up to Big Sky country with Jennifer Ryan to meet her

MONTANA MEN . . .

Keep reading for a sneak peek at

AT WOLF RANCH

A Montana Men Novel

Coming Winter 2015

*After years on the rodeo circuit, Gabe Bowden
wants nothing more than land of his own and
a woman who will claim his heart for more
than one night. When he has the chance to
buy the enormous Wolf Ranch spread, he snaps up
the incredible deal. Everything is set, until Gabe
rescues a woman on the deserted, snowy road
leading to the property, and the half-frozen beauty
changes everything.*
*Ella Wolf rushes to her family's abandoned Montana
ranch after her twin sister is murdered. She knows
she's next . . . unless she can uncover a secret hidden
somewhere at Wolf Ranch. The last thing Ella expects
is to be rescued by a rugged rancher with his own
agenda. A man who almost makes her forget how
dangerous love can be . . .*

As an unlikely partnership sparks into something so much more, and a killer closes in, can Ella and Gabe learn to trust one another before it's too late?
Three Peaks Ranch, Montana

GABE BOWDEN PUT the quarter horse through its paces around the corral, stopping him short to make an abrupt turn, then pulling on the reins to make him back up. All in all, he liked the horse's attention and readiness to follow commands. His brother Blake trained the animal well. The horse would be a fine addition to his new ranch and a big help with the cattle due to arrive in nine weeks. Gabe couldn't wait to take over Wolf Ranch. He'd worked his ass off to earn the money to buy the place, and in nine short weeks, the deal closed and he'd have everything he ever dreamed: the huge spread with wide-open meadows, rolling hills, rivers snaking out over the land, grass as far as the eye could see for the cattle. A livelihood he could depend on, and a legacy he'd leave to his kids. If he ever found a woman and had some kids.

After Stacy left him standing at the altar all alone, turning her nose up at his little ranch, the plans he had to build it into something more, and a quiet life as his wife and the mother of his children, it couldn't be just any woman. He needed to find the right woman. One who wanted the same kind of simple but meaningful ranch life he wanted. Since he bought Wolf Ranch, he had a hell of lot more to offer now than he did when Stacy left him.

If the woman of his dreams was out there, she sure as hell wasn't in Montana. He'd looked and come up bust.

Finished getting a feel for the horse, he rode over to the rail and stopped next to Blake and dismounted. He ran his hand over the horse's flank.

"You did a fine job with this one. Where'd you find him?"

"He's one of Ross's."

"Something about that guy puts me off. Don't get me wrong, his horses have the bloodlines, but I don't like the way he runs his ranch."

"Me either, but you asked for the best I could find. Sully is gentle, attentive, a hard worker, and a fast learner. He'll suit you."

"Sully? You named him already."

"I've spent the last six weeks training him. I couldn't keep calling him 'horse.'" Blake grinned and pat Sully on the white patch on his brown forehead. The horse leaned in and closed his eyes, completely enamored and content with Blake. Gabe had to admit, his brother had a way with horses.

"How do you like it here at Three Peaks Ranch?" Gabe asked.

"I love it."

Though Blake trained quarter horses for cutting cattle, he was making a name for himself training thoroughbred racehorses.

"The partnership with Bud Tucker working out? It's been a few years, you ready to get your own place?"

"Naw, I like it here. I've found exactly what I wanted and more."

"I'm glad you're happy, man."

"You must be chomping at the bit to get into the Wolf place."

"I can't wait."

"I still can't see you rambling around that huge house."

"It's the stables and pastures I'm more interested in."

"Please, that house is beyond awesome."

Yeah, it certainly would appeal to that elusive wife he kept looking for but couldn't seem to find.

"Did you get it cleaned out like the owner asked?"

"Get this, I've dealt solely with Phillip Wolf, but Lela Wolf showed up the other day."

"What's she like? Spoiled rich girl?"

"Hell if I know. I only spoke to her for a couple of minutes. I met her in the driveway. She wanted to know what I was doing there. When I told her Phillip requested I put the contents of the house in storage, she told me to leave the place alone and tore out of there. You'd have thought the hounds of hell were after her."

"So you didn't pack the house?"

"No, I did. Moving trucks showed up fifteen minutes later."

Blake frowned. "Why didn't she want you to touch anything in the house?"

"Beats me."

"Did you tell her you own the place now?"

"I don't own it until escrow closes in nine weeks. That's the deal."

"Did you tell her that?"

"She didn't give me a chance. Come to think of it, she thought her uncle sent me to find her."

Blake frowned and narrowed his eyes. "That's strange."

"I had my orders from her uncle and delaying the inevitable seemed stupid. The stuff sat in that house for the last ten years untouched. People like them, from the city, more money than they know what to do with, they don't care about all that land. Hell, Travis Dorsche took over running their prime cattle, and that guy's just this side of worthless, and they don't give a shit. So, yeah, I cleaned out the house. When the deal goes through they'll still have all that stuff sitting in the lockers Phillip rented. With those people, it's out of sight, out of mind."

"Too bad you didn't get the cattle as part of the deal. That would have saved you some big bucks getting the place set up."

"Tell me about it." Gabe rolled his shoulders to ease the ache.

"Still sore."

"I'm too old to be riding bulls and roping calves. I'll leave that to Dane."

"You won the bull-riding championship. Again."

"It felt good to beat our little brother one last time. I got ut of the seed money I needed to pay for the cattle."

"hen do you expect delivery?"

"day I move in. Things will be tough the first year. erything I have into this deal, but after that, mit."

on your way." Blake gave him a friendly pat der. "Come on, let's load this guy and get you now will pass us by here, but you'll meet it e sunset in another hour."

Gabe led Sully to the gate Blake held open and walked him straight to his truck and trailer. He unstrapped the saddle and pulled it off, handing it over to Blake, who took it inside the stables to put it on the rack. Blake walked out carrying a brush and handed it to him. Gabe tossed the saddle pad Blake's way and his brother caught it and took it back inside too. Gabe shook his head and thought of them back on their parents' ranch, always working together to get the chores done. He missed those days. Now that they were all scattered—Caleb down in Colorado with his new wife, Summer; Dane traipsing all over Texas, Arizona, and Nevada riding rodeo; and Blake here—it wasn't often they all got together at one time. He missed being with his brothers. Maybe Blake is right about him rambling around that big house alone.

He thought often these days about having a wife and kids. Seeing Caleb last month with his pretty bride, how happy they were together, made him think of finding someone special, instead of someone just for tonight, or this week, or month. Tired of roaming, he wanted to settle down to a normal ranch life like his parents shared and Caleb found with Summer. The life he planned to have with Stacy before it all fell apart.

Blake slapped him on the back, bringing him out of his thoughts.

"Go anywhere interesting in that mind?"

"Just thinking about Caleb and Summer."

"Never seen two happier people."

"Me either. Maybe that will be us someday."

"Let's hope," Blake said, surprising him with his candor. Whenever they talked about women it was to razz each other or brag about some conquest. They never talked about getting married and settling down.

Gabe brushed Sully down before leading him into the trailer and changing out his bridle for the halter. With the horse settled into the trailer, he stepped out, closed the gate, and faced Blake.

"What do I owe you for the feed and training?" Gabe pulled out his wallet, but his brother put his hand on his arm.

"Call it a housewarming gift from me to you."

"It's not necessary," Gabe tried to argue.

"It's a gift. I can't wait to come out and see your new place once you get settled."

"I'll probably need some help when the cattle arrive to get them into the right pastures."

"I'm there. Just give me a call and we'll set it up."

Gabe gave his brother a hearty hug and smack on the back. He wanted to stay, take his brother out for a beer and some food, but sunset came early this time of year. Just after four in the afternoon, it'd be dark in another hour.

Gabe sat in the cab of his truck and started the engine, cranking the heater to ward off the cold. Thirty-three degrees, the temps would plummet come dark. With the snow coming, he needed to get home without delay.

"Hey, drive careful. Sorry you're getting off to a late start."

"My own fault. I wanted to spend time with you."

"I'll see you soon. If not, definitely in nine weeks when you take over the Wolf spread."

"See you then."

"Was she pretty?"

Taken off guard, Gabe narrowed his gaze and asked, "Who?"

"Lela Wolf."

He didn't even have to try to recall that heart-shaped face, those green eyes, the sweep of her light-brown hair over her eyebrows and tucked behind the curve of her ear. She smelled like a field of lilies. Still, he'd never forget her face.

"Yeah, she's pretty." Gorgeous. Stunning. Unforgettable. Fragile, but he caught a glimpse of steel when she found out about him clearing the house and ordered him to stay out.

"Maybe she'll come back."

Gabe smirked at his brother and shook his head. Blake gave him a lopsided grin, obviously reading that Gabe indeed thought she was more than just pretty. Gabe hit the gas and left his brother in the dust, but not the thoughts he'd had of a beautiful woman in a blue coat with a face he couldn't forget.

Gabe concentrated on the slick road. Due to the earlier rain, he slowed down considerably on the back roads. When he hit the highway further north, rising up toward the pass, the rain turned to snow and slowed him even more. Way past schedule, the sun had set nearly an hour ago and visibility was getting worse by the minute along the two-lane road. If he didn't have to worry about the horse and trailer, he'd make better time. By morning, he'd need a snowplow to clear the roads if this kept up all night. Right now, it didn't look like the snow would stop any time soon.

Tired after a long day and in need of a hot drink, he scratched at his rough jaw and thought about all he needed to do when he got home. Settle Sully into the stall he'd prepared in the stables that morning. Crack open a couple of cans of stew for a late dinner and make a pot of coffee. Grab the clothes he kept tossing over the seat and take them to the laundry room. Tomorrow, he'd do all the laundry. He'd get the guest room cleaned up in case Dane dropped in for another visit.

His phone rang and he checked the caller ID. Speak of the devil. He hit the button on his steering wheel for the hands-free to answer.

"What's up, Dane?"

"Checked out your black angus beauties at my buddy's place." His brother's voice filled the truck cab. "Man, those are some prime beef cattle."

"They ought to be for what I paid," Gabe grumbled.

"Like I said, they're a bunch of beauties. Get them certified organic and you'll make a killing."

"Well, it's going to take some time, but once I get the certification and the breeding program up and running, I hope to start turning a decent profit."

"I confirmed the delivery and verified all the records and bloodlines for the cattle. You're good to go, man."

"Thanks, Dane. You saved me the trip down to Nevada. How're things going with you?"

"Rambling around, kicking ass on the rodeo circuit. I'm ranked number two behind Kurt Collins."

"You'll catch him." Gabe had all the confidence in the world his brother would not only catch Kurt but beat his ass by the finals. Dane wanted that prize money and a chance at setting up his own place.

"No doubt. Gotta run, man."

"Hot date?"

"Always. You should try it sometime. You spend far too much time alone with your horses."

"Horses are less trouble than women."

"Women smell better."

Gabe chuckled. "I've got other priorities right now."

"Doesn't hurt to have some fun."

"You're having plenty enough for me and half the men in Montana."

This time Dane laughed. "That's for sure."

"So go have your fun."

"You used to come out with me. I miss those days."

"I don't." After Stacy, he'd left his ranch and rambled around on the rodeo circuit, chasing the thrill of the ride and every woman he could get his hands on, until he woke up one morning with another buckle bunny beside him and no idea what her name was. He didn't care. She'd scratched an itch, but left him empty. They all did. He'd used them to fill up the emptiness inside him that grew with every meaningless encounter. He'd needed the thrill of the conquest, knowing he could seduce a woman into his bed. But he woke up and realized that's all they wanted from him, because that's all he had to offer. If he wanted to build a life with a woman, he'd have to have something more to offer than meaningless, mindless sex. So he came home to build something he could be proud of, a life someone would want to share with him.

"I miss hanging with you, but not the reckless lifestyle. I'll leave that to you, bro. See you when the cows come home."

"I'll be there."

Dane clicked off and Gabe smiled. He couldn't wait to see Dane when the cattle arrived. Dane promised to help him get things set up on the ranch.

Gabe didn't hold back the smile, thinking of Dane, his wild-at-heart brother, and Blake, living his dream, training race horses. Gabe worked his ass off over the last three years to pull together the money he needed for his ranch, to buy the cattle, and finally have everything he ever wanted. Still, Dane's words rang in his head. Have some fun. Seems he'd forgotten how to do that these last years living alone at his place, barely going into town for more than supplies. When it came to the women, a few new ones had moved to town, but mostly they were the same faces he'd seen growing up and none of them appealed.

He wanted something different. Something new. Someone who challenged him.

Eyes the color of spring grass, the same ones he'd thought of ever since he saw her, floated into his mind.

About the Author

JENNIFER RYAN writes romantic suspense and contemporary small-town romances featuring strong men and equally fearless women. Her stories are filled with love, friendship, and the happily-ever-after we all hope to find. Jennifer lives in the San Francisco Bay Area with her husband and three children. When she's not writing a book she's reading one.

Visit www.AuthorJenniferRyan.com for contact information or your favorite retailer applications.

Give in to your impulses . . .
Read on for a sneak peek at three brand-new
e-book original tales of romance
from Avon Books.
Available now wherever e-books are sold.

FULL EXPOSURE
BOOK ONE: INDEPENDENCE FALLS
By Sara Jane Stone

PERSONAL TARGET
AN ELITE OPS NOVEL
By Kay Thomas

SINFUL REWARDS 1
A BILLIONAIRES AND BIKERS NOVELLA
By Cynthia Sax

An Excerpt from

FULL EXPOSURE
Book One: Independence Falls
by *Sara Jane Stone*

The first book in a hot new series from contemporary romance writer Sara Jane Stone. When Georgia begins work as a nanny for her brother's best friend, she knows she can't have him, but his pull is too strong, and she feels sparks igniting.

Georgia Trulane walked into the kitchen wearing a purple bikini, hoping and praying for a reaction from the man she'd known practically forever. Seated at the kitchen table, Eric Moore, her brother's best friend, now her boss since she'd taken over the care of his adopted nephew until he found another live-in nanny, studied his laptop as if it held the keys to the world's greatest mysteries. Unless the answers were listed between items b and c on a spreadsheet about Oregon timber harvesting, the screen was not of earth-shattering importance. It certainly did not merit his full attention when she was wearing an itsy-bitsy string bikini.

"Nate is asleep," she said.

Look up. Please, look up.

Eric nodded, his gaze fixed to the screen. Why couldn't he look at her with that unwavering intensity? He'd snuck glances. There had been moments when she'd turned from preparing his nephew's lunch and caught him looking at her, really looking, as if he wanted to memorize the curve of her neck or the way her jeans fit. But he quickly turned away.

"Did you pick up everything he needs for his first day of school tomorrow? I don't want to send him unprepared."

His deep voice warmed her from the inside out. It was so familiar and welcoming, yet at the same time utterly sexy.

"I got all the items on the list," she said. "He is packed and ready to go."

"He needs another one of those stuffed frogs. He can't go without his favorite stuffed animal."

If she hadn't been standing in his kitchen practically naked, waiting for him to notice her, she would have found his concern for the three-year-old's first day of preschool sweet, maybe even heartwarming. But her body wasn't looking for sentiments reminiscent of sunshine and puppies, or the whisper of sweet nothings against her skin. She craved physical contact—his hands on her, exploring, each touch making her feel more alive.

And damn it, he still hadn't glanced up from his laptop.

"Nate will be home by nap time," she said. "He'll be there for only a few hours. You know that, right?"

"He'll want to take his frog," he said, his fingers moving across the keyboard. "He'll probably lose it. And he sleeps with that thing every night. He needs that frog."

She might be practically naked, but his emphasis on the word *need* thrust her headfirst into heartwarming territory. Eric worked day and night to provide Nate with the stability that had been missing from Eric's childhood thanks to his divorced parents' fickle dating habits. She admired his willingness to put a child who'd suffered a tragic loss first.

But tonight, for one night, she didn't want to think about all of his honorable qualities. She wanted to see if maybe, just maybe those stolen glances when he thought she wasn't looking meant that the man she'd laid awake thinking about while serving her country half a world away wanted her too.

"You're now the proud owner of two stuffed frogs," she said. "So if that's everything for tonight, I'm going for a swim."

Finally, *finally*, he looked up. She watched as his blue eyes widened and his jaw clenched. He was an imposing man, large and strong from years of climbing and felling trees. Not that he did the grunt work anymore. These days he wore tailored suits and spent more time in an office than with a chainsaw in hand. But even seated at his kitchen table poring over a computer, he looked like a wall of strong, solid muscle wound tight and ready for action. Having all of that energy focused on her? It sent a thrill down her body. Georgia clung to the feeling, savoring it.

An Excerpt from

PERSONAL TARGET
An Elite Ops Novel
by Kay Thomas

One minute Jennifer Grayson is housesitting
and the next she's abducted to a foreign brothel.
Jennifer is planning her escape when her first
"customer" arrives. Nick, the man who broke
her heart years ago, has come to her rescue.
Now, as they race for their lives, passion for
each other reignites and old secrets resurface.
Can Nick keep the woman he loves safe
against an enemy with a personal vendetta?

The woman at the vanity turned, and his breath caught in his throat. Nick had known it would be Jenny, and despite what he'd thought about downstairs when he'd seen her on the tablet screen, he hadn't prepared himself for seeing her like this. Seated at the table with candles all around, she was wearing a sheer robe over a grey thong and a bustier kind of thing—or that's what he thought the full-length bra was called.

He spotted the unicorn tat peeping out from the edge of whatever the lingerie piece was, and his brain quit processing details as all the blood in his head rushed south. He'd been primed to come in and tell Jenny exactly how they were getting out of the house and away from these people, and now . . . this. His mouth went dry at the sight of her. She looked like every fantasy he'd ever had about her rolled into one.

He continued to stare as recognition flared in her eyes.

"Oh my god," she murmured. "It's . . ."

She clapped her mouth closed, and her eyes widened. That struck him as odd. The relief on her face was obvious, but instead of looking at him, she took an audible breath and studied the walls of the room. When she finally did glance at him again, her eyes had changed.

"So you're who they've sent me for my first time?" Her voice sounded bored, not the tone he remembered. "What do you want me to do?"

What a question. He raised an eyebrow, but she shook her head. In warning?

Nothing here was as he'd anticipated. He continued staring at her, hoping the lust would quit fogging his brain long enough for him to figure out what was going on.

"I've been told to show you a good time." Her voice was cold, downright chilly. Without another word she stood and crossed the floor, slipping into his arms with her breasts pressing into his chest. "It's you." She murmured the words in the barest of whispers.

Nick's mind froze, but his body didn't. His hands automatically went to her waist as she kissed his neck, working her way up to his ear. This was not at all what he'd planned.

"I can't believe you're here." She breathed the words into his ear.

Me either, he thought, but kept the words to himself as he pulled her closer. His senses flooded with all that smooth skin pressing against him. His body tightened, and his right hand moved to cup her ass. Her cheek's bare skin was silky soft, just like he remembered. God, he'd missed her. She melted into him as his body switched into overdrive.

"What do you want?" She spoke louder. The arctic tone was back. He was confused and knew he was just too stupid with wanting her to figure out what the hell was going on. There was no way the woman could mistake the effect she was having.

She moved her lips closer to his ear and nipped his earlobe as she whispered, "Cameras are everywhere. I'm not sure about microphones."

And like that, cold reality slapped him in the face. He should have been expecting it, but he'd been so focused on getting her out and making sure she was all right. She might be glad to see him because he was there to save her, but throwing her body at him was an act.

Jesus. He had to get them both out of here without tipping his hand to the cameras and those watching what he was doing. He was crazy not to have considered it once he saw those tablets downstairs, but it had never occurred to him that he would have to play this encounter through as if he were really a client.

He slipped her arms from around his neck and moved to the table to pour himself some wine, willing his hands not to shake. "I want you," he said.

An Excerpt from

SINFUL REWARDS 1
A Billionaires and Bikers Novella
by Cynthia Sax

Belinda "Bee" Carter is a good girl; at least, that's
what she tells herself. And a good girl deserves
a nice guy—just like the gorgeous and moody
billionaire Nicolas Rainer. Or so she thinks,
until she takes a look through her telescope
and sees a naked, tattooed man on the balcony
across the courtyard. He has been watching
her, and that makes him all the more enticing.
But when a mysterious and anonymous text
message dares her to do something bad, she
must decide if she is really the good girl she has
always claimed to be, or if she's willing to risk
everything for her secret fantasy of being watched.

An Avon Red Novella

I'd told Cyndi I'd never use it, that it was an instrument purchased by perverts to spy on their neighbors. She'd laughed and called me a prude, not knowing that I was one of those perverts, that I secretly yearned to watch and be watched, to care and be cared for.

If I'm cautious, and I'm always cautious, she'll never realize I used her telescope this morning. I swing the tube toward the bench and adjust the knob, bringing the mysterious object into focus.

It's a phone. Nicolas's phone. I bounce on the balls of my feet. This is a sign, another declaration from fate that we belong together. I'll return Nicolas's much-needed device to him. As a thank you, he'll invite me to dinner. We'll talk. He'll realize how perfect I am for him, fall in love with me, marry me.

Cyndi will find a fiancé also—everyone loves her—and we'll have a double wedding, as sisters of the heart often do. It'll be the first wedding my family has had in generations.

Everyone will watch us as we walk down the aisle. I'll wear a strapless white Vera Wang mermaid gown with organza and lace details, crystal and pearl embroidery accents, the bodice fitted, and the skirt hemmed for my shorter height. My hair will be swept up. My shoes—

Voices murmur outside the condo's door, the sound piercing my delightful daydream. I swing the telescope upward, not wanting to be caught using it. The snippets of conversation drift away.

I don't relax. If the telescope isn't positioned in the same way as it was last night, Cyndi will realize I've been using it. She'll tease me about being a fellow pervert, sharing the story, embellished for dramatic effect, with her stern, serious dad—or, worse, with Angel, that snobby friend of hers.

I'll die. It'll be worse than being the butt of jokes in high school because that ridicule was about my clothes and this will center on the part of my soul I've always kept hidden. It'll also be the truth, and I won't be able to deny it. I am a pervert.

I have to return the telescope to its original position. This is the only acceptable solution. I tap the metal tube.

Last night, my man-crazy roommate was giggling over the new guy in three-eleven north. The previous occupant was a gray-haired, bowtie-wearing tax auditor, his luxurious accommodations supplied by Nicolas. The most exciting thing he ever did was drink his tea on the balcony.

According to Cyndi, the new occupant is a delicious piece of man candy—tattooed, buff, and head-to-toe lickable. He was completing armcurls outside, and she enthusiastically counted his reps, oohing and aahing over his bulging biceps, calling to me to take a look.

I resisted that temptation, focusing on making macaroni and cheese for the two of us, the recipe snagged from the diner my mom works in. After we scarfed down dinner, Cyndi licking her plate clean, she left for the club and hasn't returned.

Three-eleven north is the mirror condo to ours. I

straighten the telescope. That position looks about right, but then, the imitation UGGs I bought in my second year of college looked about right also. The first time I wore the boots in the rain, the sheepskin fell apart, leaving me barefoot in Economics 201.

Unwilling to risk Cyndi's friendship on "about right," I gaze through the eyepiece. The view consists of rippling golden planes, almost like . . .

Tanned skin pulled over defined abs.

I blink. It can't be. I take another look. A perfect pearl of perspiration clings to a puckered scar. The drop elongates more and more, stretching, snapping. It trickles downward, navigating the swells and valleys of a man's honed torso.

No. I straighten. This is wrong. I shouldn't watch our sexy neighbor as he stands on his balcony. If anyone catches me . . .